RAISING THE DEAD

D. B. SIEDERS

CITY OWL
PRESS

RAISING THE DEAD
Soul Broker, Book 2

CITY OWL PRESS
www.cityowlpress.com

Cover Design by Mibl Art. All stock photos licensed appropriately.

Edited by Amanda Roberts.

For information on subsidiary rights, please contact the publisher at info@cityowlpress.com.

Print Edition ISBN: 978-1-944728-63-2

Digital Edition ISBN: 978-1-944728-64-9

Printed in the United States of America

For Stephanie,
who always believed in me

PRAISE FOR D. B. SIEDERS

"A unique cast of characters drives this beautifully crafted tale that demands you keep a box of tissue on hand. WAKING THE DEAD is a soul-wrenching look into the decisions one must make about life and death, not only for one's self, but for a loved one. Ms. Sieders knows how to put words on paper that touch the heart, and invigorate the mind." - *4.5 Stars from InD'Tale Magazine*

"Revolution brews in the spirit world. Vivian and Lazarus encounter a vibrant cast of allies—among them mambo woman Bijoux Briggs and Vivian's sister Mae, who was disabled in life but is powerful in the afterlife —and develop a love connection despite their complicated past." - *Publisher's Weekly*

"D.B. Sieders is a unique storyteller. CROSSCURRENTS is a mix of science fiction and fantasy that is woven together perfectly. Ms. Sieders's characters are distinctive and the story is imaginative and fun." - *4.5 Stars from InD'Tale Magazine*

"For paranormal romance readers who are looking for something a little different, Lorelei's Lyric could be your first step into a whole new world." - *Romantic Reads and Such*

"Sieders delivers a well-written and intriguing supernatural world with a plot that pulls you in and characters that keep you turning pages until the very end in FIRESTORM." - *ARC Reviewer*

"In WAKING THE DEAD, there is an emotional, raw honesty in Vivian and her struggles to care for her sister, Mae. It's so rare to find a heroine, one we root for, who is not a saint but is desperately trying to do the right thing and is not always perfect." - *ARC Reviewer*

THE SOUL BROKER SERIES

BY D. B. SIEDERS

Waking the Dead

Raising the Dead

The Quick and the Dead

Chasing the Dead (Short Story)

PROLOGUE

The woman appeared on her deck.

He'd been watching her for a long time, at least by mortal standards. Flesh was such a limiting state. The departed reckoned time a bit differently than the living. It was one advantage—or disadvantage—of their eternal natures.

Of course, time had never worked in his favor on either side of eternity.

Hidden in the nearby tree line, he stared up at the back door to her home, the white of its recently painted frame eerie as it glowed in the moonlight. Deck chairs and a small table cast long shadows as a gust sent a shiver of ripples through the fabric of a large umbrella. Empty a heartbeat before, and then all of a sudden, there she stood.

She took his breath away. Always had.

She didn't step out of the back door, nor did she casually stroll up the stairs. She materialized, as if she'd conjured her body out of thin air.

Not possible for ordinary mortals, of course. She was still technically among the living. Only powerful incorporeal guardian and reaper spirits could conjure a corporeal form from the elements. But this almost-mortal woman had learned a few of their tricks, including some she hadn't bothered to share with the guardians for whom she worked.

Her auburn curls whipped in the wind as it howled through the dark night. She fought to push the rogue strands out of her face while she waited for her dark guest, or so he suspected.

She hadn't told her guardian supervisors about *him,* either. His fists clenched as emotion exploded through his body, which threatened to shatter into the dust from which it came.

Rage to be sure, and jealousy, perhaps—or, more accurately, a deep sense of betrayal—nearly consumed him, but he struggled for calm. He was here to observe, not to intervene. That would come later, and only if he caught her in the act.

Playing both sides was a dangerous game, and one that came with the risk of dire consequences.

He'd learned that lesson from a rather unpleasant personal experience.

He half-hoped he was wrong about her. The heart he now possessed longed for it.

Vivian Bedford had intrigued him ever since he'd been assigned to monitor the rare mortal soul broker. Nearly broken under the weight of an unbearable burden, she'd proven tenacious, fiercely protective of those she loved, and surprisingly cunning in her dealings with afterlife management. She'd taken the hard road, clinging to mortal life in spite of being forever bound to the world of spirits. Death would have been the much simpler choice, if less courageous.

Pride mingled with anger and jealousy.

He'd had a hand in shaping her into the formidable soul broker she'd become, and he'd paid a heavy price. But it seemed she was seeking guidance from another mentor now. Right on cue, the man in white appeared, and she welcomed the reaper with a brief but passionate kiss.

With that one act, she'd given him the ammunition he needed. Now, he only had to pick the right moment to pull the trigger.

If he could.

CHAPTER ONE

Vivian stood outside of the Nashville Zoo at Grassmere, watching and waiting. She'd almost gotten used to that, the watching and the waiting part, but this was a major multitasking day. Eleven-year old Annabelle, eight-year old Kaitlyn, and two-and-a-half-year-old Conner a.k.a. "Scooter" Clemmens, the unholy trinity, were under her care. Fortunately, the girls were cooperating with one another in the shared task of dominating their little brother.

That gave Vivian time to scope out the spirit scene.

Two warms at the entrance, one lost and lonely lurking behind the bushes...cold ones?

She gave a quick nod to the two guardians at the entrance and they returned her greeting without obvious surprise. She'd gotten pretty good at communing with the spirits around her without alerting the living. That was essential, since she didn't want to end up endangering anyone else or wind up in the nut house. Spirits remained invisible to normal mortals, but not to her, and sometimes it was still hard to sort the living from the dead—especially the powerful spirits who could assume a corporeal form for a short time and blend in with the living.

She still didn't detect any chilly spirits after a third scan of the area. Breathing a sigh of relief, Vivian reached out to the minds of the invisible guardian spirits and requested a courtesy meeting. At least, she hoped she'd sent the right message. She couldn't read thoughts like a true guardian could.

Maybe you have to actually be dead to do that.

She still wasn't sure. The details were a little fuzzy, and her not-so-forthcoming mentor guardian spirit, Ezra, wasn't helping. But she'd found she could manage to send out a sort of mental text message to those nearby. Only short messages so far; anything else still required a face-to-face. But the skill still came in handy. These included greetings like, "Hey! I'm here and I see you, but I'm no threat," or "Ezra asked me to help with this soul crossing," or "Back off, reaper, this one's mine!" Luckily, she had some spiritual firepower to back her threats up. Even luckier, she'd only ever had to face one reaper on her own. That encounter had resulted in a rather... complicated relationship. Vivian shivered. She knew enough about the darkness lurking just beyond the perception of the living to fear it.

She suspected there was far more to fear there than she could ever imagine.

Must practice a bit more. Add that to my mile-long list!

She also needed to find a way to balance normal life with her other-worldly activities, which included looking after her dear friend's darling children. Of all days and all places, why did these guardian spirits have to show up at the zoo, and on her supposed day off?

Only one way to find out, and stalling wasn't it.

Taking a deep breath, she worked on settling the kids. She gave each a juice box, handed them her smart phone so they could watch YouTube videos, and then asked them to sit tight outside the zoo's entrance while she ran back to the car. She made sure they were still in her line of sight, but occupied.

After a quick check to make sure there were no living folks nearby, Vivian opened the driver's side door and hopped into her old but reliable hybrid. The male guardian materialized in the passenger seat and his female sidekick appeared in the back. They'd both assumed corporeal forms, which surprised Vivian, though she tried not to show it. She hoped they wouldn't leave dust all over her seats when they left.

"You must be Vivian," said the man, his voice curt and dripping with disdain. He wore a well-tailored business suit with creases as sharp as the angles of his face. Probably mid-fifties when he'd died—likely sometime in the 1950s judging by the suit's style—he had aged gracefully and would have turned heads if not for the clenched jaw and deep frown.

"I am," she replied. "And you are...or were?" She raised her eyebrows and invited him to fill in the blanks. Living or dead, she didn't appreciate his tone and lack of manners. If he wasn't willing to extend basic courtesy, she didn't see any reason to offer hers.

"I am called Wallace, and my partner is Jeanne. Shall I help you disappear from view while we chat?"

"Pleased to meet you both," she said. "And no thanks. I can manage on my own." She channeled her spirit energy and became invisible. She'd picked up that handy trick through her work with guardian spirits, not to mention someone working for the other side.

Wallace's gaze went wide with apparent shock. Good. Served him right for being dismissive.

"By the way, why go through the trouble of conjuring corporeal bodies if you were planning to make yourself invisible to the living?" Vivian asked.

Wallace bristled, but Jeanne answered, her voice warm and filled with eagerness. "I wanted to practice. Gotta keep my skills sharp if I'm to fulfill my duties as a guardian."

Jeanne was the polar opposite of her companion. Young, exuberant, and engaging, her honey-colored hair hung loose on her shoulders and framed the beautiful oval of her face. She wore jeans and a T-shirt. The shirt displayed a skeletal figure cloaked in black and carrying a scythe. It read, "Are you flirting with me?"

Vivian liked her immediately.

Now safely out of sight, at least to any living folk who might wander close to her vehicle, Vivian called the meeting to order. "I'm not here on business, but I wanted to let you know I'm here and I'm...aware."

Ezra had instructed her to check in with any guardians she ran across in her daily life. "Don't be shy, Miss Vivian," is what he'd actually told her, but shyness wasn't the problem.

No, having to make lame excuses and slip away from her living companions was the problem. A big one, and one she hadn't counted on when she'd agreed to take on the role of living soul broker.

Not that she'd agreed so much as had been made the proverbial offer she couldn't refuse.

"Duly noted," Wallace said sardonically, pulling her out of her musings and back to reality.

"Any reapers in the area? I'm here with kids, so you'll understand why I don't want any trouble," Vivian said.

"There are none in the zoo, though an unfortunate will be claimed by reapers at Southern Hills within the hour," Jeanne chimed in from the back. Wallace shot her a look, but she ignored it. She put her hand on Vivian's shoulder, sending a delightful jolt of warmth and well-being into her through touch. That was another nice thing guardian spirits could do for the living.

"Don't worry," Jeanne said, squeezing her shoulder. "We're here to guard the children visiting today. You and your companions will be safe."

"Thanks, Jeanne," Vivian said with genuine gratitude. Southern Hills hospital was just far enough away for Vivian's comfort, and both reapers and guardians hung around medical centers anyway, for obvious reasons.

Even without her comment about keeping her skills up, Vivian would've pegged Jeanne for a newly recruited guardian spirit. For one thing, Vivian hadn't seen her around before, and for another, she was friendly. Like most older spirits, Wallace was not. Many older guardians she'd met weren't keen on training, nor were they too thrilled with a mortal who was able to see them, much less one who shared some of their powers.

Given Wallace's reaction to her, Vivian put him somewhere between colonial and older than dirt.

"Speaking of children, I'd better get back to the ones I'm watching. Call if you need me."

Glad to have her courtesy call out of the way, and glad she didn't stay to hear whatever snarky comment Wallace made about her offer to help, Vivian walked back to the Clemmens kids. They stopped whatever mischief they'd been up to, which their expressions of manufactured innocence betrayed, and sat at attention.

"Listen up," she said. Best to get eye contact before issuing orders. That way, she'd only have to repeat them twice instead of five times.

Vivian didn't talk to children like they were idiots or small dogs. First of all, it was irritating. Second, she'd found that they just responded better to civilized conversation most of the time, or direct commands if that failed. Kay Clemmens, their mother, had advised her to lay down the ground rules early. Like any good commanding officer, she approached the troop with confidence and prepared to brief them on the rules of engagement.

"We're all going to have a good time as long as you behave like normal people and not like monkey butts."

That got a few sniggers from the older girls.

"So," Vivian continued, "do *not* pick your noses, scratch your heinies, or pee on the floor." The last order was directed at the two-and-a-half year old, with good reason.

"Speaking of that, does anyone need to go to the bathroom?" she asked. All she got in response was a series of grunts and unintelligible grumbles.

"Okay, I don't speak caveman, so how about a 'yes, ma'am' or a 'no thank you?'"

"I want need go pee pee," came the deceptively angelic voice of Scooter.

"Anyone else?"

"No, ma'am," offered Annabelle and Kaitlyn in unison.

She left the girls on their own to peek around the gift shop, warning them not to bend, spindle, or mutilate anything, while she took Scooter to do his business. It wasn't all that bad, though truth be told she was grateful his pull-up was clean. After months of cleaning and changing her full-grown invalid sister, Mae, before she passed, Vivian didn't think she would ever be able to handle diapers.

Of course diapers were required with children, part of the whole motherhood package.

And the point of this entire exercise, Vivian suspected, was to let her give motherhood a test drive.

Kay meant well, and Vivian was glad to help with her brood, but motherhood was the last thing she needed...or wanted.

Well, at least she was sure about the first. Being a part-time liaison between the living and dead, a title she'd imagined printing on a business card more than once, wasn't really compatible with family life. It might not be compatible with Jace, the man in her life, either, but that was an entirely different issue.

Scooter interrupted her reverie with a hopeful request. "Piece of candy?"

Having been briefed by Kay, Vivian replied, "Only if you put your poo-poos in the potty."

Well, he did.

Ain't normal life grand...

———

After returning to the gift shop with Connor in tow, Vivian was confronted by a staff member and two scared Clemmens sisters. The staffer was tall, skinny, and had a hairdo that reminded Vivian of a lopsided lump of ice cream stuck on top of a red cone. She looked none too thrilled with the girls, or with Vivian.

Great. Just what I need today.

"What did you two do?" Vivian asked the girls with a hint of good-natured sarcasm.

"Are these yours?" snapped the staffer.

"Not officially," Vivian joked, "but I am watching them today—"

"Well, *ma'am*," she interrupted, clearly not softened by Vivian's attempts at humor. "Leaving them alone in a store isn't really watching them, now is it? All children must be supervised by a responsible adult."

Seriously?

"Well, *ma'am*, I had to take the toddler to the bathroom, and Annabelle is almost twelve. I think she can handle her sister for a few minutes. What exactly did the girls do?" she asked.

"Nothing!" Kaitlyn said, stomping her foot. "We were just looking."

Annabelle nodded and then stuck her tongue out at the staffer when her back was turned. Vivian shot her a warning look and then turned her attention back to the staffer. The woman pursed her lips and folded her arms across her chest, but didn't offer an answer.

"Well?" Vivian pushed.

"We can't be too careful, and other parents complained when they saw these girls on their own."

"Fine, whatever, we'll be on our way now," Vivian said. She held Connor in one hand and beckoned the girls with her free hand. She had started walking away when her backpack slipped from her shoulder, spilling the contents on the ground.

"Candy!" Conner shouted as he wiggled out of Vivian's grasp and started grabbing Skittles by the fistful.

Annabelle tackled him and tried to take the candy away. Her heart was in the right place, at least. Kaitlyn helped Vivian pick up what Connor hadn't already snatched. The staffer just stood on the sidelines and rolled her eyes.

Vivian was sorely tempted to zap the woman in her skinny ass, but resisted. It was getting a lot harder to resist these days. She was only human, after all—albeit one with some pretty superhuman powers. Still, she reminded herself that her powers should only be used for the living in need and not for petty grudges. She took a deep breath, then thanked Kaitlyn, asked Annabelle to remove her brother from the headlock in which she held him, and convinced Connor to return what was left of the candy to the plastic bag from which it had fallen. At least one other staffer had stopped to help and see if Vivian was okay, restoring some of her faith in humanity.

"Don't mind Bea," whispered the friendly voice from the even friendlier freckled face. "She just gets a little carried away sometimes. You know, she's all about the letter of the law but not the spirit."

"Thanks," Vivian replied. "I didn't think it was a big deal. The girls know not to run off with strangers."

"Do you need me to watch this little cutie while you take the girls to the ladies' room?" the staffer asked as she bent down to examine Scooter. Her nametag read "Pat."

"No thank you, Miss Pat. I think we're good to go. I do appreciate the offer." Even the kids said thank you.

Vivian turned to gather the girls and was dismayed by a surly, still-scowling Bea. *Jeez, lighten up, lady.* Before Vivian had time to reconsider zapping her, she watched in horror as a wisp of faint light whizzed past and flew straight into Bea with enough force to knock her off her feet.

Bea screamed. The girls stared for about ten seconds before bursting out laughing along with some other patrons. Vivian bent low and looked for a clear shot. Bea reached for the cashier's stand to pull herself up, only to be knocked in the head by a box of rubber snakes that fell from the counter.

The box and gravity had some extra help.

The specter she'd seen lurking behind the bushes at the entrance now hovered over the cash register in apparent admiration of his handiwork, allowing Vivian to get a better look at him. He manifested as a smoky gray form, transparent, and only visible from head to torso. She couldn't make out his features very well, but he appeared to be young, or at least he had been young when his spirit departed his body. The energy his spirit could harness projected a version of his former self, which seemed to be the preference for most guardians and possibly the only option for lost and lonely souls. Vivian was surprised he was able to muster enough strength to cause so much trouble, and even more surprised to sense warmth from him.

She'd only ever felt a rise in temperature from bona fide guardians before.

Filing away her observations for later, Vivian made sure no mortal was watching and then took her shot. A lightning-fast flash of red light and he was down. *Hey, I'm getting faster!* It seemed that she'd managed to stun him without anyone else noticing, thank God. The other shoppers were too busy enjoying the show with Bea, who looked madder than an old wet hen as she plucked the snakes out of her hair. Feeling bad, if not partially responsible, Vivian walked over to her and started cleaning up rogue snakes and other items that had fallen.

Unfortunately, Bea didn't appreciate the gesture.

"Just leave it!" she yelled.

"Hey, I'm just trying to help," Vivian said. "But if you don't want it, suit yourself."

Shrugging, Vivian glanced over to check on the specter. He was gone.

That was definitely weird and unexpected. She hadn't put a lot of energy into her stun. It wouldn't have held a guardian or reaper, but it should have held the weak immaterial spirit. Still, she'd done all she could.

She had neither the time nor the privacy to seek out the ghost apparently hiding among the living. Vivian decided to file away the rest of this odd encounter. She could always report to the guardians here or tell Ezra later.

Besides, she was *supposed* to be off duty right now.

"Okay, Clemmens children," she called. "Move 'em up and head 'em out!"

The girls stopped laughing and walked toward the door. Kaitlyn studied Vivian for a moment and then said, "You're way too nice, Aunt Viv. I would've knocked a box of toy crocodiles on her head if I were you."

"Well, don't tell your mother, but I did think about it," she replied with a wink. "Hey, where's Scooter?"

Kaitlyn pointed to another part of the store. "He's over there talking to himself."

Vivian spun around and spotted the boy in the back corner, apparently engrossed in animated conversation with no one. Toddlers. They were so weird. Good thing they were cute, too.

"Scooter," Vivian called. "Come on. Wanna go see the meerkats?"

"I coming, Aunt Vee Vee! I coming!" he shrieked with joy. As they were all walking through the door, he turned back to wave and said, "Bye-bye, Junior!"

CHAPTER TWO

After making the entire circuit around the zoo and chasing three kids in the process, Vivian understood why Kay looked tired these days. She was pretty worn out herself, but felt great about giving Kay a break. Kay appeared to have the perfect life to outsiders, but looks were often deceiving. Vivian and Sue Carlson, her best gal pal and mutual friend, had both been wildly jealous of Kay and hoped they could get so lucky when they finally settled down.

Then Vivian had found out that Kay's seemingly perfect life was anything but.

Turned out Kay had suffered from postpartum depression after each of her three children. She was still having a hell of a time shaking it after Scooter, more than two years later. It had been worse each time. Having a traveling husband and full-time work schedule didn't help either. Vivian hadn't known any of this until after she acquired her powers, which included the ability to absorb the burdens and suffering of the living in the form of light energy. Along with flashes of insight into her friend's pain, she'd also coaxed Kay into talking about it with her.

The good news? It brought Vivian closer to a friend and gave her a rare and wonderful opportunity to help the living in a very ordinary way. And since Sue had been busy with wedding plans and a baby on the way, Vivian had appreciated the company of her other bestie. The bad news? It left Vivian even more ambivalent about family life than she had been before.

The Clemmens kids were a handful, but she had to admit that they came with some great perks. One of them was definitely comedy. While waiting for the elephants, Scooter chased a horrified Kaitlyn around the sitting area, which came complete with makeshift safari tents that were cleverly situated adjacent to pampas grass-bordered habitats. It gave the illusion of a real safari adventure, especially in the heat of the muggy Tennessee summer. The walkway was strewn with hoof and paw prints.

It would have been tranquil under different circumstances. Scooter always enjoyed a game of catch-a-sister, but this time he had a very special weapon. In addition to a cry that would make a howler monkey cringe, he wielded the recently retrieved booger on an index finger as he sprinted after Kaitlyn on sturdy, chubby toddler legs.

While standing on the sidelines to watch the show, Annabelle informed Vivian that she was going to grow her boobies someday soon and hoped they would be as "nice" as Aunt Viv's. It was oddly flattering.

Another perk Vivian had discovered were the spontaneous moments of joy she witnessed every now and again between them. Annabelle, with her mother's raven hair that was cut in a stylish bob, was on the cusp of becoming a young woman. She would often, between eye-rolls and preteen snark, coach her little sister through third grade playground politics and phonics. Kaitlyn, with her wild-child hair and freckled skin, never stopped moving, or fidgeting, or twitching. Yet her unabashed song-and-dance numbers were expressions of sheer bliss and innocence. Scooter was all boy. Ox-strong, he could be mean as a snake and just as unpredictable. But when he gave hugs and uttered words of love and gratitude, she never doubted his sincerity. Plus, Vivian was a sucker for redheads—and unlike her, Scooter was a natural.

She watched them now as they scampered around what had to be the biggest playground in the greater Metro area. At least the girls were in her sight. Her heart rate shot up when she stood and looked around for Scooter, spiking higher when she didn't see him tumbling in the toddler pen.

Shit! That little monkey butt is fast!

"Connor?" she called. "Buddy, where'd you go?" Panic crept up her spine in as she scanned the area. "Hey, Kate and Anna, have you seen your brother?"

"Nope," called Annabelle. "I thought he was playing with you."

Shit, shit, shit!

She'd been lost in her thoughts for a few minutes and managed to lose the boy. Kaitlyn and Annabelle started helping her look and calling for their brother, and a few other parents joined in the search. Vivian was just about to alert the staff when she heard a man's voice call out, "I think I found him!"

She sprinted toward the sound of the voice and was relieved to find Connor at the swing set under the supervision of a dad with his two sons. Even more surprising, Wallace the surly guardian spirit stood nearby, unseen to the living and watching over her charge. She mouthed a quick "thank you" to the scowling spirit. He shrugged and then returned to examining his incorporeal nails.

"Scooter!" Vivian scolded. "What did Aunt Vivie tell you about running away?"

"I not run away," he said, giving her his biggest smile. "Junior take me swing swing."

Vivian looked at the dad, who only shrugged and said, "Hey, I found him here swinging alone and thought he probably just wandered off."

"Thank you for finding him and keeping an eye on him until I got here, sir," Vivian said.

"No problem, ma'am," he replied. "I know how it goes. Don't tell my wife, but I lose one of these little guys at least once a month."

Vivian smiled at the man, and then turned and gave her best mad face to Connor. His smile faltered when he understood that Aunt Vivie was not happy. Fighting tears, he looked down at his feet and muttered, "Sowy,"

"Well, don't go running off again, especially with strangers, okay?"

"Okay, Aunt Vee Vee."

"Let's go."

On their way back to the girls, Vivian gave a nod to the friendly guardian as she walked among the living unseen. Jeanne gave her a bright smile and gushed at the sight of Connor. Wallace, who'd just appeared at her side, deigned to return her nod before passing right through a group of tourists. Literally.

Now that was just plain rude.

The living couldn't see or feel the impact, of course, but most guardians she'd encountered didn't just plow right through the space occupied by mortals. One of the living souls included a very old, wheelchair-bound woman being pushed by a young man, presumably a relative or caregiver. Vivian guessed the woman had been in decline for some time, given her fragile appearance and the soft rays of golden light swirling around her. The light was a manifestation of her surplus of spirit energy, unused life force that tended to accumulate in the infirm.

The sight pierced her heart.

Vivian did a double-take after Wallace walked right through the woman and her chair, his movements a blur. She swore that the light around the old woman swirled and then dimmed. Vivian squinted, trying to get a better look. Then, to her disbelief, Wallace appeared in her periphery. She turned in time to watch him rush into the gift shop, arms outstretched as if ready to attack. Perhaps he'd caught sight of the rogue ghost who'd caused trouble earlier. That wasn't the weird part.

The weird part was that Wallace kept walking alongside Jeanne.

But he'd gone into the shop. Vivian could still see him dashing up and down the aisles at unnatural speed when she looked back into the shop. Her gaze darted from each Wallace until she grew dizzy. Did he have a twin? Were they both dead? What were the odds?

Or could a powerful guardian spirit be in two places at once?

"Aunt Vivie! You found him!"

Vivian turned toward Kaitlyn as she and her sister ran to greet them. Connor wriggled out of Vivian's grasp and galloped to Annabelle, who picked him up and kissed his grubby cheek. She relaxed as a wave of relief filled her. Having wrangled all three Clemmens children, she decided to herd them to her car before she lost another one.

But the image of Wallace crossing through the old woman haunted her, for lack of a better word. Or maybe it was the perfect word. As far as she understood, guardians and reapers weren't capable of absorbing spirit energy from the living. She could, but she was a living soul broker. She filed yet another observation away for later, determined to grill Ezra about it once the old coot showed up at her doorstep for another free meal and tutoring session.

She'd also have to ask about the "being in two places at once" thing.

She had a sneaking suspicion he wasn't telling her everything he knew about afterlife management. Her mentor had a history of keeping her in the dark. Fortunately, she had other sources to whom she could turn for information—for a price.

She'd have to consider carefully, but investigating this new phenomenon just might be worth it.

———

"For the last time, stop apologizing. If I had a quarter for every time I lost the little monster, I'd be a millionaire," Kay said, reassuring Vivian that she wasn't mad about the near-loss of her only son.

"I was watching him like a hawk, I swear. He's just so fast," Vivian explained. She was pretty happy that Kay wasn't mad. She'd been afraid she would be banned from babysitting for eternity.

"That's a boy for you. I swear he'll be the death of me someday," Kay replied as she handed Vivian a glass of sweet tea.

Kay's dark eyes matched her hair, which never seemed to be out of place. Her clothing, however, tended to attract lint, stains, and kid goo when she was at home. Still, she'd managed to keep her looks, humor, and bright outlook through it all, and Vivian was certain she'd earned the title of hottest mommy on the soccer field, not to mention M.I.L.F. Kay had rolled her eyes and scoffed when Vivian said as much, but she couldn't hide the twinkle in her eyes at the dubious compliment.

They'd settled in to enjoy some quiet while Scooter slept and the girls played in their room. Vivian swore that if she ever did have kids, she would definitely institute daily quiet time for her own sanity. For hours. It seemed to be working for Kay.

"So," Kay continued, "how was the rest of the day?"

"Oh fine," she said. "Except for one royal bee-yatch in the gift shop."

Kay snorted. "Oh, Anna told me all about that. Most of the folks at the zoo are kid-friendly. I mean, if they didn't get families there, they'd be out of business, right? So the beehive lady was probably just having a bad day or something. I wouldn't worry too much about it. Anything else?"

Kay was probably going for offhand with the question, but her expectant gaze gave her away.

"What exactly are you hoping for, Kay? My ovaries to hop out and start doing the happy breeder dance?"

"Nope, I was just curious," she replied coolly.

Vivian wasn't convinced. "Did Sue and Jack put you up to this?"

Kay's face fell and she said, "Jack didn't."

"So that means Sue's been sticking her big nose in my business again," Vivian said a little too sharply. "Figures."

Their friend Sue Carlson was in the midst of planning her wedding to Jack Jameson. She'd been happily shacking up with Jack, one of her oldest flames, for almost a year. At least they'd shacked up in downtown Nashville chic style. Of course, since Sue found out she was knocked up and time was of the essence for the sake of propriety and gown fittings, the big day was just around the corner. Vivian wasn't sure if Sue had told Kay the big news yet, but she suspected as much. While deciding if Jack was shacking-up material, Sue had arranged a blind date for Vivian with Jack's buddy, Herbert Jace Blakemore. "Herb" had managed to embarrass Sue and entertain Vivian when he'd finally fessed up to going by his middle name, Jace. Good call.

They'd been going out on and off ever since. Mostly on these days. Seemed her friends were no longer content with just casual dates. Vivian was clearly expected to hurry up and jump on the marriage-and-kids bandwagon.

Kay sighed. "She means well, bless her, and she just wants you to be happy. Now as far as I'm concerned, you can do what you want to with your life and time. As long as you keep babysitting, we'll be just fine and dandy."

"Thanks," Vivian said. "I'm just super-busy with work and the volunteer stuff I'm doing, and honestly I'm pretty satisfied being cool Aunt Vivie."

Volunteer was code and cover for her work with the spirit world. Oh, and it was definitely an unpaid position, so that fit, too.

Kay leveled her gaze on Vivian and said, "I know you work hard at both, and I'm sure you're very good at it. But that's work."

"Yeah, and?"

"And, well, we're your friends and we love you and we just don't want you to forget to live, that's all," Kay said.

"What's that supposed to mean?" Vivian scowled. As if she didn't know.

"Don't go getting all riled up and ornery with me," Kay retorted with equal fire. It made Vivian feel like she was about fourteen all over again and gave her a little more sympathy for the kids. "Honestly, we've been worried about you ever since Mae passed."

"Why?" Vivian asked, exasperated, though her chest went tight and she had to swallow a lump in her throat. "I'm back at work, and I'm doing something constructive with my free time. It's not like I'm holed up like a hermit in my house."

Vivian didn't enjoy revisiting her past in general, but she found reliving her time growing up with and later caring for her invalid sister especially painful.

Especially since she'd lost more than her sister.

"Nope, but then again, that's not your style," Kay said, busying herself with refilling their wine glasses. "I've known you for twenty years, Vivian. You keep yourself crazy-busy when there's something going on that you just don't want to deal with. You were a book-a-holic and binge drinker in college because you didn't want to deal with being homesick. You were a work-a-holic after that when you didn't want to face what was back home. And you were a shop-and-bar-a-holic when Mae came to live with you because you couldn't face all of the memories and baggage that came with her. Need I remind you of your nickname? What are you hiding from now, Viv?"

Vivian was flabbergasted. She swore if anyone ever called her Vivian "Betty Ford" Bedford again, she'd zap the bejesus out of that unfortunate soul. "Well, Kay, don't go beating around the bush to spare my feelings or anything. Tell me what you *really* think."

"I've bared my soul to you on more than one occasion," Kay continued, nonplussed. Her persistence was one of the things that Vivian really liked about Kay about seventy-five percent of the time. Right now was not one of those times. "I just thought you might like to return the favor."

God, she'd give anything to talk about him. She ached to talk about him.

Vivian took a deep breath, cleared her throat, and then took small leap of faith. "Look, I haven't told anyone about this, and I don't want you to either, okay?"

"Okay."

"Last year, at the end of Mae's...life, I was really having a tough time. I thought I wouldn't be able to get through it, but I met someone. He helped me."

If Kay was surprised, she didn't show it. She simply nodded, topped off Vivian's glass again, and then gave Vivian her full attention as she nursed her own glass. Kay's gaze was focused on Vivian, and her face was calm and open.

"He was there for me when I needed someone—when I needed him, and he helped with Mae. I could really talk to him, you know, tell him things. Those ugly things that I didn't think anyone else would understand, and he didn't judge."

She paused a moment as green eyes and a wicked grin flashed through her mind. Gooseflesh ran over her skin at the memory of his touch, his warmth, and his presence. She shivered as if someone walked over her grave.

How appropriate.

Kay nodded, waiting patiently.

When she found her voice again, Vivian said, "He just...he was there. He took it all, the worst and the best of me. No judgment or pity, just understanding. He had been through some similar stuff in his own life."

What he'd gone through had been arguably worse, though he'd spoken little of it. Still, she'd learned the truth. He'd been the maker of his own hell. He'd made bad choices, but in the end, he'd found redemption. She'd played a small part in that.

And he'd given her the same gift in return.

"He was my friend and a whole lot more, but now he's gone and I miss him so much it hurts." She took a deep breath. She felt like she'd just lanced a particularly nasty sore, but it was a bearable pain, a healing pain.

Kay took another sip of her wine and said, "You loved him."

"Yes, I did...I do. But I had to let him go."

Kay paused, and Vivian dreaded the next question. Kay surprised her when she simply asked, "What was his name?"

"Zeke."

Kay slid out of her chair and walked over, enveloping her in strong, steady arms and giving her a shoulder to cry on. After, Kay offered her a tissue and some tea, and they sat in silence for a short time before Kay said, "Thank you for telling me about your Zeke. I'm sorry you lost him." She stopped and appeared to consider whether to push the conversation forward or to let it be. "If you ever need to talk about it, you know I'm here."

She managed a small smile and said, "Thanks. I'm really trying to move on and live my life, I promise."

"Well, then that's good enough for me, and it'll be good enough for Sue, too."

"I don't know if it's good enough for Jace." God, she was trying. She really was. He was a good man, too. Patient. She just needed a little more time to mend her broken heart.

"Well, honey, you're going to have to work that out with him," Kay replied. "Will I see you for dinner on Saturday?"

"Of course," Vivian said, as the smile returned to her tear-streaked face. "As long as you promise me plenty of honey ham and tater salad, you *know* I'll be there!"

She stood and started gathering her things—purse, keys, though, as usual, her cellphone proved elusive. Scooter chose that moment to run into the room at Mach 5 and scream, "Surprise!" After nearly jumping out of her skin, Kay rolled her eyes and offered a warm smile to her youngest.

"Aunt Vee Vee go bye bye?" he asked.

"Yeah, but I'll be back, buddy. Okay?" she said, scooping him up in a fit of giggles and kisses.

"Junior sowy."

"Who's Junior?" Kay asked, opening her arms to accept the bundle of boy.

"No idea," Vivian said. "Connor mentioned something about 'Junior' taking him to the swings."

Kay smiled and put Connor down, sending him off to his room with a warning to play quietly instead of pestering his sisters. "Probably just some cartoon character. He's got such a big imagination. Is it warm in here to you?"

Vivian tensed, gaze darting around the room for any hidden guardians. They shouldn't have followed her here. Ezra always warned her when she'd be needed for a crossing. They never, ever showed up unannounced.

Don't you hurt them.

"Hey, are you okay? You look pale," Kay said, voice laced with concern. "You should sit down."

But she couldn't sit down. A guardian spirit's presence could only mean one thing. No, it couldn't be time for one of the Clemmens family to cross. She refused to accept it.

Panic seized her. Vivian left Kay and rushed to the girls' rooms, her barely leashed power ready to strike at any guardian spirit set on claiming one of the children. She half-expected to find one of the girls in the midst of a seizure or choking on a Lego. Instead, she interrupted a card game and earned an eye-roll from Annabelle.

Thank God they're okay.

That left Connor.

With Kay hot on her heels, Vivian threw open the door to Connor's room. He was sprawled on the floor, completely immobile. Sparks flew from Vivian's fingertips as her heart raced. No, they couldn't take the boy, this sweet, angelic child whose life had just begun. Kay reached out and grabbed her arm, getting a jolt in the process.

"Ouch!" she yelped. Then she yanked Vivian out of the room.

"What's going on here?" Kay hissed.

Vivian scrambled for an explanation, panic fading as she noticed the slow rise and fall of Connor's chest. The little guy was sleeping. "I was worried. I thought I heard something."

Kay's scowl faded, replaced by a nod and gaze filled with understanding. "I get it, especially after the scare you had with Connor. I still get jumpy sometimes and check on them at night to make sure they're still breathing."

"Sorry I almost woke him up," Vivian said.

They crept back to the living room and sat down. Kay rubbed her hand and muttered something about how Vivian needed more fabric softener. Shit. She'd almost used her spirit light in front of Kay and the kids. She shuddered to think how much trouble she'd caused, or what the consequences would be if her living friends knew about the hidden world of spirits.

But a guardian spirit had been there, and it had hidden from her. She needed to find out why. Kay's voice brought her back from her musings.

"Hon, are you sure you're okay?"

Plastering on what she hoped was a convincing smile, she said, "I'm fine. I promise. I think you're right. I'm just, you know, a little emotional after...everything."

Kay looked suspicious, but nodded and said, "Okay. If you're sure."

Vivian grabbed her in a fierce embrace and said, "You take care. Call me if you need me."

Then she bolted out the door. She needed to talk to Ezra.

CHAPTER THREE

Ezra appeared later that evening, much as he had the first time he'd called on her, strolling from her line of tall trees in the backyard and ambling up the stairs leading to the deck. He looked for all the world as if he'd just fallen off the turnip truck, clad in bib overalls, work boots, and an old John Deere cap, which was most likely how he'd looked while he was alive. He also looked pretty hungry. Unlike the first night, he arrived in time for dinner.

"Evenin', Ezra," Vivian called out from the kitchen. "Why don't you come on inside and have a seat at the table?"

She was up to her ears in flour. She could have used biscuits, of course. Canned biscuits worked great for dumplings. But tonight, she'd opted for homemade. Flour, lard, an old wooden rolling pin, and a butter knife for trimming all decorated the countertops surrounding the stove. She'd boiled chicken breasts and thighs in stock, bones in, and the shredded meat sat on a nearby plate, waiting. Now that her stock was at a low and rolling boil, she began the process of dropping dumplings into the pot, one by one. By the third dumpling, she'd registered that Ezra was behind her, no doubt smiling.

He chuckled. "You ought to add some butter to keep them dumplins from stickin' to each other and the pot."

"Who the hell made you an expert?" she snapped, though she let him drop a dollop of butter in the pot after he'd removed his hat and set it on the counter. "Besides, it's already a heart attack on a plate with all of the salt and fat. Not that it matters to you."

Ezra had been dead for over fifty years.

"Little gal, I'll have you know I helped out in the kitchen quite a bit in my day," he shot back with mock indignation. "I was helpin' my ma with biscuits and gravy when I was knee-high to a grasshopper, and I still make the best biscuits you ever did eat."

"Well, well, well, weren't you a genuine progressive? Get here early next time and you can put your money where your mouth is, not to mention your stomach," she said, turning and sizing him up. "Speaking of, you look like you're getting fatter. How is that even possible?"

She'd always assumed Ezra's appearance, like most of the other corporeal spirits she knew, was of his choosing and not subject to changes that would affect mortals. From what Zeke had told her, they were able to "construct" a body from elements in the human realm when they projected. She'd seen him do it. Their corporeal bodies were only shells that encompassed their true essence, which was almost pure energy.

Still, she couldn't help but notice that the old coot looked pretty healthy these days, to say the least.

"Aw, now, you have to understand, Miss Vivian, before I met you I'd been a wandering this old world unseen with nary a bite to eat for years. It's only natural that I build myself a big old body when I come a-callin' on you. Consider it a compliment for your good cookin'."

"Yeah, you and every other hungry guardian who happens to be in the neighborhood. I swear y'all are eating me out of house and home," she grumbled.

"You need more money?" he asked, pulling a wad of cash out of his front chest pocket. "I promised I'd pay regular for regular work. You've been a doing a real good job."

"No," she said, maybe a little too quickly. "I mean, I wouldn't mind a raise, but I need some more time to figure out how to account for the extra cash. I only work part-time now, you know, and I don't need any trouble with the IRS. The only thing I really need you to do is to tell your dumb little buddies to wait *outside* the bathroom when they come calling. The lack of privacy is getting pretty old."

"I'll let them know," he replied, chuckling. "And I got me a few associates that know a thing or two about taxes and such."

"I know a thing or two about taxes and finances," Vivian retorted sardonically. "I am a loan officer, for God's sake."

She wondered where Ezra got all of the money. Worried was more like it. She would have hated to think of herself as a grave robber.

Ezra scowled at her and puffed out his chest. "I can't abide by blasphemy. That's mighty ugly talk coming from a nice young lady like you."

"Lay off the father-figure shit. We both know I'm neither young nor a lady."

The temperature rose a notch or two, letting her know she should probably stop. She'd only seen Ezra angry a few times, but that was enough. He kept the façade of fumbling old country bumpkin, but he was one of the most powerful guardian spirits around. Still, she didn't take kindly to being bullied, and she and Ezra still had some bad blood between them.

"I ain't your daddy, but I may as well be for all the looking out I do for you and all the trouble you give me," he growled. "You're no spring chicken, but you ain't got one foot in the grave yet." He narrowed his gaze and added, "Unless you're ready to move on."

She stood very still and stared at him. While she might not like being bullied, Vivian wasn't fool enough to push him too far. His words were no empty threat. Ezra could, in fact, arrange for her to move on from this side of life if he chose. He didn't need her permission or cooperation.

After a bad moment, Ezra sighed and spoke in a gentler tone, "But I don't think that's the case. You got a stubborn streak in you that runs clean from your bull head to your big toe. You ain't ready to give up just yet. As for the rest, I reckon you know how to be a lady when you want to be."

Vivian bit her tongue and tried not to scowl. The temperature in the kitchen dropped a bit, as did her anxiety. They were okay again, for the moment.

Ezra shrugged and said, "Still, I'd be ashamed to hear you talking like that in front of our preacher friend, or your feller. They coming by tonight? You cooked enough to feed an army."

She grinned at him. She couldn't help it. "You're right. I haven't given up on life yet, so you can hold off on taking me to the next realm. The padre's on his way, but not Jace. I still haven't worked out exactly how to explain *you* to him. Don't worry. They've both heard me say much worse."

He grinned back and said, "It sure is nice to see you smile." After a moment, his face changed from jolly to serious, and he spoke again. "You've not been smiling so much these days. You doing all right?"

"Aside from worrying about guardian spirits sneaking around my friend's house, I'm peachy," she said. "What gives?"

Ezra frowned. "Don't know anything about that, and I would know if anyone in the area was scheduled to cross."

Vivian wanted to believe him, but he'd lied to her before. Oh, he'd assured her it was for her own good, but it did put a damper on their working relationship with some serious trust issues.

He cocked his head to the side and studied her. Probably reading her thoughts. Damned guardian spirits. Though it was a skill that probably came in handy when monitoring the world of the living, she didn't appreciate it when the spirits used it on her—especially since it was one of the skills she didn't share with them. Maybe she'd have to be dead to get it.

Hardly worth the price.

"I'll look into it, but don't worry. Your friends aren't scheduled to cross anytime soon. I'd tell you if they were. Now, what else is bothering you?"

"Nothing. I'm fine," she stated flatly. Then she turned and busied herself by adding shredded chicken to her stock and dumplings, hoping he'd let it go.

"No, you ain't," Ezra said to her back. "You been running yourself ragged. Want to try telling me the truth?"

Simmering irritation gave way to full-blown anger. Guardian or not, he'd pushed *her* too far. She didn't turn to face him. Instead, she moved her stockpot to another burner set on low, dusted her hands on her apron, and worked on stirring the pot of green beans seasoned with salt pork. Having held her peace for more than a few months, she decided it was time to stir the soon-to-be-boiling-over pot between them as well.

Heaving a long sigh, she finally spoke. "Well, hello, pot. Kettle calling. You've got a hell of a lot of nerve, Ezra, talking to *me* about the truth."

They both stood still for a long time, neither one speaking. Vivian caved first and turned around to face the old spirit. His head was down, shoulders slumped, and she swore that she felt a slight dip in the temperature of the air surrounding them. A touch of pity tugged at her heartstrings, but she buried it deep.

She wasn't ready to forgive him just yet.

He spoke in a very soft voice, "I reckon I've been asking for that. We need to sit down and have us a little talk, you and me."

"Won't change anything." She shrugged. "I'm still stuck halfway between the living and the dead, I'm still as beholden to you as I would have been had you collected my soul when you were supposed to, and I still lost Zeke." She had to turn away at the last.

Of all the betrayals and losses she'd faced, Zeke's loss was the hardest. It was a raw wound carved deep in her soul, one she feared would never heal.

"Child," he began. "I never meant for you to get hurt so bad. I know you loved that boy." She felt a hand on her shoulder and Ezra's healing warmth, but she pulled herself away and busied herself setting the table.

He grabbed a couple of plates and started helping, but he wasn't done talking quite yet. "You done right by him, letting him go, and you done right by sticking around and helping folks with your powers instead of giving up and crossing to the other side."

He paused, looking like he didn't know what to say. What was there to say? She'd fallen in love with the personal guardian that Ezra had sent her, but she'd wound up taking care of the debt Ezra had owed the reapers in exchange for Zeke's safe passage, not to mention her sister's, to the other side.

Then again, had Ezra told her the truth when he'd had the chance, she'd be dead. She didn't want to think about what would have happened to Mae. Or Zeke.

Clearing his throat, he offered, "I thought you was moving on with things. You been a-courting Mister Jace for a spell."

"Yeah, but..." She stopped. Jace was a good man. He was funny, smart, and he wasn't bad in the sack. Of course, Zeke had been on a whole different level. Sex with a corporeal spirit was an otherworldly experience, to put it mildly.

But that wasn't the real issue.

"Ezra, my life isn't normal. How am I supposed to work with you and your kind and keep it secret from a living man? Do I have to keep it a secret?"

"Maybe not, if you think we can trust him," Ezra said. He sat down at his usual place at Vivian's table, careful not to disturb her place settings. She'd put out the good china that she inherited from her mom, as she often did during their meetings to discuss ongoing and upcoming cases.

He spent a few moments lost in his thoughts before nodding. "Fine. I'd say it'd be all right by me if you told him. We can always have him forget if he gave us trouble. You think you'll be keeping him around for the long haul?"

"I don't know," she replied. That was the big question, one she couldn't answer at the moment.

Before they had the chance to continue their conversation, they were interrupted by a commotion outside of Vivian's back door.

CHAPTER FOUR

The flash of white light caught her eye just before a cry of shock and pain registered in her ears. Ezra disappeared in a flash as she dropped her spoon and dashed out the back in time to watch Father Lloyd Montgomery fall to the floor of her deck. The cool of the early summer evening quickly heated as rage radiated from Ezra, who'd materialized on the deck beside the priest. He practically glowed with spirit energy.

Vivian ran to the priest and cradled his head in her lap.

"Padre," she gasped. "What happened? Are you okay? Answer me!"

He opened his eyes with great effort, his breathing labored. His complexion was ashen and he seemed to be struggling to remain conscious, "Vivian," he whispered. "Danger...Ezra?"

"He's here, Padre, and he's got reinforcements." Jeanne and Wallace had appeared shortly after she found the priest. They'd fanned out with Ezra in search of his attacker. She marveled at the speed with which they moved through her backyard and the surrounding neighborhood. They floated, flew, and dashed in a supernatural whirlwind of pursuit.

The priest's coughing tore her attention away from the display of spirit power and back to his deteriorating condition. "What did this to you? Was it a reaper?"

"Don't...know...came from behind. Said to...stop." His eyes rolled back and he started slipping away.

"Father Montgomery? Padre! Oh, Jesus, stay with me," she pleaded, rubbing his face and trying to revive him. "Ezra! Jeanne! Anyone! Help!"

The guardians were nowhere in sight, apparently still caught up in pursuit of the unknown spirit assailant while Vivian sat powerless and terrified. She and Lloyd Montgomery had been through Hell together, literally, and he was the only friend she had who knew about her association with the world of spirits. She couldn't lose him. Steeling herself, she focused her mind on the padre, intent on drawing his pain and suffering in an effort to stabilize him until she could get help.

She'd only ever channeled deep wounds of the soul, the mental and emotional sort. Physical injury was still uncharted territory. She'd only managed once or twice, and that had been by accident.

Small wisps of light flowed from the limp and listless body of the priest and into Vivian, though he didn't rouse. The light was pale and she felt nothing from it. He was fading fast, his breathing shallow and slow. *Damn!*

"Padre, come on, stay with me, stay, you have to stay," she whispered. A wave of panic hit her, followed by despair and anger.

"No. I'm not going to lose anyone else. Do you hear me?" she shouted to the heavens and whatever force had done this horrible thing. Hot tears ran down her cheeks and that fueled her rage and heartache. She'd lost Mae, her sister, before she'd even had the chance to say goodbye. And she'd lost Zeke. She couldn't lose the priest, too.

She grabbed Father Montgomery by the shoulders and shook him. "You aren't going to bail on me now, you hear me? *Wake up!*"

Light poured out of her eyes, her open mouth, and out of her pores, the same light she'd seen from Zeke, brilliant white and almost blinding. Taking a small ray in through a weak breath, the priest latched onto her arm and with the last of his strength pulled her closer. He heaved a breath and drew her light again, and then another deep breath, and another as her light flowed into him.

She was relieved that he was reviving, but she was beginning to feel light-headed. The wave of dizziness nearly knocked her off balance as she struggled to rein in the power of her spirit energy.

"Padre," she said, trying to wriggle out of his iron grip. "That's enough."

He held her tightly and continued to inhale deeply. She couldn't get away and she was growing weaker. Her breaths came in shallow rasps as she tried to hold onto consciousness. Spots danced before her eyes as her vision blurred and her stomach clenched. Vivian continued to struggle, becoming more desperate. Finally, she knocked her head against his as hard as she could, and he let her go.

"Ugh." He moaned, rubbing his forehead and sitting up. Vivian leaned against the side of the house for support and tried to clear her head, taking in great gulps of air as she recovered. Her body was too warm, almost feverish, and it ached like she'd been hit by a Mack truck.

"Vivian?" came the padre's voice through the fog. "Are you okay?"

"I'm not sure," she said, placing her head between her knees and taking a few more deep breaths. "Are you?"

"I'm feeling much better," he said. His voice was louder, and Vivian figured he'd moved to sit beside her. "How did you do that?"

"I don't know," she muttered, and then slowly raised her head to look at him. "But we can talk about that later. What happened?"

"I was heading up to your front door and saw someone rounding the corner of your house. I thought it might be Ezra, so I followed. I needed to have a chat with him. When I climbed up the back steps, he grabbed me from behind. He said, 'This is a warning for you and your friends. Stop interfering in our affairs. Stop the woman.' Then he...well, I'm not sure what he did, exactly, but I thought my heart had stopped beating. I was on the ground and you came out."

"I saw a white light. You were attacked by a spirit?"

"It must have been a spirit," he said, rubbing his temples again. "Vivian, you have a very hard head."

"So do you, Padre," she replied with a nervous chuckle. Then she sat up with a jolt, which would have merited some colorful language had she not been so taken by her next thought. "We saw light...the spirit shot white light. How did you feel just before? When he grabbed you?"

"Quite terrified," the priest replied.

"No," she said quickly and with little patience. "Was it cold?"

"No," the priest mused. "As a matter of fact, it was unusually warm."

"Shit!"

"What?" the priest's concern was genuine. Vivian didn't even get a raised brow on account of her language.

"Then it wasn't a reaper. It was...but how's that possible? It was—"

"A guardian," Ezra's voice chimed in. "We got ourselves a rogue guardian, and he's after you, Miss Vivian."

CHAPTER FIVE

Vivian woke up with a killer headache and a ravenous appetite. Lucky for her, Jeanne had figured out how to work the coffee maker and also had breakfast on the table. After the events of the previous night, Jeanne had volunteered to keep an eye on her. Wallace got assigned to Father Montgomery while Ezra went off to consult with his superiors, presumably other guardians. Vivian thought the padre had gotten the shit end of the stick. She'd rather face a dozen reapers than be stuck with Wallace the surly spirit for the foreseeable future.

Vivian grabbed a cup of coffee and sat down at her table across from the corporeal spirit. It always amazed her how real they looked. Jeanne appeared as fresh and vital as any university co-ed, with her bright eyes, blond hair swept up in a neat ponytail that sat high on her head, and her capacity to scarf down food like your average frat boy. And yet, after she'd tapped out on her spirit energy, that form would return to dust as she returned to her incorporeal form.

It was magic. Zeke tried to convince her it was simply physics working in harmony with the available elements, but building a physical body that so perfectly matched that of a living, breathing person? Nope. Had to be magic. Seeing it almost made her a true believer.

Almost, but not quite. Faith and Vivian Bedford hadn't been on speaking terms for a very long time.

"So," Jeanne began, helping herself to a waffle and some sausages. "You're a true healer? That's a rare talent. There are few real guardians who are capable of that, you know."

"No, I didn't know that. I don't know much of anything, to tell you the truth. Ezra's not big on full disclosure," Vivian replied with bitterness, remembering their conversation from the night before.

"Of course not, honey," she said, her voice muffled by virtue of the wad of food occupying her mouth. "You're just a human." Like most spirits she'd met, Jeanne relished food and drink while in corporeal form.

And, like most spirits, Jeanne didn't see her as an equal. Living soul brokers were rare, and apparently ranked somewhere between unpaid interns and underappreciated lackeys in the afterlife management hierarchy. At least that was how Vivian perceived it.

She didn't appreciate it, and since Jeanne was a handy target, she'd unleash her frustration while making a case for a higher clearance level. "I'm a human who happens to be able to suck the life burdens from other humans and ease their suffering, who can toss the light with the best of your kind, and who can apparently heal physical wounds. I think I deserve a little more respect, not to mention a little more info."

Jeanne shrugged. "Fair enough, I suppose. Ezra didn't give me permission to talk about this stuff with you, but he didn't tell me not to either." Her eyes gleamed with mischief as she leaned down and whispered, "What do you want to know?"

Wow, that had been easier than she'd expected, and her heart raced with giddy anticipation. At last, a chance to get some real answers.

"First off, what's this 'true healer' business? Jesus, I just got the hang of collecting burdens of the mind and heart."

Jeanne shrugged again. "A true healer is just...well, a true healer. You know, someone who can heal the sick?"

Vivian leaned in and said, "Really? Like I can make the lame walk, the blind see, that sort of thing, or do my powers only work for spirit zaps?"

Jeanne thought for a moment. "Well, from what I understand, you should be able to heal all manner of physical injuries and ills. It's really an extension of your ability to help people with their emotional and spiritual burdens. Just be careful. Don't overdo it until you know your limits."

"You mean I have to work out how to heal bodies, too? Is that why I feel like stir-fried dog shit this morning?" Vivian grumbled.

"You just need to get your strength back, shug," Jeanne replied with a smile. "Eat up!"

Fucking morning people.

Vivian was annoyed by chirpy folks in the a.m., spirits being no exception. Still, she didn't want to blow her chance to get more information about her condition. "Okay, so as long as I eat and get some down time, I'm not in any danger if I play faith-healer?"

"Well..." Jeanne said, appearing thoughtful once more. "I know that real guardians have to return to our realm and replenish our energy—"

"How do you do that?" Vivian interrupted. She remembered Ezra telling her that Zeke had to recharge his battery after she'd zapped him by accident. That was shortly after she'd taken in his spiritual light during a very carnal union. She'd always suspected a connection between the two, but naturally hadn't broached the subject with Ezra.

"Oh, it involves a communion of sorts," Jeanne said with a vague wave of her hands.

"Is that what they call it up there in the clouds?" Vivian asked, her voice dripping with irony.

"Humph!" Jeanne scolded primly. "Not in the sense that you mean or probably 'experienced.' We don't keep corporeal form there. But, in a sense, we draw energy from one another, which we collect through our work with the living and the crossing of souls."

"Like the kind of energy Ezra and Darkmore wanted from my sister?"

Mae, her departed sister, had spent most of her life suffering from a severe disability that rendered her helpless. With Mae unable to walk, talk, or see to even the most basic of self-care needs, their mother had cared for Mae around the clock until both their mother and father died in a freak accident while on vacation. Vivian had become Mae's primary caregiver then. After unwittingly forming an association with the world of spirits, Vivian discovered that living souls like Mae possessed enormous reservoirs of spirit energy—the kind that guardians and reapers harvested while helping spirits cross to other realms.

Once she understood that both Ezra and Darkmore wanted Mae's energy, Vivian had gone to great lengths to protect her. It had almost cost Vivian her life, her soul, and had obliged her to serve as an assistant to Ezra and the guardians as a living soul broker for the duration of her mortal life.

Most likely she'd have to still serve after she passed, but she'd cross that bridge when she got to it.

"Like the kind of energy that *every* living human possesses and releases upon their crossing," Jeanne corrected, maybe a bit too quickly. She looked at Vivian and then added with a more gentle tone, "Your sister was quite special, as are all like her. We don't relish their suffering. By harnessing their suffering and the energy that comes with it, however, we can make a difference in the lives of others who suffer."

Vivian nodded. It made sense, and Jeanne seemed sincere in her convictions. Still, the idea of harnessing spirit energy, essentially the life force, of the disabled and other vulnerable, downtrodden humans left Vivian uneasy. Who decided how much energy to harvest? Which guardians took that energy? Zeke had mentioned something about allotments of energy. That suggested that someone banked it and doled it out as necessary.

Or as he or she saw fit. Vivian doubted there was much regulation. The whole afterlife operation management system seemed more pyramid scheme than run-of-the-mill corporate structure. She'd have to investigate a bit more.

Jeanne's voice brought her out of her musings and back to the conversation. "So, what else do you want to know?"

The question of most immediate concern seemed obvious enough. "What's the deal with this rogue guardian? I thought you were all on the same team."

"Most of us are," Jeanne said, taking on a more serious tone. "But there has been some dissent among the council regarding the activities of humans like you, not to mention among and about those of us in the field. It seems as though one of us has decided to take matters into his own hands."

Council? Field agents? Forget pyramid schemes. This was like the friggin' FBI!

"Glad to know you folks are having so many meetings about me," Vivian snapped. "And thanks for keeping me in the loop. You really need to work on an instruction manual for unwitting human helpers."

Vivian paused mid-rant, letting the rest of Jeanne's words set in. "Wait a minute...you said 'humans like you.' So I'm not the only one?"

Jeanne just shrugged as though Vivian had stated the obvious.

"Who are the others? Where are they? Can I meet some?" God, she wasn't alone! Until that moment, she hadn't realized just how isolated she'd been, how she'd yearned for the company of someone—anyone—who understood. Zeke had provided that when she'd first entered the world of spirits.

Unfortunately, Zeke was gone. She'd set him free. That was another part of the deal she'd made with Ezra. No guardian touched Mae's soul or stole her energy, and Zeke had to be released from forced service as a guardian spirit under Ezra. She'd paid his karmic debt after helping him face the sins that had led to his sentence, giving him peace, or so she hoped.

Wherever you are, love, I hope you're at peace. Know that I still love you and always will.

Jeanne hadn't answered, so Vivian asked again, "Can I meet some?"

"We'll see," Jeanne replied. "What else?"

Vivian sighed in frustration. Seemed she might never get a straight answer from these spirits. Picking at the bits of fruit and syrup on her plate, she said, "What's the guardian council, and why would they have a problem with humans like me, or field guardians like you?"

Jeanne took a sip of coffee, and quirked a brow as she swallowed. "Ever dealt with management?"

"Sure," Vivian said. She'd almost been one at her old firm. Not an easy job to fill, nor was it easy to accept orders from middlemen and -women who may or may not know as much about the job as their underlings.

"Ever worked *under* a manager who hasn't been out in the trenches for a really long time?"

Boy, had she ever. "Uh-oh, trouble in paradise, huh? A little disconnect between the union and corporate?"

"They mean well, I'm sure," Jeanne muttered. She pushed her plate back and cradled her coffee cup in her hands as if gathering warmth. Or maybe she was warming it up with her natural guardian energy heat.

Jeanne spoke slowly, as if choosing her words with great care. "They have to look at the big picture, things like growth, sustainability, what you might call cost-benefit analysis." She seemed uncomfortable. Whether she felt bad about sharing the inner workings of the guardian spirit hierarchy or about bashing the big boss, Vivian couldn't tell.

"Hey, if there's something going on with the higher-ups that affects me, then I think I have a right to know," Vivian said, pushing a bit. "After all, we're on the same side, right?"

"These are tough times, Vivian. So much suffering, so much work. It's not always easy to balance that with meeting their quotas."

"Quotas?"

"They need energy too," Jeanne said with another shrug.

Oh yeah. Pyramid scheme. Add in corporate greed, lack of communication between management and workers, not to mention an apparent lack of oversight, and problems were bound to follow. Vivian wondered if their realm was on the verge of an energy crisis.

Interpreting Jeanne's expression as a sign to take up another topic, Vivian asked, "So, what do we do?"

Jeanne shrugged again and helped herself to some more fresh strawberries. Vivian considered zapping her in the ass, but refrained. Then Jeanne said, "Wait for Ezra, I guess."

"That ain't gonna fly, sister," Vivian said, grabbing her purse and keys. "I've got to go by the office for a few hours and run a few errands. I'll be back after I stop by to check on Father Montgomery."

Jeanne raised an eyebrow and moved to block her. "Whoa, what are you up to? Ezra told me to keep you out of trouble. Besides, we still have to talk about your case load!" she practically squealed. "I'll be working with you now! Isn't that exciting?"

"Great," Vivian said, without much enthusiasm.

"Oh Vivian, you should be happy. We are blessed with such a wonderful opportunity to make a real difference in the world of the living. You know, Wallace says that I'm one of the most promising recruits he's had in a few decades."

Vivian sighed and pinched the bridge of her nose. In spite of her obvious doubts about how the guardian operation was run, Jeanne still had the enthusiasm of a cheerleader and apparently bought into the mission statement. She also appeared to be a play-by-the-rules kind of gal. Wait for Ezra? Not likely. That had gotten her into the soul broker business in the first place. She wasn't about to make the same mistake twice.

But Jeanne didn't need to know that. Shifting gears, Vivian said, "Maybe I'd be a little more gung-ho if I wasn't worried about my life, not to mention the padre's. He's got protection twenty-four seven, right?"

"Of course," she said, looking a little wounded. "Now, tell me what you're planning to do."

"Oh," Vivian replied with a vague smile. "I just need to check with a confidential source after I run by the office."

———

The advantage of working part-time, aside from sleeping later and avoiding at least one major office breast-talker and all around douchebag was not being stuck in I-440 traffic. Nashville and the surrounding counties were making an effort to avoid the Metro Atlanta model of growth, but traffic congestion never seemed to improve in spite of never-ending construction. Vivian's blood pressure, not to mention her penchant for swearing, had improved thanks to a later arrival time at the office and, thus, a less stressful commute.

Walking in and giving a quick nod to her colleagues out front, Vivian moved into her office, fired up her computer, and tackled a week's worth of emails with ruthless efficiency before reviewing her stack of applications in progress. She had help with credit checks, but preferred to double-check them herself before moving ahead with the paperwork. She'd learned after fourteen years in the business, and even earlier while hanging around her dad's office, 'Always look at the three C's, hon, and look at 'em in order,' he'd said. Credit equals character, capacity equals income, and collateral equals insurance for the loan to cover your ass in case of default.

That advice was worth more than half of her college courses in this business. It was pretty sound advice for life, come to think of it. Unlike her colleagues in the crumbling mortgage loan industry, she meticulously scrutinized beacon scores, debt to income ratios, and followed the 'thirty-five to forty percent what you owe to what you make' net rule.

Whether their loan applications were approved or not, she always offered frank advice to her clients. Though there was plenty of blame to go around with borrowers taking on more mortgage than they could possibly afford, she still got hot under the collar with reports of lenders fudging incomes and their dumb little appraiser buddies inflating property values. That little bit of creative accounting had left way too many families without a home or any of what they'd actually invested.

Though her supervisors over the years had scolded her for wasting time, she also offered free credit counseling when she saw good people struggling. She'd had a nose for it even before she'd acquired her spirit powers, but they definitely helped. These days, she combined both jobs by channeling the burdens of her clients in secret. And in the current economy, the burdens were aplenty. Plus, since she still only worked part-time, she tended to get more of the high-risk and desperate clients that her colleagues didn't much care for. Today's case was one of those.

"Good morning, Mr. and Mrs...." she paused and made a quick glance at the paperwork in front of her, "Ridley—"

"It's Sam," said the man in the secondhand suit and tie as he stood and grabbed her by the hand. "I sure do appreciate you meeting us today, ma'am."

"It's my job, sir," she said, returning his handshake and smiling. "And who's your lovely lady?"

"Oh, this here's Mary," he said with a big grin. "She's the best. She and our little ones."

"Pleased to meet you both," Vivian said, turning her attention to Mary. "Now, I understand you need a loan, but I wasn't clear about the purpose."

Mary looked down at her hands, clasped together hard in her lap as waves of despair flowed from her.

"We need a little help paying some expenses on the car that Mary uses to haul around the kids," he said. Vivian didn't need any otherworldly powers to hear the anxiety in his voice.

"I see," Vivian began. "But what I don't understand is why you need such a big loan from us for maintenance." She leaned forward and gave Mr. Ridley a knowing look. "I mean, if it's going to cost you that much to fix something that's broken, you'd be better off getting another car."

"Well, it ain't so much repair as it is keeping the car," Sam said.

"Oh, you don't have the title?" Vivian asked, probing. God, it broke her heart to see good folks like these fall victim to scams and sharks who preyed on the desperate and downtrodden. She'd been seeing more and more lately.

"Well, we do..." Sam winced as he trailed off, red creeping up his neck to his face. He held his fists clenched at his sides but took a deep breath to calm his emotions. Placing a hand on his wife's shoulder, he struggled to collect his thoughts, or perhaps for the courage to admit to the trap he'd fallen into.

Vivian had a pretty good idea about what was going on and decided not to mince words about it. She leaned forward and put her palms on the desk, waiting for the Ridleys to meet her gaze before speaking.

"Mr. Ridley, I'm going to give it to you straight. Your take-home pay is pretty good, so you ought to be able to keep up a car you own. You aren't so forthcoming about the issue with your car or if you even own it, so I figure you've probably got yourself in a jam and you're robbing Peter to pay Paul. You want to tell me who else you owe?"

Sam gave Vivian a hard look and replied, "I came here to get a loan, miss, not no lecture. Are you going to help me out, or do I need to take my business elsewhere?"

Vivian waited. She didn't want to wound the man's pride by way of his wallet, but she suspected these were decent folk who got in over their heads. She wanted to know why and how before she decided if she would or even could help them dig their way out. She lowered her gaze, sitting back up in her chair and taking a moment to glance at the paperwork while giving Sam time to decide if he wanted to talk or not.

She didn't look up as she heard Mary whisper to her husband, "Sam, just tell her what happened. We got to do something, honey."

"Let me handle this, baby," he pleaded.

"But we can't lose the car!" she said, her voice high with desperation.

"Mary!"

"No, I'm done pussyfooting around," Mary said, turning to address Vivian. "Miss Bedford, our youngest got real bad sick about six months ago and our insurance doesn't cover squat. We had a mountain of bills and we didn't want to go and get behind, so we took out a loan against our car."

"A title loan?" Vivian asked, heart racing as her blood began to boil.

"I know it wasn't smart, but we'd started hearing from collections agents, calling at all hours of the day and night. It was just awful. So we used the title loan money to pay down some of the medical bills, and then we got behind on some other bills and we went to some of those payday advance places to keep up after we'd burned through our savings. It's been a rough few years and I haven't been able to work like I used to with the kids and all."

"I get it," Vivian said with genuine sympathy. She'd seen this before. Title lenders loaned the working poor roughly half the value of their cars at a whopping thirty-five to forty percent interest rate per month. If the borrower couldn't pay them off, they could repossess the car. These sharks had nothing to lose, and the poor soul who took the loan was left without transportation and in worse financial shape than before. Coupled with the rat wheel of never-ending paycheck advances, these folks could work three jobs and never dig themselves out.

And there were so many—more than she cared to count in the half a mile through Antioch or Crieve Hall, be it payday advances, title loans, or pawn shops, though you would be hard-pressed to find any in the ritzy Brentwood or Bellevue business districts. Plenty of politicians made careers out of lashing out at class warfare and social justice warriors, but Vivian had counted about ten loan shark establishments on a seven-mile stretch of Nolensville Road, north of Old Hickory. The problem was real.

"So," Vivian said. "Are you ready for my first question?"

Sam eyed her with wariness while Mary nodded eagerly. Vivian smiled and asked, "How's your youngest doing now?"

"Oh, he's right as rain." Mary beamed. "Sam, show her that picture of Luke you carry in your wallet."

While the Ridleys were digging for photos, Vivian closed her eyes and focused on them, taking in nearly invisible wisps of light. The burdens borne on that light filled and enveloped her, the sleepless nights they'd spent tending to the sick child, and those spent worrying about getting by with rent, groceries, utilities, and all that they owed. Relief washed over her as she sensed the love and pride in their family and their support for one another. Flashes of the good made the bad easier for Vivian to take, like the proverbial spoon full of sugar that helped some really bad tasting medicine go down. Tucking away the heavy load, she looked at the photo of their son and smiled.

"Okay, here's what I'm going to do. You're going to get a five thousand dollar loan from our office at a good rate, and you are going to take that money and pay off every penny that you owe to the sharks. Do you owe any more on the medical bills?"

"No, ma'am," Sam said in a very business-like tone. "We paid all of that off."

"That's good, but if this ever happens again, you call me first. I've worked with docs before and can straighten things out with a better payment schedule and even negotiate your total down. They're smart enough to know that steady payments are better than nothing at all. Now then, let's go ahead and schedule your next appointment with me before we get into the nitty gritty on the term, collateral, and the paperwork."

"Next appointment? I thought we just mailed the check or dropped it by?" Mary chimed in.

"That's what you did with the other lenders. Not with me. When you come back and we're going to go over your monthly expenses and work out a budget to get you through the length of your loan with us and hopefully work on getting your savings rebuilt. You putting away anything for retirement, college tuition, things like that?"

The Ridleys stared at her in wonder. Sam cleared his throat and said, "We have some pension money through my job, but nothing for school. You know, no one's ever offered us something like this. You think we can pay you off *and* save money?"

"You can do that and more, folks, but you have to start with a budget and stick with it," Vivian replied, giddy at the prospect of helping real, living people in the ordinary world.

"Why are you interested in helping us save?" Sam asked.

"Well, for starters, it's just good business. If I get you on the right track with your finances, I'll get the money back with my cut of the interest, plus I'll get myself a customer for life," Vivian said. That was another great piece of advice her dad had given her. It was also why she liked working for a small, independent firm rather than a giant corporation. Personal relationships mattered more than bigger profits at the expense of her integrity.

Or her soul.

"You already got that!" Mary said, standing up and shaking her hand. "You work for that guy on the radio or something?"

"No, ma'am, but I'm a big fan. Stick with me and I'll have y'all shouting, 'I'm debt free' before you know it. Now let's get you on the books for next week."

Elated by her success with the Ridleys, she stuck around the office for an extra hour to help the cashiers collect and log payments. In between, she made some calls to "encourage" a few folks who were late on their payments to at least come in and talk about the issue so they could resolve it, as well as making a few solicitation calls. The work was good, but it served another purpose—avoidance.

She dreaded her next appointment so much she even considered joining Mack and Larry, their repo men, on their weekly effort to find the hidden assets of the chronically delinquent. But there would be no avoiding the inevitable. He terrified her as much as he intrigued her, but, more importantly, he was her insurance policy against the guardian spirits to whom she was beholden. Her work with the guardians wasn't exactly voluntary, and the burdens she swallowed through her work with the living took their toll on her mortal body and on her soul.

Only one creature could relieve her of those burdens, and he'd volunteered, asking nothing in return for the service. Granted, feeding on misery benefited him as much as it did her, but he'd never asked her for anything. Not yet.

She swallowed hard.

Best get on with it.

Finally, with a deep breath for courage, she packed up, got into her car, and prepared to meet the reaper.

CHAPTER SIX

Most folks who weren't personally acquainted with the region tended to associate the South with Spanish moss-laden live oaks, sprawling plantation homes, and pretty little Scarlett O'Hara-type spitfires. Nashville had spitfires, and a few plantation homes, but the similarities ended there. It got too cold for live oaks. Music City, and Tennessee in general, resembled *Cold Mountain* rather than *Gone with the Wind*. Springtime decorated the capital city and her state with blushing redbuds, dogwoods in red, white, or pink, and grand old magnolias aplenty. Magnolias had a deep-rooted history in the state. Andrew Jackson's magnolia journeyed from the Hermitage to Washington D.C. in the early 19th century by way of cuttings and as a tribute to his beloved Rachel, then back again following the loss of the original in the tornado of 1998. From the ill-fated "Magnolia League" athletic conference efforts in the 1950s to the nearby private university's insular magnolia curtain, the scent of the big ivory blooms had long permeated the air here. Vivian could smell them from the steps of the Parthenon in Centennial Park, where she sat waiting for Mr. Darkmore to arrive.

Having arrived early after helping the Ridley family, she used her first free moments since the night before to mull things over while sipping her mocha. Up until last night, she believed things were getting easier since more in the local spirit community were aware of her ability to see them, even if they weren't always comfortable with it.

Now it seemed that some were uncomfortable enough for a serious threat down.

She'd once believed the guardians were "good" spirits. At least this type was supposedly better than some of the alternatives. Warm guardian spirits were in charge of guarding the living and helping souls cross over to another realm when the time came for their bodies to return to dust. A soul was lucky if one of these showed up, since the guardians guided that soul someplace nice—a place of peace and tranquility tailor-made and custom-designed for the soul. For Vivian, it had been a field full of gorgeous black-eyed Susans in full late-summer bloom.

It had been created for her the night she met Ezra, the night she was supposed to die.

When she'd come into her powers, she'd managed to travel there. She'd seen Ezra's, too. If every human soul who ever lived a worthy life earned such a respite, surely there were billions of these small slices of paradise, numerous as the stars and just as infinite in variety and possibility.

And, conversely, there were probably slices of Hell for those souls who led less than worthy lives.

Cold spirits, reapers, transported souls to the dark realms. Vivian had taken a few trips to one of these places before, courtesy of Mr. Darkmore, and felt pretty sorry for the unfortunates whose fate included a stay there, even if most of them had done something to deserve their sentence.

At least some got out after a while, and the reapers weren't necessarily to blame. Not entirely. But some enjoyed their work a little too much for her taste, not to mention their nasty habit of tormenting the living for their own amusement, as well as their energy needs.

Then again, the guardians were plenty happy to meddle in the affairs of mortals, which was how she'd come to be in her current situation.

The reaper emerged from the parking lot, all decked out in his preferred white suit and hat. It still surprised her that such a striking man with an odd wardrobe didn't seem to attract much attention when they met in public. Odder still, unlike most spirits she'd encountered, Darkmore didn't seem to mind appearing in corporeal form out in the open. He even tipped his hat and wished passersby a good day. He was handsome and poised. The reaper's face and figure drew the gaze and enticed the senses. If she weren't so scared of him, she'd even go so far as to think of him as charming. He could be mesmerizing, but she knew better than to let her guard down.

Yet he had helped her in the past, and he still came by from time to time to relieve her of the many burdens she carried from the living. Reapers liked pain. She hoped against hope that feeding Darkmore helped save some other poor souls from the pain he could and did inflict on the living and the dead. And, since he seemed to genuinely like her, she also hoped that he might be willing to help her out with this rogue guardian stalker business.

She hoped she could afford his price.

"Hello, Darkmore," she said as she stood up and dusted off her skirt. "Thanks for meeting me. Do you like coffee? I wasn't sure, but I grabbed one for you. Ezra and the others like food and drink, so..."

She trailed off, suddenly uncomfortable, not to mention embarrassed. She'd never offered the reaper food or drink before. Normally she sought him out for a quick emotional essence dump and left his company as quickly as she could. But since she needed a favor, she'd brought him coffee.

Why hadn't she thought to do so before? Didn't he merit even basic courtesy? She'd have to think on it.

"Yes, I do enjoy coffee from time to time. Thank you," he said, removing his hat and leaning forward to kiss her lightly on the lips. She was used to that part, since it seemed to be his preferred method for collecting burdens, at least from her. His kiss came with a pleasant coolness that was part and parcel of the reaper's presence.

It was the chill that gave her goosebumps, not his kiss. That's what she told herself and would keep telling herself. He drew back and looked quite satisfied as the wisps of red light filled him. She sighed, relieved and a whole lot lighter.

"Hmm," he murmured, apparently savoring what she'd offered. "Delightful, though not as much as I'd hoped for. Money troubles just aren't what they used to be."

"Oh, well, excuse me for being short on misery," she muttered, rolling her eyes. "The Ridleys seemed pretty anxious to me."

Darkmore waved a dismissive hand. "Honestly, they have little to fear. I recall much steeper penalties for debtors in olden days. Eviction, prison, enslavement." He appeared to be positively giddy at the prospect.

Vivian gulped.

"It really is all a matter of perspective. A good deal of reality is, you know," he said, his icy gaze piercing her.

"So I'm learning," Vivian replied with as much lilt in her voice as she could muster. "I'll see if I can rustle up something a bit more savory next time."

"No matter," he replied with a small smile. "There's plenty of misery out there for the reaping."

That shut her down. Fumbling, she bent down to retrieve the extra latte that she'd brought along for him and placed it in his hand. He accepted and took a sip, raising his eyebrows after.

Uh-oh. "Not good?" she asked.

"Actually, it is quite delicious," he replied. "The chocolate is a nice touch. Quite pleasing. A favorite of mortal women the world 'round, I've observed. Thank you."

"You're welcome, and it really is wonderful stuff. There's an old saying that goes, 'Chocolate can be a substitute for men, but men can never, ever substitute for chocolate,' " Vivian replied.

Where the hell had that come from?

"I wasn't aware, but I'll have to remember that."

They settled into an awkward silence, at least awkward for Vivian. Darkmore closed his eyes and inhaled the spring air. When he opened them, he regarded the Greek columns of the Parthenon before him with interest. "The materials are not authentic, of course, but I have to admit, it's a decent reproduction. If you don't have any more burdens to share, my dear, I think I should like to see Athena. It has been centuries!"

Now or never.

"I'm fresh out of burdens, but if you wouldn't mind some company, there's something else I'd like to discuss with you."

Darkmore's eyes widened as he said, "Oh my, the honorable Vivian

Margaret Bedford, spiritual intercessor for the city's downtrodden, wishes to consort with a grisly reaper? Tsk, tsk, what would Ezra think?"

"Never mind Ezra," she said. "I have a big problem and I need some information from you and...possibly your help."

There. She'd managed to ask for his help. Now she waited for the axe to fall.

"I take it that this 'problem' does not deal with the realm of the living. Very well. I'm intrigued, which may compensate for the paltry sustenance you brought today," he said as he offered his arm. "Come along then, my dear."

With a sense of falling, she placed her hand on his proffered arm, and before she could blink, they were standing before the impressive statue of the Greek goddess of wisdom, all forty-two feet of her. She felt Darkmore's cool arm making its way around her back to support her as she shrieked. To her surprise, none of the other patrons turned in response, or even registered their presence.

Motherfucker!

"Now, now, Ms. Vivian," he purred into her ear, his cool breath making goosebumps erupt over her flesh. "Do try to calm yourself. We are in the presence of divinity."

"Couldn't we just go through the fucking front door like normal people?" Vivian gasped. Spirit travel seemed cool in theory, but in reality it just made her nauseous. Not to mention nervous.

"But then we'd have to pay," replied Darkmore.

When he was certain that she could stand on her own, he released Vivian and moved closer to the base of the statue. He seemed to be lost in admiration, as he didn't even flinch when a couple walking hand-in-hand walked straight through him. She figured that Darkmore was trying to scare her, or impress her, or both. Probably both. Vivian knew that guardians and reapers could pull off tricks like that with ease, though she wasn't quite certain if his lack of a corporeal presence extended to her. She moved out of their way just in case.

"It is a pity to keep the doors closed. The goddess would shine with more splendor by the light of the sun," Darkmore remarked.

He was right. Her headdress, toga, spear, and shield were gilded.

Vivian was more than a little surprised, not to mention impressed. In all of her years living in Nashville, she'd never stepped inside the Parthenon. It was remarkable.

"I was expecting plain marble, and not so much makeup," she said, staring in wide-eyed wonder.

"Oh no, it was ivory over bronze back in the day—I believe that's the expression. Her very dress once held much of the treasury for Athens. Hence, the gold. The mighty did, and often still do, enjoy audacious displays of wealth. Though she isn't quite on par with Phidias," he said, inclining his head toward her and spoke in a low and confidential tone. "This likeness captures the pretense of her remoteness and frigidity quite a bit better."

"Huh?" she said, astonished. Athena was real? She was going to ask him to elaborate, but was caught off guard once more when Darkmore transported them from the floor to the statue's shoulder.

He laughed. "*Parthenos* indeed! She was many, many things, the goddess, but the title of 'virgin' was dubious at best. Now then, come a little closer and tell me all of your troubles," Darkmore drawled, pulling her beside him.

Now that would be an interesting story.

"You're enjoying this, aren't you?" She had to admit, being a little closer to the reaper eased her fear of falling. She didn't think gravity would affect them in their current state, but decided to take no chances with that either.

"Of course I am," he replied nonchalantly. "After all, it is in my nature. And your troubles are always most interesting."

With a deep breath, Vivian gave her account of the attack on Father Montgomery at the hands of the unknown rogue guardian as Darkmore continued to examine the statue. She was a little annoyed by his apparent lack of concern, though he at least nodded from time to time to let her know that he was still listening. He only gave her his full attention when she got to the part about healing the priest.

"You're a healer? You are full of surprises, Ms. Vivian."

"I only just found out, and I still don't know how it works or if I can heal people with regular ills as opposed to zaps from your kind," she confessed.

"It wasn't my kind who did this," Darkmore said. He didn't seem upset, but he waited until she nodded in acknowledgment.

"So why would a guardian want to hurt someone close to me?"

"To get your attention, of course."

"No kidding," Vivian said sardonically. "What I mean is, why does this one want me to stop what I'm doing? I'm on their side." She blushed and put her head down then, realizing her faux pas.

Damn my big fucking mouth!

"What I meant is, um...I'm working with them, you know? For them. I didn't mean...look, I know from experience that it's not all black and white, and I sure as hell know that guardians aren't always the good guys."

"Which brought you to me," Darkmore said. He didn't seem smug, or angry, or even surprised. He just seemed...interested.

Good thing. Maybe he'd help her if she kept his attention and entertained him. Taking a deep breath, she said, "I need to know what I'm up against, and I'd like to find out who this so-called rogue guardian is and how to get him off my back. Can you help me?"

"That's not the relevant question, my dear."

"Then what is the relevant question?"

"You want to know if I am *willing* to help you, and what it will cost."

"Well, yeah," she answered. She was beginning to feel a bit ornery. "You don't work for free, though I would have thought you'd be concerned enough about your meal ticket to want me safe."

"Well, there is that," he conceded, smiling.

Vivian was not amused. "So, will you help me or not?"

"Yes."

"What will it cost?"

"I shall have to think on it. Do you trust me?" Darkmore asked.

"No more and no less than I trust any other spirit," Vivian answered honestly.

"It's a start. I'll be in touch."

With that, he disappeared, and Vivian found herself back on solid ground, left to wonder about what the going interest rate might be for her line of credit with Darkmore. She shuddered, knowing full well what sort of collateral he'd hold. She stared at Pandora on the statue's pedestal. *Well, I hope that isn't a bad sign.* Hope was definitely the key word.

———

"I'm perfectly fine, Vivian. I wish you would sit down and relax," the padre said for the third time. He'd set a cup of coffee in front of her in apparent hope that she would finally sit. "It's decaf, by the way. I'm sure you've had more than enough caffeine by now." He glanced at his office clock. It was already five thirty in the afternoon.

She'd decided to pay a house call to check on the padre after his brush with death by guardian. Though small and modest, as was befitting a priest, Father Montgomery's Cathedral office was as warm and inviting as the man himself. Natural light flowed through a window and illuminated the space, bathing it in golden rays fit for an emissary of the divine while dust motes swirled through the beams of light, lending an Earthly charm to the scene.

She had to admit, Father Montgomery did look great. His cheeks held a ruddy glow, and his eyes were as sharp and bright as ever. They were also full of mischief, which gave her a little surge of mischievous pride. It entertained her to no end to be a bad influence on the priest, though he maintained that one of his most important missions was to be a positive influence in her life. Seemed like they were both having some success.

"Any word from Ezra?" he asked.

"Nope." She sighed. "But he never tells me too much anyhow."

Father Montgomery nodded and took another sip of his coffee before asking, "So what do you plan to do?"

"Sniff around myself and see what I can find out."

She deliberately declined to mention her meeting with Darkmore. The padre was leery of reapers in general, and Lazarus Darkmore in particular. He'd seen Darkmore's dark realm and darker tendencies. Vivian had managed to keep her ongoing association with him a secret so far, and she planned on making sure it stayed that way.

Shifting the subject, she asked, "Are you up for an outing?"

"Woodlawn? The ICU?" he asked. Through their work with the spirit world, Vivian and the padre had learned that cemeteries and hospitals were, in fact, a good place to find residents of the spirit realms. They'd mediated a few crossings, and for those who weren't quite ready, Vivian relayed a message of hope from the priest as well as an invitation to take refuge in his home church, making it one of the most pleasantly haunted sites in Nashville.

But today, Vivian had something a little different in mind. "Nope, I thought we might run to Nolensville this weekend and see what the spooks out there have heard. What do you say? Lunch is on me," she said.

"In that case, you have yourself a date," he replied with a wink.

"If you weren't old enough to be my dad and sworn to celibacy, I'd have hooked up with you a long time ago, Padre."

"I take offense to the 'old' comment," he said with a laugh. "And besides, aren't you taken?"

She hesitated before answering. "Yeah, I suppose I am. Which brings me to my next dilemma."

Father Montgomery leaned forward and studied her, seemingly on the edge of his seat, so she plunged right in. "I'm thinking about telling Jace the truth about my situation. You know, with the spirits and all."

No need to pussyfoot around. Besides, the padre was used to confessions.

"I see," he said, then raised his eyes to the ceiling as he mused. "If you plan to maintain the relationship, perhaps even *solidify* it, then you probably should." He ignored a fair amount of sin on her part, but the relations she exercised with Jace fell under the auspices of "mortal" and "grave" in terms of Catholic dogma. He felt it his duty to encourage her to marry her boyfriend and bedmate.

Not that she hadn't thought about it—marriage—but there were so many complications, so many risks, not the least of which was whether he'd even believe her.

"I just don't know how. I mean, he's going to think I'm nuts. And, if I have to toss some light to convince him that I'm not, he's probably going to head for the hills quicker than green grass through a goose."

His expression filled with understanding and more than a little empathy. "Do you want me there when you tell him? I can certainly vouch for the veracity of your claims, and I am trained in CPR."

"That's nice of you to offer," she said and meant it. "But I think I'll try on my own first. Keep your phone handy tonight, though, just in case."

He nodded, and then almost jumped out of his skin when he turned and noticed Wallace sitting beside him. Since the padre joined her in her work with the spirit world, guardian spirits like Wallace no longer hid their powers from the priest as they did from regular mortals—powers that included assuming a corporeal form. Vivian barely flinched, though she felt for the priest. Wallace raised an eyebrow at her glare, but didn't apologize.

"Something on your mind?" Vivian snapped.

"You should get going," he snapped. "Jeanne is waiting for your assistance."

"She can wait a little longer while I finish my coffee and make sure my friend the Padre here doesn't have a coronary. What gives?"

She'd managed to get under the stuffy spirit's skin, at least metaphorically, based on the elevation in the air temperature. *Good.* Wallace and old guard spirits like him worked Vivian's nerves no end. She had encountered a few like them while working with Ezra. They didn't take kindly to mortals interfering with what they perceived as "their" work. It seemed ironic, considering that they supposedly protected the living. Vivian figured Wallace saw being assigned to guard one of her mortal friends as a demotion.

"Vivian, it's fine, really," said the priest.

"Five minutes. If you aren't out the door in five minutes, I'll escort you myself," Wallace commanded and then disappeared.

"Vivian, whatever you are about to do or say, please don't."

"What?" she asked, trying to feign innocence.

"He may be a bit gruff, but he is doing me a great service by being here."

"It's his job," she said, exasperated. "Besides, he's dead. It's not like he doesn't have eternity."

Father Montgomery gave her a wan smile and said, "'Oh, Lord, grant me patience' is a wonderful mantra. You really should try it."

He had a point, but Vivian wasn't about to concede. "Well, I just wish he didn't act like it griped his ass to be here. And what's with this 'barking orders' business?"

"Vivian, please, just let it go. Go and do your work. It is truly your calling and brings such peace to the lives of those you touch. Don't let a few barbs and your pride get in the way or diminish your joy in it."

She rolled her eyes and huffed, but nodded. In spite of everything, she knew Father Montgomery was right. She did derive a sense of purpose and accomplishment in her work with the spirits, even though it included seeing a whole lot of dead people.

Speaking of dead people... "Oh, by the way," she said, then hesitated, dreading the answer she'd get to the question she didn't really want to ask.

"Yes?"

"You haven't seen any spirits yourself today, have you? Other than Wallace?"

"No," the priest answered. "Is there any reason I might?"

Vivian sighed with relief and replied, "I was worried that healing you might have some unintended side effects. When Zeke and I...traded light, well, that's when I started seeing every guardian, reaper, and other variety of disembodied entity in the whole city. I'm glad to know it didn't rub off on you."

Of course, trading light with Zeke had been far more intimate than what she'd shared with the padre.

If he found her admission shocking, or disapproved of yet another liaison considered illicit in the eyes of the Catholic Church, he had the grace to keep it to himself. He merely smiled, added more hot coffee to her cup from his carafe, and offered her a tissue.

She hadn't meant to cry, but the thought of all she'd shared with Zeke and what she'd lost still filled her with soul-crushing grief. The priest understood and offered her quiet empathy, as he always did. Her gratitude for his unlikely friendship knew no bounds.

Placing a hand on her shoulder, he muttered a prayer in Latin. Then he said, "Go with God, Vivian, and spread your light to others. I'll see you later."

She nodded, placing her hand on his and giving it a squeeze. He was right. A soul crossing would lift her spirits and help mend her heart.

"Let me know how it goes with Jace," he added. "I'll keep you in my prayers. You deserve peace and happiness."

She smiled, then gathered her things and left the office. Focusing on Jace and what life might be like with him long-term eased her aching heart in spite of lingering doubts. Maybe she was overthinking things. Perhaps she'd spent so much time grieving—for her parents, for Mae, and for Zeke—she'd forgotten how to be happy. If she embraced her relationship with Jace and took it to the next level, maybe she could find what she'd lost.

All of a sudden, a blast of heat ripped through her body with a force that knocked her against her car and left her gasping for air.

What the hell?

Just as quickly, shivers racked her body in the wake of a bone-deep chill. She hadn't experienced anything like it since the night she'd entered the world of spirits, when she'd held Zeke's hand as the life drained from his body. It had been the one and only time she'd seen him alive. After that, he'd come back to her as a corporeal spirit. The heat and cold that had gripped her then came from the war over his soul.

And hers.

Ezra had been called to claim her soul, while Darkmore had come for Zeke. She'd saved Zeke, and in the process had put herself in Darkmore's crosshairs and in Ezra's service.

And now, it seemed, she was back in the crosshairs—but whose? And how was she supposed to stop it?

CHAPTER SEVEN

Still reeling from her encounter in the Cathedral's parking lot, Vivian fidgeted in her seat, scanning the half-full waiting room and wondering which of the souls surrounding her would receive her comfort after the guardians claimed their loved one. She assumed she'd be helping the bereaved, since the guardians normally had her take care of that part while they dealt with the newly departed. It gave the deceased soul a bit of ease, knowing that his or her loved ones had the spiritual equivalent of a lidocaine shot. Vivian channeled the initial grief and sorrow enough to numb the pain.

Often enough she returned, mostly on her own time, to help individual family members who had a tougher time letting go, or some unresolved issues with the dead.

Vivian paused to consider the contrasts between the living souls occupying this hospital, or any hospital she'd ever visited for that matter. Roughly half maintained a state of near-constant motion. Their actions ranged from the small yet rapid clicking of computer keyboards by admitting and information desk attendants to the long strides and near-sprints of doctors and nurses rushing to attend the needs of their patients. Orderlies moved patients and custodians quietly attended their duties in the background while clergy and volunteers meandered through the corridors.

They moved among the still ones.

The still ones comprised the other half of the hospital's occupants, the patients and those who watched and waited with them. Vivian herself had experienced the exhaustion born of waiting. All of those years spent in doctor's offices, emergency clinics, and hospitals with Mae taught her that waiting drains. Strange, all the hours of sitting had taxed her more than her most grueling days spent working outdoors or rushing about the office. The souls who kept vigil all around her, with their hollow eyes, light pallor, and barely stifled yawns looked drained, sapped of their vitality.

Jeanne and Wallace appeared and nodded toward the door.

Showtime.

Vivian walked out the waiting room and snuck into the stairwell. Aside from hospital staff, most folks preferred the elevator. That gave Vivian the perfect safe zone in which to become invisible and then accompany the guardians to their destination unseen.

Once she'd rendered herself invisible to the eyes of the living, Vivian nodded to Jeanne, who took her by the hand as they traveled spirit-style to their destination. The trip through the swirling vortex, no matter how many times she took it, always made her stomach lurch. If she'd had the power to shed her corporeal form, she could have just waltzed through the door like her companions did. Since she was a mortal, however, this mode of transportation became the most efficient way to get her into the room with the spirits. She'd once insisted on lurking just outside the door and waiting for a living person to open it, but that had taken too long for the guardians.

Apparently, deadlines still applied to the dead and dying.

"Are you okay, honey?" Jeanne asked when they'd reached their destination.

"I'll be fine," Vivian muttered, bracing against a wall. *Once I choke the contents of my stomach back down.*

"If you two are finished yapping, I suggest we get down to business," Wallace snapped.

Vivian glared at the old guardian, though his attitude didn't surprise her. Ezra told her not to take it personally, explaining that most of his kind weren't accustomed to having human helpers.

That didn't stop Vivian's temper or her mouth. "Who's minding my friend, the padre?"

"Ezra. The priest asked for him," Wallace said, the scowl twisting his distinguished features into disdain.

"Why?"

"That is none of my concern, nor is it yours," Wallace said. Then he gave her his back.

Jeanne touched Vivian's shoulder and said, "Don't pay him any mind. You just get ready to help these poor people." Jeanne gestured toward the bed and Vivian turned her attention to its occupant and the three people standing around her.

An old woman rested in a hospital bed, sheets nearly swallowing her small, frail body. Her thin arms rested on top of the sheets, muscles atrophied from age, or perhaps from a prolonged period of disuse.

Like Mae's.

"How long has she been like this?" Vivian asked after swallowing the hard lump in her throat.

"Several weeks," Jeanne replied. "Wallace and a few other guardians have been monitoring her. She has Alzheimer's. About a month ago, she fell and broke her hip. They tried to fix her up with surgery, but she's just too old and too far gone."

Vivian nodded. A broken hip past a certain age always drew the already departed, guardian or reaper. The injury in one so old and infirm almost always spelled death. Death meant a harvest for the spirit dwellers in charge of directing newly disembodied souls to their next stop as they journeyed to the great beyond.

Still, something was off. She couldn't quite put her finger on it, but something was either missing or out of place for the crossing to come.

"Those her kids?" Vivian asked, turning her attention to the other living souls in the room.

"Two of them, yes. The other man is her son-in-law."

"What's her name?"

"Mrs. Martin. Eleanor Susan Martin. Elly Sue."

Vivian regarded those standing around the old woman. Their faces displayed a mixture of sorrow and guilt. Drawing in a few faint streams of light, Vivian tasted that sorrow, and also felt their shared sense of relief at the impending death. They'd all taken shifts watching over her in her decline. Vivian understood, having been through the same ordeal herself. The connection she felt to these people would no doubt help her to help them.

Then it hit her—the thing that was missing.

"Why doesn't she glow?" Vivian asked.

"Glow?"

"Back when I started to notice spirit stuff around me, I saw Mae glowing," Vivian explained. "Zeke told me it was her spirit energy. He said people who get incapacitated store up a lot of energy. I normally see it in cases like these, and sometimes in the ICU."

"So do I," Jeanne replied, distracted in her anticipation to help with the crossing. "I don't know. She's probably just not been like this long enough to store up enough."

"Maybe, but—"

"Here she comes!" Jeanne cried out, smiling at the woman.

Unlike many of her companions in adjacent rooms, this woman's body rested free of IVs, tubes, and monitors, save for the small heart monitor attached to her chest beneath the standard-issue hospital gown. She wore a soft pink robe over the gown, most likely a gift from her family. They'd combed the silver strands of her hair and cleaned her skin—a final act of love as they waited for her passing. Through these details, Vivian surmised that the family had chosen to remove her from life support. A painful decision, no doubt, but the right call. Ezra once told Vivian how he'd suffered after his stroke, trapped and betrayed by a body he no longer controlled, saddened to be a burden to those he loved.

At least Mrs. Martin's condition had spared her awareness.

Whoa, what was *that*?

Vivian swore she saw flashes of light burst forth from the living. When she blinked her eyes, though, the flashes were gone.

After a shallow breath, Mrs. Martin's chest stilled. The heart monitor went flat, her daughter's soft sob the only other sound breaching the silence in the room for long moments. Vivian watched in wonder as death claimed the woman, stilling a heart that had beat for nearly a century to silence.

Unlike the other living souls in the room, she witnessed Mrs. Martin's disembodied spiritual debut. The soul didn't rise from the corpse, nor did it hover above the spectators as per Hollywood's depictions. The whole tunnel thing didn't happen, either, at least as far as she could tell from her work with the guardians.

Mrs. Martin's soul simply appeared before them.

To Vivian's surprise, she appeared much younger than the body on the bed. She also wore a rather old-fashioned dress and dated hairstyle. Still, she looked great. Vivian imagined she must have turned more than a few heads back in the day.

"What in the blue blazes?" she exclaimed, confusion blooming on her gorgeous face.

"Eleanor Susan Martin," Wallace boomed. "We guardians of the spirit world have come to bear your immortal soul to the realm of the light."

"Seriously? Y'all are angels?"

"Well, yes, ma'am—"

"'Cause y'all don't look like angels. Where're your wings?"

Vivian snorted. She wanted to fist-bump Elly Sue but figured the generation gap might get in the way.

Jeanne sighed and placed a sympathetic hand on Mrs. Martin's shoulder. Wallace looked like he was trying to squeeze diamonds through his clenched ass cheeks, which made Vivian snort even louder. Out of all the reactions of the newly dead that she'd witnessed, Mrs. Martin's was, hands down, the most entertaining to date.

Jeanne tried to get her attention. "Mrs. Martin—"

Elly Sue, however, was having none of it. She looked down at her hands and then examined her clothing and body, clearly astonished. "And how come I'm in this ridiculous getup?"

"Your spirit projection is your choice, conscious or not," Jeanne explained patiently. "Perhaps this is the form you last remembered before your mind began to slip away."

"What do you mean?" Elly Sue snapped. She placed her hands on her hips and shot Jeanne a look of indignation. "There ain't nothing wrong with my mind, young lady!"

"If we could get back to the task at hand," Wallace barked. He was such buzzkill. Why couldn't he enjoy the moment and the show?

"Who's this jackass?" Mrs. Martin asked, jerking her head toward Wallace. Then she shot Vivian a death stare. "And why are you just standing there sniggering? I'm dead, right? That ain't no laughing matter."

"I'm so sorry, ma'am," Vivian said as she struggled to regain her composure. "I don't mean any disrespect. I gotta tell you, though, your crossing is the best I've yet attended."

Vivian did her best to stifle the next round of giggles lest the newly departed woman decided to slap them right out of her.

Elly Sue eyed her warily, then said, "I'm glad someone's having fun. Who are they?"

Elly Sue had turned her attention to the living people grieving over her body. Oh, dear. This part was always the hardest. Accepting one's own death was only the first step. Accepting the inevitable separation from loved ones often proved more challenging to the deceased and could delay crossing.

In the worst cases, desperate souls refused to cross at all and lingered for days, weeks, months, or even years, stuck in a realm in which they were virtually invisible. Some came around and sought out nearby guardian spirits once they accepted their fates.

Others stayed and went slowly mad. Vivian hoped Elly Sue wouldn't be one of them.

"They're your family, honey," Jeanne answered. "Your son, daughter, and son-in-law. You had Alzheimer's at the end of your life, so it might take a few minutes for everything to come back to you. Just give it a minute. We're in no rush."

"Actually, we do need to get going," Wallace said, his tone surprisingly gentle.

"Jesse? Maggie?" Mrs. Martin spoke to her children, though they couldn't respond, of course.

"They can't see you," Vivian explained, her heart breaking for the woman and all she'd endured, all she'd missed or forgotten.

"My God, they're so grown up now," Elly Sue whispered, confused.

"Why don't you sit down?" Jeanne asked, leading the new spirit over to the vacant chair beside the bed.

"And that's me?" she asked, pointing to the body in the bed.

"It was," Jeanne replied gently. "But that's all behind you. I know it's hard. I just crossed over myself, but you're going to a much better place now."

Elly Sue's head flew back as she examined Jeanne in shock and wonder. "How come you're still here?"

"I'm a guardian," Jeanne replied. "As is Wallace. We are charged with helping new spirits cross."

"What about her?" Elly Sue said, eyeing Vivian. She probably realized that one of these things was definitely not like the others. Vivian got that a lot.

"Vivian is still mortal, but she is one of the rare mortals who can see and speak with spirits. She's here to help your family."

"How's she going manage that?" Elly Sue asked, looking back and forth between her grieving family and Vivian.

"Why don't you show her, Vivian?"

At Jeanne's request, Vivian stepped closer to the Martin clan and focused her mind and energy on them, drawing out their burdens as wisps of pale red light. She turned back to the guardians and Elly Sue when she heard the scream. It gave her a jolt, but didn't actually frighten or surprise her. Newly departed spirits often expressed shock at their first glimpse of spirit power. Jeanne grabbed Vivian's hand and they disappeared into the vortex along with Wallace and Elly Sue.

Elly Sue kept screaming through the journey and continued after they'd landed. Wallace took her by the shoulders and shook her. Vivian knew he wanted to bring her to her senses, but she thought he shook her a little harder than necessary. So, she stepped in and placed her hand on the old guardian's arm to make him stop.

The surge of energy that flowed from him threw Vivian back. She slammed against the wall, and might have taken a tumble down the stairwell were it not for Jeanne. As it stood, she got a nasty lump on the back of her head and a gash on her left elbow for her trouble.

"What the hell?" Vivian asked, gingerly cradling the back of her head, wincing as pain shot through her arm.

"Mortal, you must take care!"

The note of concern in Wallace's voice surprised her more than his sudden appearance at her side. She didn't know for sure, but she thought most of her dizziness and disorientation had come from Wallace's touch rather than her fall. Contact with Ezra, Jeanne, and a few other guardians she'd worked with always warmed her.

Wallace didn't just warm. He blazed.

All of a sudden, a new voice echoed around them. "Halt!"

Vivian, Mrs. Martin, and the guardians all turned to face the bearer of the last voice who had suddenly materialized and held Wallace in stasis with his light.

The new entity stood about five-three and wore an immaculate suit. She'd never seen someone so short or so put together in the wardrobe department, not to mention grooming. *Kind of like a GQ hobbit.* She didn't dare give that thought voice, since this spirit clearly held a great deal of power.

With his commanding stare and even more commanding presence, he held them all captive in a state of wonder and awe. "Now that I have everyone's attention, here is what's going to happen. Wallace, you are dismissed. I believe you have other, more pressing matters to attend to?"

He dropped Wallace, who looked visibly shaken. After he regained his composure, Wallace bowed and said, "Yes, Uriel."

Then he vanished.

"Ah, Jeanne," Uriel said, turning to the young guardian and giving her a tender smile. "What a pleasure to see you again. I hear you're doing quite well."

"Thank you, Uriel," Jeanne muttered as she bowed, looking as though she'd just met a king or a rock star.

Uriel beamed at her, his approval of the gung-ho guardian evident. Good for her. Jeanne deserved a pat on the back, and Vivian was pretty sure those were few and far between with a partner like Wallace.

"Not at all, my dear," Uriel said, taking her hand and bidding her rise.

"I would like for you to personally escort Mrs. Martin to our realm so we can begin her processing."

"Processing? What the hell? Am I being deported?" Seemed like Mrs. Martin had found her voice again, not to mention her attitude.

"Oh, my dear, not at all," Uriel said, taking Mrs. Martin by the hand and pulling her down to sit next to him on the stairwell. "I do apologize for this misunderstanding. Most crossings are conducted in a more peaceful and professional manner. We've had some rather unusual circumstances of late."

He looked at Vivian, and she felt as though his eyes peered through to her very soul. The only other times she'd felt a similar vibe involved Darkmore, so she figured this guy was pretty ancient and powerful. He smiled as he looked at her, but a sense of unease crept up her spine under his scrutiny.

Uriel turned back to Mrs. Martin and turned on the charm. "Do you think you could find it in your heart to forgive us?" He bent his head and brushed a kiss over her knuckles.

"I suppose I could," Mrs. Martin stuttered, clearly affected by the charms of the powerful guardian.

"Well, that is certainly a relief!" he exclaimed. "Now then, I believe Ms. Bedford has some assurances to, ah, deliver to you in regard to your loved ones. I'll leave you to it. Jeanne, once you've wrapped things up here, kindly escort Ms. Bedford back to my office before you proceed with Mrs. Martin."

"Yes, sir, of course," Jeanne said, beaming.

Once Uriel disappeared, Jeanne turned to Elly Sue and said, "Don't be afraid. Vivian is going to share some of the thoughts and feelings that she collected from your family."

"You mean she's going to do that crazy thing with the light?" Elly Sue scooted into the corner of the stairwell, putting a little more space between herself and Vivian.

"Yes, but it won't hurt a bit and it will make you feel more at ease, trust me."

Jeanne gave Vivian the nod, so she turned to the spirit of Mrs. Martin and released some of the energy she'd collected from her family. With considerable practice, Vivian had worked out how to separate the sorrow from the underlying bonds of love. She shared those bonds with Elly Sue, who smiled as she took in the light of her family's devotion.

Vivian slumped after releasing the light, weary from channeling spirit energy and achy from the blow delivered by Wallace. To her credit, Jeanne let Vivian rest a few moments before asking, "Are you about ready to go?"

"Ready as I'll ever be, I guess," Mrs. Martin said, sass clearly intact even after tasting her family's emotions. "What the hell happened with Wallace, though? And who's the honcho?"

"Uriel? Oh my, he's from the council and very powerful," Jeanne replied. "They very rarely visit the realm of the living nowadays, but when one of the council of the seven is needed, they usually send Uriel. He is the messenger, the light, the wind of the south."

"Speak English," Vivian said, head spinning. "I need to know who I'm dealing with and what he wants."

Jeanne looked at her in disbelief but quickly shook it off. With a deep breath, she said, "You probably know him as one of the archangels."

Well that was unexpected. "Archangel? Really? I thought they went by Gabriel or Michael?"

"Those two serve a different purpose," Jeanne replied.

Though she didn't buy into most of Judeo-Christian mythology of her childhood, Vivian knew enough now about the world of the dead to keep an open mind. She also knew enough to have a healthy sense of caution, since these so-called good guys didn't always act like angels.

"So am I in trouble?" Vivian asked.

"Oh don't be silly," Jeanne said, then paused, studying her. After a moment, she nodded and gave Vivian a look that was probably meant to be encouraging.

It did anything but.

Jeanne leaned in and said, "Just be respectful and try your best to watch your mouth, okay?"

Yup, I'm definitely in trouble.

———

Uriel apparently borrowed his "office" from one of unoccupied rooms in the hospital. For Vivian's meeting, he'd chosen a rather large and impressive administrative office, well-lit and furnished in dark woods. After Jeanne left to attend to Mrs. Martin, Uriel bid Vivian to sit in one of the fancy chairs on the opposite side of the desk.

"Let me start by offering an apology on behalf of Wallace. He is terribly sorry for the discomfort you experienced and your fall."

When Vivian didn't answer right away, Uriel continued. "He also apologizes for his earlier treatment of you. Apparently you've earned his respect. You must have handled this crossing quite well."

Vivian let out the breath she'd been holding, but remained on her guard. "In that case, apology accepted. Now why else am I here?"

He gave her another one of his intense stares, and it took all of Vivian's will to return his gaze. After a while, he reached into the desk drawer and pulled out a manila folder and began to thumb through the pages as he spoke. "Naturally I am familiar with your activities over the past year, including those that brought you into our service, but perhaps it would be best to begin with a review. Let's see...you were scheduled for a crossing last year, but received a reprieve from Ezra."

Flipping a few more pages, he continued. "You also assisted with the liberation of souls in Limbo along with your sister and her impressive repository of energy. Interesting. Very interesting."

Vivian took Jeanne's advice to heart and chose to remain silent.

"You do realize, of course, that such a reprieve is very rare," he said, glancing up from the pages.

"So I'm told," she replied. "Why did I get one?"

"Let's just say that Ezra has proven himself rather useful and productive over the years. He moved up in our ranks quickly by participating in some special assignments. That gets him a bit of latitude."

"I see," she said, leaning forward. This was getting interesting.

He dropped the file folder and it landed on the desk with a slap that echoed through the nearly empty office. "No, you don't, but allow me to enlighten you. While we are willing to grant Ezra a bit of latitude, that latitude does not necessarily extend to you. You've taken it upon yourself to use your powers for unauthorized assignments, I hear."

She balked. "As far as I understood, my freelance work was my business. Those were authorized by Ezra." That was mostly true. Aside from relieving the emotional burdens of people she encountered in the course of her work with the guardians, however, she also collected burdens from close friends, acquaintances, clients, and people she encountered in her daily life.

When the negative energy weighed her down, she fed it to the reaper. It was an efficient operation, allowing her to use her powers for good while keeping the reaper out of trouble—or at the very least it kept the reaper from targeting as many human souls for misery.

"Your talents are useful, Ms. Bedford, but they are by no means indispensable."

Before her earlier conversation with Jeanne, she would've argued. She'd thought herself unique, but apparently there were others like her. There were more living soul brokers caught between this world and the afterlife, and she'd bet her bank account that, like her, they worked under the supervision of guardian spirits—probably against their will.

"Is that a threat?" she asked, knowing full well it was.

Uriel offered her smile meant to charm and said, "It is fact. You are on borrowed time, dear lady. Do not forget that."

"I haven't. So does this mean you want me to ignore all of those other suffering souls out there like you have?" As far as she could tell, the living were on their own as far as guardians were concerned. With the exception of Jeanne and Ezra, she'd yet to see a guardian take an active interest in comforting souls who weren't yet slated for crossing.

That was apparently her job.

"We aren't ignoring them, Ms. Bedford, but we do have our priorities," he said, leaning back in his chair. "And the operation has grown considerably. Still, there are those of our kind who prefer to operate alone or remain unaffiliated. While we've been tolerant of late, I believe it is time to establish some firmer standard operating procedures for crossings, visitations, energy management, that sort of thing. I won't bore you with the details. I simply want to make you aware of upcoming changes. You are being watched, and not just by this rogue guardian."

Her chest went tight with an unpleasant mixture of fear and anger, but she fought to keep her cool in the face of the archangel. "Good to know. Now what does that mean for my work?"

"Follow your assignments and report *all* extra work to Ezra."

Not likely. She'd have to be more careful, more discreet with her burden collection and meetings with Darkmore. He could help. The reaper was as clever as he was charming, charismatic, and frightening. He'd want to keep his meal ticket.

She was glad he was on her side now, and she intended to keep him there—at arm's length, of course, but on her side.

Striving for casual, she nodded and said, "Fair enough. Anything else?"

"I do wonder," he said, his hands steepled below his chin, "why we haven't been getting more energy out of you."

Her insides turned to ice at the question.

Does he know about Darkmore?

She didn't think Uriel could be easily fooled by an outright lie, and she wasn't foolish enough to try. Mustering her best poker face, she shrugged and replied, "You'll have to ask Ezra about that."

"I plan on it. You may go now."

Vivian wasted no time with her exit.

CHAPTER EIGHT

Vivian paced the floor of her home, anxiety from her encounter with the archangel compounded by worry for the man in her life. The very mortal man who could and probably would be used as leverage by the higher-ups in afterlife management to ensure her compliance.

Her ties to the world of the living represented a liability, one she hadn't considered when she'd become a soul broker. If guardian spirits couldn't ensure her cooperation by persuasion or her sense of duty, she had no doubt they'd use the people she loved as leverage to get what they wanted.

Including Jace Blakemore.

Jace never showed up anywhere late. Vivian once joked that they must set the atomic clock by his internal chronometer. Had it been anyone else, she would have thought nothing of the fifteen minutes that had crept by while she wore a hole in her carpet pacing. After what had happened to the padre, though, she assumed that those closest to her were apt to be targets for the rogue guardian, not to mention the powerful archangel.

She dialed his mobile and got no answer.

Where the hell is he?

On the verge of panic, Vivian summoned Jeanne, who materialized a few minutes later. She rushed over to Vivian and proceeded to poke, prod, and examine her thoroughly and with the same alarming zeal she applied to her work as a guardian spirit.

"Honey, are you okay? Where is he? Just wait until I get my hands on him!"

"Get off!" Vivian grumbled from underneath Jeanne's arm. "It's not me. I'm worried about my boyfriend!"

Releasing her, Jeanne gave her a confused look, the kind only a natural blonde could pull off. She assumed the perky and overzealous new guardian had indeed been a natural blonde in life.

"Well, what happened?" Jeanne asked.

Vivian softened a little. At least Jeanne was genuinely concerned, and punctual. "He's late," she stammered, glancing up at her kitchen clock. "At least thirty minutes late. That's not like Jace. I'm getting a little anxious."

"I'll go check things out in the neighborhood," Jeanne said, patting her arm. "You stay put and keep an eye out for him."

"Wait," Vivian said before Jeanne could dematerialize. "Shouldn't I go, too? What if you need backup?"

"Honey, I know you hate to wait," Jeanne replied patiently. Apparently Vivian's reputation had gotten around. "But you need to stay here in case he shows up hurt. So sit tight. I'm off!"

Damned cheerleader. Shit, shit, *shit!*

She considered calling Ezra, too, but that wouldn't get her anywhere either. He'd just join Jeanne on the hunt and leave her behind.

Helpless and angry, she kept an eye on the clock, watching the seconds tick by slower than molasses in January. Just when she thought her heart might explode, Vivian heard his car pulling in her driveway. She sprinted out the door and flew into his arms. And what arms they were. Jace was a big guy with strong arms, a strong back, and a tight ass.

She'd very much enjoyed fondling, playfully smacking, and gripping said ass, which she hoped to do later that evening. After her tussle with Uriel, she really just wanted to settle down and enjoy some more basic, physical tussling with Jace. More than that, the anxiety she'd faced during the past hours had opened her eyes and her heart.

They had a good thing going, she and Jace. Why hadn't she seen that before?

She'd been so caught up in grief and angst, she hadn't taken the time to appreciate Jace and the small, precious slice of normal life he represented. He'd been her rock, her balm, a friend, lover, and ardent supporter. She vowed to keep him safe from any otherworldly threats while giving their relationship a chance to grow.

"Easy now, gal," he said, pulling away from her. "You're liable to break my back doing that."

"You've never complained about my attempts to break your back before," she said with a bright smile, relief and happiness flooding her. "You're late. I was worried. You're never late. What gives?"

He lowered his gaze and ran a hand through his hair. "Oh, I'm sorry. Stuff came up."

"It doesn't matter. You're here now. Let's get you inside and we'll have a beer. I've got some stuff I need to tell you."

He followed her in and took his favorite seat on her couch. Vivian went to the kitchen to grab a couple of beers and steel her nerves. She handed him one, took a long draw from hers, and decided to dive right in.

She was interrupted by his sultry voice and the shock of the words he uttered.

"Vivian, I think we should see other people," he said. At least he had the decency to look her in the eyes.

Too floored to say anything else, she stared at him and said, "What?"

He got up and started pacing, rambling as he went. "Baby, we've been going out for a while now, and it's been great...really great. But where's it going? I've been thinking a lot about the future lately, and I just don't see one for us."

"I don't understand," she said, coming back to herself. Then cold fury began to seep through her as realization dawned. How had she missed the signs? The growing distance between them, his disinterest in her work, and the shift in their patterns of lovemaking—fierce and desperate couplings followed by long dry spells. She'd been frustrated.

He hadn't.

"Been thinking there's no future with me lately, huh? Tell me, were you thinking about that when you happily enjoyed me sucking your dick last week?"

Their last encounter had been pretty good, as far as Vivian was concerned, and judging from his enthusiasm, it had appeared that Jace enjoyed it, too. That thought hit her like a slap across the face, and was just as humiliating.

He didn't lash back out at her. He just kept talking. Probably had rehearsed this speech a few times. "Sex isn't the problem. Sex was never a problem with us. You're a fine woman, in every sense of the word. But I'm never going be first with you. It's work and whatever it is that you do in the way of volunteering." The way he said volunteering gave her pause.

"Wait, you think *I'm* cheating on you?"

"Not with another man, no. But you have other priorities."

"Oh and you don't?"

"Yeah, I'll admit that I do. I'm working my ass off so I can settle down, start a family, live the dream, you know? I'm not sure that's what you want, or something you even can do, Vivian. And I'm getting too old to wait much longer," he said flatly.

The pieces fell into place as her heart cracked in two. Then the claws came out.

"Ah, there it is," she said, her voice low and menacing. "I think I see what's going on here now. How old is she, Jace? Did you pick her up at preschool?"

"That's ugly, Vivian, and it isn't fair. She's not the reason."

"No, your backstabbing two-timing man-whoring is the reason. I can't believe I didn't see this coming," she said, fury erupting in an unstoppable wave.

"Get the fuck out of my house" she yelled, tossing the half-empty beer bottle at his head.

"Jesus, Viv!" he yelled as he ducked. "It doesn't have to be like this. I tried to make it work, but you're always gone."

She couldn't listen, couldn't stand to look at his handsome face and think about how she'd fallen for his bullshit. His betrayal unleashed all of the pent-up frustration, anger, and anguish she'd been holding back. Jace became the perfect target.

"You didn't try. You just went off and started banging some other woman while you strung me along, you lying sack of shit. Now get the fuck out!"

He looked to be on the verge of exploding, too, but got it under control at the last with some deep breaths and visible effort. Jeanne floated into the living room, thankfully not in corporeal form. Seeing the look on Vivian's face, she had the good sense to hightail it out, too.

As Jace walked through her door, he looked back over his shoulder and offered, "I'm sorry it turned out like this."

"*Out!*" she shouted, and, finally, he listened.

————

"Honey, you don't have to keep Scooter tonight. We'll figure something out," Kay said as she served Vivian a slice of pie with a side of ice cream.

In spite of being blindsided by her worthless, two-timing piece-of-shit ex, not to mention the mess she'd landed in with the guardian spirits and their archangel manager, Vivian wasn't about to bail on Kay. Besides, having an adorable toddler around to cuddle would take her mind off her troubles. And Kay deserved a night off.

"No, it's okay," Vivian replied. "I'll be fine, and it'll be refreshing to spend some time with a nice man for a change."

"I'll just go check on the kids," came the voice of Kay's husband, Boyd. Boyd had made himself scarce as soon as Vivian showed up and shared news of her two-timing, double-crossing ex.

"Oh, hell," Vivian hissed when he was out of earshot. "I'm sorry. Boyd must be scared shitless. I have that effect on menfolk, it seems." She dug into her pie for consolation.

They'd heard, of course. Word got around pretty fast, especially when it came to cheating hearts and other parts. The Clemmens clan had gone out of their way to pamper Vivian through Saturday dinner, but it came across like coddling. That hadn't put Vivian in the best of moods. She knew they were worried about her, but she also knew they were all worried about Sue's wedding.

Vivian was maid of honor, and, as Jack's good buddy and long-time business associate, Jace was the best man.

Their breakup had been ill-timed to say the least. Then again, that was his fault, not hers. Run-ins with mutual friends had been pretty awkward. She assumed that she was expected to be gracious and just act like everything was fine, for poor Sue's sake.

Too bad she couldn't be the "bigger" person.

"Don't you worry about Boyd," Kay said. "I tell you, as soon as he heard, he grabbed the shotgun out of the safe and made like he was planning to put some buckshot in that lowlife's ass."

"He should shoot him in the pecker," Vivian quipped. "That's what got him in trouble. So, have you met her?"

Kay got quiet. That meant yes.

"Just give it to me straight. She's younger and sweeter, has firm tits and a tight ass, and feeds fucking orphans in Mumbai, right?"

And she no doubt did it all while still "being there" for Jace, putting his needs first like a good woman should and getting ready to pop out some babies to make his life complete. After that, she'd stop working, of course, and devote herself fully to motherhood and wifehood while Jace the snake cheated on her too.

Or maybe she'd cheat on him. Vivian could only hope.

"She's younger, yes. Aside from that, I don't know. We passed them in town and Jace introduced us. Viv...I'm so sorry. I wouldn't have spoken to them if Jace hadn't practically dragged us over. Boyd was going to hit him, but she, well, she looked about as uncomfortable as we felt. After the intros, we left them in the dust."

"So, is it serious?" Vivian asked. She hated herself for caring, but she had to know.

"Honey, I have no idea. I haven't talked to Jace since that day. You've got to know we're on your side, though," Kay pleaded. Vivian nodded. She knew. Didn't make it better, though.

"Look, I hate to ask, but I need to know." She sat down across from Vivian. *Here it comes.* "What about the wedding? Sue's about going crazy, and she's really between a rock and a hard place—"

"Yeah," Vivian snorted. "That must be why she hasn't bothered to pick up the phone."

That had been the worst. Sue hadn't called, texted, emailed, or bothered to check on her since the breakup. After years of nursing her other best friend through a string of nasty breakups and life's other ups and downs, not a word. Hell, Sue was the reason Vivian and Jace met and dated. Sue had invited her out on what turned out to be, unbeknownst to Vivian, a double date.

Not that the rest was her fault, but it hurt. Sue had always been there for her. She didn't know what she would have done without her when Mae was dying—when Vivian first encountered the world of spirits. Having Sue had been a lifesaver, literally. It made her absence now cut deeper.

"Vivian, she's about to get married, she's pregnant, and yes, she really is worried about you," Kay added. "She's got a lot on her plate. She didn't ask me to talk to you. I'm doing it to keep her from having one more thing to worry about. If you want out, she'll understand, but I'll give it to you straight. If you go through with being her maid of honor, you're going to have to swallow all of that anger, justified as it may be, and let the day be about her."

"Give me some credit, Kay. I won't ruin her wedding. But I just wonder why *he* has to be there," she said.

"If Sue's between a rock and a hard place, Jack's about got it double. He's got to consider his friendship with Jace, how pissed off Sue is, how pissed off he feels, too, for that matter. He's laid it out on the line for Jace, so you may be in luck if he backs out first. But don't count on it."

Kay's dose of honesty was probably just what Vivian needed, but that didn't make it go down any easier.

"I won't bail on Sue. You know that," she said, resigned. "I just don't want everyone treating me like a redheaded stepchild running around the family reunion."

"But you're not," Kay said.

"Not what?"

"A redhead," she said, managing to get it out just before dissolving into giggles.

"Hey," Vivian said, snorting ice cream as she chuckled. "That's a well-kept secret, and it'll stay that way as long as you, my gyno, and Miss Clairol don't go blabbing that the carpet doesn't match the drapes."

Mood lifted. God, she loved Kay.

Vivian put down her fork, stood up, and started clearing dishes. "You and Boyd need to get cracking if you want to get the girls to their sleepover and make it to the show on time. Can you go get the little guy ready for me now?"

"Sure thing," she said, regaining her composure. "But I should warn you. His new friend will probably be coming, too."

"New friend?"

"Oh, yeah," Kay said, averting her eyes. "Connor's got...well, he's got an imaginary friend." She whispered it like she might whisper that cousin Myrtle had herpes to her circle of church pals.

"Okay." Vivian shrugged. "That's not such a big deal." At Kay's skeptical look, Vivian continued. "Seriously, I had an imaginary friend when I was little."

"You did?"

"Yes, ma'am, I did. His name was Charley. He lived in my closet, was pitch black, had red eyes, and it scared the shit out of my mama, too." She beamed while Kay stared in apparent horror. "Anyhow, he didn't scare me. I always thought he was kind of cool, like my own personal bodyguard against the *real* monsters in my closet. I turned out normal."

She was normal at least as far as most folks were concerned.

"Well, I suppose he'll grow out of it. It's just that he seems to talk to him a lot," Kay mused.

Alarm bells rang in the back of Vivian's skull. She sat back down, swallowed hard, and asked, "Is that all?"

Kay shook her head and then shrugged, waving a dismissive hand. "I'm sure it's not related, but things just keep disappearing around the house. When I ask the kids, Connor says that his friend did it. And there are all kinds of strange noises coming from his room, and his lamp keeps burning out."

Oh, God, no.

"Honey, are you okay?" Kay asked. "You've gone white as a sheet. I'm sure you're right, he's just going through a phase right now."

"Did Connor tell you his friend's name?" Vivian asked.

"He just calls him Junior," said Kay.

That's what I was afraid of.

CHAPTER NINE

Vivian struggled to maintain the speed limit while driving Connor Clemmens back to her home, her heart racing faster than the car. She was terrified of what he might be bringing along for the ride, but getting any information out of him was proving difficult. He could speak pretty well for his age, but like all toddlers he was also easily distracted. Passing cars and trucks had captured his attention, so it took Vivian several tries and a piece of sugar-free candy to work around to asking him about Junior.

"So, Scooter," she asked, slowing down in case the answer or possibly the appearance of a wispy yet powerful spirit gave her a heart attack. "Is Junior here?"

"Yeah," he said between slurps. Connor liked to lick his candy rather than chew it. It made it last longer and maximized the damage he could do with the resulting sticky fingers.

Vivian couldn't see him or feel him, which gave her a small measure of hope and relief. Maybe Junior was simply an imaginary friend. Since Connor seemed cooperative, Vivian pressed on. "Does Junior go everywhere with you?"

"Yeah."

"Where did you and Junior meet?"

"Look at that! I see big fire truck! Weeee-ooooooooh, weeee-ooooooh!"

Shit, dogs' ears are bleeding out there! Not to mention mine. "Okay, Scooter, I need you to focus for Auntie Viv. Where did you meet up with Junior?"

"Zoo," he said, taking another slurp.

Double shit! "Oh, I see," she said, swerving to avoid oncoming traffic. "Does Junior live at the zoo?"

"Nope."

"Does he live with you?"

"Yeah. I want some more caaaaaaaaandy!"

"In a minute," she replied, pulling over and parking in a convenience store lot. She couldn't manage to drive safely and interrogate the boy, and she didn't care to experience another car crash. "And don't give me the stink-eye or you won't get anything. What does Junior look like?"

Scooter considered. Vivian was afraid she'd lost him again, so she waved the candy in front of his beady little eyes to get his attention again. He made a grab for it, but she was faster. That earned her another dose of the stink-eye.

"I want piece of caaaaaaaaaaaaandyyyyyyyyyy!"

"Tell me about Junior, then," she shot back, holding the candy out of reach. God, was she really torturing a little kid for information? No—actually, she was bribing him. That was okay. She'd seen Kay do the same often enough.

He gave her the most adorable scowl before saying, "Junior play with Conoow."

"That's really cool, buddy." She played it up, flashing him her brightest smile and leaning in as if thoroughly interested. "What do you play?"

"He crashes trucks. *Boom!*" Scooter shouted.

Her ears rang. That explained the noise.

Shaking it off, she kept up the enthralled act even as her heart raced and her mind spun. How was this possible? He was just a kid. She didn't think all small kiddos could see spirits. Babies possibly could, but it was so hard to tell. But children his age?

No, if that were the case, everyone would know about the hidden world of spirits. Children his age couldn't keep a secret if their little lives depended on it. She'd seen Connor cave when one of his sisters looked at him funny.

Still, was there any other explanation for what he described? Was his imagination that active? Active enough to conjure a friend who could crash toy trucks and move objects around the Clemmens house without scaring the kid to death?

"Wow, that must be fun," Vivian said, hoping for a logical rather than a paranormal explanation. "What else does he do?"

"He sparks light. Tickle Conoow. That's funny." He dissolved into a fit of giggles as Vivian's heart sank. The only explanation for "sparks light" was a guardian spirit.

But the spirit from the zoo hadn't been corporeal. He'd been transparent, one of the lost and lonely variety who lingered after death and slowly went mad, forever stuck in the Earth realm, as powerless as fish out of water.

Vivian gave him the candy and decided to postpone the rest of her interrogation until they were safely indoors. Jeanne had agreed to stay out of sight, but within earshot, so they'd have privacy. She hoped she wouldn't have to zap the wayward spirit and traumatize the toddler in her care, but maybe Connor would forget about it. Or, at least, no one would think twice about another far-fetched story from the kid.

She may have no other choice. No way would she let the spirit harm a hair on the little guy's head.

After she unloaded Connor and his overnight bag, both of which she had to manually haul indoors, she asked, "Do you want a movie and popcorn?"

"Yeah! Pop pop from the beep beep," he said, a pretty accurate description of microwave popcorn.

"Okay, but first you have to promise to brush your teeth and go night-night when Aunt Vivie says it's time."

"Okay," he said, toddling after her into the house.

Vivian got him occupied with some toys and went to run his bath. She ran the shower, too, and made sure to keep the door closed. Some myths about ghosts were true. She'd seen more of them than she cared to recount in her steamy bathroom. Settling Scooter in with a pile of bubbles, she closed the door and waited.

"It froggy in here," Connor yelled. Boy, his voice sure could carry for such a small guy.

"I know, sweetie, but the steam is good for your lungs," she yelled back. "Is Junior in there with you?"

"Nope."

"Oh, okay. Will you tell me if he shows up?" she asked, adding, "I can bring him a towel and some jammies, too."

"He not like water," Connor said, followed by a splash that likely emptied half the water out of the tub and onto her floor. Who knew bath time could be so messy?

Well, hell. There goes that bright idea.

She sent a mental text to Jeanne and explained the situation. Jeanne remained invisible, but sent a warm jolt through Vivian to let her know she was there and watching. After Vivian dried and dressed Connor, she put on some animated flick or another and set about nuking some popcorn. She'd just placed the bag in the microwave when her cell phone buzzed. Probably Kay.

"Hello?"

"Hey, honey. I just wanted to make sure Connor was behaving himself," said Kay. That was mother code for making sure Aunt Vivie hadn't lost or destroyed him yet.

"He's fine. Go out and enjoy yourself. And you and Boyd will have the rest of the night to enjoy each other when you get back home."

Kay laughed. Clearly that was the whole point of this exercise. Otherwise Boyd Clemmens would never have sprung for symphony tickets. "All right. Just make sure he brushes his teeth. And, Vivian?"

"Yes?"

"Try to watch your language, honey. I don't want Connor to, you know..."

"Grow up to be a trash mouth?"

"Something like that," Kay said.

"Will do," Vivian replied. A series of beeps from her microwave let her know the bag of hot and fluffy snack was ready. Had she turned it on? "Oh, gotta run. Popcorn's on. Bye."

She looked back at the microwave and registered that something was amiss. After about thirty seconds, a particularly loud pop and arc of electricity snapped her back into reality. There was no light emanating from the inside of the box, and the LED display was blank. Moreover, she hadn't actually turned the microwave on.

She mustered all of her energy and sent a flash through the kitchen, spinning to make sure to cast her light in all directions.

Fuck, I scorched the walls again.

She looked around and registered a blurry shape in the corner. It distorted her view of the back wall, like the haze of heat rising off asphalt. She heard a moan, and was up on her feet as fast as she could scramble.

"Jeanne," she whispered, hoping that the surround sound in the living room would keep Connor from hearing the commotion. "He's down. Get over here and back me up!"

When Vivian looked back at the downed spirit, she was able to watch as Jeanne formed what looked like a spherical cage from the yellow light that flowed from her fingertips. It encased the spirit on the kitchen floor, a spirit that appeared to still be too stunned to protest.

Thank God for spirit power. "I've got hand it to you," Vivian said. "That's a pretty cool trick. You'll have to teach me that sometime."

"What should we do with him?" Jeanne asked.

"Do you reckon he's the one who's been after me?"

"Could be, but I've never heard of a lost and lonely spirit with that kind of power," Jeanne mused. "Then again, he did cause some damage to your kitchen."

"Uh, most of that was me," Vivian admitted sheepishly. No amount of magic eraser or cleaner would get that out. She'd have to spring for paint.

"You have got to practice more," Jeanne scolded.

"Yeah, yeah, Cheer Captain, I know. I've been a little busy and I was a little distracted tonight."

Suddenly, a thought occurred to Vivian that almost made her heart stop. "Jeanne, will that hold him for a while?"

"You'd better believe it," she said. "What are you thinking? What can I do to help?"

Sometimes having a cheer captain was just what the doctor ordered. Vivian smiled, hoping the next few minutes would prove her fears unfounded.

"I need you to step into the living room with me, but stay incorporeal, okay?"

She looked doubtful, but nodded. Jeanne stood beside Vivian when she walked back into the living room and paused the movie. Naturally, Connor didn't take too kindly to that.

"I want my teevee," he whined.

"In a minute," Vivian said.

"I not go pee pee anymore," he shrieked, hopping to his feet and preparing to bolt.

"No, no," Vivian soothed, bending down to get on his eye level. "I need to ask you a very important question. Connor, can you see anyone in here other than me?"

Connor looked around, making a big show of scanning the room, looking under chairs, behind the couch, and inside the drawers on Vivian's coffee table. He looked in Jeanne's direction a few times and Vivian held her breath.

Please, oh please, dear God, let me be wrong.

After the longest two minutes of Vivian's life, Connor stood up and knitted his eyebrows together. If Vivian hadn't been so scared, it would have been comical.

"I not see anyone," he said. "Where's Junior?"

Vivian rocked back on her rump and sat on the floor, tears streaming from her face.

"Vee Vee cwying, poor Vee Vee," Connor said, coming over to plant himself on her lap and embracing her with his little arms. "Vee Vee sad?"

"No, sweetie," she muttered between sobs. "Aunt Vivie is very, very relieved." She held him for a few more minutes before he squirmed out of her arms.

"May I watch deeveedee?" he asked.

"You sure can, buddy," Vivian replied, turning it back on and settling him on the couch. She planted another kiss on his soft forehead and said, "I love you, Connor."

"I wuv you too," he replied halfheartedly. He was engrossed in the television once more.

She motioned for Jeanne to join her in the kitchen again. Their prisoner had regained consciousness, or whatever the equivalent state for ghosts was, and struggled against his bonds. Vivian sent a targeted blast of red light at him and he took the hint.

"That's for blowing up my microwave," she said. "Now, we've got a few questions for you."

"Let me out of here!" squeaked the spirit. She knelt down and got a closer look at him. He had regained enough strength to manifest as he had at the zoo.

"No can do," Jeanne chimed in. "You are in big trouble, mister. Lost soul or not, you just can't go around threatening guardians and their living helpers. You've got some explaining to do, starting with your powers. Are you a poltergeist?"

"I didn't attack anyone, I swear. I was just looking out for the little guy. He reminds me of my little brother," he whimpered, seeming genuinely distressed at the accusation. "He likes it when I break lights. It makes him laugh."

"Well, you scared the bejesus out of his mama, not to mention me with that stunt you pulled at the zoo," Vivian said.

"That mean old biddy was picking on Connor, and on you. She shouldn't do that," he said, looking like a petulant child who'd just been told to go to the principal's office.

"Be that as it may, you just can't go around making mischief for the living," Jeanne said. "It's just not polite."

Vivian rolled her eyes and then considered the situation. So far, Junior hadn't caused any harm to the Clemmens family, and he just didn't seem to have the firepower that this rogue guardian did. He couldn't even manage to break out of Jeanne's cage. It seemed he was exactly what he claimed to be—a lonely spirit who'd somehow befriended a small boy. She couldn't blame him. It had probably been ages since anyone had noticed him. And Connor was a charmer.

Still, she couldn't take chances. She needed to know if his intentions were evil or benign. "So, your name is Junior?"

"Yes, ma'am," he said, casting his gaze down as a sign of deference, or fear, perhaps.

"If we let you out, are you going to cause any more trouble?" Vivian asked.

"No, ma'am," Junior replied, shaking his head vigorously.

"Wait a minute," Jeanne said. "We can't just let him out."

"Why not? He's not responsible for attacking the padre and threatening me, and I don't think he means any harm to Scooter, do you?" Vivian turned to ask him.

"No, I've been looking out for Scooter." He beamed, gaze fully of pride. "And I only blew your microwave to get your attention. There was a spirit looking in your window."

"What?" Vivian and Jeanne cried in unison.

"He was staring at you, ma'am," he said to Vivian. "I couldn't see his face, but he was glowing white."

"Shit," Vivian said, panic gripping her. She'd been so wrapped up in dealing with the lost and lonely spirit she'd forgotten to stay vigilant for the rogue guardian. "Jeanne, can you call Ezra and get him over here? I don't want any more trouble with Connor here. And let Junior out, too. He can help keep watch, can't you?"

"Oh yes, ma'am," agreed Junior.

Jeanne did a little sashay and snapped her fingers, making the light cage disappear. Vivian was about to comment, but Jeanne was preoccupied with giving Junior the business about behaving himself. They disappeared for a bit, probably checking for any signs of the rogue guardian.

When they returned, Jeanne reassured her that the only spirits in the area were the regulars who haunted the neighborhood. They liked to stick close to Vivian and the guardian spirits who visited, and they'd agreed to keep an eye out for any unusual activity.

Then Jeanne turned back to Junior and resumed the scolding session. Vivian didn't think the timid ghost would give them any more trouble.

"And for goodness' sake, do *not* blow out any more lights. We've already got enough expenses to cover for Miss Vivian," Jeanne concluded.

She then dismissed Junior, who floated through the kitchen door. He must have joined Scooter, since his disappearance coincided with a shriek of delight.

"So," Jeanne began, moving beside Vivian and looking her up and down. "What was the dog and pony show with the kid all about?"

"Oh," Vivian sighed, slumping into one of her dinette chairs. "I was worried about Connor seeing spirits. I thought—"

"You were worried that he was scheduled for a crossing?" Jeanne asked, incredulous. She shook her head. "I would've told you. You probably would have known anyway. Don't worry. He's got a long life ahead of him."

"Yeah, I was worried," Vivian replied. Cradling her head in her hands to ease the dull ache, she voiced the other horrible thought that had crossed her mind. "Or worse. He might be like me."

"Is it really that bad?" Jeanne asked, apparently shocked but not without sympathy, judging from her gaze.

"It's definitely lonely," Vivian murmured. Then another thought occurred to her. "Hey, remember you said there are others like me? Can I meet some?"

"Hmm, I'll have to check. There aren't very many, and they're pretty scattered," Jeanne said, hesitant.

"I've got a phone, email, social media. I'm not hard to get a hold of." She hadn't realized until now how much she wanted—needed—to connect with others like her.

"We'll see," she said. "In the meantime, you've got me."

Jeanne put her arms around Vivian and sent warmth and comfort flowing into her. That alleviated some of her worries. It gave Vivian the peace of mind she needed and let her relax enough to curl up on the couch with Connor and enjoy some cuddle time. Ezra, who'd arrived shortly after the brouhaha with Junior, and Jeanne seemed to be having some sort of heated discussion in the kitchen, but she was too tired and drained to be concerned about it, or nosy.

When Jeanne emerged, she slipped a piece of paper on the table next to Vivian and nodded to the kitchen door. She sent a mental text along the lines of "Hide from Ezra." Vivian got the hint and slipped it between the cushions on her sofa. Ezra came out next and gave Vivian and Connor a warm smile and pointed to the door, making a circular motion with his fingers.

Oh, right, they're going to keep watch. Good.

She nodded and slipped further down under the covers with no objection from Connor. With Ezra, Jeanne, and Junior on patrol, she and Connor slept peacefully on the couch. She'd need to replenish her energy for the days ahead. She had a date with the padre and some local spirits tomorrow.

Let her guardians watch and wait. She'd be taking action, starting tomorrow with the biggest gossips this side of eternity.

CHAPTER TEN

Vivian spied the padre's car as she pulled into the gravel parking lot at the Feed Mill. It had literally once functioned in the manufacture of animal feed. The building now resembled an old country store and specialized in feeding people rather than livestock. The folks along this stretch of downtown Nolensville—though calling it "downtown" was a stretch, to say the least—had the good sense to register most of the buildings as historic landmarks. That meant they weren't in danger of demolition as the lust for good and pricey real estate continued to consume the outer reaches of Williamson County. As a result, this little section of town had an Andy Griffith vibe to it, except in beautiful, vibrant color.

There was a whole lot of ghost lore out there. Vivian had learned that most of it was complete garbage, but at least a little bit of it rang true. Nostalgia seemed to be big in the departed community, and a lot of them were old, like Ezra. Hospitals and nursing homes teemed with spirits. Cemeteries and battlefields were good bets, too. She kept her ears open for gossip whenever she visited her sister's grave, or Zeke's, but she doubted the spirits there would be very helpful for her situation. And she'd sworn to never set foot on a battlefield again after getting spooked, literally, at Stones River Battlefield. The "War of Northern Aggression" hadn't ended for some of the South's native sons even in this day and age, but they had nothing on the spirits of veterans who still lingered on.

Nolensville, with its antique stores, old churches, and even a small cemetery, was the gathering place for all manner of Music City's dearly departed when they weren't resting in peace in the marble orchard. Vivian had discovered that by accident when she went shopping there after her powers manifested. Guardians dropped by from time to time, as did lost and lonely spirits during times of lucidity, and the odd reaper put in an appearance on occasion. In addition, many of the local unaffiliated spent a good bit of time there. They had a lot of time on their hands, after all. Vivian kept on friendly terms with a few of them, trading spirit power for information or shopping tips.

They knew their antiques pretty well, as well as what the markup had been on any particular item.

She smiled when the priest hopped down from the front porch to meet her. His smile was just about the best sight she'd seen in the last few days. She even felt free to give him a big hug as he'd traded his collar for a T-shirt and jeans.

"Thanks for coming, Padre," Vivian said. "It'll be nice to have someone who can tell me if who I see is among the living or dead."

The last time Vivian popped by, she'd gotten a few stares from folks who were no doubt convinced that she was talking to herself. Father Montgomery could serve as a cover and keep her from mistaking a spirit for a live one.

"Have you had any more run-ins with this rogue guardian?" The priest asked.

"Well, maybe. I think I ought to fill you in on the whole story first. A lot's been going on the last couple of days. Most of it not great."

"Are you all right?" he asked, concern painted across his face. Part of it was a priest thing, but most was just his nature. He made confession easy.

"I split with Jace."

"I'm sorry to hear that. Was he put off by your work?" The priest maintained a neutral and conversational tone, which helped her get through the rest without exploding in anger.

"Well, he did say that he thought I would never put him first, but I didn't have the chance to tell him about seeing the dead. Then he fessed up to having another woman on the side. I spent half the morning at my doctor getting screened for any diseases he might have passed along. I mean, we were careful, but not too careful."

She didn't want to elaborate and risk getting a look or a lecture on the merits of abstinence, though there were plenty of cheating bastards out there with wives. Still, she didn't need to have the priest kick her while she was already down.

Father Montgomery didn't speak, but pulled Vivian to him and held her while she composed herself. It was surprisingly...pleasant. Not awkward or embarrassing. Then again, she'd learned long ago that the priest was only human.

And he'd allowed her to see him at his worst, just as she'd witnessed his darkest hours through his memories come to life when they'd traveled to the reaper's dark realm. They'd been to Hell and back together, and the bond they'd formed became the bedrock of her new life. Seemed she did, in fact, have someone who understood.

He gave her a final pat on the back and said, "Why don't we go grab a sandwich and you can tell me the rest? *My* treat."

Wiping her eyes, she said, "Thanks, Padre."

They enjoyed deli sandwiches filled full of Amish cheese and cold cuts while Vivian told the priest about Junior and his likely sighting of the threatening spirit who was after her. She didn't mention Darkmore, thinking it unwise to let anyone in her circle of spirits or living helpers know about her ongoing association with the reaper. Though Lloyd Montgomery was not quite as black and white in his thinking as, say, Jeanne, he didn't hold Darkmore in high regard.

How could he, after what he'd seen and experienced in the reaper's home?

How could she?

Jeanne believed that you had to choose sides, which is why she'd refused to visit the "free range" spirits with Vivian. The priest simply didn't trust Darkmore. Vivian was afraid he'd convince her not to trust the reaper either. She cherished Lloyd Montgomery, the only living man in her life who really knew her. He was, after all, the only true confidant she had this side of eternity. It was both comforting and disconcerting. But she loved him for being her friend. She couldn't bear to lose him, but feared she might if he knew of her ties to the reaper.

He couldn't possibly understand her complex...relationship, for lack of a better term, with Darkmore. Before they'd escaped his realm with the help of Ezra, Mae, and Vivian's spirit light, Darkmore had tried to save them. He hadn't wanted to enslave Vivian, to force her to work for him as the guardians did, or so he'd claimed. He wished her to choose him.

He could be as persuasive with charm as he could be with fear. And yet, he'd seemed so genuine in his distress upon finding her with the priest, angry that she hadn't trusted him enough to discuss the terms of her surrender—not that she'd intended to surrender—and...hurt that he was unable to join them when they'd ascended back to Earth.

Darkness was his home, he'd claimed. He was right. And she suspected it made his yearning for a companion all the more powerful.

No, she couldn't tell any of this to the priest. She'd have to settle for sharing what she was able and hoping it would be enough to figure out who was after her and how to stop the threat.

"So tell me," Father Montgomery said between bites. "Who do you see?"

"Well, see those clothes hanging on the rack over there?" Vivian pointed to some Amish dresses, bonnets, and slacks on the wall to the right of their table. "There are a couple of little old white-haired ladies standing underneath them and chatting each other. I'll bet you can't see them, though."

"No," the priest conceded. "Who else?"

"There's a young man sulking in the corner." Vivian tried to be inconspicuous as she cast furtive glances around the room. "I see a young couple at the table behind us, too."

"The young man you mentioned must be a ghost, but the other two are real," he said with a smile. "How do you manage to keep it all straight?"

She grinned. "I don't always. I just proceed with caution. Oh, and I almost always keep my Bluetooth in my ear so I can pretend that I'm talking on my cell. It saves me some embarrassment."

They kept chatting while Vivian worked up her nerve, and they took the burly clerk up on his offer to try a slice of pie with a side of fresh-brewed Southern pecan coffee. Vivian suggested that they take a walk down the street to see if she could discreetly engage some of the spirits in a fact-finding chat.

She settled on a well-dressed older woman sitting outside of the Three French Hens store, sending out a mental message first to get her attention. She looked Vivian up and down, raising her eyebrows at the priest before jerking her head to indicate that they should follow her around to the side of the old white two-story house for privacy.

Once safely away from prying eyes, the spirit spoke. "You Ezra's girl?" she snapped.

Father Montgomery flinched, but only because she chose that moment to make herself visible to him. She wasn't corporeal, as she was neither guardian nor reaper. She appeared a bit like a hologram, transparent and with the tendency to fade in and out, as if her spiritual transmission frequency kept shifting. Still, it took real power to become visible to the living—ordinary living folks without Vivian's special powers of perception. This spirit appeared to manage through sheer force of will.

Vivian took the priest's hand so that her sphere of invisibility extended to him. While she didn't like to be referred to as anyone's girl, sweetie, darling, or sugar, she decided to just answer the old bat once assured that they were speaking privately.

"Not by choice, but yes, I do work with him."

The woman smiled, revealing a set of gray and menacing teeth. "Yes, I do believe you must be the one, then. What can I do for you?"

"I've got a guardian gone bad on my back and I'm trying to find out who he is and how to get him off it. Have you heard anything?"

She gave Vivian an appraising look and said, "Maybe I know something, but I'm going to ask a favor of you in return."

No surprise there. Vivian had learned that you didn't get much for free in this life or the afterlife. "What's the favor?"

"My no-account grandson and his wife are squandering their share of the inheritance money I left them, or rather they're squandering the share I left for my one and only great-grandchild. I need you to put away what's left before they spend it all."

More questionably legal activity? Great...

"Uh-huh, and how in the Sam Hill do you propose I do that? I have many talents and some special skills, but I draw the line at breaking and entering," Vivian shot back, squaring her shoulders as they began the negotiations in earnest.

The old spirit smiled wider and stood a little straighter. "You'll do it because you need to know what I can tell you, and you'll be able to do it because I know all of the account numbers and pass codes."

Vivian's jaw dropped. She hadn't expected the ghostly grandmother to have a plan.

"What, you think just because I'm old and departed that I don't know how banking works? I used to work for the bank, Missy. Besides," she spoke in a low and confidential tone, "I have an account they don't know about, already set up in his name. All you have to do is just move it on over. Won't take but two minutes, I expect."

"Fine," Vivian replied. She could always enlist Jeanne or some other spirit to use a random computer to complete the transaction. It was relatively low risk, and not quite illegal. The spirit seemed of sound mind—if not sound body—so there were no ethical barriers. "Now, tell me what you know."

"Well, we've had some newcomers hanging around the past month or so, at least. It took us a while to figure it out, but we reckon it's been the same spirit all along."

"How do you mean?" the padre asked.

"Oh, we can take on all manner of forms, but we each have our own flavor, for lack of a better word," the spirit said. That was true enough. Though most spirits carried their original forms with them and manifested as such, they could channel their energy to assume any appearance if they practiced.

For a powerful guardian spirit, it provided the ultimate advantage. They could move about the spirit world incognito and assume a corporeal form that met their needs while operating in the world of the living.

"Anyway, the first time this new one showed up, it looked like a little girl," the spirit said. "We reckoned she must have run off when the guardians came to fetch her, or maybe the others. We don't judge here. All are welcome so long as they mind their manners. Scared little kids do up and run sometimes."

That was also true, and not just for scared kids. Learning of one's passing tended to come as a shock, and not all of the departed were prepared to accept their change in circumstance.

"I see." Vivian nodded. "What made you suspicious?"

"Nothing at first. We took her in and tried to make her feel at home, tell her what she needed to know about the spirit world, see if we could get her to a guardian. She seemed real interested about us, but didn't want any guardians. What she *did* want to know about was mediums."

The priest's distaste for the subject showed on his face, but Vivian was too keen on getting information to let him interrupt. "She wanted to know about the living who commune with the dead?"

"Yes. You're quick, I see," the old bat said sardonically. "We didn't think much about it at the time either. Lots of freshly departed spend a few days looking for a way to get back in touch with their loved ones. Most try themselves, but they don't know how or just don't have the energy. Hell, I can't even get enough steam to make the damned keys on the computer move, which is why I need you."

"You have enough steam to appear and chat for a spell," Vivian said, unable to resist wheedling the spirit.

"Don't you sass me, missy, or we'll part ways right now."

"Sorry," Vivian said, fighting a smile. This one reminded her a lot of her grandmother. "Go on."

The old spirit gave her the stink-eye and said, "As I was saying, we told her straight that there weren't no real mediums around these parts, but we knew of a woman who worked with guardians and had a knack for helping those in need. She had all sorts of questions about you. We told her to stick around and we'd see about Ezra arranging a meeting, but she just up and vanished."

"That's weird," Vivian said, not to mention suspicious. Lost and lonely spirits were skittish in general. Why would this one cozy up to the spirits here and then all of a sudden turn tail and run at the mention of Ezra?

The spirit shook her head. "Not really. That happens a lot around here, too. But then a few nights later, another new one shows up. This one was a little off, but we take in strays, too. He was telling wild tales about someone trying to exorcise him or some such nonsense. Bobby from across the field joked about the lady down the road who could zap the pants off him if he really wanted to be gone. He didn't come back after that, either."

"Wow, should I be offended?" Vivian said. "And I'm not that powerful. Guardians spirits and reapers can do much more damage than I can."

The spirit shrugged. "I don't know about being offended, but by the third time a new spirit came around asking questions, we'd caught his scent and knew something weren't right. We've been on our guard ever since, but we reckon he must have already found you. He ain't been back since."

"What else do you know about him?" Vivian asked.

"Nothing much, except he's powerful. Must have been to fool us so long. We've been watching for him, but we reckon he's moved on. I am awful sorry about that, but we didn't think any of our kind would mean you harm, except maybe the man in white."

"I'm not worried about Darkmore anymore," Vivian said quickly. "I mean, it seemed like we were square after we parted ways the last time. And I don't blame y'all. Just let me know if you hear anything else, okay?"

"Of course, dear," she said. "Just take care. The last one had a few questions about you and the reaper."

Oh, God. Was this what the attack was about? Were the guardians onto her? Did they know about her ongoing association with Darkmore?

The priest put an arm around her for support. "It's all right," he said, soothing. "You're under the protection of Ezra and other powerful guardians—and me. We won't let the reaper anywhere near you."

Guilt replaced fear as she regained her composure. But relief washed over her as well. The priest didn't suspect. Perhaps the guardians didn't know about her deal with Darkmore either.

The spirit nodded, encouraging. "I don't think you need to worry. My sources haven't spotted that reaper in these parts since your last run in. You're safe."

Thank Heaven for small favors. Wait, maybe she shouldn't be thanking Heaven for this. She'd have to think on it. "Good to know. Oh, one more thing," Vivian added. "What do you know about a lost and lonely spirit hanging around the zoo? He goes by Junior."

"Junior's back? Mercy me, it's been years!"

She hadn't actually expected the spirit to have anything on Scooter's little friend. Lucky break. "So you know him, then?"

"Yeah, I do. He's harmless most of the time," she said with a dismissive chuckle. "Though he seems to have a knack for moving objects with his energy. Don't ask me where or how he gets it, but I'd give my eyeteeth to be able to do what he does, if I still had 'em."

"Well, he's taken up with a little boy I know. I just want to make sure he won't hurt him," she said.

"No, I reckon he just misses his little brother. That's why he's stuck, you know."

"No, I don't know. Tell me," Vivian said. She smelled an opportunity to do some good for him and to help him move along in the process.

The old spirit grinned, clearly pleased to share more juicy stories to her rapt audience. "Let's see, him and his little brother were farm boys a ways back, doing what boys do. Tree climbing, spitting, swimming in creeks and ponds and the like. Well, one fine afternoon they were swimming in a creek that was swelled up from rain, and the little one got caught up in the current. Junior tried to get to him, but he just didn't make it."

"Poor thing," Vivian muttered to herself. "It's no wonder he's determined to look out for Scooter. Did he drown, too?"

"No, ma'am, he didn't. He hanged himself in the barn the day after they buried his brother, and he's been roaming around these parts ever since. Go easy on him, will you?"

"I will," Vivian promised. "Now how about you lay those account numbers on me?"

The old woman, who finally revealed her name to be Mildred Bluff, gave Vivian the information and they parted ways. She and the padre spoke with a few other spirits, Vivian offering to help with burdens and the priest offering prayers and intercession. Most of them were content, though. A lot of the spirits lingered on Earth to keep an eye on kinfolk. Mildred herself swore she'd only cross to the next realm when her grandson kicked the bucket, enabling her to give him a cosmic kick in the ass before she went. In the meantime, she kept watch over the little ghost community in Nolensville and apparently had a little thing going with Ezra.

Vivian was delighted to learn that he'd taken her to his realm a time or two, and that they'd enjoyed sitting a spell on his front porch swing. *My, my, Ezra you old hound dog.* She'd be sure to tease him about that next time he came to call.

Father Montgomery offered to keep Vivian company, but she decided to just head home and enjoy some time to herself. She called ahead and asked Jeanne to clear out all squatters of the non-living kind while she stopped by the liquor store for some liquid consolation. When she reached her front door, she found a small package on her front stoop. The envelope on it bore her name, written in neatly printed block letters. She picked it up and took it inside, wondering if she should call Jeanne back or Ezra. She wondered if guardians could do harm to the living via parcel, but that just seemed silly. She knew the rogue was watching, and he'd had the audacity to attack someone outside of her home, so why send anthrax? This just didn't seem like his style. It didn't *feel* like it. Shrugging, she pulled the note from the envelope and read.

Dearest Vivian,

I heard about your recent misfortune with Mr. Blakemore. While I am pleased with the opportunity to relieve you of this particular burden, the pain of betrayal and infidelity being especially scrumptious, I am truly sorry for your loss. Perhaps I can be of service in administering some karmic justice to the blackguard? Don't get yourself all worked up about it. I do not mean the most severe form of justice, of course. That sort of punishment is reserved for more serious infractions. But I can inflict a degree of suffering on him, should it please you.

Think it over.

By the way, I'll be in touch soon with some information that should help us sort out your other troubles. You do seem to accumulate them!

Regards,
  LD

. . .

P.S. Please enjoy what's in the box until you can find a suitable substitute.

Blackguard? Who the hell talks like that?

She promised herself she'd teach Darkmore some more contemporary forms of slander as she unwrapped the package. The contents brought a wide smile to her face. Of the many spirits she knew, and she knew plenty, it amazed her that the darkest of them all would be so thoughtful as to leave her a box of chocolates.

CHAPTER ELEVEN

Had it been entirely up to Sue and Vivian, Sue's condition notwithstanding, Sue's bridal shower would have involved a lot of booze, sex toys as party favors, and at least one nearly naked man dancing on the table. Several of the ladies would have joined him, no doubt, possibly rendering him fully naked. It would have been a riot, relived and embellished to the status of legend in the years to come.

Unfortunately, Sue's older sister was in charge.

Sarah Harrow, née Carlson, was a card-carrying member of the Holier-than-thou Squad and hell-bent on making sure that the formal bridal shower was not only dignified to the point of painfully boring, but she'd also invited Jace's new girlfriend. Neither scored her points with Vivian, who'd seriously considered not going. Kay promised to run interference and to treat Vivian to dinner and drinks at Holland House after, which was the only reason that Vivian finally agreed to go.

That, and Kay promised to rescue Sue as well.

When they knocked on the door to Sarah's stately suburban estate home, they were greeted by the witch herself, wearing her Sunday best and without a single hair, eyelash, or acrylic nail out of place. Stay-at-home mother of four homeschooled rugrats—homeschooled by a revolving door of nannies—Sarah Harrow had somehow managed to regain her "girlish" figure after each birth, praise the Lord, using something she called the Hallelujah diet.

Actually, Vivian suspected it was more likely due to her personal trainer Chad, but that was probably a special kind of exercise that Sarah's hubby didn't know about.

Like her sister, Sarah was blonde and built, though taller than Sue. She'd married well, obviously. You couldn't swing a house like that on a single income, at least not legally. Her husband wasn't too bad, bless him, but he was hardly ever around. Sue thought he used work as a convenient excuse to minimize his time with Sarah, but Vivian reckoned that he had to work triple hard to afford the big family and house in the affluent area. Plus, Sarah enjoyed spending like there was no tomorrow. She didn't work and used the homeschooling as an excuse, nannies notwithstanding, though Vivian thought she probably just didn't want her kids mixing with little black and Latino kids in Davidson County schools.

Sarah gave Kay and Vivian her best pageant smile when she answered the door. The calculation and cruelty hidden beneath the expression gave Vivian the creeps.

"Come on in, ladies. We're just mixin' and a-minglin' and passing out the little appetizers," she said as she stepped back and made room for them. "Why, Miss Kay, did you bring your famous homemade mints?"

"I did," Kay said cordially.

"And Vivian, thank you so much for taking care of the cake," she purred.

"Don't mention it, Sarah. I'd do anything for Sue," Vivian answered.

"Of course. Honey, we are just so proud of you for being such a trouper, what with your unfortunate situation," Sarah offered, leaning in and whispering the last.

"You mean with Jace screwing around and still being a part of the wedding?" Vivian replied, not lowering her voice.

Kay gave her a hard nudge in the rib cage, reminding her to mind her manners for Sue's sake. Sarah glared at her, but didn't comment. Instead she led the way to the kitchen and directed them to place the mints and cake on the table. Sarah hired caterers to act as servers and provide most of the food. She'd assigned Vivian cake duty so she'd "feel" like she was a part of it all. Kay's mints, however, were a rare treat and simply non-negotiable. Everyone asked her for her secret recipe, and Sarah had made it her mission to get Kay to give up the goods.

She'd yet to succeed.

The caterers busied themselves arranging platters of canapés or fruit and chafing dishes with honey-glazed ham, warm artichoke dip, and other assorted goodies. They also chattered away in Spanish as they worked, and Vivian caught a phrase or two. She smiled to herself, thinking that Señora Harrow was definitely a *puta* and wishing she could understand whatever flavor of qualifier that they'd added.

Kay and Vivian grabbed some punch and headed to the living room. Vivian recognized half of the guests, but couldn't keep herself from scanning the room, trying to guess which one of the women she didn't know was her replacement. The candidates didn't inspire confidence, as most of the younger women were drop-dead gorgeous. When Kay noticed that Vivian was digging her nails into her palms, she took her by the elbow and suggested that they sit down next to Sue.

Sue Carlson had always looked pretty, but now she definitely carried that pregnancy glow everyone always raved about. She looked even perkier and happier when she spotted Kay and Vivian.

"Hey," she said, getting up with considerable difficulty before laying a big hug on Kay, "I'm so glad you're here! How are the little ones?"

"Oh, they're fine. Boyd's got them all day and night, if necessary," she said with a wink.

"Thank God," Sue said, reaching over to grab Vivian. She held her for a long time, whispering in her ear, "Oh, sweetie! Thank you so much for coming."

"I wouldn't miss it," Vivian replied, and meant it.

"Is Sarah being Sarah?" Sue asked, resigned exasperation lacing her tone.

"Oh, yeah," Vivian and Kay replied in unison.

"At least you don't have to spend the whole damned day with her," Sue hissed. "Just stick close and get me the hell out of here as soon as we get through the gifts, promise?"

"Sure," Vivian said. "Safety in numbers, right?"

They endured an hour and a half of highfalutin Southern bitchiness disguised as polite conversation, overpriced snacks sans alcohol, and watching poor Sue work her tail off trying to give proper deference to the quality of each gift bag, bow, and specialty wrapping paper, not to mention each gift inside. Vivian didn't understand why they couldn't at least have champagne cocktails. Honestly, she'd seen Sarah's liquor stash before. They could've had any number of quality cocktails to lighten the mood, making a few tasty virgin options for the guest of honor and those who didn't wish to partake.

Of course, Sarah was of the Southern Baptist persuasion, which meant that she and her fellow brothers and sisters didn't recognize one another when they crossed paths in the liquor store. *Seriously, either live by your principles or admit they're wrong and move on. Why be coy?* She sighed. Coy just seems to go with the Bible Belt like white on rice.

After the last of the gifts, they still hadn't managed to wind the conversation down and make a graceful exit. Vivian was getting antsy, not to mention irascible and bored, so she excused herself and snuck back into the kitchen for consolation in the form of leftovers. The clicking of high heels, two sets, entering the kitchen interrupted her mid-bite. Sarah walked in with a short and friendly-looking brunette woman. When she caught sight of Vivian, Sarah grinned a feline smile, predatory and greedy.

More than that, it was full of flagrant and smug satisfaction.

"Well, Sheila, don't I feel awkward now," Sarah said, demurring. "But I suppose you two were bound to meet sooner or later. Sheila Mayweather, meet Vivian Bedford. Vivian, meet Sheila Mayweather. She's with Mr. Jace."

Sheila looked frightened. She also looked mortified and angry. Under different circumstances, Vivian might have felt sorry for the woman. She was plenty angry, but she didn't have any cause to be mortified, aside from the fact that her mouth was full and her hands were greasy. She took her time chewing as she stared a hole through both women. The silence was deafening.

Sheila spoke first. "Hello, Vivian. I've wanted to meet you."

"Have you?" Vivian said. "You know about me. That's odd, since I hadn't heard a thing about you until very recently."

Red crept up Sheila's cheeks, but to her credit, she pressed on. "Look, I didn't know that Jace was serious with you, or with anyone else, when we met. We just sort of hit it off and—"

"Let me save you some trouble, okay? I don't really want to know the details of how you and Jace met. I don't want to know what you two do, how or where you do it, and I don't really want to know you. I'm not going to cause any trouble for you so long as you don't cross me and don't cross my path too often. Understand?"

"Fine by me," Sheila replied. Sarah seemed satisfied, and turned to leave with Sheila. Vivian wasn't going to let her off the hook so easily.

"Not so fast, Sarah. I'm not finished with you yet," Vivian said, anger welling from deep within.

Sarah turned on her heel and glared at Vivian. After Sheila was out of the room, Sarah said, "Excuse me? You come into my home, you behave rudely to one of the guests at my sister's bridal shower, and then you have the audacity to order me around in my own kitchen?"

"Cut the shit, Sarah. You've been planning this little stunt since I walked in, so don't get all high and mighty on me."

"High and mighty? I'm right with my family, I'm right with my community, and I'm right with the Lord, which is more than I can say for you. Honestly, Sue used to be a good girl until she started running around with you. Now look at her—pregnant out of wedlock. At least she's getting married, though. She's doing the right thing. You on the other hand, whoring around and taking my sister with you—"

The damn broke and Vivian let loose, barely leashing the spirit light that coursed through her veins, swirling and ready to break free.

"Whoring around? Look who's talking," Vivian said, low and with false calm. "You forget, I've been running around with your sister long enough to know a little bit about you. Those late nights sneaking out in high school, even after you met Mr. Harrow," Vivian said, abandoning all pretense of civility.

What Sarah didn't know was that Vivian had poked around in her black heart throughout the tirade she'd endured, and she had more ammunition for her effort. She'd use it, going in for the proverbial kill.

"Sue likes to tell tales," Sarah replied tartly. "I've always been a lady."

"The kind of lady who leaves her children with a nanny while she's out meeting a certain married gentleman from the First Self-Righteous Church of Middle Tennessee?" Vivian asked. She watched as Sarah's eyes went wide and the triumph disappeared from her expression. A surge of power rushed through Vivian, as did a hunger to inflict suffering upon her opponent and taste the wretched woman's misery.

She moved dangerously close, letting her words slice daggers into the psyche of her opponent. "Daddy goes away a lot, doesn't he? And you can only drown your loneliness in the sea of Jack Daniels for so long. You'd leave him, but you're afraid. Not afraid of what the Almighty might think, but afraid of what the congregation would say, what the neighbors might whisper, what damage your reputation would suffer."

"Th-that's not true," Sarah said, gooseflesh erupting over her arms. "Please, stop."

Vivian grabbed her arm to keep her from bolting and leaned even closer to whisper the awful truth in her ear. "The children don't concern you, but the money does, doesn't it? So you found someone who's safe. He'll fuck you nicely on the side but won't risk his own finances by ruining his marriage, so he keeps quiet. He wouldn't even talk if he suspected what you do, would he?"

Vivian leaned back to examine her handiwork. A voice in the back of her mind warned her. Her conscience, perhaps? Her better nature? The new hunger that gripped her urged her to continue her assault on the horrid soul in front of her, so ripe for the harvest.

"Stop," Sarah pleaded again. Her skin was pale, her breathing shallow, and she would have fallen over had she not backed herself against the kitchen door.

"Have you submitted his hair samples yet, or are you afraid to find out for sure if he's been your baby daddy twice over? Think of the scandal, the shame. Oh, I see that you do think of it, but the things he does to you," Vivian continued, reveling in Sarah's shock as unbidden memories of the passion and frenzy of acts never performed in her husband's bed filled her heart and mind.

She looked at Vivian, and knew that Vivian knew.

"Stop!" Sarah screamed. "I knew you weren't right with the Lord, but I didn't know you were a witch. I rebuke thee in the name of Jesus, I—"

Vivian shot a blast of red light at Sarah's mouth, silencing her mid-scream and causing her to collapse onto the tiled kitchen floor. She stooped down next to the woman and grabbed her shoulders so she couldn't scramble away.

"Now then," she said, "I'm going to talk and you're going to listen. If you're a good girl, I might let you have your voice back. Nod if you're picking up what I'm throwing down."

Sarah nodded, or perhaps she was just shaking all over. It didn't matter. Vivian knew that she had her attention.

"Now then, I'm fixing to leave your little soirée, and I'm taking Kay and your sister with me. I'll walk out and prepare to thank you for your gracious hospitality while you stay here and pull yourself together. I expect you can do that, right?"

Sarah nodded again. Vivian could see the sweat on her brow and the tears in her eyes. She'd wet herself out of fear. Vivian thought back to the time when she'd first encountered the dark realm of the spirit world. She'd confronted her own darkness there. This time was different. This time she was not afraid.

That fact should have disturbed her more than it did.

"I don't expect you'll feel like telling tales about me or messing with me in general after this. Beside, who would believe you? I *do* expect that you'll behave a little bit better from now on, and not just when I'm around."

Sarah nodded vigorously and Vivian flashed her a wide smile. "I have some interesting friends with eyes and ears just about anywhere you'd care to go, and some places you wouldn't. I think you've figured out by now that you don't want to be on my bad side."

Vivian rose and scowled at the pitiful sight before her. Sarah scooted out of the way and Vivian stepped over the mess on the floor and cracked open the kitchen door to look out at the crowd of ladies in the dining room. They were all occupied, so Vivian turned and told Sarah she had five minutes to clean up the kitchen and herself. Inhaling deeply, she absorbed the red light of wickedness that floated from Sarah Harrow.

It wasn't a burden willingly given, nor taken in secret. She'd ripped this darkness directly from a human spirit and it felt and tasted entirely different from anything Vivian had yet experienced. After she recovered, Vivian shot a jolt of red light at Sarah's mouth to release her voice before walking away without a second glance.

———

Holland House Bar and Refuge was busy, but not overly crowded. After the bridal shower from hell, that wasn't a bad thing. Kay was delighted to be someplace where munchkins weren't allowed. This hip East Nashville bar with meal service was strictly twenty-one and over. Vivian was just happy to have made it out without her nerves fraying and to have her mind on something else. She'd had some time to think about what she'd done to Sarah, and decided that she was better off not thinking about it for a while. Alcohol would help, and she was grateful that Kay was driving tonight.

But sooner or later, she'd have to face this shocking, new dark side she'd unleashed.

It was warm enough at the end of April to sit at a table out front underneath the pergola. Since the guys who'd robbed the bar a few months back got caught in another holdup, folks could breathe a bit easier. According to the proprietor, business had boomed right after. East Nashville didn't have the best reputation, in spite of the new hip watering holes and modern condos. Still, the element of danger had its appeal and many of the city's locals and transplants enjoyed a little walk on the wild side along with their fancy cocktails.

Vivian didn't have to worry, of course. Seemed she might be one of those elements of danger, come to think of it.

"So, Kay," Sue said during a gap in the conversation. "Now that we're away from polite society, I've got a question for you."

"Here we go," Kay replied with a roll of her eyes. "You've got that naughty look in your eyes."

Vivian chimed in, "No, Kay, she's the woman of the hour. Let her have the floor. Besides, I'd like to see where she takes this little brain cell misfire."

"Okay, here goes. Did the sex get better when you were pregnant? I mean, like, a *lot* better?"

Vivian, already half drunk, almost fell out of her chair laughing. Sue looked a little embarrassed, but not much. The old Sue emerged from behind the façade she'd kept up while at her sister's place. Kay, bless her, kept a straight face and appeared to give the question some serious consideration.

"I can't say it was great with my two girls," Kay mused. "In fact, I just couldn't get there, so to speak, to save my life, and not for lack of trying. I mean, Boyd was a trouper and we even bought—"

"Oh, Jesus, no more," Vivian cried. "I really don't need to know that much about your sex life, or I'll never be able to look at Boyd again."

"Grow up, Vivian. I'm serious. Besides, you're the one who said I could have the floor. I just can't get enough of Jack. It's like I'm on girl Viagra and steroids," Sue said, whispering the last part.

"Then I think you're having a boy," Kay said. "When I had Scooter on board, I was woman, and boy oh boy could the neighbors ever hear me roar! Maybe it's the male influence. Who knows? I say just be happy and go with it while it lasts."

"How long will that be?" Sue asked.

"Until your back aches, your feet swell, and the hemorrhoids hit. By the way, the hemorrhoids also interfere with the only comfy position after around month eight and—"

"No more, no more," Vivian roared between giggles. "Or I swear to God I'm getting an elective hysterectomy tomorrow!"

"No, Vivian, you can't! This is a rite of passage, you know," Sue snorted.

"Besides, Annabelle, Kaitlyn, and Connor are going to need someone new to corrupt after they're done with Jack Jr.," Kay added.

"I'd love to help y'all out," Vivian said, still stifling laughter and slurring her words a bit. "But unless I rob a sperm bank and grab a turkey baster, my prospects aren't so hot right now."

"Oh, no," Sue said before clapping her hands over her mouth. She looked from Vivian to Kay and back again, trembling as tears started to fall. "Vivian, I didn't mean...I shouldn't have said...oh, Jesus I'm such an insensitive bitch!"

"No, honey, that's your sister," Vivian said, laughing. She turned to Kay, pointed at Sue, and whispered, "What's going on with her?"

"Don't worry. It's the hormones. They get worse as things move along." Kay signaled to their server and pulled her wallet out of her bag. "On that note, I think we'd better call it a night. When one gal pal is bawling and the other can barely stand," she said as she patted Vivian on the back, "the party is *definitely* over."

"Oh, by the way," Sue said between sniffles. "I hope y'all don't get sick."

Vivian snorted. "Don't worry, I can hold my liquor with the best of 'em."

"No, I'm serious," Sue said. "I just got a text from my sister. She's at the hospital with horrible stomach pains. They're going to admit her."

Vivian froze. Clearing her throat, she said, "Is she going to be okay?"

Sue waved a hand. "It's probably something she ate. I told her to take it easy on the pasta salads. Mayo goes bad fast. Anyway, I just hope it isn't some stomach bug. It—"

She missed the last part during her dash around the corner to vomit up the contents of her stomach. Karma was apparently an eye-for-an-eye kind of bitch.

CHAPTER TWELVE

Kay was kind enough to help Vivian into her house without breaking anything, herself included, but Vivian drew the line at Kay's offer to help her into her jammies. She remained shaken, but not helpless. All she really wanted was to dive straight into bed, clothes and all, and just let the alcohol remaining in her system take its sedative effect. There were way too many things she just did not want to think about.

And damn it all to hell, she still had to find a date for Sue's wedding rather than face the humiliation of going stag in front of Jace and Sheila, not to mention Sarah. It was too bad that Jeanne had other plans. She materialized as soon as Kay left and brought more karmic retribution with her.

"What in the name of all that is good and righteous were you thinking?" Jeanne's voice screeched from the hall. At least she was nice enough not to barge in the bathroom.

"What?" Vivian called back, not exactly feigning ignorance, but not exactly admitting guilt either.

"That little stunt you pulled on a mortal in broad daylight? Where you could have been seen? Our powers are only used for good—"

"Oh, get off your high horse, Jeanne. I wouldn't even be able to pull stunts like I did if *that* were true, and you know it. Ezra broke more than a few rules with me, so lay off. She was asking for it."

It didn't excuse Vivian's actions or misuse of power, but she wasn't about to concede the point to Jeanne.

"You can't just go around and use your gifts for personal vengeance. There are some serious consequences," Jeanne said.

Vivian came out of the bathroom clad in her jammies and tried to look contrite, even if she didn't exactly feel it. She looked at Jeanne and asked, "So, are you going to rat me out?"

Jeanne gave her a hard look but didn't speak. Vivian's buzz was intact, but her happy drunk state faded fast thanks to the guardian realm's number one party pooper. She remembered Uriel's warning, not to mention the fact that her actions had landed Sarah in the hospital, and decided it was time to break out the big guns.

"Jeanne, I'm sorry, okay? I was mad and I let Sarah get to me," she pleaded. "Seriously, that was pretty low, parading Jace's new piece in front of me for spite. You have to grant me that."

"It was mean, yes," Jeanne said, trying not to soften. "But still, you can't do things like that."

"I know, I know, and I promise I'll work on that. So pretty please with a cherry on top, don't tell, okay?" Vivian paused, then added, "I'll make those brownies you love..."

"With the melted Ghirardelli chocolate squares instead of coco powder?" Jeanne asked.

Gotcha. "Of course. I know how much you love the real thing."

She was champing at the bit, and Vivian could tell, but she didn't want to let Vivian off that easy. "Fine. I'll only tell Ezra."

"What if he decides to tell the Grand High Inquisitor of the Guardian Realm, or whoever's in charge of your little outfit?" Vivian protested.

"He won't," Wallace said.

Vivian almost jumped clean out of her skin when the old guardian appeared. Jeanne's eyes widened, which made Vivian think she wasn't expecting him. *Great.*

Just as Vivian braced herself for a fight, Wallace gave her a soft smile and said, "Ezra will protect you from any guardian who means you harm. Now we just have to figure out how to protect you from yourself."

What the hell? Wallace didn't like her. He'd made that perfectly clear. So what was with the one-eighty?

"Of course, he'll probably think of some penance for you. If I were you, I'd butter him up with some more home cooking and a few more of those western flicks he likes," Wallace said, smiling. She hadn't even known the guy had teeth.

"Um, okay. I guess I can do that," Vivian said with a hint of caution. Perhaps Wallace sensed her hesitance, since he walked toward her slowly and placed a hand on her shoulder. She felt a quick surge of warmth and comfort. He then released her, nodded, and disappeared.

What the ever-loving fuck?

"Jeanne, what just happened?"

"Wallace is trying to make amends."

"Seriously? I though he hated me."

"No, not at all. Look, I know he seems gruff, but he's a good guardian. He's just old school. You threw him for a loop at first, but he does respect the work you're doing with us."

Stranger things have happened. Just go with it.

Shaking her head, she said, "Well, I guess we can have him over for movie night, too."

"Just pick one that has some cute guys in it, though, since I'll have to watch it with y'all, too."

"Good idea," Vivian replied, yawning.

"Well, I'll let you get some shut-eye now. The next time someone tries to get your goat like that, why don't you just try spitting in her iced tea, or ruining her dress, or punching her, or something more...human?" Jeanne said.

Sound advice. She only hoped she could take it. Now that she'd had a taste of the dark side, one that she'd found a little too satisfying, she'd have to be on her guard lest those appetites take over again.

"I'll bear that in mind. Good night," Vivian muttered as she pulled the covers over her head.

———

The alarm clock read 4:17 in bold, red digital numbers. She barely had time to feel irritation at being awake so early once she registered the cold. A hand closed over her mouth before she could scream. That didn't stop her from kicking.

Released from the grip but still unable to speak, Vivian scrambled out of bed and onto her feet by way of pure adrenaline and prepared to strike. Light sparked from her fingertips, the only other light visible in her dark room aside from the alarm clock readout. She heard a grumble from the corner of the room and shot a blast.

Unfortunately, it revealed nothing and left yet another an unsightly black smudge on her wall.

"I suggest you cease and desist now, Vivian, unless you want to receive another reprimand from your personal guardians," came a familiar cool voice. He sounded a bit breathless.

"Damn it, Darkmore! Why can't you just show up during normal hours or make an appointment or something?" Vivian growled. She settled herself back on her bed and waited for the reaper to appear.

He was on top of her before she knew what hit her, and this time he was smart enough to immobilize her legs. A surge of raw terror and rage rushed through her. Staring into his cold blue eyes, she registered hunger, not for her body, but for the powerful and deadly emotions surging through her mind and spirit.

It excited him and he inhaled deeply, drawing in the red light flowing from her mouth with his breath.

She felt him shiver and heard him moan, a reaction she'd never witnessed before, and she struggled to hold onto her will even as the fear and anger drained from her being and left her relaxed and at peace. How was that possible?

The sensation of his more carnal excitement jolted her back to reality and into action. She shoved him off of her with all the force she could muster, dismayed and confused at her own mixed feelings. He didn't fight or speak. He seemed to be in the throes of some sort of rapture.

Rapture this!

Vivian slapped him as hard as she could across the face. He slowly returned from his reverie and placed a hand on his cheek. "That was a bit of a mood killer," he said, chuckling.

"You're lucky I didn't hit you where it would hurt a lot worse," Vivian shot back, and meant it. God, how could she have been so foolish, forgetting exactly what he was?

He sat up and looked at her, or so she thought. She couldn't see him well enough to tell in the darkness, so she reached over and turned on the lamp beside her bed. The bastard was smiling at her. It would have made her rage all over again, were it not for the angry red mark that graced his cheek. He kept staring, which made her even more uncomfortable. She pulled the covers up over her flimsy pajamas.

"You want to tell me what that was all about?" she asked.

"I apologize for being so forward," he said as he bowed his head. He sure didn't look sorry, though.

"Forward? You attacked me."

"Yes, and I apologize for that, too. My intention was to merely rouse you from your sleep and tell you what I've discovered about your unidentified enemy. I was...distracted by your spirit essence."

Vivian gave him a sour face. "My 'spirit essence,' huh? Wow, at least you're original."

"You shouldn't be so flippant," Darkmore said, apparently having regained his composure. "There is something different about your energy, Vivian, the way you taste."

The way he said "taste" made her feel dirty and excited, the contrast in reactions as uncomfortable as the reaper's presence. Fear crept up her spine and she didn't like it. Given the choice, anger was always better than fear.

Lifting her chin and mustering what false bravado she could, she said, "Now that we've established how delicious I am, can we talk about what you've discovered?"

"Ah, yes we can. As a matter of fact, the trail left by this particular guardian was quite similar."

"Similar to what?"

"To you."

Wherever this was going, she probably wouldn't like it. "Could you be a little more specific? I'm afraid I don't have my Cryptic Reaper-Speak-to-English dictionary handy."

Darkmore didn't answer right away. He seemed to be lost in thought. Vivian would have complained, but remained too bone-tired to muster any more really good snark. Besides, she reminded herself, he was helping her. At her request. And the chocolates had been nice.

A random and unexpected kindness from such a creature as Darkmore. Who would have thought?

"His energy has the same flavor, for lack of a better word, as yours," Darkmore said at last. "You look puzzled. It appears there is much you've yet to learn of our kind."

"You think?" she quipped. Seemed she had a little snark left, after all.

"Then allow me to enlighten you, my dear," he continued, ignoring the tenor of her remark. "All of our activities—by 'our' I mean those from the spirit realms, of course—those activities require a considerable amount of energy. Whenever we expend our energy, a trace is left behind for a time. It is possible to learn something about the spirits who have frequented a particular place by their trace energy."

"Well, I'll be damned," Vivian muttered, flopping back down on the pillow to alleviate the pounding in her head. "Even the dead leave behind forensic evidence. I guess we'll have to call Horatio Caine and Gil Grissom."

"Who?"

"Never mind. So do you know the spirit who's after me?"

"Something about his energy is familiar," Darkmore mused. "But I've been in this business for quite some time. I encountered many flavors and varieties of spirits."

"So where does that leave us?" she asked, frustrated. She'd hoped for more.

"For starters, I know where he's been and his mood."

"I know where he's been, too," she groaned. "And I can guess his mood. What else you got?"

"Well, beyond the little bohemian colony in outer Williamson County, he's been tracking you for months now." Darkmore paused to drink in her reaction. He tried hard not to show his enjoyment, but not too hard. "Every ICU, nursing home, and private residence you've visited bears his mark."

"How did you know where to look?" she asked as familiar, piercing dread filled her, like knives in her belly.

"I tracked your energy as well, and naturally I've been keeping tabs on you. Don't look so surprised. After all, you are my meal ticket, as you so eloquently put it," he said with a smile.

His smile did nothing to quell her anxiety. "As to the matter of mood, I'm afraid I have more bad news. It seems he's feeling particularly vengeful. Yes, vengeful with a side of spite and indignation. That's why it's so similar to you right now. It's quite irresistible."

"Huh?" she said, hoping he knew less than she believed he did. Did he realize how much the guardians for whom she worked hated him? Maybe he realized the truth. Maybe that's why the rogue guardian was after her. What if it came after him?

No such luck. "Do try to keep up, my dear," Darkmore said with a hint of impatience. "Or are you just being coy?"

Noting her look of confusion, Darkmore waved his hand and continued, "I'd wager you've been a bit of a naughty girl today, at least in terms of your powers. Tormenting the living? Perhaps for personal satisfaction, or as punishment?"

"Oh my God, Sarah," Vivian said, covering her face with the pillow in mortification.

"Well, well," Darkmore said, sounding for all the world like a proud parent. "I was wondering how long it would be before you took your talents in that particular direction."

"It was a mistake," Vivian groaned from underneath the pillows. "I got mad and I got cocky. I shouldn't have done it."

"That's Ezra talking, not you. Be honest. Are you more upset about the act itself, or about how good it felt?"

"Do I have to answer that?"

"If you don't want to answer me, that's fine. It would be best to answer yourself, however. Want my advice?" he asked.

"Will I like it?" Vivian said, doubting it.

"Never make it personal, Vivian. That's the key to maintaining control."

She peeked out from behind the pillow. It wasn't the answer she was expecting. "Is that your secret to success?"

"Of course. I very much enjoy my work, mind you, and take a certain degree of satisfaction in doling out cosmic justice, but it's only work," he said.

"Really? It's only work," Vivian said with incredulity. "Just your average day at the office, huh, carting off souls and spreading misery and suffering, blah, blah, blah? Some daily grind."

"What makes you think my business is so different from yours?" he said. He didn't seem angry. Merely curious.

"For starters, I don't drag people off to Hell," she said, stating the obvious—and most relevant—point.

"There's so much more to my work than that, but if you want to follow that line of logic, what do you call loaning money to the desperate and downtrodden and then confiscating their belongings when they cannot repay you?" he asked.

She balked, outraged by the insinuation. "That's not the same and you know it. I screen potential clients very carefully and base my lending on what they can afford. I work with clients and offer free credit counseling and advice on fiscal discipline—"

"Ah, discipline," he interjected. "You aim to teach your clients."

"Of course."

"And what if they fail to heed your advice and default on the loan?" he asked, his calm irritating and frightening by turns.

"Then I have no choice but to sic the collection agencies on them or send out the repo men. It's not like I make them make bad choices, but I do need to try to get the money back. I mean, someone has to pay the piper one way or another and—"

"Exactly."

Damn, he was slicker than owl grease.

"So wait, you're a karmic debt collector, or an enforcer for the afterlife mafia. If people can't pay off in this life they pay you in the next?"

"Growth, particularly spiritual growth, is often painful, Vivian. *Life* is often painful, but it does teach us a thing or two, and it builds character. Not everyone who travels to my neck of the woods stays forever, and when they emerge, I'd wager that I've taught them a thing or two."

"Your interest rates are waaaaaaay higher than mine," she replied. Then another thought occurred to her. "What happens if someone skips out without paying up? Do you have a piper to pay?"

"Everyone answers to someone," he said.

His tone and expression shut her down. She wasn't sure she wanted to know about Darkmore's boss.

Shaking her head, she said, "Well, this has all been very enlightening, but what's your point?"

"A warning, if you will," he said. "Using power such as ours for personal vendettas is a tricky business. One who seeks vengeance must dig two graves, one for one's enemy and one for oneself."

"Uh-huh," she said, with a note of caution. "And I suppose you and Ezra are still learning that lesson, what with your personal vendetta that got me into this business in the first place?"

Vivian always figured she was smarter than the average bear, so to speak, but Darkmore probably had her beat by a country mile. At the very least, hanging around for a few millennia made it pretty hard to win an argument against him. He'd probably heard just about all of them in some form or fashion. Her only weapon was the truth.

The truth was that she'd been a pawn in a game of vengeance between Ezra and Darkmore, the reaper who'd once tormented his soul. She'd paid the price—losing Zeke and being caught between two worlds. What had that little grudge match cost them?

"Well," he conceded. "Even the oldest and wisest of us need a little reminder every now and then. It cost Ezra. It has cost me, too, you know."

She did. Darkmore had come for Ezra when he was a mortal man, no doubt seeking a surplus of powerful spirit energy stored in his incapacitated body. He'd tormented and tortured him, but somehow Ezra managed to hold onto his soul. When last they met, Ezra was a powerful guardian spirit and had the means to get a little payback. Ezra claimed Zeke's soul, which was owed to Darkmore. In the process, Ezra had failed to collect Vivian and left her in Limbo, where she remained to this day.

"No, I didn't know," she said, puzzled. "I mean, I would have gone with you to set Zeke and Mae free, if it had come to that, but I just thought when Mae...passed, that we were, you know, square."

She had, in fact, almost become Darkmore's, but a last-minute reprieve came in the form of her sister's demise. Mae's death and crossing released enough spirit energy to satisfy both the guardians and the reapers, or so she'd thought.

"Oh, that," he said, laughing. It was strange, the laughter of the reaper. If she hadn't seen his darker side, she'd almost believe it to be genuine. "No, my colleagues and superiors were more than satisfied with the outcome after your last visit. Were you worried?"

"Maybe. A little," she replied, eyes lowered. "I got a visit from one of the guardian council members. He seemed a little less than thrilled with my performance and a little too curious about where I'm keeping my energy."

"Do tell."

She recounted her story from the hospital during and after Mrs. Martin's crossing. At the mention of Uriel's name, Darkmore sat up a little straighter. That counted as a major reaction from the reaper.

"Uriel came to see you? I was under the impression that he doesn't get out of the office much these days. He was rather more active in my time, when he took on the persona of one of the revered seven."

"Come again?"

"The archangels had their first heyday amongst God's chosen, post-exile," he said with a wave of his hand. "Though naturally Uriel and his brothers have been around much longer. He's a bit of a bean counter for the guardians from what I understand. Try not to make waves and he'll likely forget you as easily as he forgets most mortals."

She hoped Darkmore was right. Changing the subject, she asked, "So if the...account with Zeke, Ezra, and me was settled, how do you figure you're in the red?"

"Don't you know?" he asked.

For a split second, she swore she saw something in his eyes. She couldn't look into them too long. While his corporeal form was that of a man in his prime, his gaze often betrayed him. It was ancient, wise, and terrible to behold when he revealed a glimmer of his true identity. Yet, for an instant, it held something that should not have been there, or at least something she could not reconcile with what she knew him to be.

She must have been too weary, worried, and perhaps wishful.

"You should sleep, Ms. Vivian," he said. When she looked at him again, his gaze showed only a glint of his mischief.

"Wait, so what now? You tell me that a vengeful guardian has been after me since, well, pretty much since I got into the business of working with the guardians? I don't get it. I've only ever worked up close with Ezra and Zeke, so how can I have personally offended any other guardian?"

"All very good questions," he conceded. "I daresay it will take a little more time to get the answers."

"So what am I supposed to do now? Just sit around and wait until he comes after me or someone I love again?" Nope. Not an option. She'd take action with or without the reaper's help.

"What else did you have in mind? Do you propose to draw him out in the open? Your little stunt this afternoon may do the trick."

"Well, if it doesn't, maybe I'll need to try a little harder," Vivian mused, remembering how Sarah made her blood boil by baiting her. It wouldn't take a big act of defiance to goad an angry guardian into coming after her. But how would she trap him?

She couldn't, but maybe he could. "Darkmore, do you think you could take on this guardian in a fight and win?"

"It depends on the guardian," he replied. If Darkmore was surprised by her question or by the line of logic that inspired it, he didn't let on. "At the very least, I could defend you and yours. And, if you're looking for a way to incur his wrath, I'm sure I could come up with a use for your talents."

"I'll bet you could," she said. As much as she hated to admit it, she'd always wondered what it might be like to work with a reaper. Come to think of it, Darkmore was the only one she knew personally, so of course it would have to be him.

"Think it over, Ms. Vivian. You still owe me a favor, after all."

Since she couldn't get back to sleep, Vivian did just that, trying not to think of the debt she owed the reaper, or whether or not she'd enjoy paying up.

CHAPTER THIRTEEN

Vivian sensed Ezra in her house when she returned home late the next afternoon. She could also tell he was pretty pissed. It may have been a pleasant seventy-five-degree spring day in Music City, complete with a light breeze, but it felt like a sauna when she walked inside. Guardians tended to run on the warmer side, but they blazed white-hot when riled.

The old spirit stood in her kitchen, puffed up like an old bullfrog and shooting daggers out of his eyes. Vivian felt about two feet tall and wished she were about anywhere else.

"Little gal, I ought to turn you over my knee and tan your hide. Don't you ever do something like that again, you understand me?" he said, voice low and full of menace. He didn't yell, which gave his words all the more punch.

"I'm sorry, Ezra, I really am," she pleaded. "I didn't mean to, but Sarah Harrow is just such a conniving, vindictive, and meddlesome hag. Did Jeanne tell you what she did?"

"The Good Book says to turn the other cheek. And if that won't work for you, you could at least try to control that temper of yours," he said, his face growing redder by the second.

Best let him get it out of his system and take it like a grownup, she figured, and braced herself for the next round.

He paced back and forth as he berated her, growing hotter with each step. "You ain't a guardian, but you're mighty close. We don't abide by revealing ourselves to nobody livin' except when it's do or die, and we sure don't abide by using our powers on the living for spite. I don't care how bad that person's acting."

"You're right," she said, throwing her hands up in the air in frustration. So much for taking it like a grownup. "I'm not a guardian. I never wanted to *be* a guardian, or close to it. I'm human. I make mistakes. I can't abide being bullied by the likes of Sarah, but I do promise that next time I'll just punch her lights out. With my fists, mind you, though after yesterday I don't expect there'll be a next time."

"I reckon you're right about the last," Ezra conceded. He was trying to act mad, but she thought she'd softened him up a bit. She could always hope.

But just in case...

She pulled a DVD out of her shopping bag and handed it to Ezra. "Here, why don't you pop this baby in the DVD player and I'll warm up the brownies and get some drinks for us, okay?"

She hurried off to the kitchen and set the oven on low, and then shouted, "Hey, I'm gonna need a new microwave."

"You don't have to go a-yellin', you know." Ezra's voice came from directly behind her and she jumped.

Damn it.

She thought she'd get used to the random disappearing and reappearing acts someday, but she always jumped. When she turned, she could see that the old coot's ear-to-ear grin.

"I hate it when y'all do that. You know that, right?" she said. Though her heart still raced, she got a measure of relief in seeing her guardian smile. Bribery worked. She'd have to thank Jeanne for the advice.

"'Course I do," he said, obviously pleased with himself. Turning to her broken microwave, he shook his head back and forth and asked, "What happened to that durned contraption, anyway?"

"Junior."

"Oh, that's right," he said with a chuckle. "Jeanne told me old Junior was back and took up with one of your girlfriend's young 'uns. In that case, I reckon we do owe you. How much they run?"

"About two-fifty, three to four hundred for a good one," Vivian replied.

"Lord have mercy, when did everything get so costly?"

"Inflation, Ezra," Vivian said with a sigh. They had this conversation every time she asked for compensation or for cash to cover spirit-associated expenses. Vivian figured he must have been a real tightwad back in the day.

She rolled her eyes and said, "You think that's bad, why don't you stroll through Best Buy sometime? If you can spring for it, I'll get us a nice flat screen, forty-two inch plasma and a Blu-ray player. I've already got a good surround sound system to work with. We could have a decent home theater system for movie night."

He cocked his head and looked at her. "Well, we might be able to work out something. Got many westerns in Blu-ray?"

"They sure do," she said, grinning. The old spirit loved westerns almost as much as he loved baked goods. "So, am I forgiven?"

He appeared to consider before saying, "As long as you behave yourself, I reckon we can let it be for now. But you need to be careful, and not just about breaking the rules. You're making it hard for me to keep you safe from this rogue guardian."

"And from Uriel, too?" she asked, remembering the threat she'd received from the archangel. She'd been meaning to ask Ezra more about him. "I thought you were on the same team?"

"Mostly, but you shouldn't get on the bad side of either."

"I'm sorry," she said, meaning it this time. She figured Ezra would be in a heap of trouble if word got around. Still, she'd have to consider Darkmore's offer if her guardians didn't come up with any leads soon.

"You know," he began, a little hesitant. "I only want what's best for you, to keep you safe."

"I believe you," she said.

"We never did finish our little talk we started that night when all of this bad business began."

"No, we didn't."

Ezra had used his own life story as a way of introducing her to the world of reapers, guardians, and the afterlife. It hadn't been a pretty story. He'd suffered a stroke and been subjected to torment by Darkmore while trapped in his own battered body before the guardian spirits set him free.

He'd never told her exactly how he'd managed to escape the reaper, nor had he shared what he'd done to attract him in the first place.

She wasn't certain she wanted to know.

She sighed, then said, "And if it's all the same to you, I'd really rather not finish it tonight. All I want right now is to kick back, eat some brownies, and watch Kurt Russell and Val Kilmer play Wyatt Earp and Doc Holiday."

"*Tombstone*, eh? Now that ought to be a good one," Ezra said, beaming. "But I do want to clear the air and come clean with you on a few more things. I reckon you've earned it. I've found out a few more things that I should tell you, and a few that I should've told you a while back."

"Okay, let's do that, but not until we solve the mystery of the rogue guardian. Between that, Sue's wedding, and life's little curve balls, I don't think I can take much more, Ezra."

He nodded, then reached out and put his arm around her, sending out warm rays of peace and harmony, which she happily and gratefully accepted. "Now let's get down to movie night."

Ezra enjoyed the Old West tale, especially the gun fights. He told Jeanne and Vivian that he'd been a crackerjack shot back in his day when the young guardian joined them. Wallace showed up, too, and remained friendly.

Jeanne seemed to enjoy the man candy on screen almost as much as Vivian did. It made her wonder if Jeanne missed her old life. Judging from her corporeal form, she'd been quite young and pretty when she died. Aside from the whole Pollyanna happy-crap thing she had going on, she would have made a great gal pal. Did she get lonely? Did she miss her friends or perhaps a special someone whom she'd left behind? Maybe she had a little "love in the afterlife" thing going on like Ezra did. Vivian would have to ask her sometime.

After the movie was done, they enjoyed some sandwiches and sodas before Wallace excused himself so he could get back to guarding Father Montgomery. Vivian offered them beer, but both spirits declined. She wondered if guardians weren't allowed to drink, but she remembered that Zeke had enjoyed it.

Zeke—the ache that would never heal. Not that she really wanted to heal. She feared she'd forget him, and that would be far worse than any lingering pain.

Jeanne took her up on a glass of Riesling. Figures she'd go for the sweet stuff. Ezra still declined. Figured he'd be the party pooper.

She bid them goodnight earlier than usual after the movie, letting them know she'd yell if she needed them. It would be better to have them out of the way if Darkmore showed up again. Besides, after last night, all she wanted was to sleep for about twelve hours.

Too bad, then, that a very agitated Junior showed up in her bedroom just as she was dozing off. Seemed there was trouble at the Clemmens household and he wanted her to go with him and help.

Figured.

———

Vivian knocked on the door with soft taps so as not to wake the children, as the doorbell surely would have done. She could hear Kay's footfalls and noted the slight shift in the blinds that covered the door frame windows. When she didn't open the door right away, Vivian spoke.

"Kay, it's Vivian. I know it's late, but can I come in, honey?"

"Give me a minute," replied Kay's muffled voice from the other side. It sounded raspy and rough.

"Are you okay?" Vivian asked. If Junior's frantic call to arms hadn't scared her already, Kay's voice surely would have put her over the edge. The agitated spirit was hovering just behind Vivian.

"Junior," she hissed. "Back off!"

"You gotta get in there. She's gone crazy and she's going to hurt someone, I'm telling you," Junior said. He was in such a state of panic he could barely manifest.

According to Junior, Kay had had a very bad night with the kids. Boyd had been gone for nearly a week total, with only a brief stay at home the night of Sue's shower, and Kay been getting snappier and more irascible each day. Tonight, she'd lost it and yelled at the kids for about thirty minutes straight, slamming doors, throwing household items, and collapsing in her closet in a heap of bone-chilling wails. The kids were in bed, but Scooter was pretty scared.

It scared Junior enough to make him fetch Vivian.

"I've got this, I promise," Vivian said. "You want to be a guardian? Then go and look after Scooter. He's probably still scared, too, if he's still awake."

That seemed to calm him, from what Vivian could tell by the fuzzy lines of the face he projected and from the drop in temperature. Good thing, too, since Vivian started sweating on account of his radiant heat. He nodded and disappeared, giving Vivian just enough time to get it together before Kay opened the door.

What Vivian saw shocked the hell out of her.

Kay Clemmens was one of the most poised and centered women she'd ever met, but no one would have guessed that looking at her now. Her eyelids were swollen from the force of angry tears shed and yet to be shed. Normally smooth and even, her complexion was mottled with angry red blotches. And she hadn't stopped shaking since she opened the door.

Instead of her normal elegant attire, she wore her rumpled pajamas, a ratty old bathrobe, and it looked like she hadn't bothered to comb her hair in about three day, and her eyes were filled with desperation, rage, and now embarrassment upon meeting her friend at the door in such a state.

"My God, honey, what happened?" Vivian asked, reaching out for Kay.

"Oh Vivian, I'm sorry..." Kay collapsed in her arms, fresh sobs wracking her body. "You caught me at a bad time, I'm sorry...I'm normally not like this, I—"

"Don't worry about it. Let's just get you inside, sit down, and you tell me what's going on."

Kay released her grip on her friend and moved aside. Vivian walked in, taking a moment to look around the Clemmens' home. The state of the living room mirrored that of its co-owner. Books were scattered on the floor, as were all manner of toy trucks, cars, puzzles, dolls, and other items that rendered the carpet below nearly invisible. Kaitlyn and Connor had been at it, no doubt. Signs of Annabelle were less obvious, but still discernible to

Vivian's trained eye. She always left her laptop and homework strewn out on the family computer desk in the adjacent study. Judging from the candy wrappers and empty soda cans pushed off into one corner, she'd had a bad case of the study munchies.

Vivian followed Kay into the kitchen, which was also unusually messy. Kay hated dirty dishes piling up. It was one of her biggest pet peeves. And yet, a sizable stack rested in both sides of the divided sink, jutting out of stale water, discolored bubbles floating along the water's edges.

"Sorry about the mess," said Kay, with a sniff. She shifted the dishes on the right side of the sink to the left, drained the water, and washed her hands before filling a couple of mugs with water. After she placed the cups into the microwave and set the timer, Vivian grabbed a towel, refilled the right side of the sink with fresh hot water and some dish soap, setting to work.

Settling into an old routine from days as roommates, Vivian washed and rinsed the dishes while Kay dried and put them away, pausing only to retrieve the cups from the microwave and make hot tea with honey for them. It was a comfortable routine, and both women worked in silence until the task was complete. Vivian wiped down the counters and Kay nodded with satisfaction.

Grabbing the mugs, Kay bid Vivian to follow her into the living room. She set their cups down on the edge, cleared some of Kaitlyn's markers and drawings, and then placed one mug in front of Vivian while she curled up on the opposite side of the couch and took a sip. Vivian watched as her friend closed her eyes and exhaled deeply. Kay looked so weary and much older than her thirty-nine years, a shadow of the vibrant woman who rescued both of her best friends only a few nights ago and carried them through an evening of shared laughter, not to mention helping haul a drunken Vivian and distraught and pregnant bride-to-be Sue home.

How had she gone from that woman to this wreck in such a short time?

"So," Vivian began, "I take it you've had a lousy day?"

"I've had better," Kay replied, opening her eyes and looking at Vivian. She set her mug down and grabbed a basket full of loose clothing and set to work. Vivian followed suit, falling into another old and comfortable routine.

"Are these the same old baskets we used to keep at the duplex?" Vivian asked, eyeing the white wicker baskets lined up in front of the fireplace. Parts of them were still white, but years of bumps along brick and door frames, not to mention bumpy rides in the back of various clunkers driven by young women scraping by on student or startup salaries, had left their marks. Flecks of paint were peeling from sections of the weave, and some parts had been stripped bare to reveal pale wood byproduct that for a miracle managed to hold together.

"The very same," said Kay with a wan smile. "Every year I tell myself I'll throw them out and get something fancier, but I just never get around to it. Or maybe I just don't want to. They remind me of the good days, I guess."

"Oh, yeah." Vivian snorted. "The good days of maxed-out credit cards, ramen noodles, and Saturday night meetings of the Lonely Hearts Club Dateless Roommate Society."

"Yeah, somehow, those days don't seem so lonely anymore," Kay muttered.

"You and Boyd okay?" Vivian asked. "Did you have a fight?"

"No," she snapped. "It takes two people to fight. Two people in the same place for more than two hours at a time."

Kay kept at the clothing as she spoke, Scooter's poor little blue jeans bearing the brunt of her growing frustration. One of the snaps hit the wood off the coffee table with such force that Vivian jumped a little after Kay slammed it down. She steeled herself. Kay's fuse was lit and she was getting ready to blow. Vivian had been on the giving end of such eruptions often enough to recognize the signs, and she knew that Kay would feel better after she got it all out.

Kay struggled with one of Kaitlyn's shirts, a hoodie. The hoodie part was getting the better of her in her efforts to fold it neatly.

Three, two, one. Here we go.

"He's gone. He's always *gone* and I'm always the one left behind to clean up the mess when he goes!" Kay screamed the last, getting up and throwing the hoodie across the room. When that didn't satisfy, she threw the teacup at the fireplace.

"Boyd loves you," Vivian said.

It was the wrong thing to say. She had sense enough to know that. But, she also had sense enough to know that adding a little accelerant to the fire would make it burn out faster, even if it made it burn with a more furious heat.

"He loves the convenience of me," she hissed, spinning around and channeling her anger toward Vivian's façade of calm. "*He* can get up and walk out of the fucking door to do his job without a second thought about feeding three people, yelling to get them out of their damned beds! We do the same fucking thing every day, but they still whine, they still cry, they still won't just do anything for themselves, so I'm left with no time to go to the toilet or brush my teeth without someone hanging off my tits! 'Help me with my sweater, help me with my shoes, help me wipe my ass. Mama, mama, mama, *mama*!'"

She paused for breath before unleashing another wave of frustration. "He's still in the fucking bed watching the news while I'm up scrambling. Or behind the computer while I'm putting food on plates and milk in cups before I've even had the chance to take a sip of coffee—I swear to God I haven't sat down for a meal without inhaling my food and getting up five times to do for someone else since Holland House. Does he not *see* it?"

She was on a roll now. Vivian sat and listened, and waited. This needed to run its course. Better that she listened to it than the kids. Maybe Boyd needed to hear some of it, but not like this. Not in the heat of anger, with Kay's face red and the veins in her neck straining. She'd yelled so much and so loudly that she would probably be hoarse for a few days.

But there was more. Vivian sat there and took it all, giving her all the time she needed to exorcise her demons.

"I can't count the number of times he's walked out the door when I've been dead with a cold or even sick with a stomach flu, curled up on the couch in agony while he trots off to work without a care in the world. 'Call a neighbor, call a friend.' How can you just walk away from your wife when she's hurting?"

"I don't know," Vivian said.

"He's never missed a day of work for a sick kid, or spent the night in the hospital with a baby hooked up to IVs after watching her scream through a spinal tap, or seven hours in the ER waiting for stitches. It's always me.

And then he tells me when I fall apart to just deal with it...or worse, he says, 'I thought you were stronger!'"

"Wait, he said what?" Now Vivian was starting to get pissed off.

"Oh, God, Vivian, I've tried exercise, I've tried therapy, I've been on more meds for longer than I ever dreamed of, but it always comes to this—I spend half my life alone, looking at happy families out and about on weekends and hating them."

She put her face in her hands as exhaustion flowed off her in waves. "I've got three kids, but no man. I'm always the one alone at the restaurant while the other couples cuddle, laugh, share, and hold hands. I hate them because they have what I want and need but will never have. I've been the third wheel on dates with you and Sue more times than I care to remember. Boyd loves his job. He'll never leave it. He'd leave me first."

"Kay, I'm so sorry, I had no idea you were dealing with all of this," Vivian said, guilt and regret filling her to the brim, and this guilt was all her own. How had she missed this? She should've been there for Kay.

"Oh, Vivian," Kay said, looking up and meeting her gaze. "What am I going to do? How am I going to go on like this? My children are afraid of me half the time because I just can't keep it all in—like tonight! I just want to crawl in a hole and never come out again, but who would take care of them. I feel so...so..."

"Trapped," Vivian said. She said it calmly. No accusation, not question, it was merely a simple statement of truth between two friends.

"Yes, God forgive me, but that's it," Kay whispered, tears falling.

Good. She's gotten it out of her system. Now I can help her with some of the aftermath.

Vivian held out her arms and held Kay close while she shuddered, sobbing. Kay said, "What you must think of me, getting all worked up about three healthy children and being a little tired when you had Mae and...I'm so sorry I laid all of this on you—"

"Shh," Vivian whispered. "It's okay. I'm only mad at you for not calling me sooner, for not letting me know how bad things had gotten."

"They aren't always like this," she said weakly.

"No, but I'm sure it happens more often than you've let on to anyone."

Vivian thought, and she thought hard. Kay was one of her closest friends, practically family. *No, she* is *family*. She'd lost everyone else, her folks, Mae, and Zeke. She refused to lose anyone else dear to her, or to let a loved one self-destruct. She'd come over with every intention of helping Kay, both in the conventional way and by using her special gifts. Guardian spirits and archangels be damned, if this wasn't her calling—taking in heavy burdens like the ones Kay bore—then what was?

And maybe this time Kay could help her, too.

"Kay, I'm going to help you, but first I need to ask you to make me a couple of promises. Can you do that?"

Kay looked at her with confusion, but nodded.

"First, I need you to promise that what happens here stays between you and me. No one, and I mean *no one* else can know. Promise?"

"Um, Vivian, I don't want to sound ungrateful or anything, but my days of experimenting with...that sort of thing ended during our second year of college."

"What?" Vivian asked before understanding dawned on her. "Oh, no, I'm not offering *that* sort of help. Although, that does explain a lot about your falling out with that really hot Brazilian exchange student."

Hmm, never knew you took that particular e-ride. Well, there'd be more time to delve into that sordid topic later.

"Okay," Kay said, recovering. "What's the second promise?"

"Do you trust me?" Vivian asked.

"Yes."

"Then promise me you won't scream." Before she had the chance to react or get too scared, Vivian grabbed Kay's arm and focused her mind and heart on her friend.

Kay's gaze grew wide as she felt the shocking heat of Vivian's spirit energy pulling hers, and she shrieked as she watched thick waves of red light flow from her body into Vivian. Kay tried to pull away at first, but Vivian gripped her even tighter, until she could feel the waves of relief wash over Kay as she took in her turmoil and pain. It was always a strange and somewhat uncomfortable experience, drawing out the darkness within people, but with her closest friends the process was more intense, almost overwhelming.

She was an intruder into Kay's heart and soul, and thus tried her best to ignore specific images for the sake of privacy. She'd experienced her share of darkness, still did, and she didn't relish the idea of having someone close to her knowing all of that. She could have just taken it all in on the sly, or when Kay was sleeping. Maybe she should have.

But after all she had endured during the past year, she was just weary of secrecy.

Someone ought to know about her, other than the padre, someone who'd known her longer, before she'd become a soul broker. That would be kind of nice. It might even lighten her load a bit.

After the light stopped, Vivian released Kay and gave her a minute to recuperate. She needed a minute herself, come to think of it. Processing and storing other people's baggage until Darkmore got around to taking it off her hands took more than a little concentration. When she came back to her senses, she found Kay staring at her with wide-eyed wonder.

"Wow," Kay said. She didn't seem to know what else to say.

"Tell me about it." Vivian sighed. It had been a long night and she was pretty drained.

"No, actually, I think you do need to tell me all about it," Kay said, leaning forward and touching her hand with a bit of hesitance. Vivian wasn't sure if Kay was afraid, or maybe just trying to reassure herself that Vivian was real.

She couldn't really blame her. It was a lot to take in.

"It's a pretty long story."

"I'll put on some coffee."

Over the next hour and through at least two cups of coffee, Vivian told Kay everything, from the beginning. She told her about guardians and reapers and how she came to be associated with them, relating the little mix-up that left her somewhere between the realm of spirits and the living and saddled with her "gift" of collecting burdens of the soul. She told Kay about what she'd traded to save Zeke and Mae, her departed younger sister whose incapacitation in life made her untapped spirit energy a valuable resource.

Kay listened as she recounted her terrifying trip to the dark realm of the reapers and how she had freed Zeke from Ezra and had freed Mae from

Ezra and Darkmore. In exchange for the freedom of their souls, Vivian told Kay about how she now worked for Ezra.

She left out her ongoing association Darkmore. It was the one secret she couldn't afford to share just yet.

"You mean you have to work for them, like a slave or something?" Kay asked, appalled.

"More like indentured servitude, I think," Vivian answered. "I'm mostly free to help who I choose, but I have to report to him and do a little freelance on the side, emphasis on free."

"They don't pay you?"

"It's complicated, but they do get me extra cash when I'm running short."

"Do you get dental?" Kay asked with a wry smile. She was definitely feeling better.

"Nope, and the hours are a bitch," Vivian said, grinning back at Kay.

"Speaking of," Kay asked, taking a serious turn. "How did you know to come here in the dead of night and help me out?"

"Oh," Vivian said, thinking it would be best not to mention Junior if she wanted Kay's newly minted tranquil state to hold. Vivian just told her that word got around through the spirit grapevine.

"You mean they're everywhere? Like in people's houses?" Kay said, leaning in to whisper and casting furtive glances around the room.

"They can come and go pretty much anywhere, but don't worry. As a general rule, they respect the sanctity of house and home. Except mine," she added as an afterthought, "Since they found out about me, a lot of them feel just fine about crashing on the sofa, raiding the fridge if they have enough energy to muster a body and eat, and using my computer and TV. Don't even get me started on the mess they've made out of my DVD collection!"

"Interesting life you lead, Vivian," Kay said with a smile. Then she became thoughtful again. "Thank you for telling me."

"It feels pretty good to share," Vivian replied honestly. "Now, you need to get to bed and you need to stay there until late in the morning."

"Oh I feel better now, thanks to you, and the kids—"

"No arguments. You may feel better now, but what I did is just a temporary fix, not a cure all. You need some rest. I've got my overnight bag, so I'll take care of the kids tomorrow morning. Then we're going to call your doctor to see about getting you something to help. You probably ought to talk to Boyd, too, and see about some marriage counseling."

"He won't go. And I really don't want to go back on those pills, especially after all that brouhaha that celebrities started about postpartum depression and medication."

"Make the appointment for when Boyd's at home and make him get in the fucking car. Believe me—he'll go. You're just going to have to be the one who sets it up," Vivian said, holding up her hand to stop Kay's protests. "Not fair? Probably, but fair doesn't matter, results do. As for the meds, those celebrities don't have medical degrees last I checked. Bottom line, you can't go on like this. It's time to get some help."

"Okay, fine," Kay said, too tired to put up much of a fight, "I surrender."

She stood up and gave Vivian a big hug before heading off to bed. Before Vivian made her way to the Clemmens' guest room, she peeked in on Scooter. He was sleeping soundly while Junior hovered over him, ever watchful. Vivian nodded to the specter and shut the door. The girls were sleeping peacefully, too, thank goodness. Satisfied that everyone was well, Vivian settled herself into bed.

A knock at the bedroom window had her grumbling as she stumbled out of bed and over to see which spirit had decided to disturb her this time. She pulled back the curtain and peered into the darkness. Nothing. Perhaps the spirit in question had trouble manifesting?

All of a sudden, the glass grew very warm as cold shivers of fear ran up her spine. She backed away, arms at the ready to defend herself with the energy she'd harvested. An invisible force scratched at the glass, etching a message for her.

You work for the dead, not the living. This is your last warning. We are watching.

CHAPTER FOURTEEN

Vivian woke with a jolt when the first rays of dawn flooded the room. How she'd managed to doze off was beyond her. Glancing at the window, she wasn't surprised to see nothing but clear glass. That message had been for her and her alone.

Remembering the events of the previous evening, she quelled the panic that had started to rise. She was safe in the Clemmens home, more specifically in their guest bedroom.

But she was not alone.

Turning to her side, she smiled at the sleeping child curled up next to her. Connor was angelic in his slumber. It was probably the only time he was angelic, but she took a moment to bask in the tranquility of his innocence. She scooted closer to the warm bundle of boy and pulled the covers around him. Wrapping her arms around him made left her warmer still. She dozed next to Connor and was able to forget all of her troubles for a few moments of blessed peace. When she woke once more, she offered a sleepy smile to Junior, who was hovering over the bed and watching over them.

"Good morning," she whispered.

"Mornin', Miss Vivian," Junior whispered back. "I hope you don't mind about Connor. He normally runs to his mama and papa's room when he gets up, but after last night..."

"No, this is good," she said with a sigh, stretching a bit. "Actually it's kind of great. And Kay needs some more rest. You were right to come and get me. You did well."

Junior must have been brimming over with pride, since the temperature rose a few degrees. He looked down at what would have been his feet and muttered something. Careful not to wake Connor, she shifted a bit and slipped from the cherubic little guy's side so she could move to sit on the other side of the bed and speak with the spirit. That gave her the chance to get a better look at him.

"I don't know if it's because of the daylight or something else, but you look a little..." Vivian struggled for the right word, not wanting to offend him, but also not quite believing what she was seeing. "You look a little more...um, a little more real, for lack of a better word."

She took a closer look as his big brown eyes got a little wider. They seemed to match his hair, which appeared to be almost amber. "Did you have freckles?"

"Yeah, I did," he muttered, staring at Vivian in wonder. "You can see them?"

"Mhmm," Vivian said, looking him up and down. "I can see your legs, too." She reached out with trembling fingers and tried to grasp his arm. It wasn't solid, but she could feel a change in the space it occupied. Junior could as well, apparently, since he shuddered.

"What's happening to me?" he asked. He seemed scared.

"I'm not sure," Vivian said. Then she added, "I don't think it can be bad, though, right? It looks like you've got enough spirit energy to appear more substantial."

"Does that mean that I could be a guardian?" he asked in a hushed tone, dropping his gaze again. "I mean, that's what you said last night."

"Honestly, I just said that to get you off my back," she admitted. "But maybe."

He looked back up, and Vivian didn't miss the hopeful expression gracing his features now that they were coming in a bit more clearly. "I've wanted to, um, you know, help for a while, like the guardians do," he stammered. "But I always figured I'd be stuck down here in Limbo. I mean, it's better than Hell, I reckon, but I've been here a long time."

The way he said long made Vivian's heart ache.

She wondered if it was true, then, what she'd been taught about suicides. The Catholics had them pegged as forever condemned, and most other faiths frowned on taking one's own life. She didn't see what all of the fuss was about, personally. Jack Kevorkian was kind of creepy, but she could imagine and had imagined pulling the plug, or having someone else do it, if she ever got as badly off as Mae had been. Why prolong suffering like that?

Even if she believed in God, she couldn't imagine why an almighty and supposedly compassionate deity would force someone to endure such a state. Was Junior really condemned to wander the Earth forever as a lost and lonely soul simply because guilt drove him to end his life after he lost his little brother? That just seemed too cruel.

"Junior, what exactly happened when you died, if you don't mind my asking? Didn't a guardian come to get you? Or maybe a reaper?"

He didn't seem to mind, but it took a while before he answered. Maybe he just had trouble remembering. He did tell her he'd been around for a while.

"Well, it's funny. I was expecting to be sucked right down into the pit of Hell right after I jumped from that rafter. I mean, that's what they tell you will happen if you go and interfere with God's plan. But I just went and did it anyhow. I knew I couldn't go on without Scout."

"That was your brother?"

"Yeah, that's what we all called him. His real name was James, but everyone knew him by Scout and he liked it that way. He was a rascal, that boy. Three and a half and he could climb a tree faster than a wiry little squirrel. He could snatch apples faster than the neighbors could grab a switch and run after him. He could swim—"

Junior stopped there. The pain on his face would have been evident even without the clearer projection.

"It wasn't your fault, you know. These things happen." It was a cliché, and a really bad one at that, but Vivian believed it to be true. She wasn't sure what else to say. So, she just decided to listen.

"Me and Scout did everything together, at least, when I wasn't in school. Some of my schoolmates didn't like looking after their little brothers and sisters, but I did. Scout and me were thick as thieves, and I loved him more than anything. I only looked away for a second," he said, staring at her. He seemed to be willing Vivian to believe him. Or, perhaps, he was still trying to convince himself.

"I'd told him over and over again not to get too close to the creek unless I was there with him. He was a good swimmer, but we'd had so much rain. He fell and maybe he hit his head on them rocks, or just got caught on a branch, or…I don't know. He was gone. All I wanted after that was to go away, too."

Vivian reached out and put her hand where his shoulder would have been, had it been solid. She took in a few wisps of light to ease his burdens a bit. He gave her a look of pure gratitude and continued. "So you can imagine how confused and mad I was when I got up off the ground and realized that I hadn't gone anywhere."

"You mean, your spirit just landed on the ground?" Vivian asked. She felt bad for him, but was fascinated all the same. She'd never actually gotten around to asking any of the other spirits she knew what happened after they departed their bodies. She knew, of course, that it wasn't all tunnels full of light and angel songs for the redeemed any more than demons and flames for the damned.

Still, she'd expected something a bit more dramatic.

"Yeah, I guess," Junior replied. "Only it must have been a few days later, since I didn't see myself hanging up on the rafters. At that time, I just thought I'd managed to goof up my own death. I sat on the ground for a while and then decided I would just go on in the house, grab some of Ma's biscuits and pinto beans, and figure out how to get it right the next day. But I couldn't actually open a door. I just fell through it. Things got real bad for me once I found out I didn't have legs, either."

"What happened then?"

"I kept close to home for a while, but it was kind of hard to watch my Ma and Pa grieving over two lost boys instead of just the one. I didn't know I'd end up hurting them so bad. The last time I saw my body was at receiving friends. I didn't watch them lower me in the ground, though."

Vivian swallowed hard. "I can see why you wouldn't want to see that."

"Anyway, after that, I just sort of wandered around. I tried to get noticed by the living, but no one could see me. Not then, anyhow. I spent a little time with some other spirits, like the ones in Nolensville. They said they could probably get a guardian to come and help me, but I figured this was my punishment for James and for killing myself, so I'd just take it like a man. I could at least do that."

Her heart went out to the lost and lonely soul, and she vowed to find a way to help him. "So, how did you get so you could move objects and talk to little kids?"

"Oh, that happened a few years after I died, or maybe ten or more. It's hard to say. I can't seem to keep up with time like I used to."

Time is a little different on the other side.

That's what Zeke had told her. Apparently time was a little different for the departed still trapped on Earth.

"Anyway," Junior said, "I was watching some little 'uns play and I spotted this little towhead boy running around. Scout was a redhead, like Scooter here, but there was something about him that reminded me of my brother. Maybe it was his laugh, I don't remember. I do remember getting closer to him and being scared half to death, so to speak, when he started talking to me. I started following him around and we kept each other company until he outgrew me."

"Wow," Vivian said. "I can see the appeal. Were you able to move objects, too?"

He nodded. "Yeah. I found out that if I thought real hard, I could make things move. I kept practicing until I got really good, and every time I met a new little boy who wanted to be my friend, it got easier and easier. It made life less lonely, anyway. Plus, I was able to look out for the little guys."

"So the only living people who ever see you are kids?"

"I guess so," he said with a shrug. "I mean, other than you. I sure was glad to meet Scooter. He reminds me so much of Scout. I've been looking out for him and making sure he doesn't get himself into trouble when his mama's busy or when his sisters aren't looking. He's a handful."

"Don't I know it," Vivian replied, remembering how scared she had been when he went missing at the zoo. Then it hit her. He didn't actually need her help. He'd already found his place, even if he didn't realize it.

"You know what?" she said, bursting with excitement. "It seems like you've found a purpose instead of a punishment. And it seems to me like you're getting rewarded for it."

"How do you figure?" he asked, gaze wary but hopeful.

"Well, you said you started getting stronger once you took up with the first kid who saw you, right?" She held up a finger.

"Yup."

"Has it gotten a little easier to move things and to project yourself with each new kid?" She said, holding up a second finger.

"Well, yeah, it has," he said, scratching his head. "But I always have a little trouble just after the kids stop seeing me. They seem to outgrow me around four or five. I'm pretty sad for a year or two after that."

"That makes sense," she said. "But you seem to have built up a lot more energy since you've been around Scooter." She held up a third finger, ticking off another item on her mental checklist of guardian duties.

He nodded, a grin slowly spreading across his boyish face.

"So, maybe you've been working to become a guardian spirit all along, and you just didn't know it," she said, spreading her hands wide.

"You really think so?" He seemed positively giddy at the prospect.

"I do," Vivian said. "In fact, I'm going to have a talk with Ezra and Jeanne about it to see if there's anything they can do to help."

"You'd do that for me?" He seemed stunned, which made her heart break as she fell in love with him a little more. If ever there was a guardian spirit, Junior was it—the real deal.

"Of course I would! You've been taking such good care of my favorite little man here, it's the least I can do." She leaned over to ruffle Connor's hair. He wiggled a bit and shifted, but then returned to a peaceful slumber.

"Now, do you think you'd be up for helping me out with breakfast for the Clemmens clan?"

"Why, sure," replied the giddy spirit. "I like them. It's almost like I'm a part of a family again."

She grinned and then added, "Just, please, for the love of Pete don't blow up anything in the kitchen, okay?"

———

"Auntie Viv! Auntie Viv! Hooray, Auntie Viv!"

Kaitlyn wasn't known for her dulcet tones. Aside from the high frequency of the squeal, which she suspected could make dogs' ears bleed, Vivian was pleased with the greeting. Kate was a morning person in the making, but she was just so darned cute about it. She flew into Vivian's arms and planted a big kiss on her cheek.

"What are you making?" Kate asked.

"Coffee, for starters," Vivian replied, kissing her back and settling her on the ground.

"Can I have some?"

"No, you may not."

"Awwww, why not?" Kate asked, her not-so-dulcet tone going an octave higher.

"Because you aren't old enough yet. Wait until college. That's when you'll need it," Vivian answered. That seemed to satisfy her as she turned her attention to what was on the counter.

"Ooooh, biscuits," she said, licking her lips. Can I help?"

"Sure. Grab your apron and let's get started."

Vivian had her elbow-deep in Crisco and Martha White when Connor came bounding down the hall calling out, "I hungry, I hungry!"

His surly older sister was walking close behind, shooting daggers at the back of his head with her gaze.

"Morning, all," Vivian said. "Connor, we're having biscuits, gravy, and sausage. It's not ready yet, though. I want you to go potty with Anna while I cook, okay?"

"No," he whined. "No! I don't wanna go!"

"Fine, 'cause I don't want to take you," Anna shot back.

Damn, no wonder Kay had been at her wits end. A few more minutes of this, and Vivian's head might explode along with her temper. Squaring her shoulders and giving each of them her best stern look of authority, she said, "I didn't ask either of you, and I'm not asking now. I'm *telling* you to do it!"

With much reluctance and a few more dirty looks, the youngest Clemmens kid accompanied the oldest to the bathroom. In the meantime, the middle child helped Vivian finish folding the biscuit dough after she added the buttermilk.

As they were stamping out some rounds, Kate asked, "Is Mama still mad and sad?"

Figuring honesty was the best policy, Vivian said, "Not as much as she was. You worried?"

"Yeah."

"I think she's going to be okay. But if you ever get worried or scared, you can always tell your Aunt Viv about it."

"I know that."

Kate was apparently satisfied with Vivian's answer, since she didn't bring up the subject again. When Kay woke up, she looked better and seemed to be in better spirits. Coffee helped. Connor seemed unaffected by the previous night's events, which relieved Kay.

Annabelle remained sullen and refused to speak to her mother.

Steeling herself, Vivian decided to have a little chat with the girl during kitchen clean up and while Kay took Kate and Connor out for some errands.

"So," Vivian began. "You're still pretty ticked off at your mom, huh?"

"I don't like it when she yells so much. It scares Kate and Connor," she replied, her gaze never leaving her work at the sink.

"Does it scare you?"

"Not anymore. Except when she yells at Dad. I don't want them to get divorced."

"I don't either," said Vivian.

"My friend Megan's mom and dad got divorced. She spends a lot of time at her grandma's while her mom works and her dad spends time with his new girlfriend."

"Hmm," Vivian replied. She didn't want to lead Anna too much. She figured she'd get more out of the girl if she just let Anna reveal what she wanted to share in her own time and in her own way.

"I'd hate it if my dad started going out with some skank."

"I would, too," said Vivian.

"Like the skank Mr. Jace is going out with?"

"I don't like it," Vivian said, trying not to let her composure slip. "But there's nothing I can do about it. Besides, we weren't married."

"I don't want to get married ever. Or have kids."

Vivian could tell that Anna was trying to get a rise out of her and was smart enough not to take the bait. Again, honesty was the best policy. It was easier for Vivian, too, since Anna wasn't her kid.

"I don't think I do, either," Vivian said.

Anna gave her a funny look. "Really?"

"Really."

"You don't like kids?"

Vivian flicked her on the rump with a dishtowel, which earned her a squeal and a smile.

"No, I like kids just fine. But, for starters, I don't have a partner. And my life's pretty complicated."

"You gonna put that on social media?" Anna asked, looking mischievous.

"Smartass," Vivian shot back. "It just looks like a really tough job. But I think it's one of the most important jobs you could have."

"Do you think Mom wishes she didn't have us?" Anna blurted out.

Vivian looked straight at her and said, "No, I don't think that at all. I think she loves you more than life itself and that she's working really hard to be the best mom she can be. She's tired and she's depressed. Do you know what depressed is?"

"I guess," Anna said, shrugging.

"Tell me."

"It means that she's sad, like she was just after Connor was born," Anna said, gaze dropping.

"That's right. It's like being sick, only not with a cold. It's a sickness in your mind. I had it, too, when I was little. I had it later when Mae died."

"But you're okay now, right?" she asked, meeting Vivian's gaze again.

Vivian nodded. "I'm close enough. Your mom will be, too."

"I hope so," Anna said. She looked hopeful. Skeptical, but hopeful.

"You can help her, too. You can help out around the house and get your brother and sister to do the same. They'll listen to you better than they will to your mom and dad."

"Okay," she said. "I can do that."

"Good. So, what are we going to do today?" Vivian asked. She'd told Kay to go out and get a massage or a pedicure while she took the kiddos for the afternoon. Since Kate and Scooter normally got to choose where to go, she figured it was Anna's turn.

"How about we head out to Radnor Lake? I like the turtles."

"Sure thing. You know, I saw some wild turkeys last time I was out there. And I caught a big, ugly brown toad—"

"Ewwwwww!" Anna screeched, clearly horrified by the thought.

If they could joke again, Anna must be feeling better. She hoped to talk to her a little bit more in the afternoon, but at least she could reassure Kay that her kids would suffer no long-term damage from her mommy melt-down. She also sent Boyd a text message so she could speak to him about the situation. Not wanting to be meddlesome, she was still sufficiently worried about her friend to want to get Boyd on board with the program.

Besides, a part of her was curious about his side of the story. It was and would always be Vivian's natural inclination to take Kay's side, but after what happened between her and Jace, she figured she could use some more insight into the male psyche.

She just hoped she didn't wind up losing control and unleashing her fury on Boyd like she had on Sarah, especially after last night's warning message. Then again, she couldn't very well go about her life and work in fear. If what Darkmore said was true, and he was willing to defend her and those she loved, then maybe she should take his suggestion and try to draw the rogue guardian out in the open. Perhaps she could channel her unique energy into more than simply a solid defense—perhaps she could attack.

At the very least, she could bring the fight out of the shadows and face it head on.

Because one thing was certain—she could and she *would* continue to work for the living, no matter who was watching.

CHAPTER FIFTEEN

"I want more wiggle worms, Aunt Vee Vee!" Connor screamed. Ever since she'd pulled out that first slimy nightcrawler from her back garden and showed it to the boy, he'd been hooked on worms. She wasn't sure if it was legal to dig in the park, but she figured letting Scooter dig in one small spot just off the trail wouldn't hurt. Kaitlyn was busy chasing butterflies, which left Vivian and Anna sitting on a nearby bench at Radnor Lake and sharing what was left of the Goldfish cracker and yogurt-covered raisin snack stash.

"So, what's been going on with you these days?" Vivian asked.

"Nothin' much," Anna muttered.

"Nothing? It's been a like a month or so since the zoo, and you mean to tell me that nothing important has happened in all that time?"

"Is this like one of those heart-to-heart talks like they have in all of those stupid movies on Lifetime?"

"No, this is me trying to have a civilized conversation with someone I care about. Someone who's waaaaaay too close to becoming a surly teenager," Vivian said, giving her a shove. "Anyway, what's going on with school? What's going on with boys? Are you experimenting with drugs, alcohol, or cigarettes? That sort of thing."

"Yup," Anna said between bites. "This is definitely turning into a heart-to-heart." At least she said it with a smile.

"And?"

"And school's okay. I'll be glad to be out, though. Boys are boys. Most of them are dumb and loud and act like they don't have a lick of sense. And I haven't tried any drugs or cigarettes."

"Ah-ha!" Vivian said in mock triumph. "Now we're getting somewhere. Boys don't have a lick of sense most of the time, and men aren't much different. But let's get back to the last. I didn't hear you confirm or deny experimentation with alcohol."

"I guess you're talking about Jace, huh? We saw him a couple times and Dad looked like he wanted to hit him. Mom wasn't real nice either, and she didn't even fuss at Kate when she asked him why he was such a big meanie poop-head," Anna said, her voice and expression overly animated.

Vivian was touched, but she wasn't fooled by the distraction ploy, "Well, that's pretty cool of your mom and dad. Now, back to the subject of you and booze..."

"Fine. I had a sip of wine at Lacy's house when I went for a sleepover. Just a sip," she said, pleading her case as if she were on the witness stand. "And I didn't even like it. It wasn't sweet. It tasted like cough syrup, only way grosser."

Ugh. Probably the cheap stuff. Good thing, too. It would be harder to argue with a tween who'd sampled fine wine and enjoyed it. "So you aren't going to be trying any of that stuff again, right? Not until you're much older?"

"No, I'll be good, I promise," Anna swore. "Just don't tell Mom. Please?"

"That's good, and I won't tell your mom," Vivian said. "But in case you ever forget to be good and find yourself in trouble, I want you to promise me one thing."

"What?"

"You'll call me. No matter what time of day or night, call me. I'll come and get you, no questions asked. Understand?"

"Yeah," Anna said, offering her a lopsided grin. "I will."

They sat in silence for a few minutes and watched Kate manage to coax a small white butterfly to land on the tip of her finger for about a nanosecond before Scooter scared it off. To her credit, Kate didn't hit him.

She decided instead to join him on a worm hunt while Vivian and Anna cheered from the sidelines.

Anna looked Vivian up and down and said, "You know, I think you should have some kids, Auntie Viv."

"Well...maybe someday," Vivian said with a small, dismissive wave of her hand.

"You'll meet someone nice. You have to," she said, then her gaze went wide and she latched onto Vivian's arm in a death grip. "And you have to do it before Auntie Sue's wedding. You can't show up without a date while Jace is walking around with that hoochie mama!"

"First of all, it doesn't work like that," Vivian said, ignoring the lurch of anxiety forming in her gut. Damn, she'd forgotten about wrangling a wedding date.

"Like what?" Anna said, bring her attention back to the girl.

"Like, with a deadline," Vivian replied with exasperation. It was a sad day indeed when her love life, or lack thereof, was under scrutiny from an eleven-year-old. "Second of all, where on Earth did you hear the term 'hoochie mama'?"

"At school," she replied primly.

"Well, don't go repeating everything you hear at school, especially not where your mother can hear. She'll probably think you've been picking that stuff up from me."

"It's okay." Anna grinned. "I learn even weirder stuff from my science teacher. Sometimes."

"Like what?"

"Like if you put sodium metal in the toilet it will explode."

"Please tell me you didn't test that yourself," Vivian said.

"Nah," Anna admitted. "But some of the guys wanted to."

"What else?" Vivian asked.

She thought about it for a minute and said, "Oh, we also learned that this summer is going to be the year of brood nineteen."

"What?"

"You know, cicadas?"

"Oh, right," she said. "The ones that come and go every thirteen years, right?" Vivian asked. God, she still remembered the last time they'd hit, shuddering as visions of red eyes danced in her head along with the deafening buzz that came along with them.

"Yeah, they're supposed to be, like, a Biblical plague or something."

"They sure are. I remember the last time they popped out," Vivian responded. "Back when you weren't even a nasty thought yet."

"Um, yuck!" Anna replied, with her face screwed up. Vivian knew that Anna had been around long enough to know about the proverbial "birds and bees." Vivian also knew that Anna was guaranteed to have a mini-conniption fit whenever she was reminded that her parents enjoyed nature's way.

She found it highly entertaining.

"Anyway," Anna said when she'd recovered. "You are going to find a date for the wedding, right?"

"It's a week away. That's cutting it a little close, honey," Vivian replied as anxiety returned in full force.

"Don't you know any cute guys?" Anna asked.

"Not really," Vivian muttered. *At least none that are walking in the world of the living.* Then again, she did know of at least one attractive spirit, but that was simply out of the question. Wasn't it?

Her face must have betrayed her thoughts, since Anna's next words were, "Ooooooooh! You *do* know someone. You should ask him to be your date. It will make Jace crazy-jealous!"

"Why would I care about making Jace jealous?" Vivian asked. "It's not like I want him back, and I don't really care what he thinks."

"To get even," Anna said with a shrug, as if it were obvious. "Besides, you might actually have fun if you bring a cute guy."

With that, she got up from the bench and ran to join her siblings and their growing pile of squiggly worms, leaving Vivian with plenty of food for thought.

"Connor, do *not* eat that," Vivian yelled just as the boy was dangling a worm above his open mouth.

"It's not the worst thing he's ever eaten," Annabelle said with a sigh.

Vivian had the sneaking suspicion that Anna was right about that, too.

———

Vivian sat at her desk, fidgeting. She didn't like coming to the office when she wasn't working. But she needed privacy, and she would have privacy for her meeting, privacy that would not be possible at her home. Ezra had been staying closer than he usually did, as had Jeanne.

While waiting, she looked over the accounts and checked a few emails. The Ridleys had sent her a thank-you message and let her know they'd paid off the title loan sharks. They promised to bring in their first payment, along with their little one, in a few weeks.

Here's hoping.

Some of her other clients were delinquent and she was afraid she'd have to send the repo men after them. She made a few notes to call them or pay a home visit first, since she didn't want to have to resort to taking the stuff back. It wasn't easy or fun for anyone, and they never recouped their losses on resale.

Exhaustion threatened to overtake her as she sat, so she got up and paced around a bit. She couldn't afford to let her guard down, even though what she was planning definitely constituted a major breach of caution. Maybe she should just call it off. But she'd already summoned him, so she couldn't, right?

Oh, hell.

She rubbed her tired eyes and wondered for the thousandth time if she should just run out right now.

No, he'd just find you and grill you, then scare you, and then laugh his ass off at you.

Maybe that was what truly scared her. Rejection was almost as scary a prospect as any reaper, guardian, or ghost she'd ever encountered. Of course, when last they met, he'd still seemed...interested. His level of interest was intense and frightening, but she just needed him to be a convincing escort. Nothing more.

"I do so love to watch you when you are at war with yourself," came a whisper from behind her.

She should have expected it, but the sudden appearance of Lazarus Darkmore never failed to catch her by surprise and scare her. This time, not only did she shriek and curse, she also fell to the ground and twisted her ankle in the process. She wasn't sure what hurt more, her injury or her pride.

Before she knew what hit her, she was lifted from the floor and placed on a nearby chair. The next sensation she registered was that of intense cold coursing through her injured limb as the reaper massaged it with his cool hands. She tried to jerk away, but his grip was firm and insistent.

"Shh," he soothed. "Relax. This will help."

"How do you know all about the proper treatment for sprains?" Vivian asked, wincing as his hand found the center of the pain.

"I know much about injuries, Vivian, and not just those of the soul. Better?"

"Yes," she groaned, relieved his coolness soothed the sting and swelling. "But I don't know if I'll be able to walk out of here."

"Didn't you mention that you were a healer?" Darkmore asked politely.

"Yeah," Vivian replied. It hadn't occurred to her that she could heal herself. *Might as well try.* She tried to remember how she'd managed to heal the padre, but it was all still a blur. She'd been desperate then, and she hadn't tried since. She took a deep breath, closed her eyes, and focused on the ankle, but nothing happened.

"Shit," she cried in frustration. "I don't know how to do this yet."

"Shh," Darkmore said again, his voice low and hypnotic. "Calm down. Take a deep breath."

She managed to calm herself with the help, she suspected, of some cool and calming energy emanating from the reaper. She smelled cool spring rain and almost felt a soothing breeze. Then, she heard his voice.

"Try this," he said. "Close your eyes and pretend someone you know and love is injured."

"That's just silly," she said, discomfort and humiliation in the presence of the reaper making her more irascible than usual.

"Just try it, please. Think of your friend the priest, or maybe one of the children you were with this afternoon, the little boy, perhaps? Pretend he's here now and he's distraught and in pain. You can hear him crying. He's asking you for help. Can you hear him, Vivian?"

She could. She saw Connor with his face screwed up in agony, crocodile tears falling, and asking for Aunt Vee Vee to make it all better. She focused on that image of Scooter and willed him to get better. The burst of light from within the room brought her back to the present.

"Did it work?" she asked, opening her eyes. She was mortified to find they were filled with tears, and she quickly set about wiping them away.

"See for yourself," he replied, his voice no longer so close. She looked up and realized then that he'd moved to the other side of the room.

She stood and gingerly placed her right leg on the floor, testing it against her weight. It felt a little stiff, but it was definitely on the mend.

"Wowzers," she exclaimed. "It actually worked!"

She heard him chuckle from across the room and it made her smile in spite of her lingering embarrassment and fear.

"What's so funny?" she asked, trying her best to sound mad.

"Oh, I was just amused by your reaction, particularly by the fact that it was devoid of profanity."

"Well," she grumbled as she walked toward him. "I *have* been working on it, and I was around kids today. How'd you know about that, by the way? Been keeping tabs on me again?"

"Always."

"So," she mumbled, having recovered from her injury and the distraction it caused. God, was she really going to ask him? "Thanks for, um, you know, helping me work out this healing thing."

"My pleasure," he said. "Now then, down to business."

"Business? Oh, right, yes, let's get to it, since I'm sure you're busy and all..." Vivian was getting nervous, not to mention tired. It must have showed, since he took her hand and led her to her desk chair, bidding her to sit.

"You look tired, my dear. Busy day?"

"Yeah, and the night before was busy, too. I took in some serious burden baggage last night, from a friend. It's always harder to push it aside when I know the person. And I got another warning from my guardian stalker."

"I can help with the first part at least," he said, leaning in and pressing his cool lips to hers. Determined not to let that make her even more edgy, she forced herself to calm and savor the contact. She didn't have to force the relaxation and peace that followed releasing the spiritual burdens she carried.

But for the first time, she let go of all thoughts and worries and just focused on Darkmore's kiss. That was a first.

It must have been good for him, too, or else he was just happy to be savoring the delicious pain he'd reaped from Vivian. She was a bit taken aback by the look of bliss painted across his chiseled features. Strange that the horrors of human life could be such sweet sustenance for creatures like Darkmore.

That should make him seem all the more evil in her eyes. She still feared him, but she couldn't think of him as purely malevolent. What did that make her?

"You must stop warring with yourself," scolded the reaper. "Or, at the very least, institute a temporary cease-fire. Savor this moment. You are lighter, as is your friend Kay, and I am fuller and closer to fulfillment. No need for such angst, my dear. Everyone wins in our little game."

"Sorry," she muttered, yawning.

"You'd best be off to bed now. Shall I deliver you to your home and spare you the drive?"

"What about my car? Oh, and there's Ezra and Jeanne. They're guarding my place like Fort Knox, and—"

"Shh," he said, lifting her in his arms and pulling her into the vortex. She really should be annoyed at this new habit of his, shushing her and coddling her like she was a child. She was a little annoyed.

But, she was also a little grateful, albeit grudgingly so.

When she opened her eyes, they'd landed in her backyard. He'd had the foresight to bring along her purse and house keys.

"What about my car?" Vivian asked.

"It will be here in the morning. And now, I should bid you good night."

"Wait," she blurted out. "I...I still need to ask you something."

"I'm afraid I don't have any more news on your attacker as yet."

"No, it's not about that—it's, well, it's another favor actually."

"Another favor?" Darkmore asked. She had no idea if he was intrigued, amused, or angry. She could be pushing her luck instead of entertaining him, for all she knew.

"Yes. See, my friend Sue is getting married in a week. You remember Sue, right?"

"Yes, the young woman whose body I possessed while we negotiated the terms of our first exchange of favors."

Well, Hell's bells, you had to go and bring that up, did you?

It was true. Back when she'd first met Darkmore and worried that he was out to drag her off to Hell, he'd taken control of Sue's body to get Vivian's attention. It worked, and it had scared her. The memory didn't inspire courage or trust in her now.

But what other choice did she have, other than the humiliation of showing up alone?

"Well, like I said, Sue's getting married next week, and I'm invited. I'm a bridesmaid, actually."

"I see. Would you like to relieve her of her burdens in honor of the day? I would be happy to take them."

"That's sweet," Vivian replied. She thought she meant it. "I have a problem, though. Jace, my ex, is the best man and he's bringing the woman he dumped me for to the wedding. I don't want to have to go alone, and I don't really have any prospects, so…"

Darkmore stared at her. Either he wasn't getting it, he wasn't believing it, or he just flat-out wasn't interested. Her pride had already taken more than a few nosedives on account of the reaper. What was one more?

"So," Vivian said after a deep breath for courage. "I wanted to know if you would be willing to escort me to the wedding."

There. The invitation was out, and she couldn't take it back. Now it was up to him.

"You want me to be your escort," he said. It wasn't a question. He appeared to be thinking it over. "I am to be your wedding date?"

"Well, yes," she said. "I mean, if you aren't doing anything else that day."

He kept staring, which made her blush. Blushing made her mad. She was just about to storm off after telling him to forget the whole thing, when he answered.

"I'll pick you up on Saturday."

With that, he disappeared.

CHAPTER SIXTEEN

"Rise and shine! Wakey wakey, eggs and bakey!"

"Jeanne, I'd kill you right now if you weren't already dead. You know that, right?" Vivian grumbled from beneath the covers.

"Well, it's not my fault that you were out so late last night. Where were you, anyhow?"

"I had to see to go see about a boy," she muttered with a small smile, remembering her encounter with the reaper. If nothing else, he'd make a great conversation piece. With his fine features, courtly manners, and attractive figure—not that she'd been looking...much—he'd turn heads while on her arm, giving the guests something to talk about other than how Jace had dumped her for another woman.

She might actually have a good time after all.

"Ohhhhh, that's wonderful," Jeanne cried, plopping herself down on Vivian's bed and bouncing up and down in excitement. "So you've met someone new? Tell me, tell me, tell me! I want details."

"Jeanne, were you like this in life?" Vivian asked, trying and failing to stop her aching head from spinning.

"Like what?" she asked, looking confused.

Vivian thought for a moment and decided that she really didn't want to hurt her feelings. After all, the young guardian had been working extra-hard to protect her. She really shouldn't be so mean.

"Um, you know, a bubbly morning person. We've been hanging out for a while, but I don't know anything about you," Vivian said, hoping to change the subject before she managed to hurt Jeanne's feelings.

Jeanne thought for a while. Vivian wondered if she was having a blonde moment, but it turned out that she was just thrown for a bit of a loop with the question.

It was apparently a new one for her.

"Sorry, I'm not trying to be impolite," Jeanne began. "I'm just not used to talking to people anymore. I mean, we aren't used to speaking with the living. You have to understand, most of the living can't see us, even when we're looking out for them or helping them. When we help someone cross over, they're usually too shocked by dying to ask us much of anything, except for where we're taking them."

"Oh," Vivian said. "I guess I didn't think about that. Well, if you don't want to talk about it I'll understand."

"Don't be silly," Jeanne replied with a bright smile and renewed enthusiasm. "I don't mind at all. And I'm tickled pink that you're working so hard to be nice."

Vivian let that one slide, since she supposed she deserved it. She hadn't been the most pleasant person to deal with these days. Now that she thought about it, it seemed downright impolite that she hadn't asked Jeanne about herself before now.

"So what were you like in life? What did you do for a living?" Vivian asked.

"I was a student before I crossed over," she said with a shrug. "And I was pretty much like I am now. You know, sorority girl, gung-ho in class, that sort of thing. Don't you dare roll your eyes."

"Sorry. Habit. What were you studying? Child psych, pre-nursing, dental hygiene?"

"Pre-law," she replied with another shrug, this time looking a bit more smug.

"Really," Vivian said. "You don't strike me as the pit-bull type."

"Oh, I can be," Jeanne said, smiling.

"What happened to cut your life so short, if you don't mind me asking?"

"Melanoma. I spent some time in tanning beds, and I liked the sun. I still do, actually, but I don't have to worry about cancer anymore."

"Wow, I'm so sorry," Vivian said. She was no stranger to tragedy, but such a matter-of-fact declaration of death from this perky guardian threw her off. Life was fragile and the proof of that sat right in front of her.

"Don't be," Jeanne said. "Things in the afterlife are pretty interesting, and challenging. I like the work."

"Did you choose it? I mean, how much of becoming a guardian has to do with being chosen versus volunteering?" She couldn't see Jeanne being coerced, but she'd just assumed that everyone working in afterlife management had gotten into the business on a debt repayment plan. Vivian certainly had.

"Some of us have to do it, but I wanted to. As soon as I popped up out of the hospital bed I was ready to go," Jeanne said.

I'll just bet you were.

Curiosity piqued, Vivian asked, "What about those who have to? Is it like a punishment, Purgatory, the draft?"

"Oh, I don't think I'm supposed to go into detail about those who have to serve," Jeanne said. She added in a whisper, "It's a private matter between the conscripted and the mentor guardian."

"Says who?" Vivian asked. She'd had just about enough of secrecy and stonewalling.

"What do you mean, 'says who?' Who are you to question the rules?"

"I'm someone who's affected by them, for starters," Vivian said. "And I question everything."

"Oh, Vivian," Jeanne offered, speaking as though she were dealing with a precocious child. "This isn't like your average office gossip. It's very personal. Some people who die in the middle of their lives, or even at the end, leave behind a mess. I'm not talking about little mistakes either. I'm talking serious issues."

"I know. I've seen it before," she said, remembering Zeke. "So it is a punishment?"

"Nope. It's a shot at redemption."

She must have rolled her eyes because Jeanne got mad—mad enough to turn the kitchen into a sauna as her gaze burned a hole right into Vivian. No longer the bubbly co-ed, Vivian was confronted with the guardian's otherness and its power for the first time.

Jeanne stood, blazing, and spoke with a voice Vivian had never heard before.

"Vivian Bedford, you may be a different sort of mortal, but mortal you are. There are things you do not yet understand and, whether you choose to believe in them or not, you must respect the rules and the nature of our realm or—"

"Or what?" Vivian asked, standing. If the room was a sauna before, Vivian's added heat turned it into an inferno. "You'll kill me? Reap my soul and make me work on the chain gang of eternity? That's what your friend Uriel implied. Seems like I'm in the irons already, so what was my crime? Who are any of you to act as judge and jury?"

Jeanne didn't speak or strike, so Vivian continued her tirade. "I am mortal, yes, but I've seen how your kind operate. I know enough to understand that you aren't so different from us. You help some souls but you like to leave others hanging out to dry, like Junior and all of those lost souls down in Nolensville. What did Junior ever do wrong besides feel terrible about losing his little brother?"

"It isn't so easy to make things right. I can't just snap my fingers and cross Junior over, or make someone do the right thing instead of the wrong thing, or make you behave. But we are not the same. We—"

"The only difference I see between guardians and humans is just that guardians have more firepower." She held up her hands and let the spirit energy spark out of her fingertips, brighter and more powerful than before. Then she leveled her gaze on Jeanne's and said, "But then again, so do I."

Jeanne's gaze went wide with surprise, and perhaps a lick of fear. "Vivian, you don't want to go down this road. I'm telling you, if you make more trouble and start abusing your power, rogue guardians are going to be the least of your worries."

The temperature was near unbearable, but Vivian refused to back down. Jeanne, Ezra, and all of the other guardians charged with protecting her seemed to spend more time ordering her about and warning her of the dangers of her powers and situation than actually solving any problems. And now, on top of that, Jeanne wanted her to put her faith in some sort of afterlife probation and community service program? Vivian wondered if she herself was a part of such a program, even though she was still living.

What had she ever done that was so terrible? And who were the dead to decide?

Jeanne sighed and backed down first. She walked over to the kitchen sink, ran a dishtowel under the faucet, and tossed it to Vivian, who was covered in sweat. Jeanne remained dry, of course. Lucky her.

Vivian mopped her face and the back of her neck and muttered, "Thanks."

After about five minutes of literal cool down, she hoped their bad little moment had passed. She figured she'd hit the shower and take care of the rest. It was going to be a busy day. Manicure and pedicure at eleven followed by a ladies' lunch. The mean part of Vivian was looking forward to seeing Sarah again. After that, they needed to pick up their dresses and transport them to Scarritt Bennett, and once they arrived, they needed to make certain most of the decorations were in place. The flowers would be delivered on the day of the wedding and Sarah was in charge of overseeing their placement. Sue put Sarah in charge to keep her busy so she wouldn't annoy Vivian. No doubt Sue wanted to keep Big Sis out of her own hair as well.

No doubt Sarah would be happy to stay out of Vivian's way after their last encounter.

After scrubbing herself, shaving, and drying her hair, Vivian made her way back to the kitchen. Jeanne was gone, at least physically, for which Vivian was grateful. She could appear at any moment or if Vivian happened to call, but it was nice to be alone. Vivian hadn't realized until now how much she'd missed her privacy. She wasn't antisocial, but it would be nice to have the option to mingle with the living or dead on her own terms and schedule. Now she had a few hours to kill before the hustle and bustle of the day began.

She grabbed a cup of coffee and went to her living room, intent on catching up on the news while she calmed down. She was about to plop her rear end down when she noticed a slip of paper sticking out from between the cushions. She picked up the note and read it.

BriggsonfireMS2010 Online ID. You wanted to meet someone like you, so here's how to find him.

She remembered, then, that Jeanne had given her the note when they caught Junior. Jeanne must have put it back in plain view before she left. Vivian stared at the note for about fifteen minutes while she let her coffee sink in and then grabbed it, sat down behind her desktop, and set about loading her IM and creating an ID before she changed her mind.

After about thirty minutes and ten tries for a unique ID, she sent a request for contact to this mystery man. She didn't expect much, since most normal people would already be at work on a Friday morning. To her surprise, however, she received a message about five minutes later.

BriggsonfireMS2010: Good morning.
HauntedVivTN1975: Hello.

Vivian stared at the screen for a moment, wondering how she was supposed to start a conversation about seeing dead people. If Jeanne was right about him, then he saw them, too, and shouldn't be fazed at all. If not, he'd think she was nuts. While she was musing, another IM popped onto her screen.

BriggsonfireMS2010: You still there?
HauntedVivTN1975: Yes. I was just thinking about how to start this conversation.
BriggsonfireMS2010: *I see dead people. They're everywhere.*

HauntedVivTN1975: Very funny.

BriggsonfireMS2010: I was whispering, too. Pulled the covers up to my neck and everything.

HauntedVivTN1975: You're in bed?

BriggsonfireMS2010: Laptops are handy. You should get one.

I'll just bet they are. Hoping he wasn't a pervert or serial killer, Vivian decided to dive right in.

HauntedVivTN1975: I got your contact information from a local guardian. You know them, too?

BriggsonfireMS2010: Yes. My guardian friends told me someone might be in touch. How long you been in the know?

HauntedVivTN1975: About a year. Long story. I work with them. Today I wish I didn't.

BriggsonfireMS2010: LOL—I understand. Been there myself. I'd be interested in getting your story sometime.

HauntedVivTN1975: I'd like to know yours, too. Have you had any trouble with them?

BriggsonfireMS2010: Trouble?

Vivian thought for a moment. It was a risk, of course, confiding in a stranger. A human stranger might be in more jeopardy than a spirit should he become a target. Of course, Jeanne wanted Vivian to contact him, and she probably had more than one reason. She decided to test the waters and let him decide.

BriggsonfireMS2010: You still there?

HauntedVivTN1975: Yeah, just thinking. I don't want to put you in the middle of some bad stuff. It might not be safe for you.

BriggsonfireMS2010: OK. I should tell you that I met the guardians while serving in Afghanistan. Almost got blown up by an IED when they showed up. Had a few scrapes on account of them since then. That's the CNN version.

HauntedVivTN1975: Soldier? I get it. You can take care of yourself.

BriggsonfireMS2010: I hold my own. What's the deal?

HauntedVivTN1975: Rogue guardian. Doesn't like me interfering with their business. Tried to hurt a friend of mine to make me stop.

BriggsonfireMS2010: Why aren't the guardians on top of this?

HauntedVivTN1975: Not sure. Say they're working on it, but they don't tell me much.

She paused again, and then decided she might as well be straight with him. It was strange, but this form of communication lent itself well to candor. Maybe it was because she didn't really know the guy, or maybe because she couldn't see him. It didn't matter. She wasn't in the mood to be coy.

HauntedVivTN1975: Someone from the other team is helping me.

BriggsonfireMS2010: Reaper?

HauntedVivTN1975: Yeah. Long story.

BriggsonfireMS2010: Must be a good one. Tell me sometime?

HauntedViv1975: Sure. Hey, what do you do, by the way?

BriggsonfireMS2010: Besides hang out with the dead?

HauntedViv1975: Yes, smartass. Are you still military?

BriggsonfireMS2010: Army reserve. Not active. Firefighter now. You?

HauntedViv1975: Finance.

BriggsonfireMS2010: Business OK in this economy?

HauntedViv1975: OK. Enough to get me by.

BriggsonfireMS2010: Married? Kids?

HauntedViv1975: Personal question.

BriggsonfireMS2010: Don't have to answer. Just making convo.

HauntedViv1975: No and no. You?

BriggsonfireMS2010: Nah. Situation isn't conducive to it.

HauntedViv1975: Lonely?

BriggsonfireMS2010: Sometimes.

HauntedViv1975: Me too. Glad I'm not alone in all this, you know?

BriggsonfireMS2010: Yeah, I know.

HauntedViv1975: Where are you?

BriggsonfireMS2010: Jackson, Mississippi. Not too far off, Tennessee girl.

HauntedViv1975: Tennessee woman! By way of Nashvegas.

BriggsonfireMS2010: I stand corrected. Still friends?

HauntedViv1975: I'll let it slide just this once. Gotta go now. Best friend getting married tomorrow. Chat soon?

BriggsonfireMS2010: Sure. You take care of yourself now, Ms. Tennessee.

HauntedViv1975: Vivian Bedford. I'll try. You do the same.

BriggsonfireMS2010: Sure thing, Vivian. Waylon Briggs signing off.

HauntedViv1975: Bye.

Vivian turned off her computer feeling much better than she had before her chat. She wondered if Waylon Briggs the fireman was tall, dark, and hotter than July? Giggling to herself at the prospect, she figured she'd find a way to dig out that information sometime in the next few chats. At the very least he'd made her smile. And she didn't feel so alone.

Another message popped up on her screen.

You were warned, yet you persisted. There will be consequences.

A lick of fear shot through her followed by anger. She let more sparks fly from her fingertips as she stared at the screen. Then, willing the energy back into her body, she typed a message back.

. . .

Maybe you should be worried about consequences.

A beat passed, then another message appeared.

See you tonight.

CHAPTER SEVENTEEN

Vivian managed to relax after her nail treatments and lunch in spite of Sarah Harrow's presence. She'd barely looked in Vivian's direction and hadn't spoken a word. If Sue or anyone else involved in the wedding found this strange, they didn't let on. A twinge of guilt hit her for a few moments, but then she remembered the images that flashed through her mind—images of Sarah's inner darkness and worst sins.

Maybe she'd given the woman something to think about. Perhaps it was part of her penance, as Darkmore claimed.

Moving on, she decided to put her talents to some genuine, unambiguous good uses.

Sitting in the courtyard of Scarritt Bennett, she wasn't sure exactly what she should be doing. Sarah was busy with the decorations, Boyd Clemmens was helping Jack and Jace the cheater carry stuff inside, and Sue was resting so her feet wouldn't swell so much that her wedding shoes no longer fit. That left Vivian on her own. At least she'd been able to snag a cup of coffee from the nearby Front Porch gallery and coffee shop. She took it back out and sat in a small courtyard on the center's grounds, admiring the view.

Nestled between Vandy and Music Row, and sitting in the shadow of downtown, Scarritt Bennett center exuded an unexpected tranquility for such an urban setting. The high, Gothic towers and surrounding trees gave Vivian a sense of seclusion, and she fully expected Mr. Heathcliff to emerge from one of the high arched doors, or perhaps a monk might peer through one of the aged stained-glass windows. Come to think of it, one might just do that. She closed her eyes and tried not to dwell on any spirits who might choose to appear before her at any moment. She wanted to focus on the location and the pending nuptials. It was a great place for a wedding in spite of the fact that, typical for the Bible Belt, all events had to be alcohol-free. Hence, the reception that followed would be held elsewhere.

Vivian pulled out a copy of some frou-frou girlie magazine she'd picked up from the nail bar, hoping that some light and mindless reading would take her mind off ghost-spotting while she waited to catch her target alone.

Okay, calling this stuff mindless was pretty generous.

She flipped past the sea of ads and obviously faked testimonials of sexual exploits that belonged in your average episode of *Sex and the City* rather than the annals of the average woman's repertoire. *Over-priced couture? Check. Celebutard interview? Check. Requisite article on how to give the best blowjob* ever? *Check.* Seriously, how many variations did men need? In her experience, any technique guaranteed a big finish and a mountain of gratitude. If you were lucky, you might even enjoy reciprocity. She wondered if men's magazines provided handy-dandy tips, too, but snorted at the notion. Still, some writer could sneak in an instructional article in between workout and auto maintenance pieces, right? Something along the lines of *How to Toss Her Salad Like a Master Chef?*

She'd started daydreaming about firemen when Boyd Clemmens sat down next to her. Finally. Now was her chance to talk to the man in her crosshairs.

He looked and smelled sweaty. The mean part of her figured that Jace hadn't been pulling his weight, but it was probably just the fact that today's forecast was sunny and unseasonably warm. Tennessee weather was tricky and fickle. You could have snowstorms that shut the city down in March followed by an eighty-degree surge two days later. Vivian was just glad that the last batch of tornadoes didn't strike the city this time around. More torrential rains were in the forecast for tomorrow evening, but it shouldn't affect the wedding or reception.

"Hey, Viv," Boyd said, wiping his brow. "Got a minute?"

Do I ever. "Sure. Want me to grab you something cold to drink?"

"Nah, we'll be heading out for a bachelor dinner after this. Someplace with BBQ, beer, and no dress code." He chuckled. Then he got serious, clearing his throat before he said, "I wanted to thank you for taking care of Kay and the kids the other night. I'm sorry you had to get involved in our private mess."

"You don't have to apologize," she said, her gaze turning hard. "Not to me and not for Kay."

Boyd sighed, "I guess you'll be blaming me, too. Just like she does."

"I didn't say that," Vivian said, holding up her palms in the universal sign of "I come in peace."

"Well it sure seems that way," he said, voice hoarse. He looked away and seemed ready to walk away.

They were both on the defensive. That wouldn't do anyone any good. Vivian decided the least she could do was to listen to Boyd's side of the story. Maybe she could help him as well, depending on what he said and how he said it.

"Look," Vivian started again. "I didn't mean to come across as judging you, okay? I love Kay and I don't like to see her hurting. I know you don't either. Did she talk to you at all? Tell you how she's been feeling?"

"Yeah," Boyd said, staring off into the distance, his brows furrowed and face tight. He looked older, weary. Kay wasn't the only one suffering it seemed. "It's pretty much the same story every time. I've heard it at home and I hear it when I'm on the road and can't do anything about it. I don't know what she *thinks* I can do, anyway."

"What does she say?" Vivian asked.

"That I don't listen, that I'm not there when she needs me, that I don't care. It's not true, but I can't sit around and cry with her when she gets like that. It won't help. Besides, I've got to stay focused on the job and on getting home safe. It's hard to do when she's yelling in the phone. Sometimes..."

"Sometimes what?" she asked. She wanted him to just say what he was thinking, even if she didn't like it. She'd been there for Kay and listened. It was the least she could do for Kay's husband.

"Sometimes I don't even want to come home. I know it's not right, but who wants to walk into a hornet's nest? Does she really think I like being away from her and the kids? I mean, does she think I'm out partying and living the high life? I'm not doing this for fun and I'm sure as shit not doing this for my health. It's my job. It's how I put food on the table and keep a roof over our heads."

Vivian didn't like it, but she could see his point. She didn't relish listening, but maybe if he got his mad out with her then he wouldn't have to take it out on Kay. And he was hurting, caught between what he saw as a man's duty to provide and a stubborn man's inability to give his wife what she needed—reassurance, understanding, compassion, and the dreaded sharing of feelings. The whole "men must be macho and swallow their feelings" thing really sucked.

She sat in silence and let him rant.

"She knew I worked on the road when we got married. I don't know what she expected. It's not like I can quit with all our mouths to feed, school clothes, ballet and soccer, college funds, you get the idea," he said. Vivian nodded.

"Besides, she's the one who wanted a third, not me," he added with some bitterness. He looked to Vivian for some reaction, but she'd shifted her features to neutral. She'd had a lot of practice with that over the past year.

"I don't know why I'm telling you all of this," he muttered.

She shrugged. "I have one of those faces. People tell me all kinds of things. I'm a good listener. It's my superpower."

A small smile ghosted across his face, then he blew out a long breath and said, "I love my son and nothing's going change that, but it's been hell since he was born and it's not getting any better. Sometimes I think the only reason we're together now is for the kids, but even that's not going to be enough unless something changes."

"Do you love her?" Vivian asked.

"Of course I do. But that's not always enough."

"Is it enough to go and get some help?"

Boyd scowled, "Oh, so that's why she's bringing up the therapist again, huh?"

Time for some tough love, big boy.

"Yeah," Vivian said, scowling. "She figures since she's throwing stuff and you're running away, what y'all are doing ain't working out so hot. Am I right?"

"How's some damned shrink who's just going to take her side anyway supposed to help? All Kay does is bitch and moan and when I try to give her some pointers she just gets pissed off at me. I can't fix her."

"No, you can't," Vivian agreed.

"No, I can't—wait, what did you say?"

"I said no, you can't fix her. What's more, you shouldn't try." Vivian waited for it to sink in. He clearly hadn't expected it. Of course, he wouldn't like the rest, but maybe it would help in the long run.

"You're agreeing with me?" Boyd said with incredulity.

"Look, Boyd," Vivian said, putting a hand on his. "I'm going to let you in on a little secret. You don't have to offer advice, you don't have to 'give pointers,' or do any other such nonsense that tells her you think you know better than her. All you have to do is listen."

"Listen? You mean just sit there and not say anything while she goes off like she does every other week. How in the Sam Hill is that going to change things?"

Men. They really didn't get it. Then again, Kay probably hadn't told him what she needed either. Hard to do in the middle of a fight, as Vivian knew all too well from personal experience.

"Well, for starters, she probably won't yell at you anymore. I get that you think you're helping by making suggestions, but you're not. All you're telling her is that she's not good enough and she's not capable. Worse yet, you're telling her that the man of the house knows best— "

"I said no such thing," Boyd snapped.

"That's what she's hearing," Vivian snapped back. "And what's this about telling Kay you thought she'd be stronger?"

"See," Boyd said, standing and getting ready to storm off. "I knew you'd take her side."

"Boyd Clemmens, you turn around and sit your ass back down right this minute," Vivian said as she jumped off her seat. Her tone must have gotten his attention, since he turned. He didn't sit. *Stubborn jackass.*

"I mean it. After I came to the rescue of your family, that's the least you can do. You owe me that much."

That did it. He still looked as mad as a mule chewing on bumblebees, but he sat. Vivian drew in a deep breath and sat back down, too.

"Now, listen up. You and Kay need to get your shit together or else you aren't going to be any good to anyone, not to each other and not to those three kids caught in the crossfire. What you're doing isn't working. You want your wife back and happy more often than not, then go and get some help."

"I'll think about it," Boyd said, grudgingly. It was probably the best she'd get out of him.

"Don't think too long, or else you're going to be thinking somewhere with half your stuff," Vivian said.

With that, she stood, wrapped her arms around him, and kissed him on the cheek. She took in his burdens on the sly while she was at it, then grabbed her purse and headed for the parking lot, hoping he would think about it.

As she walked away, she looked back over her shoulder, crinkled her nose, and said, "And take a shower. You stink to high heaven!"

———

"So, you gonna tell us who this mystery man is?" Sue asked.

"Nope," Vivian said between sips of her blueberry margarita. "You'll just have to wait until tomorrow."

"Not if you keep downing the booze we won't," Kay chuckled. Vivian, Sue, and Kay had all headed out for their own low-key bachelorette dinner at Taco Mamacita. The late afternoon was cooler, so they'd taken advantage and walked. Even though it was her big night, Sue's delicate condition made alcohol a no-no, so she graciously agreed to be the designated driver. She seemed to enjoy her virgin 'rita almost as much as she was enjoying the chips.

"Watch the salt," Kay offered. "It will just make the foot swelling worse. And you don't want high blood pressure right now."

"Fine," Sue said, deflating. "Can I at least have some cheesecake?"

"Of course, hon. My treat," Vivian said.

"Seriously, though, where'd you find a guy on such short notice? You didn't...I mean, he's not a, a *man whore* is he?" Sue whispered the last, making Kay and Vivian giggle.

"No, I'm not that hard up," Vivian replied.

"Did you find him online?" Kay asked.

"No, and he's just a friend," she said. God, she needed to change the subject before they asked too many questions. It was risky enough bringing the reaper in public, let alone under the scrutiny of her friends. Then inspiration struck. Leaning back, she said, "But I do have a chat buddy in Mississippi. He's a fireman."

"Vivian!" Sue cried, jumping up and giving her a big hug. "You're back."

"Overkill, and not so fast." Vivian gasped, which made Sue loosen the death grip on her neck. "I haven't met the guy or even seen a picture. We've just got a few things in common."

"Oh?" Kay replied. She raised her eyebrows and Vivian gave her a small nod. Kay added, "Well, I think it would be very nice to get to know someone who understands you."

Wouldn't it just.

"Promise you'll be careful, okay? You never know about folks on the net these days. He might be a psycho killer or some sick pervert. Just make sure you meet someplace public," Sue warned.

"He lives in Mississippi, for Pete's sake. It's not like I can just run out and go meet him for coffee."

"But definitely keep chatting and see where it goes. If nothing else, you'll get a good friend out of the deal," Kay said. "Now let's see about ordering some real food and getting you ladies home for the night. I don't want to watch two zombies tottering down the aisle tomorrow."

———

Vivian couldn't sleep right away after Kay dropped her off, so she retreated outdoors. Her backyard had always been her sanctuary. It was even better this evening since she had the place to herself. Perhaps Jeanne had had the good grace to tell the other spirits to clear out. Or maybe she'd been afraid of another epic meltdown.

Still, she was grateful. Vivian had almost forgotten how glorious solitude felt, and she reminded herself to thank Jeanne the next time they spoke. She should thank Jeanne for telling her about Mr. Briggs, too. Maybe apologize for their argument while she was at it?

Nah. Vivian had to admit that while standing up to a full-fledged and powerful guardian of the spirit realm might be foolhardy, it had felt pretty damned good.

She breathed in the scents of honeysuckle and freshly mown grass, and she took in the eerie beauty of the moonlit night and of dark clouds rolling across the night sky as she watched them moving through tall tree branches. It soothed her and gave her a chance to think over the events of the day and night. She'd enjoyed the meal and the company of her two best girlfriends, which both pleased and surprised her. She'd been worried about this night since it was Sue's last hurrah as a single gal. It seemed like it ought to be a turning point of sorts, like their relationship would change somehow after tomorrow.

The last thing she wanted was more change. Still, amid the laughter and love of the evening, she didn't get the sense that a chapter was ending in her life, and for that she was grateful. The fear remained, but the longer she examined it, the more she became convinced that it had nothing to do with her friends on this side of life or maybe even the other side.

That was a scary prospect.

She slipped off her house shoes and walked down to the yard, reveling in the feel of the grass beneath her bare feet while admiring the shine of her polished toes. They caught the nascent light from the streetlamps. She didn't see any fireflies, but decided she'd probably best get back inside before the mosquitoes ate her alive. She stopped on her stroll back to the stairs of her deck when her foot brushed something wet and living. Not being the squeamish sort, Vivian bent and allowed her finger to seek out the creature. She picked it up with gentle fingers and walked it up the stairs so she could get a better look at it.

The light revealed it to be an insect, a pale green creature with red eyes and the uncertain movements of a newborn. It was rather large for an infant. She reckoned it to be about an inch in length. She regarded it as its sluggish legs examined the flesh of her palm beneath them. She got the sense that the nymph's red eyes were taking her in as well. Smiling, she carried it back downstairs and allowed it to crawl from her hand onto the bark of one of her trees. It seemed more eager once in contact with this terrain, perhaps in response to some primal instinct akin to that which brought it from the depths of the earth below after many long years of waiting. It was the instinct that compelled it to rise and complete the metamorphosis so long in coming.

A warm wind blew, setting her on edge. Change was coming. Would it be for good or ill? And would she be ready?

CHAPTER EIGHTEEN

Vivian got dressed and ready to go thirty minutes early, which left her plenty of time to wonder if asking Lazarus Darkmore to be her wedding date had been such a good idea.

It also left her ample time to wonder what he would wear, if he would show up to get her in a car, if he had or even needed a car. How would he get a car anyway? And where and how he would get a car anyway and keep it? What kind of car he would drive? Could he even drive?

This was such a bad idea.

It was selfish, really, now that she had time to reflect. Her pride demanded that she one-up Jace since he'd be bringing Sheila. That, and fear of being seen as pathetic and lonely, kept her from going solo. Of course, she probably was pathetic if her only options for a date consisted of a pool of dead men, and the one whom she'd chosen was pretty much the embodiment of the grim reaper, albeit suave, handsome, and sometimes charming.

She fidgeted, sat down, and tried to skim through an old issue of *Time*. The cover was framed in red and emblazoned with a good bit of red font in front of a tableau of black and white figures in free fall. It posed the question, "What if there's no Hell?"

Oh that's just perfect...

She put it down when she could no longer pretend to concentrate, and then ran back to her bathroom to check her hair, makeup, and to make sure her body shaper was keeping all of her flaws strategically hidden. Why was she doing this? She looked good enough, and anyway, it was Sue's big day, not hers. It wasn't even a real date.

Vivian was making a mental note to remind Darkmore of that fact when the doorbell rang. She walked through the house and prepared to answer the door, wishing once more that she'd reminded him not to wear white.

The sight that greeted her at the door left her utterly speechless, a fact not lost on her caller. Whether it amused him or pleased him was more difficult for Vivian to determine. At least his smile seemed genuine. He'd dressed in a black suit rather than a tuxedo. She hadn't expected under-stated from such a being. It fit well, obviously tailored, and his tie was a bril-liant shade of crimson. *Of course.* The only things brighter than the tie were his icy blue eyes. He'd left the Stetson at home, giving Vivian the chance to take in his white-blond hair, carefully combed away from his face. He'd toned it down a bit, blending gold and a few strands of honey blond in. She was glad that he didn't look too otherworldly. Still, a man like Darkmore would garner attention anywhere.

She was glad for that, too, and couldn't stop the smile and giggle in reaction.

"Good evening, Ms. Vivian," he said, offering a bow. He kept a gentle-manly distance, though he still gave her the once-over with his gaze. All of her. "You look stunning."

"You look pretty good yourself," she replied, "Oh, that reminds me, what are we going to call you tonight? Darkmore isn't...well, it isn't normal here, and we mortals tend to come with a first name."

"What did you have in mind?"

She stood aside and gestured for him to come inside. "I don't know. Do you have a first name, other than Lazarus? That's a bit...old-fashioned, too."

"I've had several."

"Several?" Vivian asked, turning to face him.

"Yes, several. I've lived many mortal lives."

Oh, now this was interesting!

"Well, which name was your favorite?" she asked, curiosity eclipsing her lingering anxiety.

He thought for a long moment and then said, "I was once known as Hesperus. It means evening star."

It fit. The man—no, the form he'd chosen—was breathtaking. Clearing her throat, she said, "Well, you don't look Greek and that really isn't a name you hear around these parts anyway. What else you got?"

"Hmm, I went by Aisly when I lived as a maiden in Britannia."

"What? You were a *woman*?" She almost shouted in surprise.

"Of course, Vivian. One cannot hope to understand the complexities of the human experience unless one has lived as both man and woman."

"I think I need to sit down for the rest of this conversation," she said, indicating that he should sit across from her in one of her old, oversize armchairs. He'd given her a lot of food for thought in the past few moments. How fascinating it must have been to live so many lives. What he must have seen, done, and experienced through the years, centuries, eons?

"Hey, how old are you anyway?"

"In human years? I cannot say. I have been around for a very long time."

"Did you start out as human? Were you born a man? How did you become a reaper?" Vivian supposed she shouldn't barrage him with so many questions, but she couldn't help herself. She was sure she'd have interesting company tonight, if nothing else. Of course, she'd worked out by now that his personal research on the human experience was probably a means to improve his skills as a grisly reaper.

He certainly knew his quarry well.

"As to your last question, I think I'll save the answer for another time, but yes, my origins were quite conventional. I was born the son of a slave in Mesopotamia a very long time ago and that is how I lived my first life."

If remembering his past affected him, Vivian couldn't tell. She didn't think it polite to ask directly, "Well, I guess that explains the name you use now. But you're so...blond." Foolish, but it was all she could think to say.

"One so ancient as I can shed the attachment to early physical incarnations. I find this form appealing. Don't you?"

"Oh, yes, you're quite a looker," she replied, trying not to blush. He smiled, so she guessed she hadn't succeeded. "Anyway, back to your name. How about Robert? Robert Darkmore?"

"Are you partial to that name, Vivian?" he asked, leaning back and giving her his best come-hither look.

"Cut it out," she said. "No, I'm not especially attached to the name, but it fits."

"How do you mean?"

"Well," she stammered. "I was thinking of Robert Redford."

He leaned forward and thought for a moment. She was afraid she'd offended him, or maybe he just didn't know who Robert Redford was. Then again, he'd said he liked westerns. *Butch Cassidy and the Sundance Kid* ringing any bells?

"Robert it is," he said with a nod. "Do you have any other concerns about this evening?"

"Yes. What if someone asks you how we met?"

"I'll just tell them it was through work," he replied with a wicked grin.

"Very funny," she shot back. "But that's actually not a bad cover. So you'll just tell them that you work in finance, then. No, wait, I've got it! You can say you're a repo man. That's not far from the truth."

"Repo man?"

"You know, repossession? That means you're the guy who gets stuff back when folks can't make their payments, like cars or boats."

"Ah, I see. That fits indeed. Am I your lover, or merely an acquaintance?"

Heat crept up her cheeks. "Let's just keep that a mystery," she replied with a smile.

He rose and took her hand, bidding her to do the same. Vivian tensed. She was sure he was going to kiss her, just as she was sure that she would respond. One of his talents was seduction, and he often used that along with his beauty and charm to bend the will of the living and newly dead to darkness. While she was drawn to him, Vivian was still doggedly determined to hold onto her free will. Instead, he placed another hand on the small of her back and guided her to the door.

"Oh, I should mention, I'll be needing your services the day after tomorrow," he said.

"What for?" she asked. She was on edge now, assuming that he was ready to collect the debt she owed him.

"Nothing you cannot handle, I assure you," he said with a smile. "I'll give you the details later. In the meantime, you should concern yourself with nothing other than enjoying this fine evening."

"Oh, hang on," Vivian said, scrambling back up the stairs, "I almost forgot Sue's gift." She grabbed the white envelope and dashed back to him as he held open the door.

"Such a small package," Darkmore commented as they walked toward his car. "You know, the last wedding I attended involved an exchange of livestock."

"Oh," Vivian said. She got distracted by the red Prius that was parked in her driveway. That induced another battle of the giggles. She had been expecting something more exotic. "Um," she continued, "well, I thought Sue and Jack might find a gift card more useful than a cow."

"Goats."

"Or goats," she conceded. "Do you dance?"

"Like Fred Astaire. Shall we?" He even held the door open for her and helped her in. Vivian heaved a deep breath and tried as hard as she could to relax and look forward to the night ahead.

———

They meandered toward Scarritt Bennett Center on foot, having opted for free parking some distance away. Vivian wasn't sure if he was being cheap or if he just wanted a chance to talk some more. At least his innate coolness was keeping her from sweating like a pig in the long bridesmaid gown.

"Oh, FYI, I don't want to know when anyone in attendance is going to die, or where they might be headed, except for maybe Jace," Vivian said.

"I can dispatch him for you, if you like," Darkmore replied, casually.

"No, no," she said. "Tempting as that sounds, I think I'd just like to avoid him until we have to walk down the aisle together."

"Fair enough."

"So, can I ask you something?"

He smiled. "You just did, but yes, I am willing to indulge your curiosity."

"Is it better to live as a man or as a woman?"

He laughed out loud before replying, "Dare I reply to such a question from you? You might strike me blind as Hera did Tiresias, depending on my answer and your own views on the subject. Both forms experience joy and sorrow in equal measure. If you wish to know my personal preference, I'd have to go with male, but I was born into a male body the first time around, so perhaps I am biased."

"Well aren't you diplomatic? You'd make a fine politician. Is that how you got the gift of foresight?"

"My, my, I'm impressed! To think I believed that all of the tales of old were forgotten. Foresight is part of the package for high-ranking reapers, guardians too. I have dabbled in politics from time to time, which has helped in my current occupation."

His grin turned mischievous. "Now it's my turn. Why did you ask me to accompany you to this event?"

Vivian thought for a moment. She didn't want to lie, since he'd probably know anyway, but she wasn't sure about all of the reasons herself. "For starters, Annabelle told me I had to take someone," she said.

"Annabelle?"

"My friend Kay's oldest daughter. Oh, speaking of, you won't scare any of the children there, will you?" Vivian asked.

"Of course not," he replied with a dash of indignation, "I prefer to spar with those capable of holding their own. Now, back to you. Did you seek my company based solely on the whim of a child?"

Persistent, aren't you?

"No. I didn't want to be alone, but I didn't want to just settle for some random guy. I thought you would be interesting company. Plus, I still owe you. I was hoping you'd have fun. Good enough?"

"Yes, that will do for now," Darkmore said, his gaze twinkling. Yeah, he saw right through her.

She was just about to breathe a sigh of relief when she spotted Boyd, Kay, and the kiddos heading their way. Slipping into panic mode, she struggled to psych herself up for the first in a series of what she thought would be awkward introductions.

Darkmore gave her hand a light squeeze. He then let go and sauntered over to Vivian's friends.

"What a delightful evening for a wedding," Darkmore drawled. Boyd and Kay stared at him and Kay couldn't seem to pick her jaw up off the sidewalk. Kaitlyn and Annabelle beamed and made a beeline for the reaper. Connor sulked beside his father. At first, Vivian thought he was probably sour at the prospect of keeping tidy and behaving like a civilized person. Then she realized that Junior was nowhere in sight.

He'd probably high-tailed it out when he saw Darkmore.

"Hiya," Kaitlyn said, forgoing her usual stranger anxiety. "Are you Aunt Vivian's date?"

"Yes, young mistress, I am," he said, stooping to the girl's level. "Is that quite all right with you?"

Kaitlyn considered as she eyed him with unabashed curiosity, the kind only a kid can manage. And get away with. "I guess, as long as you give up your evil ways, rescue her, and take her back home on time."

"Kate!" Annabelle scolded.

"What?" Kate asked as she shrugged her shoulders. "That's what Flynn Rider did in *Tangled*."

"I'm not familiar with that particular tale," Darkmore said, appearing to give the matter serious consideration. "Perhaps you could tell me more."

"Flynn starts out as a thief, but he's not really bad. He ends up rescuing Rapunzel from her mom. Well, she's not really her mom, she was just pretending, and then..."

Vivian watched and tried to stifle a chuckle while Darkmore listened to Kaitlyn's rambling plot summary. Annabelle gave Vivian the thumbs-up on the sly. Boyd and Kay still couldn't seem to put two sentences together.

"Mistress Kaitlyn, I promise I shall do my utmost to be worthy of your

Aunt Vivian's regard," Darkmore said as soon as he had the opportunity to get a word in.

"Oh, and you should probably kick Mr. Jace in the—"

"Kate, that's enough!" Mama Kay found her voice just in time.

"Ah, you must be the lovely Mrs. Clemmens," Darkmore said, rising and taking Kay's hand. "It is an honor to meet you. My name is Robert Darkmore."

"It's certainly...nice to meet you, too," Kay said, still flustered. Darkmore had that effect on people even when they weren't aware of his other-worldly status.

A red-faced Boyd stepped up and insinuated himself between his wife and the reaper. "Mr. Darkmore," he said, offering his hand in a very pointed way.

"Mr. Clemmens, I'm delighted to meet you and your lovely family," Darkmore replied, taking his hand and giving it a firm shake.

"So, you're looking out for our Vivian this evening?" Boyd asked.

"She's quite capable of holding her own. I am, however, in charge of her happiness for as long as she requires me," Darkmore said.

"All righty then," Vivian chimed in. "Time's a-wasting. Let's go and get you settled, *Robert*. I've got to do my duty and find Sue."

"Oh, we'd be happy to look after Mr. Darkmore for you," Annabelle said, trying her best to sound grown up.

"I'm not sure that's necessary—" Vivian began.

Boyd cut her off, "You're right, Vivian. Let's get inside and get you kids settled and let Vivian take care of her friend."

When Kay and the kids started to protest, Boyd continued, "I'm sure we'll have plenty of time to get to know all about Mr. Darkmore at the reception."

After the Clemmens family scurried off, Vivian turned to look at Darkmore. She was feeling a bit helpless at her friends' reactions and worried about how he'd feel. He simply looked amused, which made her feel a little better. At least he was having fun.

"Go on in," he said, bowing and planting a small kiss on her hand. "I'm sure I'll be fine on my own for a while."

It's not you I'm worried about. She thought twice before uttering that sentiment aloud.

"Hey, wait," she said, pulling him back. "I didn't even think to ask. Can you, um, you know, go into a church?"

Darkmore stared at her for a long moment, then turned and strolled right into the chapel looking like Lord High Smug, the show-off. God, he was going to give her a heart attack. Vivian took the scurrying option as she rushed off to find the bride and her witch of a sister. She carried with her the cool and refreshing feel of Darkmore's lips on her skin as she ran.

Along with the sparks of power flying from her fingertips.

CHAPTER NINETEEN

After Vivian found Sue and helped her squeeze into her undergarments and dress, which was a delicate operation to say the least given Sue's expanding waistline, Vivian found herself with more time to kill than she'd bargained or hoped for. At least Sarah managed to hold it together and not make her fear of Vivian obvious. She sensed it, and every now and then caught a wary or disapproving glance, but it was about as obtrusive as background noise from a distant radio. She could tune it out.

What she couldn't tune out was the feeling that had been tickling her innards for weeks. The tickling morphed into gnawing and she felt the urge to go outside and get her head on straight if she hoped to get through the next hour without blasting the hell out of someone in the wedding party.

She settled on ducking into one of the smaller corridors between buildings to avoid the gathering throngs in the main courtyard. Sue and Jack had a lot of friends and family. They were well on their way to having their own family soon enough. They had the home, the marriage, and the baby on the way, not to mention good jobs and a bright future. She was trying superhard to be happy for them and failing miserably.

Misery loved company, or in this case, it seemed to attract the type to bring more misery. Jace walked out of one of the side doors and made his way toward her. Vivian considered moving on, but sheer stubbornness kept her in place. He didn't own this particular space and she'd be damned if she'd leave it.

He looked her up and down, but managed to be respectful about it. It would have been less upsetting for her had he leered. "You look great, Vivian," he said with a smile.

"So do you," she replied. "You must have left your horns at home. Or does Sheila have them?"

"I suppose I deserved that, but she doesn't."

"Then she's definitely more than you deserve," Vivian said. She took some of the bite out of her voice. His apathy had deflated her anger a bit.

"You're probably right about that, too, but she makes me happy. What about this new man you brought along? He do right by you?" Jace asked. He seemed genuine in his concern.

"So far so good," she said. That was about as honest as she could get about Darkmore. She had to admit, though, it pleased her no end that Jace noticed and seemed worried about his replacement.

"Are we going to get through this like civilized people?" he asked. Again, he managed to ask without inspiring any anger. There was no accusation in his voice. She'd have to work harder, she reckoned, if she wanted to get a rise out of him.

"I can if you can. You'd better run along back to your young miss before she starts to fret," she replied.

He regarded her for a moment. She could tell he was mad and was fighting awfully hard to hide it. That would have been a turn-on and the beginning of some serious steam about a month back.

Not anymore.

"You know," he began with a sad, wry smile lifting to the corners of his mouth, "of all the things I miss about you, and believe me, there's a lot, I think I miss your fire most of all. It was worth all the rest while it lasted."

She shivered even before Darkmore put his hand on her bare shoulder. Had he just appeared? Jace looked a bit taken aback, but maybe it was just because he'd put his foot in his mouth.

"She is rather a live wire, is she not?" Darkmore purred. "And her worth is immeasurable. You must be Jace."

Vivian gulped and, remembering her manners, got on with the introductions. "Yes, um, this is Jace Blakemore. Jace, allow me to introduce Robert Darkmore."

Jace mumbled something along the lines of "nice to meetcha" before bowing out. Darkmore watched him the entire time. When they were alone once more, he gave Vivian his attention.

"You could always change your mind and secure my services, you know. According to your friend the priest's dogma, I'd be well within my rights. Treachery, synonymous with betrayal, is a mortal sin."

"So is lust, and by that rationale I am just as guilty and got what I deserved," Vivian said without emotion.

"Well, that particular sin doesn't rank quite so high." He stared at her with his intense blue eyes. "Still warring with yourself, I see," he said softly. "What shall I find in there in the way of other deadly sins?"

He sucked in a breath and closed his eyes to savor it, as one might a fine wine while trying to unravel its complexities.

"You won't find gluttony or sloth," she quipped with a dash of tartness. It was her go-to defense in uncomfortable situations. "I'm certainly not lazy!"

"Nor avarice," he murmured. "You have a healthy sense of pride and understandable envy with regard to the happy bride."

She gasped, abashed that he'd spoken her ugly little truth aloud.

"Don't beat yourself up about it, Vivian," he said, eyes opening. "As I said, it is understandable given your circumstances, and a natural human reaction. You should worry more about anger."

Eager to change the subject, she said, "But you didn't taste greed, huh? I thought greed and envy would be in the same flavor family."

"Not quite," he said. "You don't even realize how interesting that is, do you? You, who have been graced, or cursed as you might think, with remarkable powers, have yet to use them for personal gain or to harm others in any meaningful way."

The last he offered with a wink. She supposed Sarah would recover, then.

"That's me," she said with bitterness. "Selfless to a fault. A real giver."

"Why so glum?"

"Look how far it's gotten me," she said.

"Don't be too quick to dismiss this quality, Vivian. It may save you in the end."

Before Vivian could ask him what he meant, they were interrupted by the minister.

Showtime.

———

Vivian put on her best and brightest smile as she strolled down the aisle with her arm linked with her philandering ex's. It was amazing what a girl could accomplish when she put her mind to it. In Vivian's case, she pictured Jace neck-deep in a frozen lake, screaming in agony while wolves chewed on his face. That was all Darkmore's doing, no doubt. He certainly painted a vivid mental image.

The ceremony itself was short and sweet. Vivian cried along with Sue and Jack as they promised to love, honor, and cherish one another until death they parted. She had to wonder if they could find their way back to one another from beyond the grave someday. She'd seen some spirit "couples" holding hands and appearing for all the world, at least to those who could perceive them, as being deeply in love.

Whether they'd found one another after crossing from the land of the living was still a mystery.

Some of her tears were for those who'd lost their loves, and who still might. She spared a tear or two for Kay and Boyd, hoping they'd find a way to mend their marriage. She spared a few more for her parents, who would have loved to witness such a beautiful ceremony.

She cried for Zeke, too, and the raw, gaping wound he'd left in her heart.

While the ceremony was short, the staged and stilted photography session just after soon became as painful to Vivian as her forced smile and cramped toes. She couldn't believe how long this apparent Annie Leibovitz wannabe was taking. Plus, she was antsy and worried about how Darkmore was getting along. Now that the reverent part of the ceremony was over, she knew he'd be swarmed by curious family and friends, not to mention single horny women. Maybe a few married ones, too, judging from Kay's reaction.

She wasn't sure how she felt about this hypothetical attention.

"Just a few more, I promise. You're doing great," Sue whispered. It was then that Vivian realized she'd been frowning.

"Sorry," Vivian muttered.

"Don't be. We'll get you back to that tall drink of water in no time," Sue teased.

"Stop it," Vivian whispered back, hissing.

"What?" Sue said, feigning innocence.

"Keep that up and I'll work in a jibe about you wearing white during my toast," Vivian shot back.

"Ladies, ladies, let's focus," said Ms. Taskmaster. "We're losing the light and I want to get some nice sunset shots."

Vivian wished for a Snickers bar, since she clearly wasn't going anywhere for a while.

A flash of white caught her attention in the periphery, chased by radiant warmth. No, this could not be happening. She wouldn't let it happen.

"It's so hot out here," Sue whispered before flashing another bright smile for the camera.

Vivian couldn't breathe, she couldn't think. All she could do was stand in front of the camera, frozen and terrified, hoping the rogue guardian wouldn't unleash his fury on her family and friends before she could summon Darkmore.

Or before she was forced to abandon all pretense and attack in the open.

CHAPTER TWENTY

By the time they arrived at the Union Station Hotel, Vivian was a bundle of nerves on the verge of exploding. She'd barely uttered a word in the car. Between lingering worry over the rogue spirit who might or might not decide to crash her best friend's wedding reception and the reaper who'd be forced to wreak havoc if the guardian did show up, she had a lot on her mind. It certainly made keeping up appearances difficult.

There were more than a few cracks in her fragile façade of calm.

If this bothered Darkmore, he didn't let on. He observed the speed limit, obeyed all traffic signals, and had the good grace to let folks merge. The only time he spoke during the drive was to tell Vivian that she was magnificent during the ceremony.

She didn't feel magnificent, but she appreciated the sentiment.

She'd hoped to have a few moments to brief Darkmore on modern etiquette in the parking lot, but he opted for valet. He offered his arm and she took it, gripping a little too tightly. He smiled, winked, and together they walked into to building for the reception, him looking about as happy as a tick on a fat dog.

Vivian was astounded. The room was full. If there were a fire marshal of the spiritual persuasion, he'd be lighting a fire under the dead to get them the hell out of the room. Departed spirits lingered, floated, and walked among the living as far as her gaze could reach.

Vivian ducked down a corridor and tried her damnedest not to hyperventilate.

Darkmore didn't try to coddle her this time, which was good. He did speak quietly and send rays of cool, calming blue light her way. Vivian devoured them and felt slightly better. When she could speak, she asked, "Who invited undead Nashville?"

Darkmore chuckled. "It wasn't me, I can assure you." He slid down the wall and sat beside her. She was grateful for the time to recuperate, and also for the fact that she wasn't alone.

"They're here for the party," Darkmore continued. "Festivities, especially milestones like births, marriages, or deaths, tend to draw spirits. Some are relations, no doubt. Others are simply lonely and wish to be close to vitality."

He leaned closer and whispered in her ear, his breath causing shivers that had nothing at all to do with the cold. "And I do believe a few have come to see you, Vivian."

"Why on Earth would they want to see me?" she asked.

"You are becoming rather famous in our circles. We don't get many living souls mingling with us. They are curious, too. Some want to gawk, some would like your assistance, and others wish to protect you. In spite of the reluctance of the guardian council to accept you into the fold, most don't take kindly to a rogue in their ranks."

"Good to know," she said. "Not that I'm not grateful for the support and protection, but I don't think I can make it through the rest of the night if I have to be worried about sorting the living from the dead."

God, she hated feeling so helpless, and she didn't want to ask him for more help.

Wait, maybe I don't need help with this one.

She closed her eyes and silently sent out a mental text, opening her mind wide so that all of the spirits waiting just around the corner would pay attention. The little jolts of electricity she felt coursing through her made her think it was working.

. . .

Hey, folks, I'm glad to see so many of your kind are here to celebrate Sue's big day, and I'm really and truly honored that so many of you want to know me and protect me.

Fortunately, she didn't have to say it out loud, though it was damned awkward. Conversations in one's head often were.

Here's the thing, though. I'm still not used to coping with so many of the dead, especially in a room full of the living. I might get confused and slip up, or I might not be able to get through my toast to the bride. I hate to ask, but would you mind staying out of sight for a few hours? I promise I'll make a graceful exit early and let you get back to the party after I leave.

She waited. Nothing. None of them disappeared or exited stage right. Or left. They all just stood rooted to the spot. Closing her eyes, she sighed and gave it one last shot.

Please? I'd be happy to meet with you a few at a time over the next few weeks. Just give Ezra or Jeanne a shout. They manage me.

She was pretty sure that she'd laughed at the last. She waited, afraid to open her eyes.

"I do believe that did the trick, Vivian," Darkmore said when she finally took a peak. He was only an inch or two away from her face. She lowered her gaze and he rolled back on his heels.

"Shall I go make certain?"

"No," she muttered, knowing perfectly well that he could track any spirit for a few miles, if not more.

"Then, please, will you do me the honor of escorting me into the reception? I'm famished!"

Great. Another hungry corporeal spirit.

Feeling a little less than confident, Vivian stood and took Darkmore's hand, pausing only to fuss over her dress. It was wrinkled, of course, but it probably would have been by night's end anyhow. They walked at a stately pace, even when she tried to rush things along. Darkmore stopped and bid her take in her surroundings. The dark wood tones, low recessed lighting, and the sweeping arches of the vaulted ceiling were warm and inviting. Vivian couldn't help thinking that it must have been a bitch to renovate and modernize, but she was glad they'd left the old clock and the board with the train schedule as a nod to the past.

It seemed to just stand still, observing, without doing anything. Darkmore didn't appear to mind. Then again, he had oodles of time relative to her short existence. He probably spent a great deal of time just watching and waiting for the right moment to swoop down and steal souls. No, that wasn't fair. He didn't steal them. The souls to which he could stake a claim deserved it.

It was easier to swallow, however, when one didn't know the soul personally.

She couldn't make herself believe that Zeke had deserved damnation, no matter what he'd done in life. That was probably why Darkmore had warned her not to make things personal. God, she hadn't been a saint herself, and the guardians had certainly found her to be less than saintly these days.

And here she was, cavorting with a reaper and enjoying his company. What did that say about her?

"Shall we mingle?" Darkmore asked.

"Let's," Vivian replied. In for a penny, in for a pound.

The reception was casual in the sense that everyone was able to hit the buffet line and sit where they pleased before the toasts and speeches. Vivian's went off without a hitch, save a few more tears. In spite of her envy, she expressed her sincere wish—and it was sincere—for a lifetime of happiness and love for her dear friends, Sue and Jack.

She tuned out for Sarah's speech.

Darkmore proved to be quite adept at social graces for a non-Southerner. He tolerated the prying questions and artfully evaded those that proved to be too personal, or uncomfortable for Vivian. Boyd warmed to him after a lively discussion about football. Jace shot surreptitious glances their way when he wasn't chatting up Sheila or the friends that they apparently now shared. She wondered if she'd ever be comfortable with them. She decided to leave that question for another day once the music began.

Apparently she'd spent so much time immersed in her own personal angst that she'd missed the cake cutting. If she was ever going to get back to normal, Vivian figured she'd have to work harder at living in the here and now.

She faced the last Jace hurdle when he asked her to dance to the second song, just after the bride and groom christened the floor with Shania's "Still the One." It was a good song for Jack and Sue, given their history. Edwin McCain's "I'll Be" played second. Vivian would have preferred "Your Cheating Heart," for her obligatory appearance on the dance floor with her ex, but it wasn't her call. Swallowing some more of her pride, she accepted his proffered hand and they joined Jack and Sue, as well as Sarah and her husband James. She noticed that Sarah looked more relaxed, even happy in the arms of her husband.

Interesting.

Jace didn't talk, thank God. He held her at a comfortable distance and Vivian was surprised to find that she felt...nothing. Jealousy lingered just below the surface, and she was certain she could muster it along with righteous indignation, but swaying to soft music with the man she'd once considered spending her life with—she was blessed with indifference.

Did Darkmore do that, or did she?

Darkmore tapped Jace on the shoulder, and her ex let the reaper cut in. Vivian took his hand and found that he hadn't lied about being able to dance like Fred Astaire.

She certainly didn't feel indifferent while they moved in time to Smokey and the Miracles.

"Are you having a good time?" Vivian asked.

"Of course. Did you think I would not?" Darkmore said in her ear. His cool breath made her shiver.

"I don't know. I guess I just figured you'd had much more interesting company in all of your years." Wow, that was pathetic. Was she seriously fishing?

"Define 'interesting.'"

"Kings? Queens? Great warriors? Intellectuals? Take your pick," she tried not to sound small.

"Ah, some things never change. You mortals reckon relative value on a different scale than we do," he replied, spinning her around in a way that made her appear to possess more poise and grace than she could've ever claimed on her own.

"Really?" she said after catching her breath.

"Certainly. Beneath the surface, you are all the same, really. The same flesh, sinew, and bone. Strip away the trappings of mortal glory and what's left?"

"So all souls are the same?"

"I didn't say that," he said, his gaze growing intense.

"Then what are you saying?"

"Death is the great equalizer. I've encountered bland kings and delightfully rich beggars. I have indulged in carnal discourse with all manner of mortals, as well as more celestial exchanges. What merits consideration in the afterlife has little to do with wealth or talent, nor even great deeds as far as you would consider them noteworthy—though deeds matter, of course."

"I see," she said, considering. It made sense. So the question that remained was—what did merit consideration? And interest.

"Why don't you ask me what you really want to know, Vivian?"

"Why don't you tell me, since you apparently already know?"

It seemed their standoff would continue a bit longer, since the music changed and allowed Darkmore to show off even more fancy footwork. Vivian wasn't an easy lead. She'd been told enough and she knew from her few forays into dance lessons that it was true. Darkmore managed quite nicely, though, leaving her breathless and exhilarated after three more songs.

"Lazarus," Vivian said when she'd recovered, "I want you to do something for me. Walk over there to Kay and ask her to dance. I want you to make her feel like the most beautiful woman in the world, like she's treasured and worth more than her weight in gold. Think you can do that for me?"

Darkmore did as Vivian requested, which gave her the chance to grab a drink of water and visit the ladies' room. She wasn't at all surprised to find it full of spirits. She was, however, surprised to find Junior there.

"Junior, what the hell? You shouldn't be here, especially in the women's restroom," she scolded.

He looked sheepish, but shrugged. "This is as close to women as I can get."

Men! Dead or alive, they were all perverts.

"And you can just mosey on outta here right now while I take care of my business. Alone."

"Why are you with that reaper?" Junior asked.

He seemed scared. She couldn't blame him, really. He was unaffiliated and had spent a lot of time worrying about whether his suicide had condemned him to eternal damnation.

In his position, Vivian would be looking over her shoulder, too.

"Because I needed a date and he said yes," Vivian replied. "He's not here on business and he's not here for you. Besides, you're looking better and better by the day. You're practically a guardian already."

It was true. She could see him clearly now from head to toe. He wasn't corporeal, but it was a start.

"Jeanne's been talking to me about, you know, working with them," Junior said with obvious hope.

"That's great," Vivian replied, trying to be happy for him. "Just be sure to read the fine print on the contract."

He gave her a quizzical look but then shook it off. "All right. You sure you're going to be okay with the reaper?"

"His name is Darkmore, and yes, I will. You trust me, right?"

"'Course I do! Can I peek in on Scooter?"

"Go for it. I'm sure he's driving the nanny crazy right about now."

Vivian was just stepping out of the ladies' room when she ran into Kay, who looked out of breath and a bit overwhelmed, but still glowed. Darkmore must have done his job quite well.

"Vivian," she gasped, dragging her by the arm and leading her to a couple of unoccupied chairs in the lobby. She sat across from Vivian and stared a hole through her with glittering eyes. "Your Mr. Darkmore...he's quite a dancer!"

"Don't I know it," Vivian said.

Speaking of Darkmore... "So, where'd you leave him?"

She waved a hand in the general direction of the reception area, a serene smile still painted across her face. She'd have to thank the reaper for going above and beyond the call of duty.

When she arrived back at the reception, she was surprised and a little miffed to find Darkmore deep in conversation with Sarah. Now she'd have to go and talk to the witch if she wanted to get her date back. And she'd have to resist the temptation to zap her.

Watching from a distance, she spotted the thin stream of pale red light that he drew from her and smiled in spite of herself. Of course he'd be hungry. Human food was one thing, but Darkmore needed the sustenance of raw human emotion, the uglier the better.

She could hardly blame him. Sarah was a smorgasbord.

She kept watching until Sarah's hand landed on the reaper's arm. That was enough. Vivian marched over and put on her best fake smile, saying, "Sarah, I see you've met my date, Mr. Robert Darkmore."

"I have," she purred. She didn't even have the decency to act afraid. Not until Vivian shot a few eye-bullets her way. "Robert was kind enough to rescue me from a few of my more eccentric aunts."

Eccentric was code for batshit crazy. *Look who's talking.*

"I see," Vivian replied. "I'll be taking him back now, if you don't mind. I figure we have about another thirty minutes before your folks start requesting Ronnie Milsap and I want to be out of here by then. Shall we?"

"Of course," Darkmore said, winking at her. "I'll see you around, Mrs. Harrow."

They walked back to the dance floor and enjoyed more slow songs. She allowed herself to lean into him a little more and to enjoy the closeness. He must have enjoyed it as well, since he pulled her in and started stroking her back with his long, talented fingers. She found herself wishing they had a room waiting upstairs. But they didn't.

Probably for the best—fantasy was one thing, but risking her body, and if she was being honest, her heart with the reaper was quite another.

They made their goodbyes and rode back to her house with little conversation, and she was left with the nagging thoughts typical for any really good date. Would he kiss her? Should she kiss him? Would it lead to other things? Was he even interested in her beyond her powers and the fact that she was a "food source?"

He handed her out of the car and walked to her front doorstep. She was tense and figured he must have been, too, since she was feeling his chill. She looked at him and waited.

"Thank you for the lovely evening, Vivian," he said, low and smooth. "I haven't had a night out in a very long time."

"I doubt that's true," she said.

"Touché, dear lady. To be more specific, I haven't had a night out for the sole purpose of my own pleasure in a very long time. I tend to be a bit of a workaholic, you know," he said, stepping closer.

"Well, you know what they say about all work and no play?" she whispered. Then she gulped.

It must have been the sign he was waiting for, since he closed the distance between them, pressing her to the door and placing his lips on hers. They were cool, but she didn't think she'd have to worry about temperature. It was the kind of searing cold that burned and she pulled him closer and grabbed the nape of his neck with such force that he snarled. Kissing the reaper was incredible. He had to throw her off with some force when he decided to break the kiss.

When she could catch her breath, all she could ask was, "Why?"

"I'm old-fashioned," Darkmore said. He was a little breathless, too. "I'll not have you yet. Not until you know what it is to be mine."

"What if I don't want to wait?" she asked.

He closed his eyes and turned his face up to the night sky. He seemed to be drawing in the tangible world around him, tasting the air and the earth. It was humid tonight. Rain was just around the corner. If she had to guess, she reckoned he was warring with himself a little as well. She didn't think that happened very often. He opened his bright blue eyes and regarded her, having reached some decision.

"You have unfinished business. We'll continue ours in a few days' time. I'll find you then."

Then he disappeared in a burst of scarlet light.

CHAPTER TWENTY-ONE

Stunned and disoriented, she walked into her home, shut the door, and locked it. She didn't bother with the lights. Reality seemed bright and harsh enough.

While she wasn't the type of girl to put stock in fairy tales, and she'd convinced herself that Darkmore wasn't a suitable suitor, she had to admit that his departure hurt. She'd been hoping that this strange and magical night would last a bit longer. Maybe a lot longer. They could have cooled off long enough to sit and talk for a bit.

He could have come in for a cup of coffee or a nightcap, at the very least.

She stood in her foyer and pondered the state of her romantic life, along with life in general, and didn't like what she saw. If she had any prospects at all, surely a corporeal spirit would have to be it. Her attempts with normal, breathing men—okay, *one* attempt—hadn't worked out. Would any other mortal be willing to make the sacrifice it would take to be with her, not to mention the energy that she owed to dwellers of the great beyond? He'd have to sacrifice a family, at least for the foreseeable future. It would be too dangerous. Any guardian, reaper, or pissed-off spirit would just have to threaten a child of hers and it would be over. She'd destroy that spirit or die trying, and their child would wind up dying and going...who knew where?

Not a pretty picture, to say the least.

Sighing, Vivian walked to her bedroom, allowed her grateful feet to slide out of the pumps she'd worn, and slipped out of the gown. Looking in the mirror, she removed the delicate undergarments as well and stood naked in the half-light cast by the bathroom light she'd left on. Her hair was still in place, and the makeup and illumination played well with her features. She could almost feel the sensation of Darkmore's fingers caressing her arm as they danced. Her lips still burned.

No need to start something that won't be finished.

Slipping on her robe, she padded to the kitchen to seek some liquid consolation.

Outside, the rain fell hard and fast as it often did in early summer. The rumbling thunder moved closer. Flashes of white pierced the darkness of her kitchen as she poured a shot of smooth, dark whiskey into her glass. She didn't bother to chase it, taking a long draw instead and letting the burn slip down her throat and warm her body. She'd left her windows cracked and could hear the wind whipping through her maples and jostling her deck chairs. Closing her eyes, she smelled the earth and damp musk released from the ground by the relentless pounding of the rain. That earthy, primal scent beckoned her and she imagined the porous ground as it drank in every drop, pulling it deep within until saturated, sated. Another flash, this one closer.

Vivian was not alone.

Her first instinct to spin and fire in all directions, but she stood paralyzed by fear. Her bravado evaporated as the reality of her situation sank in. She'd been stupid. She was alone, unprotected, and he knew it, the rogue guardian who'd surely chosen this moment to strike.

Her battle with her guardians, dismissal of the other wayward spirits that night, and Darkmore's departure had left her defenseless save for her own powers. She doubted she could control them enough to defeat an experienced guardian. Maybe she could subdue the rogue until help arrived or she could escape. All of this careened through her mind in the space of seconds. Another flash.

He was there.

He lurked in the shadows of her kitchen, a tall and imposing figure. Sparks flew from her fingertips. No flight. He was too close. She'd have to fight. She stood her ground.

Another flash.

He was bare. She'd seen enough to know that he'd arrived fully corporeal and ready. The air around them was thick and redolent with mutual anticipation mingled with fear and...heat. It was a familiar heat, one she thought she'd never feel again. She wanted that heat like she'd never wanted anything in her life.

She wanted *him*.

Fear morphed into longing as her greatest desire stood just out of reach. *Come to me now.*

He was on her and she saw raw hunger his green eyes.

Lust, anger, and fear intermingled with disbelief and primal need. He didn't utter a word. Lifting her onto the kitchen counter, he slipped her robe off, leaned her back, and was inside of her in the space of a heartbeat.

Vivian shrieked and he roared. Forcing her body up to meet him, her mouth located his and she attacked, unleashing wave after wave of passion. He growled and pushed her back down, pinning her shoulders to the granite and holding her immobile as he impaled her. She managed to break free so she could grip his back, clawing him from shoulders to his ass to spur him on. His relentless movements didn't let up until she convulsed beneath him.

She couldn't breathe, but she used adrenaline to her advantage and pushed hard against him even as he pinioned within her. Pausing long enough to raise her and allow her to wrap her arms and legs around him, he lifted her again, still joined, and moved them to the kitchen table. He broke a vase of flowers in the process.

She clung to his neck and shoulders with all of her might as he pushed her back down. She tried to find his mouth again, but he was insistent.

"Don't fight me, Vivian," was all he said.

She wanted to fight him. To scream and rage at him for leaving her, to beg him to never leave again.

To grovel and beg his forgiveness for sending him away.

She relented and leaned back on the table, bracing herself for him. She rested on her elbows and found some leverage, but he made it clear that he was in charge. It seemed to be what he needed. She cried out as he began to move within her at a furious pace. Tears streamed from the corners of her eyes. Her back ached. He kept going and going and she didn't want it to end, even when her arms screamed for her to let them down. She came again and came hard. He soon followed and collapsed on her. She drank in the light that emanated from his spent form.

She hadn't realized how thirsty she'd been until she took his light. It coursed through her and filled her. She wasn't sated, but the night was young yet.

They lay together a long while in silence while recovering and shuddering with aftershocks. She couldn't think of anything to say yet. She simply wanted to stay there forever. With him. But she was getting really sore. She tried to nudge him so she could shift to a more comfortable position, but he pushed her back and embraced her with a ferocity she'd never felt from him before.

In the end, she surrendered.

"Fine, Zeke. You win."

———

The rain still pounded when she first awoke, though the thunder was more distant. It was still dark. The clock on her nightstand read 3:08 a.m. *Zeke must have carried me to bed.*

"Zeke," she cried out, stiffening. She sat bolt upright and cast her gaze about in the darkness, fearful that it was all a dream. Or maybe he'd left. But it was still warm.

"I'm here," came a voice in the dark.

"Where are you?"

"Over here," he said. As her eyes adjusted, she made out his outline and the contours of his body. He sat in her mother's rocking chair, which occupied one corner of her bedroom. He didn't move a muscle. She found his stillness more unnerving than his earlier aggression. She threw back the covers, seeking some relief from the rising temperature.

"Why are you all the way over there?" she asked.

"I was watching you," came his reply.

She wanted to grab him and pull him close to her. *You came back to me!* Something about his demeanor held her back. Anxiety crept through the thin veil of peace, threatening to tear it to pieces.

She didn't go to him. She waited.

"You were with the reaper tonight," he said. It wasn't a question.

"He's helping me, Zeke," she said. She tried to remain calm. "There are some things you should know. He's been an insurance policy against Ezra and he's been helping me track down a guardian who's out to get me. I'd like to tell you about it. I...God, I've wanted to talk to you for so long."

"I'm listening."

She took in a deep breath and told him everything. It took a while. He'd been away for a year. She looked at the clock again, which now read 4:27 a.m. It felt cooler. She didn't know if that was good or bad.

"Will you come here beside me?" she asked. She hoped her voice didn't sound as small as she felt.

She waited, cloaked in a blanket of guilt. She didn't know where it came from or why she felt it, but guilt persisted. Tears threatened, and she closed her eyes to hide them.

Come back to me. Please, oh please come back to me.

After a moment, strong arms enveloped her, holding her in a vise grip. She returned the embrace, tears falling freely. His sweltering heat dissipated, replaced by the welcome simmer of comfort.

"You were kissing him," Zeke whispered into her hair.

"I thought you were lost to me, that you'd gone someplace better. I—"

"I didn't like you kissing him," he said. He released her from his fierce embrace long enough to claim her mouth. He was still possessive. At that moment, she was more than happy to be claimed.

When she stopped to catch her breath, she asked, "How did you get back? Will you stay? Can we—"

It was difficult to speak with strong hands stroking her tender flesh.

"He's been here, too. In your bedroom," Zeke said, his voice roughened with anger or desire, perhaps both.

"Nothing h-h-happened," she gasped. Zeke had clever fingers.

"Nothing like this," he hissed as she groaned. He had a clever tongue, too.

"Zeke," she whispered. There was so much she wanted to say, reassurances to be given and received. All she could manage was, "Stay with me, please."

"Shh," he whispered. "Talk later. Love now."

CHAPTER TWENTY-TWO

There was something deliciously sinful about fucking on your kitchen table and then having your friends over for lunch. She and Zeke had managed to christen every place setting over the past few nights. She couldn't stop smiling, though she felt a little pang of guilt. Then again, she *did* clean and disinfect the table before serving lunch, so she gave herself full permission to enjoy the private joke.

The guilt and confusion she experienced whenever she thought of the reaper was much harder to bear. Still, she tried to focus on the bliss. Zeke had come back to her. That's all that mattered.

"You seem relaxed," Kay offered with a knowing smile.

Vivian smiled back but didn't offer any details. It was killing her, since Kay was one of two living persons who knew about her ghost lover, but she hadn't had a chance to tell her that he'd come back. She could tell Kay. She wanted to tell Kay, but something niggled at the back of her mind and stilled her tongue.

"Give me a hand with these, will you?" Vivian said, handing Kay one tray of deviled eggs.

"You think there's any room left on the table?" Kay muttered, balancing the tray with one hand while using the other to slide a plate of sliced honey ham out of the way.

"I don't want anyone to go home hungry," she said.

No danger there. She had enough to feed a small army. An army of aunts, Sue's in particular. Sue Carlson-Jameson's father's sisters were funny about weddings and funerals. They never attended. So Vivian agreed to host a luncheon for them and the newlyweds, along with a few other close friends and family, before the Jamesons left for their honeymoon in Vegas.

"So," Kay began. "Are you just going to keep grinning like a fool or are you going to tell me what happened with your friend Mr. Darkmore?"

Another pang of guilt stabbed her in the gut. "It's a little complicated," Vivian said. The ringing doorbell chimed to announce a reprieve from her interrogation. "Look, I'll tell you all about it later, I promise."

"Just a hint," Kay whispered.

"Zeke's back," she blurted out. The look on Kay's face was priceless. It felt wonderful to say it out loud. She wondered why she'd been so hesitant.

"We *will* talk more about this later," Kay said. Her voice left no room for argument.

Vivian scampered to the door to bid Sue, Jack, and Aunts Hazel and Etta welcome. Boyd arrived with the kids in tow shortly after, as did Father Montgomery. His appearance was unexpected. Though he tried to politely bow out when he realized that Vivian had company, she yanked him inside, offered him some sweet tea, and introduced him all around.

The aunts' reaction alone was worth it. They didn't trust Catholics. Vivian could see the wheels turning beneath silvery gray up-dos. They were probably torn between grudging approval of Vivian's interest in religion and suspicion that she'd corrupted the older gentleman in the Biblical sense.

The priest himself seemed more somber than normal, which gave Vivian pause.

Between the heart-attack-on-a-plate Southern fare and the Clemmens' kids' antics, Vivian didn't notice the pointed stares of the padre until it came time to pass around the banana pudding. Junior had been flitting through the kitchen and waving, but she'd assumed he was just entertaining Scooter. Then he wound himself around the light fixture above her kitchen table and flashed a note reading: "Trouble coming."

Great. So much for a normal day.

She shot him a helpless look, which prompted him to whisper something in Scooter's ear.

And then all hell broke loose in Vivian Bedford's home.

Scooter slid under the table. That in and of itself wasn't unusual given his age and general tendency toward mischief. But Scooter didn't squeak. Something else had.

When he emerged from under the table he bore a wicked grin and an agitated rodent.

"Mama, Aunt Vee Vee, look! I got mouse! I got a mouuuuuuuuuuuse!" he cried with delight.

Kay screamed, "Connor, put it down before it bites you!"

For once, Connor listened to his mother and plopped the mouse down onto the table. The dazed rodent sat frozen until Boyd's failed attempt to whack it with a serving spoon. It somersaulted over the mashed potatoes and straight into Aunt Etta's lap.

Aunt Etta screamed as she stood and knocked over her chair, which fell on Annabelle and knocked her to the floor. Boyd continued his pursuit with the serving spoon, joined by Jack, both men uttering colorful combinations of foul language that would make their wives blush later and would no doubt be repeated by at least one of Boyd's children.

Aunt Hazel pushed her ample frame into the corner of the kitchen while Vivian ran and snatched up her broom.

"Jack, block the doorway," Vivian yelled as she tried to herd the vermin toward him. It zigzagged in a serpentine pattern in response and they almost lost it under a loose board below her lower cabinets.

With agility borne of maternal instinct or, perhaps, from her college years running cross-country, Sue leapt and slammed a bowl over the mouse. Boyd and Jack scooped it up and went out back to release it while Connor moaned and whined to have it back.

The whole fiasco accomplished putting an early end to the party, which had apparently been Junior's intent. Jack and Sue packed up the agitated aunts while Boyd gathered the kids. Kay offered to stay behind and clean-up, which left her with Vivian and the padre.

Junior opted to accompany Connor, which would probably make

Boyd's drive a little more serene—okay, a lot more serene. It also saved Junior from the exorcism Vivian had planned for the troublesome spirit once she got her hands on him again.

A dollop of gooey yellow pudding dropped onto her shoulder, apparently having fallen from the ceiling. Vivian sighed. Apparently, the exorcism would have to wait.

———

Vivian brewed some coffee. After she served her remaining guests, she settled on the love seat across from Kay and the priest, who shared the sofa. She took a moment to enjoy the confused and anxious look on Father Montgomery's face.

"Don't worry, Padre," Vivian said. "You can speak freely in front of Kay. She knows all about my friends from the other side."

"I'm glad you have a confidant," Father Montgomery offered. "And someone else to look out for you. It seems you need it."

Oh, boy. Here we go.

Both Kay and the padre spoke at once, leaving Vivian lost in the cacophony of warning voices. She made out the words "trouble," "reaper," and "Zeke," but nothing more. Holding up a hand, she was about to ask them to speak in turn. They ignored her though, as they began speaking to one another.

"Wait, Robert Darkmore is a *reaper?*" Kay asked with a touch of disbelief.

"Ezekiel is back?" the padre asked simultaneously, his brow furrowed.

"Hello, I'm still in the room!" Vivian shouted over them. "What's all the fuss about?"

"Vivian," the padre began, keeping a low tone and level voice, "you've been summoned before the guardian council. Ezra sent me to tell you."

"Why? And what does that mean" Vivian asked as anxiety pierced her gut like a thousand tiny knives. "And why isn't the old coot here to tell me himself?"

"I don't know the answer to your last question. As to the first...perhaps it has something to do with the company you've been keeping," he answered.

"My company is my business. Ezra doesn't own me, the guardians don't own me, and part of my keeping company with Darkmore is to make certain of that," she said as she hopped up off the couch.

"While I'm certain you believed you had good reasons for turning to Darkmore, I am very worried about the consequences," the priest said. "He is not to be trusted. He—"

"He's a reaper?" Kay repeated, realization dawning, "Oh my God, you mean he's the kind who drags souls off to Hell?"

"Well, technically no," Vivian said. "It's more like a form of Purgatory."

"But Vivian, what on Earth are you doing with some...some *thing* like that?" Kay asked, a look of horror blooming on her face.

"Look, I know it sounds bad, but he's been protecting me." Vivian paced around her living room as she tried to explain the inexplicable.

"From what?" Kay asked.

"From one of the so-called 'good' guardians. One of them doesn't approve of my extracurricular activities and he's decided to threaten me and my loved ones, like the padre here," Vivian said, gesturing to Father Montgomery. "That's why I turned to a reaper."

"But, Vivian, what you told me about last year," Kay said, gulping. "About that place you went, that terrible, dark place—he was the one who took you there, right?"

"I know, I know," Vivian replied, trying to think of a way to explain. "He started out that way, and I'm still afraid of him sometimes, but after we sorted things out with Ezra's cosmic debt, he's been helping me."

"Helping?"

"Yeah," Vivian said. She stopped pacing and stood before her friend. Taking a deep breath, she started, "Remember the other night when I came by and helped you?"

"How can I forget it?" Kay asked. She looked a little embarrassed, but the priest reached over and squeezed her hand, then nodded to Vivian so she could continue.

"You know how you felt better after I took in that light from you?" Vivian asked.

"Yes," Kay replied with a bit of caution.

"Well, that's how I was able to make your burden lighter."

"Come again?"

"I'm not sure exactly how it works," Vivian said. "But guardians, reapers, and, well, me...we can channel spirit energy through light. The spirits collect and use life force energy when souls cross, but my talents are a little different."

Kay blinked, apparently struggling to process the impossible.

"I can channel energy from the living through emotion. I take in burdens—suffering—from the living through light energy."

"You mean you were able to feel what I was feeling? Know what I was thinking?" Kay asked, clearly mortified.

"I wasn't trying to pry and I can't read your mind," Vivian reassured her friend. "But I can feel the pain from the burdens that I carry."

"How do you manage?" Kay asked.

"That's where Darkmore comes in. He stops by from time to time to relieve me of those burdens."

Father Montgomery gave her a sharp look and asked, "You mean Darkmore has been taking them off your hands all this time?"

"Yes," Vivian admitted. She felt as though she was sitting on the witness stand being grilled by a ruthless prosecutor. "You didn't think I was keeping all of that stuff inside me, did you?"

"No, I was under the impression that it was Ezra's responsibility to help you with...disposal."

"Well, Ezra isn't all that responsible, in case you hadn't noticed. Besides," Vivian said with a shrug, "reapers feed off suffering."

"You mean he *likes* it? That's just awful," Kay said, shuddering.

"It's not like that," Vivian said. Her automatic defense of the reaper should probably have troubled her more than it did. "It's his job to dole out suffering to those who make others suffer. If he comes calling on you, odds are you've done something to deserve it. And like I said, he's been helping track the rogue guardian and he's delivered some useful information, not to mention his protection."

"But to what end?" the priest asked, his voice pleading. "I was there with you in his dark world last year, remember? He wanted to own you and claim your soul."

"Vivian," Kay tried to chime in.

"And what did Ezra want to do? What right did he have to interfere with my life like that?" Vivian's pent-up resentment broke through the barrier she'd constructed over the last year.

"Guardians aren't any better than us, any better than the reapers. Look at all of the souls they've left behind to rot here in Limbo. You've seen them, Father. Not all of them want to stick around here. And one of their own attacked you."

"Vivian," Kay spoke again.

"I don't pretend to have all of the answers, Vivian, but I think you should talk to Ezra and trust his judgment—" the priest said.

"He lied to me from the first moment I met him," Vivian said, her volume rising with her anger, giving voice to the outrage she'd felt since his betrayal came to light. "He almost cost me Zeke."

"Vivian!" Once Kay had their attention, she asked, "What do you know about the guardian who's after you?"

She hadn't expected that question. She was ready to go off on the padre again, but Kay had caught her up short. She took a few deep breaths and sat down again before she spoke.

"He doesn't like what I'm doing, apparently," she answered, wondering where this was going. "I have no idea why, aside from the fact that the guardians want to keep their power structure intact and want to control me."

"Was Zeke a guardian?" Kay asked.

"Yes," Vivian said with a note of caution. "He was training with Ezra. Why?"

"Ezra claimed him from Darkmore," Father Montgomery added quietly.

"What are you getting at?" Vivian asked.

"So Zeke did something to deserve the likes of the grim reaper?" Kay asked.

"No," Vivian said. "Yes, but he made amends. That's why he agreed to work with Ezra." That's why he'd agreed to stay with her. She'd come to him as he died, borne witness to his darkest hour, held his hand, and had seen him through. He'd thought that if he could save her, it would make up for his failures as a husband and father. He needed redemption.

"Well, which is it?"

Vivian threw up her hands in exasperation. "Zeke made some mistakes and he paid dearly for them, but he's more than made amends. Darkmore does some things I don't like, but he's been helping me with my burdens and with some guardian-gone-bad, so he's not the bad guy."

"Seems hard to tell who's good or bad," Kay said thoughtfully.

"Vivian," Father Montgomery said, brows furrowed. "Where has Zeke been all this time?"

That one stumped her. She hadn't actually gotten around to asking him that. They'd been too busy celebrating his return, so to speak. As far as she knew, he'd crossed over to the great beyond, his own personal paradise. She'd asked Ezra to see him safely to the other side. It had been part of their deal.

Then somehow, he'd come back to her. But...spirits didn't come back from the great beyond.

What if he'd never left?

"You don't think..." Vivian said as a cold chill ran from her spine down to her toes.

"A rogue guardian shows up just before Zeke reappears? An angry guardian who seems bent on making you suffer?" Father Montgomery said carefully. "One who's angry with you for breaking the rules, perhaps where he was concerned?"

"Honey," Kay said, grabbing her hand, "we're just worried about you. We—"

Vivian jerked her hand back, stammering, "No. You've got it all wrong, Zeke loves me. He'd never hurt me. He's a good man."

"He's a man who abused and neglected his wife and family and then abandoned them," said Father Montgomery.

Vivian interrupted, "He made a mistake. He—"

"You sent him away, Vivian."

"I was trying to set him free," Vivian said, heart racing as fear and doubt crept into her heart and soul. It couldn't be. Not Zeke.

"He must have been hurt and angry, perhaps angry enough to retaliate?" the padre said, his cold logic slicing through her defenses.

"No, no, I won't listen to this." Vivian stumbled backward. Summoning her energy, she focused on getting out, getting away, getting someplace where no one could destroy her peace and happiness.

Away, take me away, please oh please take me away!

She disappeared with a flash of red light.

CHAPTER TWENTY-THREE

Vivian opened her eyes and experienced a moment of shock. She'd expected to land in the spirit realm. Honestly, she'd hoped that she could travel back to her field of black-eyed Susans that bordered a cool babbling creek. After all, that's where she'd landed the last time she'd been upset enough to warrant a quick exit from reality. It was her place of peace. It had been there that she'd learned the truth from Ezra. She should have died in the same car crash that claimed Zeke's life. Darkmore the reaper had been coming for Zeke, and Ezra for Vivian. Only Ezra had broken the rules at the last minute and left Vivian alive.

Unfortunately, his decision had also opened a permanent link between her and the world of spirits. And it had cost her Zeke.

She hadn't landed in her own private paradise this time. Instead, she stood outside of the Longhollow residence, the home that Zeke had shared with his family in life. She didn't know why she'd landed there, and she wasn't really sure she wanted to find out.

Rendering herself invisible, Vivian sat on the front porch steps to gather her thoughts. *Damn you, Padre!* He'd given voice to the gnawing doubts lurking in the back of her mind, and she hated him for it.

On the one hand, the Zeke she knew was gentle and protective. He'd helped her care from Mae and guarded her against Darkmore when he was after them both. Zeke had comforted her, helped her face her inner darkness, and loved her.

He understood your darkness because of his own.

That much was true. In life, Zeke felt burdened by a wife he'd "had" to marry, an autistic son, and another disabled child on the way. The night he died, he was running away from those terrible burdens.

Don't pussyfoot around the truth, Viv. He damn near assaulted Jenn and cleaned out the bank accounts. He was an abuser, a thief, and a coward.

Darkmore, get out of my head!

She could almost hear him laughing and wondered if he was capable of implanting himself into her subconscious. Maybe he served as her voice of reason because he'd never lied to her.

At least not as far as she knew.

She placed her head in her hands, but could not hide from the unwelcome truth. Zeke had been a philanderer and a cold-hearted bastard to his family in life. He'd felt cheated by fate and he ran away. Hell, she'd wanted to run away from the burden of caring for her sister, Mae, too. She was just as bad.

But you didn't.

No, she hadn't. She'd always come back. And she'd even helped Zeke face his sins before leaving him in her field of gold and green. All she'd wanted was to free him from his guilt and his obligations in the afterlife so he could move on to his own paradise.

But what if the padre was right? What if, instead of free, he'd felt abandoned?

So that left the big questions that she'd been avoiding since Zeke stormed her kitchen and took her on the counter. Why hadn't he moved on? Where had he been all of this time? What did he want now?

Why don't you ask the most important question, Vivian? The relevant one?

Having an internal dialogue with the reaper's voice in her head didn't help, but he was right, of course. The relevant question now, as then, remained. If Zeke was all of those horrible things in life, what did that make him in death?

She'd landed at his old home. She'd most likely landed here for a reason. To answer her questions about Zeke's present, she'd have to delve into his past again.

She'd have to talk to his widow, Jenn Longhollow.

————

"Vivian," Jenn cried, enfolding her in a warm embrace. "I haven't seen you in ages! What a nice surprise. Please, come on in."

Vivian stepped into the house and looked around. It seemed brighter than the first time she'd visited, as did Jenn. She smiled at the toddler in the corner, who struggled to pull up and support her cherubic frame on chubby legs.

"Michelle's getting so big," Vivian said, walking over and stooping down to get a better look at the child. Michelle gave her a wide, toothless smile and reached out for her. She took the girl's hand and lifted her, tossing her into the air and catching her again as the toddler rewarded her new playmate with squeals of delight.

"Lord, don't I know it," Jenn said. "Have a seat. Can I get you anything to drink?"

"No, thank you," Vivian muttered as she tried to get the squirming girl settled on her lap. "I just dropped in to check on you and chat for a while. Is this a good time?"

"You're in luck," Jenn answered. "Zeb's at school and Michelle's about ready for her nap. Lou's taking us out tonight, but I have a little time before I need to get ready and go pick up my little man."

"Lou sounds like good people to me," Vivian said with a smile.

"He is," she said. "Oh, I meant to tell you, Zeb's got so many new words now. His therapists are blown away. It's like someone turned on a light inside him. I hear him practicing all the time in his room, talking to himself."

That was wonderful news on both counts. Jenn had been reluctant to enter the dating scene after Zeke's death. She was convinced that no one would be interested in a widow with two kids, one whom needed a lot of extra resources. Zeb's autism had been classified as moderate to severe when diagnosed, but apparently he'd been improving by leaps and bounds.

As for Jenn's new flame, Lou Mitchell was an old friend who came into her life shortly after Michelle's birth and just wouldn't take no for an answer. Jenn eventually caved in and they'd been happily dating since. He was great with the kids, and patient with Jenn.

"That's wonderful news on both counts," Vivian said.

"Yeah, Lou is really, *really* great," Jenn said, blushing a bit and looking away.

"Really, really, huh?" Vivian teased.

Seemed as though Lou's patience had paid off. Vivian was happy for her and relieved to have the opportunity to ease her way into the awkward questions about Zeke. She still wasn't sure how she might work the conversation around to him.

"Let me put Little Bit down for her nap and we'll have some girl talk," Jenn replied. She picked up Michelle, who resisted even as she rubbed her fists in her eyes, and walked down the hall.

Vivian stood and walked around the living room. She had befriended Zeke's wife the previous year and helped ease her burdens, and she dropped by from time to time to check on her and help out with the kids. Though she genuinely liked the woman and Zeke's children, she'd never quite managed to shake the discomfort she felt in the home that Zeke had shared with his family during life. For starters, they'd both shared the man, or in Vivian's case the spirit of the deceased man. It wasn't technically infidelity on his part, since Zeke's marriage ended upon his death, but it still made things uncomfortable.

Not to mention that her current errand required deceiving both Jenn and Zeke.

Vivian's gaze traveled over the photographs scattered haphazardly on end tables flanking the sofa, lining the walls, and adorning the mantel over the home's fireplace. Jenn had kept most of the photographs with Zeke, probably more for the children more than for herself. She imagined that Jenn still had mixed emotions about her departed husband.

Vivian couldn't really blame her.

Jenn returned to the living room and plopped down on the sofa, kicking her feet up and making herself comfortable. At least, she would've looked comfortable were it not for the deep crimson filling her cheeks.

"So, I normally wouldn't talk about this sort of thing," Jenn said. "But I swear there is just something about you. I've always found it easy to talk to you, you know, since we first met."

"I just have one of those faces," Vivian replied. She'd gotten that a lot, even before she started working with spirits.

"So when I first started seeing Lou, there wasn't much of a spark, if you get my drift."

"Uh-huh."

"It wasn't his fault," she said quickly, waving her hands in apology. "It was all me. Zeke had his faults, but magnetism wasn't one of them, and neither was stamina."

Tell me about it!

On second thought...please don't.

Vivian cleared her throat and said, "I can see that. He was a good-looking man."

"He was, but it was much more than that, if you knew him."

Yes, she knew more than she could ever admit to Jenn.

"Anyway, a few months after we started dating steady—" She lost it then and started laughing.

"What?" Vivian asked, fighting a chuckle herself even as she chided herself. This was one of the stranger conversations she'd had lately, and that was really saying something.

"Well, aside from sounding like a teenager for talking about going steady, I *feel* like a horny teenager all over again." Her cheeks turned a deeper shade of crimson.

"Good for you," Vivian said. "If anyone deserves some happiness and satisfaction, it's definitely you."

"Thank you. You know, I just never thought a man could change so much. I mean, it's like he just got some, um, skills overnight," Jenn said. "Like a light bulb went off." Her smile faltered a bit, and Vivian sensed her nervousness.

"So what's the problem?" Vivian asked.

"Oh, it's silly," she muttered. A shadow crossed her face and Vivian began to feel a bit of raw nerves herself.

"It's just that..." Jenn trailed off, creased her brow, and then leaned in closer to Vivian and whispered. "It almost feels like he's been a different person since then."

"Different in what way?"

"Well, when we're together, you know, like *together*...it's almost as if he's grown more intuitive, like the way he talks or, um, touches. It's like he has some sort of new energy."

Alarm bells sounded in the back of her mind as disbelief morphed into suspicion. If Zeke hadn't crossed when she left him, if he'd chosen to stay on Earth, or hide on Earth, where would he go? He hadn't come to her, and only one other place held Earthly ties for him.

"Vivian?" Jenn's voice brought her back to reality. "Are you all right? You've gone pale."

"Sorry," Vivian muttered, struggling to gather her thoughts as she rose. "No, um, I think I'm probably fine. I should get going. You need to get ready for your date, right?"

"Are you sure?" Jenn asked, looking doubtful "You don't look well at all."

"No, no, I'm fine," Vivian said, embracing Jenn and drawing out some of her worries in barely visible wisps of light. She took in a little extra to alleviate any suspicion Jenn might harbor over her sudden departure.

She also held onto her a little longer than usual to get as much spirit essence as she could gather. She had to be sure.

When Vivian released Jenn, Zeke's widow seemed a bit disoriented but much less worried. Jenn walked Vivian to the door and told her goodbye. Vivian managed to transport back to her home before reality struck and she collapsed in a heap on her kitchen floor.

Putting two and two together—from Lou's change in energy level to Zeb's seemingly miraculous response to therapy—there was only one plausible explanation.

Like it or not, she had her answer.

She knew where Zeke had been.

———

After her fits of sobbing eased, Vivian stood up and glanced at her kitchen clock. Her trip to and from the Longhollow home had taken about fifteen minutes, mortal standard time. Her tears had given her a measure of release, leaving her exhausted and numb. An odd sense of gratitude filled her for that. Perhaps she could collapse into bed and block out everything for a while. She hoped Zeke would make himself scarce tonight. She feared any confrontation.

What would I say, anyhow?

Accuse him of infidelity? He'd been staying with his wife, and it appeared his only interference had been providing Jenn's new man with an energy boost. In some twisted way, it was probably Zeke's way of making up for what a terrible husband he'd been while alive. How could he stand it, though, lingering in his former home and watching a new man take over his role? And what about the children? He'd clearly been trying to help with his son, but at what cost?

God, was he torturing himself? Because she'd sent him away?

She didn't want to think about it, and she didn't want to ache over it. She'd just gotten him back, or so she'd thought.

But she'd sent him away, as the padre so cruelly reminded her. And she'd been with Jace, and almost been with Darkmore

Damn it, I will not feel guilty about this.

Without guilt, the only familiar territory left for Vivian to traverse was anger. Rage that she normally kept locked deep within her soul threatened to tear loose and wreak havoc. All that she'd endured at the hands of spirits over the past year flooded her, all that she'd lost and all that had been denied her. They'd robbed her of her freedom, a normal life with a husband and children, and now Zeke. Ezra had made her give him up, had promised to help him cross, but he clearly hadn't.

She wanted to pound her fists into pillows, then later on the cold, hard floor. She wanted to throw things. And she had even more destructive means of channeling her anger.

She gave into the urge to use that power.

A flash of red light erupted from her right hand and smashed one of the dirty glasses that rested on her countertop. It was a clean shot, with just enough power to send shards flying without scorching the wall behind or granite below. She fired again, sending a serving platter careening to the floor with an ear-splitting crash.

Another shot and pans crashed to the floor. Another took out a second glass.

"Vivian," a quiet voice spoke from behind her.

She spun around ready to attack the bearer of the voice, but managed to stop the light. Her fingers burned with the searing heat of unreleased energy and she hissed. A mixture of pain and comfort filled her through the burn, as if the damage to her flesh could ease the damage to her heart and soul.

Father Montgomery stood before her, his calm demeanor almost concealing his fear of her. He stood still, not daring to step closer, not even after she dropped her hands. He spoke again in the same quiet tone, "I was going to wash those for you."

"Is that why you're still here?" she asked, matching his quiet tone. "Or did you plan on gloating as well?"

"You know me better than that," he said.

"Do I, padre?" she asked, turning away from him.

"Perhaps no better than I know you."

That got her attention. She spun back around and faced him, waiting for an explanation.

"I've always been honest in my dealings with you. Always. You, on the other hand…"

"What's that supposed to mean?" she asked as another wave of rage began to build within her.

"All this time? You've been associating with Darkmore all this time?"

"Yes, I have," she spat. "What are you going to do, *Father*? Curse me to Hell? I can do without the judgment."

"You really don't get it, do you?"

"Apparently I don't, so why don't you explain—"

"Damn it, Vivian, you lied to me!" he yelled.

She opened her mouth to protest, but he cut her off. "How could you keep something like this from me?" he snapped. She'd never heard the priest lose his cool before. Not until now. "After all we've been through and seen together, how could you turn to that…that demon?"

"I was protecting you," she shouted. "And I was protecting myself."

"But with that creature?" Father Montgomery rose and crossed himself. "Has he spread his sin to you, then, as well as his lies? Have you been sleeping with him as well?"

She rose and crossed the space between them. He stood his ground, though the slight recoil in his posture and features betrayed his preparation for a deadly strike. Vivian held onto her self-control, but only by the barest thread. She didn't cast her light at him.

Instead, she slapped him across the face.

Stunned, perhaps even more so than the priest, she turned and took slow, measured steps toward her couch. She tried to control her breathing, which came in rapid gasps. She couldn't stop her hands from shaking, but she'd be damned if she'd shed another tear. She sat on her sofa and stared at her hands, hands she kept clasped together in a tight knot on her lap.

"Vivian," came the uneven voice of the priest. "I'm sorry, I…"

"Please," she whispered. "Just go."

She heard him sigh but refused to look up, part in stubbornness and part in shame. She'd hit him hard enough to leave an angry red mark on his left cheek. After long moments passed, she listened to his heavy footfalls moving to her front door. Closing her eyes, she focused her energy and exhaled, willing her healing light in the direction of the priest as he retreated. She could at least heal his flesh, if not the gap between them.

"Ezra will be here tomorrow night," Lloyd Montgomery said, just before he closed the door behind him.

CHAPTER TWENTY-FOUR

After a restless night and too-quiet morning, Vivian needed a distraction to calm her nerves. She started with the mess she'd made in her kitchen, picking up the larger shards of broken glass and double-bagging them in heavy-duty trash bags. The smaller shards were tougher to spot. She did a thorough sweep-and-mop job after cleaning the splattered remains of food and beverage from her countertops and wall.

At least I didn't scorch anything this time.

While she was at it, she decided the whole house could use a scrub down. She dusted every nook, cranny, and smooth wooden surface, including her baseboards and the nastiness that rested atop her ceiling fan blades. Both Vivian and the vacuum got a workout. Her floor and upholstery had never looked better.

She'd scrubbed the bathrooms and cleaned the windows by late morning and still couldn't turn off her mind. Had she not made a deal with her spirit tenants to help out with the yard work at night in exchange for food and lodging, she probably could have killed at least another two hours in the yard.

Damn, damn, damn.

She considered calling Jeanne, but figured Ghost Barbie would lose her shit when she found out about Vivian's extracurricular spirit world activities. She didn't want to drag Kay any further into this mess, especially with her troubles and the potential danger to the kids. At least Junior could offer some measure of protection. He'd promised Vivian to keep an eye on the Clemmens family while the rogue guardian remained at large.

She couldn't think about the padre. Not after last night.

She ached for Zeke.

But she didn't want to have the inevitable confrontation yet. She had bigger fish to fry. First and foremost, she needed to find out what the grand high inquisitors at the guardian council might want with her. Plus the elusive rogue guardian remained at large.

And, thanks to Kay and the padre, she worried that the rogue guardian might be Zeke.

She fired up her laptop and was relieved to find Waylon online. He might know something. If not, at least he could keep her from going stir crazy with the wait.

BriggsonfireMS2010: Hello again. Still in trouble?

HauntedVivTN1975: Up to my neck in it. What do you know about the guardian council?

BriggsonfireMS2010: Jesus, you really are in trouble!

HauntedVivTN1975: Thanks. I feel so much better now.

BriggsonfireMS2010: Sorry. I don't bullshit. Especially about this stuff. You shouldn't either. What can I do?

HauntedVivTN1975: Fine. No bullshit. I've been summoned before the council. I don't know why, but I can think of at least three reasons.

BriggsonfireMS2010: Hit me.

HauntedVivTN1975: I blew my cover with the reaper. They know I've been working with him. And the rogue guardian is still after me.

Vivian paused. She waited for him to tell her she was royally screwed. She also needed to wipe the tears from her eyes and stop her hands from shaking.

. . .

BriggsonfireMS2010: What's the third, Vivian?

BriggsonfireMS2010: You still there?

HauntedVivTN1975: Yeah, I'm here. It's bad.

BriggsonfireMS2010: I've seen bad and probably done worse. If you don't want to share, that's fine, but there's not a lot I can do if I don't know what you got yourself into.

BriggsonfireMS2010: If you tell me, I won't judge. I'll try to help.

With a deep breath and a swallow to clear the ball of anxiety and guilt from her throat, Viv started typing.

HauntedVivTN1975: I fell in love with one of the guardians I met last year. He was the kind they force to work for them because he did some bad stuff in life. Understand?

BriggsonfireMS2010: I get it.

HauntedVivTN1975: Long story, but because I loved him I made a deal with his keeper to set him free and let him cross over. Only he didn't go. He came back.

BriggsonfireMS2010: So what's the problem?

HauntedVivTN1975: For starters, he's been hanging out at his wife's house.

A full minute passed. She fidgeted in her seat and worried that she'd lost her only lifeline. She placed her fingers on the keyboard and typed the rest before she had the chance to lose her courage.

HauntedVivTN1975: He was mad when he came back. Some of my friends think he might be dangerous.

BriggsonfireMS2010: What do you think?

HauntedVivTN1975: I don't know what to think, what to feel, or who to trust. It's pretty sad when the most reliable spirit you know is the grim reaper.

BriggsonfireMS2010: You got some firepower?

HauntedVivTN1975: Yes.

BriggsonfireMS2010: Use it when the time comes. Don't think. Just fire. Can you do that?

HauntedVivTN1975: I think so.

BriggsonfireMS2010: Don't think. Know so.

HauntedVivTN1975: Okay, Okay, I know so!

BriggsonfireMS2010: When's your summons?

HauntedVivTN1975: Tomorrow night.

Briggsonfire2010: Can you get some more energy?

HauntedVivTN1975: I don't know. Why?

BriggsonfireMS2010: Look, there are only two things the guardian higher-ups care about—energy and order. Don't swallow the Kool-Aid about duty, purpose, helping lost souls, and the living. The ones in the trenches may believe in the cause, but those in charge just want to stay in charge.

HauntedVivTN1975: The guardians and reapers tried to take my sister last year. She was special. Trapped. You know what that means?

BriggsonfireMS2010: Yeah, I know. Big generator for Casa del Dead. What happened?

HauntedVivTN1975: I made a deal to free her, too.

BriggsonfireMS2010: And they just let her go?

HauntedVivTN1975: When she died, she passed through the reaper's realm and let go of a lot of light energy. Took a bunch of souls with her. That squared all of us with the reapers and the guardians.

BriggsonfireMS2010: No. If she got away, you ain't square.

Vivian froze. She couldn't breathe. She couldn't think, save for a single plea reverberating through her fractured mind.

No!

. . .

HauntedVivTN1975: No. That's not right. I kept my end of the bargain and I work for the guardians.

BriggsonfireMS2010: Oh, I see. The guardians in your neck of the woods are good for their word, huh? Real honest types.

Vivian stared at the screen. Long seconds passed. Minutes. She lost track.

BriggsonfireMS2010: That's what I thought.

BriggsonfireMS2010: I promised you no bullshit.

BriggsonfireMS2010: You still there, or you running away with your little white bobtail tucked between your legs?

HauntedVivTN1975: Fuck you.

BriggsonfireMS2010: Please, Miss Scarlett, that all you got?

HauntedVivTN1975: FUCK YOU!

HauntedVivTN1975:   Jalodiasnkldfafsdnklafkn;kadfbjkadfsbjknadsb-jkladfsbjkldfabkjbjkbjkbjkvbvvzcxbmzvn,.cmxvzmn,.fkndjjkafddhjksadfs;hkdhkl;

BriggsonfireMS2010: Well you can swear like a soldier. When you're done smashing the keyboard, how about fighting like one?

HauntedVivTN1975: What do I have to do?

BriggsonfireMS2010: You need energy. Lots of it.

HauntedVivTN1975: That's a problem.

BriggsonfireMS2010: Guardians sucked you dry?

HauntedVivTN1975: Nope. I suck in burdens from the living and they leave me stuck with them. So I feed them to the reaper.

BriggsonfireMS2010: Then the guardian in charge of you has some serious explaining to do.

HauntedVivTN1975: What do you mean? Guardians are supposed to live off light and goodness. Reapers take in burdens. How do you know so much about this stuff anyhow?

BriggsonfireMS2010: I'll answer the last question later. First, energy is energy. Guardians can run off the dark stuff when they need to. Reapers aren't so choosy, either. You said you trust your reaper pal?

HauntedVivTN1975: As much as I trust any of the sorry bunch.

BriggsonfireMS2010: Get to him double quick and gather as much energy as you can.

HauntedVivTN1975: For what? So I can just give it to the council?

BriggsonfireMS2010: I told you to use your firepower when the time comes.

HauntedVivTN1975: You want me to take on the guardian council? Are you nuts?

BriggsonfireMS2010: I want you to get yourself out of there alive. If they take your life they'll own your soul. I want you to get out, lie low, and get to Mississippi as quick as you can after. We can help you then.

HauntedVivTN1975: Who's we?

BriggsonfireMS2010: Get here. We'll talk then.

BriggsonfireMS2010: Get up, Vivian. Clear your chat log, lock and load, then get the hell out.

HauntedVivTN1975: How do I know I can trust you?

BriggsonfireMS2010: You don't, but what other choice you got?

BriggsonfireMS2010: You still there?

HauntedVivTN1975: How will I find you?

BriggsonfireMS2010: I got to go work on that now.

HauntedVivTN1975: In case I forget later, thank you.

BriggsonfireMS2010: Thank me by staying alive. GO!

Vivian cleared her chat log as instructed and kept panic at bay by getting to work. She grabbed the suitcase packed with clothing, cash, and other essentials she'd been keeping since shortly after beginning her work with the spirits. Once loaded in her car, along with enough nonperishable food and bottled water to last a week or two, she drove it to a secluded spot near home and parked, traveling back spirit-style. After a moment's hesitation, she summoned Junior and asked him to look after the Clemmens clan, and asked him to seek out Jeanne and Wallace to take care of the padre and the Longhollows. The eager spirit was happy to oblige, no questions asked.

She did not permit herself to grieve over the potential loss of her home, her friends, or her life as she'd known it. There would be time for that later.

She hoped.

Locking her back door, she stood on her deck and looked out over the expanse of her backyard. Her eyes lingered on the line of trees where Ezra had first appeared, when it all began. She breathed in the familiar and comforting scents, listened to the din of cicada calls, and soaked in the waning light of the afternoon sun.

Then, steeling herself against the tears, she summoned the reaper.

CHAPTER TWENTY-FIVE

She kept her eyes closed and focused on her breathing as they moved through the swirling vortex. She also clung to Darkmore's arm, though she felt a little uncomfortable with the implied intimacy of such contact, especially after Zeke. Guilt waged war with fear of the reaper, which led to an even fiercer battle with the guilt lodged deep in her heart. After their last encounter, Vivian felt obliged to trust Darkmore.

She owed him that, didn't she?

Besides, he was the only being she could trust right now. She remembered his tenderness and her response, but these memories were making her mind feel as though it were swirling through the vortex rather than her body as thoughts of Zeke's return and her response to him kept flashing through her mind as well. Darkmore shuddered, which probably meant that he was enjoying the turmoil raging through her.

Would he be flattered, jealous, or amused if he knew the cause of her turmoil? Perhaps he would be angry. She wasn't sure she wanted to know.

"Vivian," he whispered, his lips close to her ear. "We're here." She must have been so lost in thought that she failed to register their exit from the vortex.

"Oh, excuse me," she muttered as she removed herself from his arms. It seemed she'd been clinging to his entire body rather than his arm.

"I don't mind," he replied with a small smile. Aside from the smile, his expression was unreadable. After a moment, he asked, "Why so glum, my dear? Does the thought of returning the favors I granted you make you uncomfortable?"

"It's not that," she muttered.

"Still at war with yourself, I see," he said, gazing at her with unnerving intensity. "And even more so than before. Care to share?"

"Maybe later."

"Definitely later," he whispered, giving her shivers that had nothing to do with his cold reaper energy. "Are you ready?"

"As ready as I'll ever be."

He placed his hand on the small of her back and urged her forward with gentle pressure, speaking in a soft, low tone as they walked through what appeared to be a hospital corridor. "We will be working with an associate of mine tonight, and one of her human assistants. I would have told you sooner, but I only just found out. This particular case has some rather...interesting possibilities."

God, she wasn't sure how much more she could handle.

"As far as your role, I believe we will require your healing powers for this assignment. It may be a bit taxing for you, but I will be there to provide relief should you need it."

"Healing? Really? I thought you and yours were more of the hurting kind," Vivian said, half-joking, but only half.

He didn't smile, which did nothing to alleviate her worry. Instead, he stopped and turned to face her before saying, "I will provide relief and support, as well as protection, but this is no laughing matter, Vivian. We come for the reaping, ever watchful of the darkly sweet and deadly harvest."

She started to protest, but he held up a hand, palm open, to silence her. "We also come for justice. Many from whom we reap, and those whom we reap, call to us with their evil. Be on your guard and do exactly as I tell you."

He raised his other hand to stop her burgeoning protest. "I tell you this for your safety and the integrity of this task, not as an order. Your involvement is your choice. I doubt you've ever received a similar offer from your guardian friends."

"No, I haven't. But I am in your debt, so this is a bit of an obligation."

"True, but you'll have the choice to withdraw your assistance should you find yourself unable to complete it."

"Wait a minute," Vivian began, just a bit belittled by his last comment. "You think I'm not strong enough to handle this? After all I've been through the past year, with you and on account of you and your kind?"

He became very still, and the temperature surrounding them plummeted. His voice remained low, but it was even colder than his presence. "You believe you've seen true evil, in its magnitude and delicious splendor?"

The way he said delicious sent a shiver up her spine. It took more conviction than she thought she possessed to hold steady and keep her eyes on his, but she did. When his composure returned and the temperature rose a few degrees, he said, "We shall learn, then, the strength of the metal from which you were molded."

"Fine," she said, her voice a bit sharp. "The only thing I ask in return is spirit energy. Lots and lots of energy."

She felt as well as saw his intense scrutiny. If he was curious about the reason behind her request, he didn't ask. She thought about telling him, but then thought better of it. Finally, he stood straight, nodded, and said, "I think we can arrange that. Consider it a bonus, if you will. Shall we?"

They continued walking, which gave Vivian a few more moments to think. That wasn't a good thing, as it gave her more time to dwell on Darkmore's words and wonder if she was up to the challenge.

Sure, she'd been to some dark places, some within her own soul, and she'd tasted pain and suffering from the living that nearly drove her to her breaking point. Still, she'd survived. More than that, she was able to keep coming back for more. Yet Darkmore, ancient and wise, witness to the spectrum of humanity's wickedness and cruelty, was most assuredly qualified to take her down a peg or two.

What she'd seen and experienced in her thirty-six years could not compare to that, she realized. Then, she was afraid.

Breathe in, breathe out. If she could breathe, she could move. If she could move, she could face the darkness ahead. All of it.

She was snapped back into awareness as they approached a room flanked by two police officers. They were in an ICU. Vivian had been in and out of hospitals enough to recognize the unit. The police and staff took no notice of them. Darkmore must have concealed them with his spirit powers. She questioned that conclusion when a sleek female physician smiled and walked toward them, heels clattering against the tiled floor.

She was even more shocked, and a little angrier than she should have been, when the lady doc planted a sensual kiss on Darkmore's lips.

Anger turned to dismay when she realized that the clattering hadn't been a product of high-heeled shoes. Rather than black pumps, her shapely calves tapered into slender, delicate ankles that ended in hooves. Cloven hooves.

"Uphir," Darkmore purred. "How lovely to see you again." Ever mindful of his manners, Darkmore turned and touched Vivian on the arm as he offered an introduction. "Allow me to present Ms. Vivian Bedford, spiritual intercessor and healer. Vivian, this is Uphir. She is called the demon's physician by some lower life forms, but I prefer to think of her as the spirit realm's supreme authority on all matters medical."

Uphir looked at Vivian with shrewd, calculating eyes, the eyes of a predator sizing up the value of a potential kill. Vivian hated her right away. She was pretty sure the feeling was mutual. Naturally, Uphir's projected form was quite attractive. Vivian consoled herself with the notion that the illusion probably hid scales.

"Darkmore," she purred. "I didn't realize you had acquired an... assistant. I thought you preferred to operate solo. She looks so *new*. I would have expected you to acquire a partner with more experience in the art of reaping dark pleasures."

She didn't think that Uphir was being particularly complimentary. Or nice. Vivian didn't feel like being nice either. Darkmore probably saw it coming, so he spoke before she had the chance.

"Vivian is here of her own accord, freelance, if you will. She normally works with the guardians, but we have developed a rather satisfying rapport."

"I see," Uphir said, gaze wide in what seemed suspiciously like appreciation. "She's a healer, you say? In that case, I believe she will prove most useful indeed. Shall we proceed?"

They were interrupted by a noise from behind, part cough and part grumble. Vivian turned and almost burst out laughing at the source of the sound. In retrospect, she was glad for her uncharacteristic level of self-control. She was in the company of powerful dark beings, after all.

Only this one didn't look especially powerful. He looked downright comical.

"Oh," Uphir said, not bothering to hide the touch of bored disdain in her voice. "This one's a new recruit for my legion. He prefers to be called Lothar, but you may refer to him as Earl. It is the name that his mommy gave him, after all."

Earl's pride evaporated instantly, replaced by the chilly mixture of humiliation and resentment. *Well, if you work for demons and go around dressed in that getup, what do you expect?* Earl was decked out in some sort of black leather and cape combo, accented by a pitchfork. He apparently had been granted some demonic powers of projection, since his head was green and adorned by a panel of spiky protrusions. These were probably supposed to look menacing.

They might have, if you couldn't still see the rest of him. Earl stood about five-five in his heeled boots, and the rest of his frame was woefully small. Vivian thought he must have been bullied quite a bit in life, assuming he'd left life behind. He could have been trapped in some sort of limbo as she was for all she knew, but she imagined that the small man before her willingly traded his soul in exchange for the power that he lacked on his own. That, or he was just a little too into role-playing games. Vivian had to wonder why he was here.

If Darkmore found his appearance odd, he didn't show it. He simply nodded and turned back to Uphir. "We'd best get started."

Turning back to Vivian and Earl, he added, "Please excuse us while we talk shop and strategy for a moment. We'll be back in a jiffy." Vivian glared at him, and damned if the reaper didn't wink just before he disappeared behind the door of the ICU suite.

Asshole.

She wasn't sure what she should be doing to fill the time, but conversing with Earl was not high on her list of options. Unfortunately, he seemed eager to chat with her.

"So," he said, giving her the once over. "You're freelance? Like to spread it around a bit? Nice."

She wondered if she could get away with zapping him, but settled on the silent treatment. She had to conserve her energy for bigger battles later. Maybe he would take the hint.

He kept staring at her.

Maybe not.

"I'm strictly on team demon, myself. Most of the players on this side don't like to share, if you catch my drift," he continued. He actually wiggled his eyebrows. *Pathetic.* "But Darkmore's a pretty good score, too," he offered in a reassuring tone.

She still didn't bother to answer, preferring to count the cracks in the ceiling instead. But she was getting more irritated. For starters, she didn't like hospitals. Too many bad memories with Mae. Plus, every time she'd visited a hospital since Mae's death, it had been for work. That meant consuming burdens and pain, which was uncomfortable at best, downright unpleasant at worst.

She wasn't looking forward to tonight's prospects, and Earl wasn't helping to improve her focus, or her mood.

"So, what do you do, besides heal? I'm a tracker, see," he continued, not waiting for her to answer. "I can detect a spirit from light years away. And I can tell whether the spirit is a reaper, guardian, lost and lonely, or..." He hesitated. Vivian hoped he was getting ready to shut the hell up, but he finished with, "Well, I'll just leave it at that. Some of this stuff is classified, and I don't know how much I'm allowed to divulge."

He positively beamed. Perhaps he was pleased with his use of a big vocab word. More likely, he was reveling in his perceived superior status.

Vivian knew she shouldn't feed the troll, so to speak, but she'd had about enough.

"Look, Beelzebubba, I'm here as a favor for Darkmore. I just want to go in, get the job done, and get out. Your babbling is making it difficult for me to get in the zone, so can we just drop the idle chit chat?"

"Fine," he snarled. "Sure, Red, why not? You don't look like all that, anyhow."

She really thought about zapping him then, but she held her power in check, as well as her tongue. He wasn't worth it. Besides, she felt a small measure of pity for any fool who had such obvious issues for which to compensate.

At the sound of Darkmore's beckoning voice, she shifted into high alert mode and prepared as best she could for who or what was waiting behind that door.

Vivian entered at Darkmore's request, followed by Demon Boy. Hospital disinfectant assaulted her senses, which almost covered the festering scent of old sweat and older blood. The smells emanated from the man at the center of the room, lying motionless on the standard issue hospital bed. The bits of his flesh that weren't covered by bandages, blankets, or tubes were covered in angry purple bruises or were sickly gray. His greasy salt-and-pepper hair needed a wash, as did his body.

Vivian had spent enough time in the presence of death to feel it and smell it. This unfortunate man reeked.

Uphir busied herself doing normal doctor-type things, like checking the man's vitals, while her minion sulked in the corner of the room opposite Vivian. Darkmore stood beside Vivian at a polite distance and waited. After perusing his chart, Uphir bent over and licked the man's face with a slender forked tongue, the sight of which made Vivian jump. The others remained unfazed.

"Well?" Darkmore asked.

"He's on his way, but not too far gone. I think we should give it a try," Uphir said, casting her gaze upon Vivian.

Darkmore turned and addressed Vivian. "We need you to try to heal Mr. Rockford."

"I'm no doctor, but he looks like he's in pretty bad shape to me," Vivian said. "I've only ever fixed up a sprained ankle and a spirit blast injury. What's wrong with him anyway?"

"He was beaten," Uphir answered. "And the victim of multiple stab wounds. He's suffered severe internal injuries as a result. Start with those.

The superficial cuts and bruises are not especially important. We need him to recover. And we need him conscious."

Vivian was about to ask what interest a demon and a reaper had with curing an injured human, but Darkmore took her hand and squeezed hard. She took the hint and remained silent as he led her to the side of the bed.

She looked down at the man, unsure how to begin.

Darkmore spoke to her in a soft, low tone, asking, "What did you do for your friend the priest?"

"I grabbed him, shook, took in some of his light," she said, struggling to remember. "Then he took in mine."

"Then perhaps you could do the same for Mr. Rockford," he suggested. "I'll be right here."

She was grateful for Darkmore's presence and reassurance, though she was loath to admit it. She placed her hand on Mr. Rockford's and squeezed. He didn't respond. No surprise there. Taking a deep breath, she focused her energy on the unconscious man so she could draw in his burdens. She saw the small wisps of yellow light flow from him, a sickly green shade that made her stomach turn. Steeling herself, she inhaled.

Her stomach turned even more.

She tasted lust, perversity, and greed. This man harbored sickening thoughts and desires and Vivian fought the urge to recoil from them. Instead, she forced herself to inhale again. Revulsion and rage shook her as she felt his depravity and degradation, which he not only accepted, but relished.

Disgusted, she tried to release his hand, only to be gripped tighter as his eyes flew open. He pulled her closer as she fought. She registered a wail of sheer horror, and then realized it was her own.

No, no, *no!*

He ripped the light from her being, sucking in the healing rays into his broken body even as she choked on the evil drawn from his wretched and decrepit soul. She fell deeper and deeper into the chasm as the light left her and filled him.

Too much...you're taking too much! Stop!

She couldn't breathe. He'd kill her if he kept at it.

Suddenly, a whirlwind of ice swept in and all around her. Rather than causing more agony, it soothed her burning flesh. It bore her up from the depths and lifted her back to the light. Only then did she succumb to oblivion.

———

Something was being forced into her mouth and she fought like hell to dislodge it. Fear gripped her and she thrashed. She would not taste more of that man's darkness no matter what she owed Lazarus Darkmore.

Darkmore...

"Darkmore," she croaked. "Make it stop...he's killing me."

"Shh, Vivian, it's over," he soothed. She felt his hands near her mouth again and snarled, pulling away while baring her teeth to bite.

"None of that now, my dear," he said, stilling her head with strong, insistent hands. "Drink, now."

It wasn't a request.

She almost spit before she realized that he only offered water. It cooled and soothed as it traveled down her raw throat. She must have screamed a long time before blacking out.

Once her addled brain caught up with reality, she did spit as she tried to speak.

"No, you need more. And this, too," he commanded, placing something solid into her mouth even as she protested. "Relax. It's just an energy bar."

"What the hell happened out there?" she asked, opening her eyes and then wishing she hadn't. The harsh glare of hospital halogen made her head hurt.

"I'll tell you after you eat," he answered.

"Fine," she said, snatching the bar from his hand and tearing off a bite. She gave him what she hoped was a squint-eyed look of pure damnation while she chewed.

"Ah, there's the Vivian Bedford I know and love," he said. He smiled too. He had the audacity to smile. Had she the strength, she would have lunged at him.

"You've done well, my dear," Darkmore said, lifting her from her place on the floor and cradling her in his lap. "Mr. Rockford is making a remarkable recovery."

"Whampf on Erfth d'd h' do?"

"Don't talk with your mouth full. It's rude. Not to mention incomprehensible. I could also do with fewer dirty looks."

Vivian chewed. Her eyes adjusted and she also took in her surroundings. Once finished, she said, "I asked you what on Earth did he do. And while we're at it, why on Earth are we in the bathroom?"

"What he did is irrelevant. You have fulfilled your obligation and have acquired the energy you desired, although I suspect you'll find it less than palatable. I moved you to the bathroom so you could recover in peace, and so we would not disturb Uphir and her minion while they work."

"So that's it? That's all you're going to tell me?" she asked, trying not to get too comfy in the reaper's lap.

"That was my plan, yes," he said, shifting his blue eyes slightly to the left. "When you are ready, I shall be happy to see you home."

"No, I don't think so," she said as she hopped off his lap and reached for the door. "I want to know what you got me into."

"I wouldn't do that if I were you. You might not like what you see."

"I already don't like what I've seen. Darkmore, his light was so...I mean, it was revolting. I've never tasted anything so vile."

"Mr. Rockford has been rather a naughty boy. Uphir doesn't come topside for just any old offense."

"What did he do?"

"I'd rather not tell you."

"And I'd rather you not make decisions for me. I want to see what's going on out there. Are you going to stop me?"

"No," he answered. "Free will, Vivian. For better or worse, that's what you get with me."

She nodded, turned, and opened the door before she could change her mind.

CHAPTER TWENTY-SIX

If Vivian had tasted evil in the spirit energy of Mr. Rockford, she surely witnessed pure evil when she opened the door to his hospital room.

The sight that greeted her chilled her to her soul.

Rockford's body was chained, his wrists and ankles encircled by barbed metal that held him taut and tore into his flesh, the bonds held him suspended in midair above the bed. His face contorted in anguish and his mouth gaped, but no sound escaped. His captors did not permit him the luxury of screaming, or even writhing. He remained completely immobile as both Uphir and Earl repeatedly sliced his flesh with curved daggers.

They took their time, piercing his tissue with slow, agonizing jabs. Once embedded, they turned the blades to inflict maximum damage and pain, and then pulled up, down, and around to create angry, gaping wounds. The wounds didn't bleed. Instead, they released more of the sickening yellow light that Vivian had tasted. The smell of it made her stomach turn almost as much as the sight of their torture.

When both Uphir and Earl paused and placed their mouths on the open wounds, sucking and slurping, she ran back to the bathroom and vomited. Darkmore was kind enough to lift the toilet lid for her.

Still gagging, she looked up at him, her face smeared with tears. She managed to gasp one word between bouts of nausea.

"Why?"

Darkmore looked at her, his expression inscrutable. His voice, however, held a trace of sorrow. "I did try to warn you, Vivian."

"You had me heal him," she whispered in disbelief. "I cured him so they could torture him? Why?"

"Vivian—"

"Tell me why!"

"Mr. Rockford is a predator, Vivian. He preys upon children in the worst way possible. This is his punishment."

"He's a pedophile?"

"Child predator seems more appropriate, don't you think? There is no love in the unspeakable acts he prefers, I can assure you. He has subjected dozens of young girls and boys to—"

"Stop!" she screamed, her already-raw throat protesting. She felt even sicker than she did when she saw the demon and her novice savoring the tastes of torture. Her innards clenched even tighter when she saw the look of longing and hunger on Darkmore's face.

Oh my God, he wants to feed, too.

"Why not let him die?" she asked.

"It isn't his time."

"You mean he'll survive?" she asked, disbelieving. Disbelief morphed into anger when an even more sickening thought occurred to her. "What then? You won't just let him go, will you?"

"It isn't his time, Vivian."

She launched herself at him, hitting any patch of his corporeal form that she could reach, tearing and clawing in unchecked fury. He didn't strike her back or fight her, except to deflect her stronger blows.

"Is this what you call justice? You made me heal him? And when you and your demon friend are done having your jollies he'll be free to hurt other kids! How could you?"

"Never make it personal, Vivian."

"*I* healed him. *I'm* the reason he'll live. It *is* personal, Darkmore! Goddamn you to Hell!"

"Vivian—"

She slapped him across the face and asked, "Who did he hurt?"

He didn't answer, so she slapped him again. "Answer me. He's here in the hospital for a reason. I figure it has something to do with his extracurricular activities, so you're going to tell me who he hurt and where I can find that person, and you're going to do it now."

He looked at her and appeared to consider her request. When she moved to strike him again, he grabbed her hand and pulled her close to him, his face millimeters from hers. Holding his rage and hunger in check by the smallest of margins, he said, "Wait here. I'll take you to her when I'm finished."

Darkmore released her, walked through the door and closed it behind him.

———

She heard the door open about ten minutes later, when Darkmore returned from his meal. She didn't look at him. She couldn't. She accepted his proffered hand without looking into the face of the reaper. The same hand that had soothed her through fear, caressed her as they danced, and comforted her. The hand that she knew held and tormented Rockford and countless others through his long existence as he relished unfathomable suffering.

They swirled through the vortex and landed in another hospital room occupied by a little girl who looked all of six years old, perhaps in the same house of healing her tormentor occupied. She slept. Thank God she slept.

Vivian released Darkmore's hand and walked toward her, seating herself upon the bed beside the child. She stroked her soft hair and noticed the bruise below her right eye. Thinking of her other, unseen injuries brought hot tears to Vivian's already-swollen eyes.

She leaned forward and focused her energy on the girl. "Give me your hurt, baby," she whispered, taking in her burdens in wisps of soft, violet light.

She tasted the devastation and wept.

Then she willed the child to take in her healing light until Darkmore's icy grip tore her away.

She finally looked at him, ready to protest, but he stilled her mouth with his finger. "That's enough, Vivian. You've done all you can for her."

"No, I didn't. I—"

"I know you want to make it all go away, but you cannot. No one can."

"Will she be okay?"

"Time will tell. You helped. More than you know."

She thought for a moment, long and hard. She had acquired the energy she needed to face the guardians. Dark and terrible energy coursed through her veins, filled her body, mind, and soul, as powerful and rich as it was dangerous.

She also feared that a part of her liked it. Then she made a decision.

"Take me back to Rockford," she said.

He raised his eyebrows at her, perhaps out of curiosity or maybe out of suspicion. Perhaps both.

"I give you my word that I will not kill him," she said. "But I need to go back."

"Why?"

"You'll just have to trust me, Darkmore. I believe I've earned it."

As she prepared to launch into an argument for her case, he reached for her and transported her back to Rockford's room. Uphir had traded the hateful blade for a wicked-looking whip, which she put to use by flogging the wicked man. Earl sat sprawled in the corner of the room, his eyes glazed with what could only be described as satisfaction.

Uphir's face held the same look of rapturous contentment. They were nearly full.

Uphir stopped mid-strike and turned to face Darkmore and Vivian. "Well, well, well," she said. "Your little helper came back for more. I wouldn't have thought it. She's quite a find, Darkmore. You should hold onto this one."

"She isn't mine to hold," Darkmore replied.

Uphir looked surprised, a look Vivian didn't imagine graced her features often. "Oh?"

"I'll only have her when she comes to me freely, not out of obligation."

Uphir shrugged. "Suit yourself. We're finished here, unless you care for another helping," she said to Darkmore. Then, turning to Vivian, she added, "Or perhaps you'd like another taste? It is sweeter from the wound, but the last leavings hold a rich, savory quality."

"No, thank you," Vivian said. "Just stand back out of my way."

Eyes wide, Uphir managed to sidestep Vivian's burst of red light energy aimed at Rockford. He found his voice as the blast hit and his wail echoed through the room and beyond. Darkmore seized her and pulled her into the vortex before she had the chance to hit the monster again.

———

"Darkmore, you're hurting me," she cried, trying to extricate herself from his punishing grasp.

He spun her around to face him. She'd never seen his rage before. It chilled to the bone, and scared her more than he had during their first terrible meeting.

"Explain."

"Darkmore," she gasped. "Ease up, I can't breathe."

"Explain!"

"I didn't kill him! The worthless piece of shit will live."

He eased his grip, but didn't release her. She struggled for air and fought against the darkness threatening to engulf her so she could get her bearings.

"Where are we?" she asked.

"Hospital parking lot," he said, then he growled and tightened his grip. "I may give you to Uphir if you don't explain yourself to my satisfaction," he said in a cold, smooth voice. She hoped he was kidding, but she couldn't be sure.

"I promised I wouldn't kill him, but I couldn't just let him go free without doing something to stop him. So I gave him what the girl gave me. I gave him her suffering."

Darkmore stared at her long and hard. The temperature around them dropped again and she waited for her doom. He moved in.

He claimed her lips and took all of the suffering that remained. He didn't let go after. Instead, the reaper deepened his kiss and poured his dark passion into her every pore. As abruptly as he'd started, Darkmore broke off the kiss and cocked his head to the side.

"What the—"

Darkmore's smooth voice interrupted her. "Mr. Longhollow, I presume," he said, grinning, "It's been far too long since our last encounter."

Oh my God.

Zeke. He was here.

CHAPTER TWENTY-SEVEN

Zeke emerged from around a shadowed corner of the emergency department entrance. He looked from Vivian to the reaper, and back. Vivian unwound herself from Darkmore's arms and stepped back. She didn't go to Zeke.

"What are you doing here, Zeke?" she asked.

"I followed you," he said, gaze locked on Darkmore. She'd never seen him so predatory, so focused, and so ready to attack.

"Why?"

"Because you're in trouble." Heat surrounded her in thick waves, engulfing her in a punishing inferno. God, could it be? Was he really the rogue guardian set on stopping her in her tracks?

"How did you know?" she asked.

"I told him."

Vivian spun around and came face to face with Father Montgomery. The shock of seeing the priest superseded the shock of Zeke's appearance, but it didn't diminish her fear. She looked from Father Montgomery to Zeke, and back to Darkmore, unsure where or how she could begin to sort out her current spirit world mess.

"This evening has certainly taken an interesting turn," Darkmore said.

"Perhaps we should find someplace more private for our little impromptu soiree?"

"We have things to discuss in private," Zeke said, turning his burning gaze to Vivian. Then he spoke directly to Darkmore. "We don't need you."

Things were about to get ugly. *Think, think, think!* She had to find a way to protect the priest and herself from Zeke, possibly Zeke from himself, and Darkmore—

No, he'd probably be okay.

"He's not the one," said Father Montgomery.

Now Darkmore took his turn looking from the priest to Zeke, and then back at Vivian.

"Oh, my dear," Darkmore said softly. "You thought..."

"I don't know what to think anymore!"

"You obviously thought you could trust him," Zeke growled, jerking his head toward the reaper.

"Now's not the time," the priest said. "Your summons is upon you, Vivian. Are you prepared?"

"I...I'm out of energy."

"What?" Zeke and Darkmore asked in unison.

"Look, I was supposed to stock up on spirit energy so I could defend myself against the guardian council, and I had it. But I had to let it go. If anyone has any bright ideas about how I can get around this, now's the time."

"If that is all you required, why not simply ask?" the reaper asked. If she didn't know better, she'd swear he was hurt.

"Because, Darkmore, I owed you."

"You wanted to come here with him," Zeke accused.

Darkmore turned to Zeke and said in his cold, hard voice, "That's right. She came here with me. She faced the darkness, faced her obligations. She's a fighter, Ezekiel, not a runner. She's better than you."

"Stop it," she cried. "Please."

"The truth is a double-edged sword, is it not?" the reaper said. Zeke's face contorted in rage, grief, and agony as Darkmore circled, taunting him with the darkness he'd created in his life.

"Vivian set you free, made the ultimate sacrifice, and what did you do?

You squandered her gift. You didn't move on, did you? Was it because you wouldn't, or because you couldn't?"

"She gave me away," he growled, anger and anguish seeping from every pore. "She threw me away!"

"No, baby," Vivian whispered. "No, I didn't want to hurt you, I wanted you to find peace."

"So you went back to your old life, your old patterns, back to hurting the ones who loved you," Darkmore continued. "You certainly didn't come back to thank your savior."

"She was with someone else, a living man, I wouldn't stand in the way of that."

"Stand in the way? You were perfectly happy to stand in your wife's way, so to speak, and to interfere. Old habits die hard, even when we depart the mortal realm. When will you stop hurting her? Haven't you done enough?"

"Darkmore, stop it!" Vivian shouted.

She ran to Zeke, her tears falling as freely as his. He pushed her away.

"No, I let you be. Even as I ached for you, I left you to live your life with your mortal man. But then he left...he left you because you couldn't give yourself fully to him. Not with what you are, not with what you can do. So I came back. But then you turned to *him!*"

Vivian tasted his jealousy and bitterness. It tasted almost as sour as her own.

"A year, Zeke. You walked this world for a whole year and not one word. Not one sign. I ached for you, too. My heart broke the night I let you go."

"Stop it! Both of you just stop. We don't have any more time," the priest said, his words laced with desperation, "Vivian, it's time to go."

"Wait, I thought Ezra was supposed to fetch me," she said, panic setting in.

"He can't."

"What? Why not?"

"The council already has him, Vivian," Father Montgomery said.

This was bad. Really, really bad.

Vivian looked around at her companions, wondering which, if any, she could trust. She wondered which, if any, she would put at risk. She took a deep breath, and then made her decision.

"Padre, Darkmore, I need to speak to Zeke. Give us a minute," she said. Darkmore flashed a wicked grin as he placed his hand on the priest's shoulder. She caught Father Montgomery's horrified expression just before they disappeared.

She turned back and looked at Zeke, aching to take him in her arms yet fearing to touch him. They had no time to say all that they needed to say to one another. A pang of regret sliced through her, knowing how she'd hurt him, how they'd hurt one another. With no time for apologies, or comfort, she waited for his gaze to meet hers. After a few long moments, his green eyes lifted and the sorrow she saw there pierced her soul.

"Zeke, I need you to take the padre back and look after him," she said, keeping her voice steady and holding his gaze. "I need you to protect him. Please."

He looked at her for a moment. She expected anger, but she swore he looked confused. She shook her head and said, "Zeke, please, protect him, and Kay and her family, and Sue, and...and, please, baby, they're all I've got left in the world. Please?"

"I won't run away," he said, words uttered in a hoarse whisper. "I'm not running."

Damn it, there's no time for this.

"Zeke...if you love me, you'll guard those I love and keep them safe."

"I won't let you go do this alone—"

"Please! Zeke, I swear I'll return if I can and we'll work it all out."

"Do you love him?"

"Zeke, now is not the time."

Zeke's embrace enfolded her and his mouth stopped her protests. He poured his light into her, filling her with his rage, regret, and jealousy. Then he filled her with his fierce and frightening love.

"I will fight for you, Vivian," he said. Then he disappeared.

———

She almost wore a hole in the asphalt as she paced through the parking lot, waiting for the reaper. She grew more anxious with each passing minute. For the first time in hours, she had time to think the situation through.

The council had Ezra. If she could trust her chat buddy Waylon's warning, that meant Ezra had a lot of explaining to do about his failure to collect their cut of her spirit energy. She'd no doubt have to explain herself as well.

Why didn't he just take what I owed him?

She kicked the curb in a fit of frustration. Ezra! Ezra and his half-truths, Ezra and his omissions, Ezra and his lies. That's why she'd turned to Darkmore in the first place. She didn't trust Ezra.

She couldn't trust him.

Another disturbing thought stopped her mid-step. She looked up at the hospital, at the window to the room that held Rockford and his tormentors. His wicked deeds in life had drawn Darkmore and the demon.

"Darkmore?"

"Yes, my little Pandora?" he asked. His expression was somber, and his eyes held a bit of sadness.

Dreading the answer, she asked the question that she should have asked a year ago. "What did Ezra do to make you come for him?"

CHAPTER TWENTY-EIGHT

He didn't answer, so Vivian grabbed him by the shoulders and said, "I'm expected stand before the guardian council here in a few minutes. I'd kind of like to know what I'm up against and why."

"You don't have to go, you know," he said.

"I don't see any other option."

"You may come with me," he whispered, pulling her so close that her face was a breath away from his. "If you do, the guardians cannot claim you."

"What about my friends? What about Zeke?"

"We can protect your friends."

"And Zeke?"

He pulled her closer, moving his cool lips to her ear, "I do not make this offer lightly, Vivian. I have only extended such an offer to a mortal once before." Heaving a deep breath, he continued, "Though you sorely test my patience, I am willing to indulge you. I will take Zeke as well if you wish it. He was meant for me and my realm, as you well remember."

She didn't know what to think or what to say. He'd given her an out, the perfect escape clause. And he'd take Zeke. That request had come from desperation. She'd never thought Darkmore would share.

Never in her life and trials had she felt more tempted.

She pulled his face to hers and kissed him, devouring him with her gratitude and sorrow. When she released him, he simply asked, "Why won't you come with me?"

"You said it yourself. I'm a fighter."

"Ah, there's the Vivian Bedford I know," Darkmore replied. He smiled at her, a wicked and knowing smile. Then, she felt herself fall into the swirling vortex.

———

As soon as she landed, she looked all around for the reaper so she could hit him.

"You bastard! Where are we?" she screamed.

He'd fucking kidnapped her.

She received no answer, which only made her anger burn hotter. She looked around, wondering where he'd taken her and how she'd escape. It wasn't dark or cold, not like the last time she'd come to Darkmore's realm. Instead, a dense sheen of fog surrounded her and obscured her view.

"What happened to all that talk about free will?" she yelled. "Because this sure as shit doesn't qualify."

Her legs lurched beneath her of their own accord, jerking Vivian and making her stumble through the fog until she felt her body press against a cold, hard surface. She willed her arms, apparently still in her control, to push herself away, but her feet remained rooted to the spot.

This would be much a lot easier if you'd work with me instead of fighting.

She tried to scream, but the unknown force that held her legs in its control seized her throat and stifled her outburst. It forced her to take in large gulps of air, which alleviated her physical distress but did nothing for the fear and outrage that gripped her mind.

If I release your voice, will you be a good girl?

She tried to scream again, but to no avail.

That's what I thought. Why don't you hear me out first, and then we'll discuss a sharing plan.

Realization dawned. The unbelievable, high-handed, fucking bastard had possessed her.

You didn't leave me much choice, Vivian.

She willed him to release her.

No. You're going to need some backup if you are to get through a council trial.

Wait. Was he telling her that he actually brought her to the guardian council?

Of course. Free will, remember?

But—

I couldn't exactly stroll through the front door with you, now could I?

He shouldn't have. He—

As much as I'd love to continue this conversation, I suggest we save it for later. I'll give you back your arms, legs, and wayward tongue so long as you follow my advice. Refrain from speaking until I tell you and do not under any circumstances fire until I give the order. Understood?

"Fine," she muttered.

Good girl. You may thank me properly later. Or attack me. Either way, it should prove a delightful diversion. Shall we?

"Where are we going?" Vivian asked.

If memory serves, I believe any direction will suffice. The gates will appear when they are ready for you.

"Will they be pearly?"

If that is what you envision, then yes.

"What do you mean if that's what I envision?"

Much of the physical manifestations in our realms, when made for the benefit of mortals and newly released souls, are based upon the expectations of the subject.

"So none of this is real?"

The spirits are as real as you, Vivian. The setting is dynamic and tailored to your vision, though in this case I suspect they'll strive to present an air of supreme authority. Home court advantage, if you like.

Vivian remained silent for a little while, allowing her body to adjust to the presence of Darkmore and her mind to process information overload.

Normally, the human subjects of spirit possession remained unaware during the period of occupation. It certainly felt strange to her.

"Is this as weird for you as it is for me?"

Not at all, but I have extensive experience. Besides, I've been itching to get inside of you.

"Very funny, asshole."

Sticks and stones. Whether you're willing to admit it or not, part of you has been itching a bit as well.

"You never did answer my first question," she said, changing the subject.

Ah yes, back to Ezra. What has he told you of his life as a mortal?

"He told me he'd been a tobacco farmer, husband, and father. I assume he was a man of faith. He told me that you tormented him after his stroke." Vivian tried to keep her tone neutral. Reapers tormented the living and dead, as she had recently witnessed. As she'd also observed, those souls often did something to deserve it, though she didn't put it past any reaper or guardian to interfere with the living or dead out of spite or ulterior motives.

Oh, he became very pious later in life.

"Which implies that he wasn't always like that. He once told me he had the zeal of a convert. Like Paul."

Darkmore's laugh echoed in her mind.

Indeed, though perhaps St. Augustine would make a better comparison, as in "Lord, save me from my sins, but not quite yet."

"So he was a bad man before?"

For a time, I suppose. Of course, moral relativism is a bit of the norm in my circles, just as it is for the guardians. He did change, though not necessarily in the way he'd have you believe.

"What's that supposed to mean?"

Let's just say he liked to play both sides when it comes to our kind, rather like you.

Vivian opened her mouth to comment, but the thinning fog interrupted her. She suspected they were near the meeting place. That gave her an idea.

"I'll be asking a lot more about that later, believe me, but let's get back to the whole 'manifestation of setting' business. If it's based on what I expect, then I can change it if I change my expectations?"

You're catching on. What did you have in mind?

"Something a little more to my advantage," she said. She closed her eyes and concentrated on the familiar image held in her mind. When she opened her eyes, she stood before a closed door.

Did it work?

"One way to find out," she said. With that, she placed unsteady fingers on the doorknob and opened it.

CHAPTER TWENTY-NINE

Walking through the door, Vivian saw three corporeal spirits seated around a familiar conference table that she'd modeled after the one at her office. She recognized Uriel, looking as poised and polished as he had during their last meeting. Other than the table, bland office chairs, and their occupants, the rest of the setting remained cloaked in fog. At least she had her round table. It leveled the playing field and placed them as equals, at least in her mind. She tried to hold onto that image as her confidence faltered.

Uriel spoke first. "Good evening, Ms. Bedford. Thank you for joining us." He gestured to an empty chair in invitation.

"Good evening, Uriel," she replied, looking around the room before taking a seat.

Ask for an introduction.

"May I be introduced to the rest of the council?"

"Of course," Uriel said. "Allow me to present our brother Raphael." The tall and imposing spirit seated on Uriel's right nodded. "And our brother Gabriel." Gabriel, beautiful in his projected form, smiled at Vivian and nodded. "My brothers, may I present Vivian Bedford, mortal woman and assistant to our guardian Ezra."

How interesting. Uriel only brought his brethren who helped fight against the Watchers. Confused? Allow me to bring you up to speed, then.

The Watchers were guardian spirits who chose to mate with human women and impart their knowledge to mortals—a big no-no back in the day.

Ask why you've been summoned, and do try to be polite about it.

"May I ask why you have summoned me here?"

"We have evidence that you have continued to use your spirit powers for unauthorized activities. What's more, you've failed to report them to Ezra. I recall warning you about that."

"Where is Ezra?" she asked.

"He is in the company of our brothers at the home office. Do not fret, my dear. He is quite safe, I assure you. All quite informal, as is this little get-together." Uriel waved his hand. "Now, let's get back on track. Do you care to confirm or deny your activities?

Answer him honestly.

Vivian hesitated, her bravado giving way to fear. She didn't believe Uriel's claim regarding Ezra's safety. Given what Darkmore told her about the makeup of this particular council, she questioned her safety as well.

Answer the question.

She had no choice, she supposed. Then again, she figured she could dodge answering Uriel directly, since he seemed content to pussyfoot around with his interrogation instead of just asking what he really wanted to know.

It could buy her a little more time to devise an escape plan with Darkmore.

"I don't deny it. I used my powers to help a few friends out with marital and relationship issues, but that hardly seems important in the grander scheme of things."

"Come now, Ms. Bedford, you disappoint me. Coyness does not become you."

"You're right. It doesn't. It doesn't become you, either. How about you tell me about your energy management plan?"

Uriel's eyes widened a fraction, and the up-until-now-immobile Raphael cocked his head slightly to the left. Gabriel raised one lovely, arched brow. Vivian figured those qualified as astonished reactions from the ancient trio. She almost winced as she waited for Darkmore's response, but then she decided to dive right in before he had the chance to talk her out of it.

"I pay attention, and I'm not stupid. I know you targeted my sister because of her energy, and a lot of the crossings I've attended are similar. Disabled or incapacitated mortals? Weary friends and family who look a little peaked? That little stunt Wallace pulled at the zoo? You're siphoning off their energy, aren't you?"

Uriel smiled, and it chilled her to the bone. "Payment for the ferryman."

"And what about all the others who suffer?"

"We get to them when we can, of course, but this is, for lack of a better term, a business we're running, Ms. Bedford. A very lucrative one, I might add."

"Meaning?"

"Meaning," he began, rising from his chair and seating himself on the top of the table, "perhaps we could come to some sort of mutually beneficial arrangement, if you're willing to work with us. You are a businesswoman, are you not?"

"Not that kind."

"No? Let me sweeten the deal for you, then, by informing you that your little side projects do not interest me. We're all about pro bono and charity, aren't we, my brothers?"

Gabriel spoke, his voice as beautiful and mesmerizing as his face. "Our guardians are free to assist those who cannot offer full payment. Most of them do. We are not heartless."

"Of course not," Uriel chimed in. "But you must understand, it takes a great deal of energy to accomplish our tasks. If we did not focus on paying clients, as it were, we would not have the resources to operate at all. Ask your reaper friend sometime. He'll tell you the same thing."

You could ask him about his interest rates, or why human souls require assistance in crossing at all, but I think it might be wiser to hear his offer and request some time to consider it. Get them to let you leave this realm.

"So what's the deal?"

Raphael laughed. "I like this one. She has her mentor's cunning and survival instincts."

"Perhaps…" Uriel mused. "Very well, our proposition is as follows: you advance and move on to special collections."

Vivian narrowed her eyes in disgust.

"Come now, it's not as if you haven't the stomach for it, or the *taste*," he said, leaning closer to her ear so he could whisper. "I know about your visit to Mr. Rockford this evening."

"So you're proposing to move in on reaper territory?"

"You may have noticed that the lines are rather blurry. You wouldn't have to sneak around anymore. You'd be operating with our full support."

Vivian froze as realization dawned on her. "*You* sent the rogue guardian after me."

Uriel laughed. "We had to test your convictions. Not to mention your abilities. Mortals often need a bit of a crisis in which to find and hone their skills, you being no exception. Your healing abilities were quite an unexpected bonus. I wonder what else we might discover?"

Vivian opened her mouth to protest, but Darkmore stilled her tongue.

Wait! See what else he has to say.

"Oh, don't get me wrong. There are still guardians within our ranks who believe that humans have no place here, but that was never our intent. The Nephilim, not to mention mortals in your situation, might have continued their work and existence had they worked with us rather than against us."

"So your rogue doesn't know about your plans?"

"He is rather zealous, but do not fear. Our soldiers remain ever loyal. Don't believe me? He could have attacked any number of your loved ones, yet he chose the priest."

"So?"

"Doesn't she know?" Raphael asked.

"It would seem that she does not. Your friend has moved on, at least from the mortal plane. I do not believe he has crossed to us quite yet, but he's been in decline for several months, and was therefore our safest target."

Vivian couldn't breathe. She couldn't think. Father Montgomery. No, he couldn't be dead. She was just talking to him. He couldn't be!

Vivian, listen to me. Your life and soul depend upon it. They don't have him yet. You heard that yourself. Tell them you're interested in their offer and ask to think about it. Tell them now!

"I...I'm feeling a little overwhelmed. I need some time to work all this through." She allowed her tears to flow freely. They were genuine. She hoped they would interpret her turmoil as human weakness. To her shame, she admitted to herself that a good bit was human fear and wavering.

If she accepted their offer, she could keep her loved ones safe.

"What about Zeke?" she asked.

"What about him?"

"Will he be safe?"

"All we ask for is discretion. And payment. We've been monitoring Zeb."

"That's sick!" She understood all too well that reapers and guardians targeted the most vulnerable humans and sapped their considerable spirit energy reserves, but the thought of any of them harming Zeke's autistic son made her stomach roll and blood boil.

"It's business. No real and lasting harm would come to the boy. You could persuade Ezekiel to see reason, I'm sure."

She knew she couldn't keep control for much longer. She needed to get out of there. She rose and took a step back, careful to keep the waterworks going. "I need to think about this."

"Of course you do," Uriel said patiently. "Just don't take too terribly long. You aren't under our protection yet."

The sound of Uriel's mocking laughter echoed as she ran back into the fog.

CHAPTER THIRTY

"You can let me go now," she shouted. Then she collapsed on the ground and curled up into a ball of tears. She had enough of her faculties still intact to be mortified at the display, especially with Darkmore still around, but she'd reached her breaking point.

Then a cool breeze caressed her skin. Taking in a deep breath, she smelled honey and citrus, and her throat felt soothed, as though she'd taken a long drink from a clear mountain stream. She could feel Darkmore, but she didn't see him.

"Please, just go," she pleaded. She was too weary to bear his scrutiny.

Go? And leave you to wallow in sorrow and self-pity? I think not. It wreaks havoc with your complexion, you know. Besides, you're rather tasty at the moment.

"I can't do this," she whispered.

What happened to my fighter?

"She realized that she's in over her head and can't do this alone."

Oh, don't fret. I do believe you've earned yourself a few reinforcements.

"What?"

Try sitting up instead of wallowing. It does tend to change one's perspective.

She sat up and took in her surroundings as best she could, given the darkness. They appeared to have landed in a clearing surrounded by tall trees. The crescent moon glowed through a few scattered clouds, along with quite a few stars. *Not a lot of street lights, then.* She noticed a few round bales of hay scattered throughout the field and caught a whiff of cow patties. On her feet and ready to complain, the first flash of white light caught her off-guard and almost made her jump out of her skin.

Jeanne and Wallace materialized, flanked by the padre and Junior, now in full corporeal form and beaming with pride. Before she could speak, Mildred Bluff's transparent manifestation emerged through the trees at the opposite end of the field, followed by all of the ghostly residents of Nolensville. She also recognized a host of spirits from Woodlawn Cemetery, many of whom she'd befriended when visiting the graves of Mae and Zeke. Just when she thought she could not be more overwhelmed, Mrs. Martin came too, bringing at least twenty other corporeal spirits with her.

"How did you—"

Before she could finish, Jeanne ran up and wrapped Vivian in her arms, filling her with the warmth and comfort of her guardian nature. Junior joined her, as did the padre, and for long moments she stood wrapped in their circle of peace, drawing in their strength. She longed to stay there forever.

But she had way too many questions. Not to mention an apology to deliver.

"Padre, I'm so sorry for everything. I...I didn't know."

"I didn't want you to know, Vivian," the priest said, taking her hand. "You had enough to worry about. It was just my time. Ezra was kind enough to give me a heads-up and help me with the planning."

"Did it hurt?"

"No, dear, not at all."

"So, are you a guardian?"

"I'm a newly-minted freelance agent," he said with a smile. "It seems you've awakened the rebel in me."

"What is all this?" Vivian asked, turning and looking at all of the spirits surrounding her.

"Oh, Vivian, I'm so sorry that I kept you in the dark, but I was afraid you'd...well, you'd be you and do something rash."

"Too late, but you might as well tell me now."

"It would be safer to get you to Mississippi and let Waylon explain. His allies can protect you until we're ready to strike."

"Whoa there, let's rewind and try that again. Allies? Strike? What have you gotten me into?"

Jeanne looked at the priest, who nodded and took Vivian's hand. "There is dissent among the council and guardians, as we told you, in regard to mortals working alongside them. I'm sure you've gathered by now that the conflict runs much deeper."

"Ah, hell!" Mrs. Martin shoved her way through the crowd as she spoke. "Cut to the chase, why don't you? The guardian higher-ups are running an energy racket at the expense of the souls they're supposed to serve!"

"Honey," Jeanne said, trying to soothe. "We're getting to all that."

"It's not that complicated. They've got a bureaucracy that makes the federal government look efficient. I've been waiting for 'processing' so long I swore I was back at the DMV!"

"You're one of the lucky ones!" Mildred Bluff chimed in. *Great, let the battle of the biddies begin.* "At least they came back for you. Look around. See all of these good folks they've left in limbo or just plain left?"

"Anyway," Jeanne said. "Many field agents don't like it and we've been conducting crossings in secret."

"And opening more channels so spirits can find their own way," Junior added. "But it's not enough."

"Like-minded guardians have been working for centuries to change things, either by outnumbering and outvoting them, or by starting a rebellion."

That statement floored her. Anger and indignation at the methods used by the guardians was one thing, but a rebellion? Visions of epic battles from Revelation to *The Iliad* flashed through her mind and she became seized by panic.

"Vivian," Jeanne said, pulling her chin up with warm fingertips so that their gazes met. "We need all the help we can get. We need you."

"And if I refuse?"

All of the spirits focused on her and she felt the temperature ratchet up.

For once, she was grateful that Darkmore hadn't listened to her when she'd asked him to vacate her personal premises. He sent waves of soothing cool through her in defense. Clearly, she hadn't pleased the rag-tag rebel alliance with her response.

"Since your kind dragged me into your affairs—unwillingly, I might add —I've been a slave to whoever wants a piece of me. I've never had a choice! Not from Ezra, not from the council, and not from you now."

"Do you think we have a choice?" Jeanne shot back.

"You volunteered. I didn't."

"So you'd walk away from us? Give up on all of these beautiful souls you've helped and just let them languish along with the living who need you?"

"Of course she would," boomed the voice of Wallace. "There's a reason for the council. There's a reason why we don't share our power with mortals. They are weak-willed and selfish. They have no place with us."

Oh my God.

The rogue guardian was Wallace. He'd been there the night Father Montgomery was attacked. He hated her, resented her powers and her work, and he believed in council—a council he'd apparently been working for.

As realization dawned on Vivian, she shoved the guardians flanking her away and dashed forward to deflect the blast of light from Wallace. She managed, but her light didn't block one ray that hit her in her shoulder.

Vivian, get down!

"Darkmore, get out. Get the fuck out of me now!" she cried.

The pain in her shoulder seared, but adrenaline trumped it and she shot back. Wallace flashed out of the way, and her blast knocked over a tree instead.

"Jeanne, Padre, get the others to safety!"

Many wispy spirits disappeared into the trees along the perimeter while Junior herded those in a panic away to safety. Jeanne and the priest flanked Vivian, casting blasts of light wherever Wallace appeared. She'd never seen a spirit move so fast. Uriel and his buddies must have given him premium fuel. Fuel harvested from the living in their dying hours. Payment. Tribute. Folks like Mae and their families.

"Playing hide and seek? Too scared to come and fight face to face?" she said, taunting.

"What are you doing?" Jeanne asked, grabbing her by the collar.

"We can't let him get away," she gasped, the wound in her shoulder searing more under Jeanne's grip. "He'll keep on sucking the life out of people and giving it to those self-righteous assholes on the council. We've got to stop him now."

Jeanne nodded and clasped hands with the padre. Their mental texts were too rapid for Vivian to fully grasp, but they appeared to be in negotiations with the rogue spirit. Vivian stumbled over to the tree line and leaned on a hickory. She didn't dare sit. She didn't think she'd be able to get up.

"Darkmore, help me out here. What do you have on Wallace?"

Not much, I'm afraid. He's a true believer in the cause and he has a grudge against Ezra. Try that one. You both have that in common. While you're at it, you should repair your shoulder.

"You should get out."

Nonsense. I haven't had this much fun in years.

"What if I die? What happens to you and your soul?"

An interesting question. I suppose you'll just have to keep us both safe.

"This isn't a game. I don't want to cause you harm any more than I want these souls to suffer."

I know. That's what I'm counting on.

Damn him. He knew her Achilles' heel and he was using it against her. She focused her energy on the wound on her shoulder and managed to reduce the agony to a dull ache. The rest would have to wait.

"Hey, Wallace," she yelled. "I had an interesting little chat with Uriel tonight. Raph and Gabe were there, too. If you think they're going to just hand Ezra over to you in exchange for taking me out of commission, think again."

A temporary cease-fire let Vivian know that she had his attention. Now she'd have to keep it.

"He's been playing both sides and they know it. What's more, they gave him the green light. He's good at hauling in massive loads of energy. You think they're going to just let their top producer go? They played you, Wallace. They're playing all of us. It's what they do."

"You lie, mortal. You would do anything to save your worthless life and hold onto your power."

"No, I wouldn't. If I could give this curse back, I would do it in a heartbeat. All I ever wanted was a normal life. But Ezra showed up and he wanted my sister. I didn't give her to him, and I won't give all of these souls over to you or anyone else either."

"I have no interest in these pitiful abominations who have betrayed our kind and our ways. There is no room for the unaffiliated. You all must choose!"

"Free will, Wallace. Every soul has that right."

"Not you."

She whirled around and found herself face-to-face with Wallace. He grabbed her by the neck and lifted her, his blazing hand burning her neck as he choked the life out of her. She struggled, gasping for air. Her frail human body could not withstand the onslaught.

"Don't fight, woman. It will hurt less. I shall claim you and bring you into the fold, where you belong. The others will follow."

Vivian's consciousness ebbed away. Terror gripped her, but not at the prospect of death. If death solved problems, she might have chosen it over a year ago. No, she feared enslavement. She would not serve them. She kicked.

Wallace's sudden release of her came as a shock. Surely her pathetic defense hadn't done that. She looked up and saw Wallace grimace. When he turned, Vivian saw the raw, charred flesh through his shirt.

"Serves you right!" Mrs. Martin shouted as she delivered another blast. "Leave me waiting in a damned office for a century!"

A century? Dear God, how long have I been gone? She shook that thought off and scooted backward, placing distance between herself and the two guardians locked in battle. Wallace shot Mrs. Martin in the stomach and she flew backward, slamming onto the ground. Then he turned back to Vivian.

"You are ours now, Vivian Bedford," he said as he raised his arm and fired.

She fired almost simultaneously, shrieking in horror as both blasts caught Darkmore. She felt his presence depart her body too late to stop her stream of light energy or to move them out of the way.

"No!"

The impact sent him careening to the ground between them. She grabbed Darkmore's hand and took a long draw of his darkness. Then she sent it to Wallace.

His face became a mask of rage, anguish, and finally resignation. His corporeal form disintegrated, and Vivian caught a glimpse of his soul as it folded and fell into the swirling vortex. She didn't know where she'd sent him, but she hoped he'd have a hard time getting back to the human realm to hurt anyone else anytime soon.

Jeanne and the priest ran toward Vivian, trying to help her off the ground. Junior emerged from the tree line with several spirits in tow. She shook them off and turned to Darkmore.

"Darkmore, damn it, get up!"

His corporeal form did not bear any obvious signs of physical injury, but she knew the blasts had taken a toll. He didn't move or respond. Her touch did not rouse him.

"This isn't funny. Get up right now and help me clean up this mess."

"Vivian, perhaps—"

"No, Padre," she said, shaking off the hand he'd gently placed on her shoulder. "He isn't dead. He was already dead so he can't be dead. He's here somewhere." She rose, raging and screaming at the gathering throng. "Tell me where he went! What happens when y'all get hit! Don't you just regroup and form another body?"

"Honey," Jeanne began. "His body is still here."

"So where is he?"

"If a reaper loses a life while in corporeal form, he must go back and begin again."

"Begin again? What the hell does that mean?"

"He'll start over as a new spirit."

"Darkmore? At the bottom of the reaper chain?" she asked, incredulous. She'd seen a bit of the reaper hierarchy and politics during her last visit to Darkmore's realm. Someone as old and seasoned as her reaper would have made more than a few enemies, and those he'd stepped on during his rise would no doubt revel in kicking him on the way down.

She couldn't stomach it.

She fell to the ground and straddled the reaper, ripping his jacket and shirt to expose his chest. She knew that guardian bodies sometimes maintained a heartbeat, having heard Zeke's. Whether they kept it up as a ruse to blend in versus having an actual blood-pumping capacity, she had no idea.

Since she didn't have anything else to go on, she listened for Darkmore's and detected the sluggish and erratic rhythm. His breathing was shallow and labored. She stroked his face and pleaded with him to stay with her. Closing her eyes, she placed both hands on his chest and focused her energy on him.

The healing power flowed freely, so desperate was her desire to save him. His arms shot up and his strong hands clasped her to him. He took in her blinding light, latching his mouth onto hers.

She collapsed atop him, gulping for air and recovering from the energy transfer. His arms encircled her and stroked her back. His touch gave her shivers, but not from his innate coolness. "Vivian?"

"Yes?"

"As much as I enjoy the closeness, would you mind removing yourself from me? I cannot breathe."

She pulled herself away and hopped to her feet. That maneuver turned out to be a bad idea, since she lost her bearings and would have fallen backward had the priest not caught her. Jeanne surprised Vivian by waltzing right up to Darkmore and offering her hand. He accepted and she pulled him to his feet. Vivian struggled to escape the priest's arms so she could run to Darkmore, but the reaper held a palm up. He seemed out of sorts.

"Darkmore?"

He surveyed the spirits around him. Some leaned in for a closer look, others shrank back in fear. Fresh fear gripped her as well. She couldn't face another ghostly showdown tonight.

"Listen up, everyone," she shouted. "This is Lazarus Darkmore, and yes, he's a reaper. But he isn't going to hurt anyone here. I promise. He's been helping me."

"You don't have to worry about me harming anyone here, Vivian," Darkmore said softly, lifting a sharp stick from the ground.

"I know," she whispered out of the side of her mouth. "That's what I just said. Pardon me for saying so, but you seem a little off your game."

Darkmore took the pointed end of the stick and jabbed it into his forearm. Vivian screamed. He winced, but then stared in fascination at the blood flowing from the wound. So did Jeanne and the priest.

"Why the hell did you do that?" Vivian shouted, freeing herself and running to the reaper. She grabbed his arm, ripped out the branch and healed him.

"It was a test," Darkmore whispered, his voice hollow.

"A test for what?" she asked. "What are you trying to prove?"

"That you are a truly gifted healer."

He examined his body with mild curiosity, as if noticing it for the first time.

"Say something that makes sense," she said, dreading the answer.

"Your powers worked a little too well, my dear. I'm tethered to this corporeal form now."

Understanding dawned as consciousness faded.

The last thing she heard him say was, "You've made me a mortal."

THE END

Thank you for reading! Did you enjoy?

Please Add Your Review! And don't miss the Soul Broker novels with book 3, THE QUICK AND THE DEAD. Turn the page for a sneak peek!

SNEAK PEEK OF THE QUICK AND THE DEAD

She floated in the place between here and there...what was it called again?

"Between life and the afterlife."

Her body materialized. Her body, but not her body—she'd never had this kind of body before she moved to the afterlife. Not that she remembered very much from that time, the time before she came to the place between here and there and...someplace else. That place had been dark, filled with many sad and hurting things, many angry things and they hurt one another. It was a place of great suffering for the things there.

"Souls. You freed thousands upon thousands of souls." The voice was one she knew. He was from the time before the afterlife, just before she moved on to the afterlife. Before she died.

"I..." The word formed and sounded strange to her. Her voice before the afterlife hadn't been in her control. She'd learned some words from Mother and Father and Sister, and others from television, but speech had been impossible for her then.

The bearer of the voice, the man—and not man, wearing a body not his own from before the afterlife—touched her hand, holding it in his larger, warm hand.

She gasped.

"Hello, Mae. It's good to see you here."

His hand was so warm, and it filled her with comforting warmth that seemed to come from the inside out. "You were there...*before*. You brought...something to me and to Sister. It was...nice, but more than nice. I'm sorry. Words are hard."

He smiled, his eyes a lovely shade of green, his hair dark, his face... beautiful, but that wasn't what people said about men. Her thoughts clarified, and she breathed deeply, without pain or the crunching rattle in her chest like before, when she'd been alive.

"It's all right," the man said. "It'll come to you. I had a hard time, too, but maybe not so hard as you. I was able to, *ah*, I was, um..."

Her lips curled into a smile. She loved smiling. And laughing, but it seemed a little wrong to laugh at the man as he struggled to find words. His cheeks were red, and he looked away. Strange. She didn't like it. Her mouth turned down in response to her anger. It reminded her of the before time when people didn't want to look at her. People pretended she was not there, talked around her, and she could never talk to them because her body didn't work like their bodies.

"Look at me and say words to me. I am not invisible."

"No, you aren't," he said, meeting her gaze with a lopsided grin. "You're a lot like her. I didn't realize it when we first met. You were different. I was afraid to say that, to say something stupid like I was normal and you weren't when we were alive. It seemed rude."

She shook her head, confused. "I *was* different. There is nothing rude about what is true."

He sighed, pulling his hand from hers. She missed the heat and the feeling that was more than nice. Running a hand through his hair, he walked around the place between here and there. Most of the others who crossed through this space were eager to move on. Grey, silent, without scent or taste or texture, it was the place that the others used to travel from the afterlife to the world of the living. For her, it was a place of calm and respite, the place that reminded her of the time before, when she'd been alive.

She was not alive now, but she had not yet gone to the place that awaited all departed souls who chose forever. It wasn't time. This place between here and there was home enough for now. She took a tentative step, marveling at how her legs supported her body and allowed her to move when she wanted. And she was high, standing, looking at the man without stretching her neck—she could control her neck sometimes when she'd been in her own body before the afterlife, but it was hard. People were always above her when she was in bed or in a chair.

Now she was tall, and she could walk. She wanted to run. When she tried, her feet became tangled and she fell forward. The man caught her.

"Easy. You have to learn to walk before you can run. As far as the truth not being rude, well, I'll take your word for it. And in the spirit of being honest, my normal was nothing to be proud of. I wasn't a nice man when I was alive, especially near the end."

She let him ease her back up to stand. When he tried to pull away from her, she held on to his hands with hers, refusing to let go. "You were nice when you came to me and to Sister. You helped me, and you helped her. She was sad and angry. You helped. What is the word for that?"

He made a strangled sound somewhere between a laugh and a sob. "Comfort. I wanted to give you both comfort and peace. It was my job, but I would have done it anyway."

She smiled. "You said I was like her. You mean Sister?"

He nodded, then he met her gaze again, his filled with anger and worry. She knew anger and worry. Mother, Father, and Sister had been angry in the time before, and worried—about her.

"Why are you worried?" she asked. Something deep inside the core of her being awakened. She'd unleashed it when she'd moved to the place between here and there and then beyond. Power. Power to do something to help.

His face relaxed. Had she given him comfort and the thing called peace?

"I'm worried about your sister, Vivian. She's in trouble. I...let her down and now she's in trouble. I need you to help her."

"Of course I will help Sister. I love her."

He tightened his grip on her hand and whispered, "I do, too."

"What is your name?" she asked. She'd forgotten. When she'd known him before she moved to the afterlife, he'd talked more to Sister. To Vivian. That was Sister's name, but to Mae, she would always be Sister."

"I'm Zeke. I was your guardian, and Vivian's guardian, for a while. But she saved me. You saved a host of souls. And if we can save Vivian now, we might just save every soul alive now and yet to be."

————

Don't stop now. Keep reading with your copy of THE QUICK AND THE DEAD available now. And sign up for the City Owl Press newsletter to receive notice of all book releases!

Don't miss Soul Broker novels with book 3, THE QUICK AND THE DEAD available now! And find more from D. B. Sieders at www.dbsieders.com

———

Afterlife management is tightening the noose. Can a living soul broker break it?

Vivian Bedford is on the run.

Her alliances with reapers and demons, and talent for freeing trapped souls, doesn't sit well with the Archangel Guardian Spirit council, and now Vivian's time is running out.

Meanwhile, reaper Lazarus Darkmore, is trapped in corporeal form. With she and the reaper on equal footing, Vivian can no longer deny her feelings for him. But the ghost of a past lover leaves her stuck between two men and two very different worlds.

Her only refuge is a band of other living soul brokers and their brewing rebellion.

The resistance is small, but their skills, weapons, and leader are impressive. When a traitor in their ranks threatens to bring the whole operation down, Vivian's fight for survival turns into a battle to save the rebellion and root out the turncoat.

Vivian will need her wits to keep the danger at bay while restoring Lazarus to his former state and liberating a group of imprisoned souls who may be the key to toppling the corrupt Archangel Guardian Council's monopoly on soul crossings once and for all.

But doing so just might cost Vivian everything. Will she prevail in a the war for her love...and her soul?

————

Please sign up for the City Owl Press newsletter for chances to win special subscriber-only contests and giveaways as well as receiving information on upcoming releases and special excerpts.

All reviews are **welcome** and **appreciated**. Please consider leaving one on your favorite social media and book buying sites.

For books in the world of romance and speculative fiction that embody Innovation, Creativity, and Affordability, check out City Owl Press at www.cityowlpress.com.

ACKNOWLEDGMENTS

I thank my dear friends Stephanie Moore and Ronald Wuister. They were instrumental in my writing journey, read the first drafts, and gave me a wealth of great advice and encouragement. I'm grateful to my Music City Romance Writers sisters and brothers. Their support and knowledge base about everything from craft to marketing has made me a better writer and better business-minded author. Thanks to my agents, Victoria Lea and Natalia Aponte, for believing in the story and this series.

I am eternally grateful to Yelena Casale and Tina Moss of City Owl Press for the wonderful opportunity. I'm delighted to have such supportive and collaborative publishers! Thanks to Amanda Roberts for her fantastic edits, and to Mibl Art for the beautiful cover art!

And most importantly, I thank my family. They are my biggest supporters, fans, and greatest source of inspiration.

ABOUT THE AUTHOR

Award-winning author D.B. Sieders was born and raised in East Tennessee and spent her childhood hiking in the Great Smoky Mountains and chasing salamanders, fish, and frogs. She loved to tell stories while sitting around the campfire.

She is a working scientist by day, but never lost her love of telling stories. Now, she's a purveyor of unconventional fantasy romance featuring strong heroines and the heroes who strive to match them. Her heroes and heroines face a healthy dose of angst as they strive for redemption and a happily ever after, which everyone deserves.

www.dbsieders.com

facebook.com/DBSieders

twitter.com/DBSieders

goodreads.com/dbsieders

amazon.com/D.B.-Sieders/B00D18ZPOY

ABOUT THE PUBLISHER

City Owl Press is a cutting edge indie publishing company, bringing the world of romance and speculative fiction to discerning readers.

www.cityowlpress.com